PRAISE FOR JOSEPH FLYNN AND HIS NOVELS

"Flynn is an excellent storyteller." — *Booklist*

"Flynn propels his plot with potent but flexible force."
— *Publishers Weekly*

The President's Henchman
"Marvelously entertaining." — *ForeWord Magazine*

Digger
"A mystery cloaked as cleverly as (and perhaps better than)
any John Grisham work." — *Denver Post*

"Surefooted, suspenseful and in its breathless final moments
unexpectedly heartbreaking." — *Booklist*

The Next President
"*The Next President* bears favorable comparison to such
classics as *The Best Man, Advise and Consent* and
The Manchurian Candidate."
— *Booklist*

"A thriller fast enough to read in one sitting."
— *Rocky Mountain News*

The
Daddy's
Girl
Decoy

A JIM McGILL NOVEL

Joseph Flynn

Stray Dog Press, Inc.
Springfield, IL
2016

ALSO BY JOSEPH FLYNN

The Jim McGill Series
The President's Henchman, A Jim McGill Novel [#1]
The Hangman's Companion, A JimMcGill Novel [#2]
The K Street Killer A JimMcGill Novel [#3]
Part 1: The Last Ballot Cast, A JimMcGill Novel [#4 Part 1]
Part 2: The Last Ballot Cast, A JimMcGill Novel [#5 Part 2]
The Devil on the Doorstep, A Jim McGill Novel [#6]
The Good Guy with a Gun, A Jim McGill Novel [#7]
The Echo of the Whip, A Jim McGill Novel [#8]
The Daddy's Girl Decoy, A Jim McGill Novel [#9]
McGill's Short Cases 1-3

The Ron Ketchum Mystery Series
Nailed, A Ron Ketchum Mystery [#1]
Defiled, A Ron Ketchum Mystery Featuring John Tall Wolf [#2]
Impaled, A Ron Ketchum Mystery [#3]

The John Tall Wolf Series
Tall Man in Ray-Bans, A John Tall Wolf Novel [#1]
War Party, A John Tall Wolf Novel [#2]
Super Chief, A John Tall Wolf Novel [#3]
Smoke Signals, A John Tall Wolf Novel [#4]

The Zeke Edison Series
Kill Me Twice, A Zeke Edison Novel [#1]

Stand Alone Novels
The Concrete Inquisition
Digger
The Next President
Hot Type
Farewell Performance
Gasoline, Texas
Round Robin, A Love Story of Epic Proportions
One False Step
Blood Street Punx
Still Coming
Still Coming Expanded Edition
Hangman — A Western Novella
Pointy Teeth, Twelve Bite-Size Stories

Published by Stray Dog Press, Inc.
Springfield, IL 62704, U.S.A.

Copyright © kandrom, inc., 2016
All rights reserved

Visit the author's web site: *www.josephflynn.com*

Flynn, Joseph
  The Daddy's Girl Decoy / Joseph Flynn
  432 p.
  ISBN 978-0-9974500-0-2
  ISBN eBook 978-0-9908412-9-6

Printed in the United States of America

PUBLISHER'S NOTE
This is a work of fiction. Names, characters, places, and incidents are either the product of the author's imagination or are used fictitiously; any resemblance to actual persons, living or dead, events, or locales is entirely coincidental.

Book design by Aha! Designs
Cover photo courtesy of iStockPhoto.com

DEDICATION

For Catherine, just because.

ACKNOWLEDGEMENTS

Catherine, Cat, Anne, Susan and Meghan do their level best to catch all my typos and other mistakes, but I usually outwit them. Please be kind. Even Ty Cobb didn't get a hit every time at bat.

AL
Reader
Discretion
Advised
Contains Adult
Language

CHARACTER LIST

[in alphabetical order by last name]

Ah-lam, wife of Tyler Busby
Eugene Beck, assassin/thief, formerly U.S. military
Abra Benjamin, Special Agent, FBI
Gawayne Blessing, White House head butler
Ellie Booker, independent news producer
Philip Brock, (deceased) Democratic Congressman from
    Pennsylvania
Tyler Busby, fugitive billionaire wanted by FBI
Edwina Byington, the president's personal secretary
Celsus Crogher, retired Secret Service SAC
Byron DeWitt, Deputy Director of the FBI
Deirdre "Didi" DiMarco, WWN news show host
Darren Drucker, billionaire co-founder of ShareAmerica
Carolyn [McGill] Enquist, first wife of Jim McGill
Patricia Darden Grant, President of the United States, second wife
    of Jim McGill
Bahir Ben Kalil, (deceased) personal physician to the Jordanian
    ambassador to the U.S.
Dr. Hasna Kalil, twin sister of late Dr. Bahir Ben Kalil
SAC Elspeth Kendry, head of the Presidential Protection Detail
Carina Linberg, novelist, formerly a colonel in USAF
Aurick Ludwig, gun lobbyist
Donald "Deke" Ky, Jim McGill's personal Secret Service bodyguard
Leo Levy, Jim McGill's personal driver
Jim McGill, president's husband, aka The President's Henchman
Galia Mindel, White House chief of staff
Jean Morrissey, Vice President of the U.S.
Thomas Winston Rangel, conservative intellectual/strategist
Putnam Shady, head lobbyist of ShareAmerica, Sweetie's husband
Margaret "Sweetie" Sweeney, McGill's longtime friend and police
    partner; Putnam's wife
Welborn Yates, the president's personal (official) investigator,
    Air Force colonel

CHAPTER 1

Friday, March 25, 2016
McGill's Hideaway, The White House — Washington, DC

McGill couldn't remember a time when a phone call from one of his children had hit him so hard. His elder daughter Abbie had called, upset. He would have cursed at the top of his voice upon hearing what she had to say if he didn't think that would scare Abbie further.

In the most even tone he could muster, he said, "Give it to me one more time, honey."

The encore recitation didn't have quite the same impact, if only because McGill thought he was already as angry as he could possibly be.

Abbie said, "I've been seeing this girl around campus the past few days."

She was in graduate school at Georgetown, pursuing a master of arts in conflict resolution — of all things.

"I had to look twice the first time I saw her, Dad."

"She looks that much like you, honey?"

"Yeah, almost like twins separated at birth. You and Mom didn't flip a coin to see which one of us you'd keep, did you?" she asked, going for a note of levity.

McGill said, "Unh-uh. The only thing better than one Abbie

would be two of you."

A small sob reached McGill, stoking his ire further. Proving his outrage might be boundless in this case. Somebody was scaring the hell out of his first-born. He didn't have a handle on everybody who was involved, but he thought he knew some of the guilty parties. They'd be hearing from him soon, and their ears would likely ring for years.

"The second time I saw her," Abbie said, "I thought I'd say hello, kid her about the resemblance between us. But she stepped into a building, and I'd have had to chase after her. I thought she might have been busy and not in the mood for a conversation. Heck, she might not have thought we look at all alike."

McGill said, "But thinking about it, later, you decided she couldn't miss the similarities."

"Not unless she's blind, and I didn't see her using a cane." Abbie paused, long enough to draw her father's curiosity. She must have thought of something new.

"What is it, Abbie?"

"The thought just struck me. The way this girl entered the building? It was abrupt. As if she'd noticed me noticing her. She took the first opportunity she had to duck out on me."

McGill hesitated, but asked, "You're sure that's not just your imagination?"

"Could have been except for what happened the next two days."

"Go on," McGill said, accepting that his daughter had things right.

"I saw her again, yesterday, and this time she was walking right toward me. She gave me a glance as she passed by, like I was no one special. But I was stopped dead in my tracks. My mouth might have been hanging open for all I know. She breezed right by, though, never gave me a second look — even though she was wearing *exactly* the same clothes I was."

Unlike the first time he'd heard the story, McGill asked a question, "We're not talking a school hoodie, jeans and sneakers here, are we?"

"Oh, my God," Abbie said. "I just realized that's what we were both wearing the day before, when she ducked into the building." Abbie continued in greater detail than she had previously. "Yesterday, I had a paper to present to the class. So I was wearing a light gray blazer, a French vanilla blouse and a deep plum, knee-length skirt. Dad, *so was she.* Any normal young woman would have stopped dead in her tracks the way I did and shared a laugh, at the least."

McGill asked, "She didn't even frown?"

"No, I might have been invisible for all she knew." Abbie took a deep breath and let it out. "What was even worse, I felt silly telling all this to Teri."

Secret Service Special Agent Teresa Kinney headed Abbie's security detail.

"But you did," McGill said, "and that was exactly the right thing to do."

"I had to, Dad. I didn't want to start freaking out. Even if this girl's just your garden-variety stalker, that's bad enough. But being the President's step-daughter, I couldn't take any chances."

"No, you can't. Give me the ending once again."

"This morning, I talked to Teri before going to class. She said I was doing exactly the right thing, and there's never anything too small to bring to her attention. I felt better right away, but just before I got to class I thought of something I forgot to mention to Teri. This girl looks almost exactly like me, but she's probably an inch or so taller. I noticed that when she walked right by me. I ran out to see if I could catch Teri ... and I saw her maybe a hundred feet away, talking to the girl I'd been telling her about."

"And Special Agent Kinney didn't look like she was questioning her, possibly in a harsh tone of voice?"

"Teri did look like she *was* scolding the girl, but not like she was questioning her. It was more like when Kenny, Caitie and I were kids, and you gave us *a good talking-to.*"

For just a moment, McGill couldn't help but smile. "Not you so much, sweetheart."

"Okay, thanks, but you know what I mean. I got the impression Teri and this girl know each other. The idea that my lost twin is with the Secret Service scared me more than anything else. I mean, what if Teri's gone rogue or something? I know that's crazy, but the whole situation is."

"You said you closed the door to the building you were in before they saw you, right?" McGill asked.

"Yes, at least I think so."

"And you're in your thesis adviser's office?"

"Door closed and locked, yes."

"Would you like to spend the weekend at the White House while I get all this worked out?"

"Yes, Dad, I would."

"Okay, honey, I'll send Deke and Leo to pick you up right away. With orders to Teri and the rest of your protection detail to stand clear."

"Dad, I feel kind of foolish, but so much better, too."

"Never hesitate to call me, kiddo. I'm *always* glad to hear from you."

What McGill didn't say was nobody ever truly died of embarrassment.

Other causes of mortality, however, were innumerable.

Nagle Warren Mansion — Cheyenne, Wyoming

The two leading candidates for the Republican nomination to become President, Senate Majority Leader Oren Worth and General Warren Altman, United States Air Force chief of staff, retired, met in the library of the fanciest bed-and-breakfast in the Cowboy State. Worth and Altman had both gone to college in Colorado: the School of Mines for the senator and the Air Force Academy for the general. But Altman had also been born in Colorado while Worth arrived in the world in Utah. They might have held their meeting in Denver, but the senator didn't want to cede the home-state edge to the general.

After 33 primary elections and caucuses to that point, Worth held a pledged delegate lead of 739 to 608 over Altman. The magic number needed to win the GOP nomination on the first ballot was 1237. Nine hundred and forty-four delegates were still available to be won in the upcoming contests.

Worth had the statistical edge to win the nomination, but Altman had recently won Arizona, an unexpected and unpleasant turn of events for Worth, and the general's poll numbers in remaining races made it look like either of the two men could arrive at the convention in Philadelphia that summer as the front-runner, if not the outright winner.

There was only one other candidate remaining in the race with them, Representative Hale Eddy, a moderate House member from Austin, Texas, and he was regarded as more of an obstinate bystander than a viable alternative. Worth and Altman viewed each other as the only obstacle between himself and a general election contest with Vice President Jean Morrissey.

The party hierarchy had commissioned a poll to see which of them would do better against the VP. The result was a wash: both of them would lose by three to five points. Interestingly, though, a combined ticket of the two of them, with either on top, would just squeak past Morrissey. Desperate to regain the White House, the party leaders had persuaded both men to meet privately and see if they could work out an accommodation. The two men would join forces with one of them claiming the Presidential slot and the other agreeing to become Vice President.

After both of their political teams had concurred that the meeting would be held in neither man's home state, they consented to a compromise location: Wyoming. It bordered both Utah and Colorado and had the proper rugged, Western atmosphere.

By mutual agreement, the two principals agreed to meet without advisers or handlers to accompany them. They wanted to take each other's personal measure. Not see who had the most adept strategists and fundraisers working for him. In the end, it always came down to who the best man was — or most recently the best woman. Damn Patricia Grant to hell.

The meeting, as proposed by their negotiators, would start with a toast to the proposition that one of them would become the next President, using the scripted line, "Here's to my presidency."

Worth had brought with him a bottle of Yamazaki Single Malt Whiskey; Altman had arrived with a bottle of Jack Daniel's Old No. 7. Each man thought he spotted a weakness in his opponent's choice, but they both kept their thoughts to themselves.

Once their drinks had been downed, their advisers left the room.

The room was furnished with facing leather wing chairs placed in front of a lit fireplace. A set designer couldn't have done better. Then again, maybe one had been called in.

The senate majority leader said, "I won't insult you, Warren, by asking if you'd like to be my Vice-Presidential running mate."

The general offered an icy grin in response. "Only because you wouldn't want me to do you in once we were both in office."

Worth had the self-confidence to laugh. "True enough. There is more than one avenue to the Oval Office. But I could certainly have the Secret Service keep a close eye on you. Thing is, neither of us sees himself as anyone else's number two."

Altman knew what was coming next. He wished he'd had another whiskey in hand, but he held Worth's gaze without further fortification.

The senator delivered as expected. "The thing is, Warren, you've never made it all the way to the top, have you? Oh, you were chief of staff of the Air Force, all right, and had four stars on your shoulder, but you never became Chairman of the Joint Chiefs. You know, the nation's *highest* ranking military officer, the guy the President turns to in the most awful of times."

Altman knew Worth wasn't done and waited him out.

Better to let the other guy expend all his ammo before you counter-attacked.

"On the other hand," Worth continued, "I was the founder and the CEO of a multi-billion dollar corporation, and I'm now the majority leader of the United States Senate."

The implication that Worth's logical, maybe inevitable, next step was the presidency didn't have to be voiced. The subtext was Worth could finance his campaign far beyond whatever amount Altman could wheedle from his donors. The combination of Worth's history of achievement and his wealth had been enough to scare off all but the most delusional competitors, Hale Eddy, and a half-dozen others, who never stood a chance of winning the Republican nomination, six of whom had now dropped out.

The only real challenger was Warren Altman.

Despite his disadvantages, the general was serious competition.

That was why the party had called for this meeting.

They didn't want their two best chances to win the election to tear each other to pieces.

Altman knew all that and counter-punched. "You're right about what you just said, Senator, but you skipped right past the most significant advantage I have. I've not only served in the military, unlike you, I've flown *combat* missions. I've dropped *bombs* on our nation's enemies. You might not think something like that counts as much as it once did. After all, there hasn't been a President who's seen combat since Kennedy. The last combat vet who ran, John Kerry, got Swift-boated and lost. But I'll tell you right now that kind of bullshit won't work on me."

Altman leaned forward. "The world is only getting more dangerous and I think the military candidate's time has come around again. I think a man with my record will make the general election voters feel safer than any businessman or politician possibly could."

Worth had, of course, considered that point of view and found it at least plausible if not entirely persuasive. He wasn't at all surprised by the card Altman had just played, but he thought it worthwhile to meet with him anyway. There was nothing like seeing a man up close to take his true measure.

Worth said, "So we'll each give it our all, and neither of us will be intimidated or bought off."

Altman laughed. "Come on now, Senator. Who could possibly

buy you?"

Worth smiled. "No one I know of, and I don't see you as being motivated by money either."

The general shook his head. "Got all I need."

"So may the better man win, right? We'll both fight hard but fair," Worth said.

"Hard as we can, I'm sure. Dirty only if the other guy does first."

"And despite the polls, we're both sure we can beat Jean Morrissey."

Altman nodded. "Can't have another woman President."

"No, we can't."

The general said, "There's one more thing you should think about, Senator."

"What's that?"

"It's almost inevitable these days that a President will wind up with blood on his hands, one way or another. As I said, I've already got blood on mine. You should ask yourself if you're up to the task."

Oren Worth's eyes narrowed. "Oh, I have *no* worries about that."

With that, the private meeting broke up. Party officials filled the room, and a photographer got a shot of the two men shaking hands. Everyone put on a happy face, even though the party chairman and his cronies silently cursed that neither of the two SOBs could find the grace to accept the Vice-President's spot on a dream ticket.

The party chairman didn't ask for a pledge that the loser of the primary fight would support the winner in the general election. He'd had enough disappointment for one day.

McGill's Hideaway, The White House — Washington, DC

McGill called Kenny out in Palo Alto; he got his son's voice-mail.

"Hi, this is Ken. Sorry I missed you. Call you back as soon as

I can."

McGill's surprise on two counts all but pushed aside the disappointment he felt at not reaching ... Ken? Where had Kenny gone? The scamp he'd known all of his life. Well, all of his son's life. But he supposed once a young man went off to college, to begin the studies that would lead to a career in medicine, he could adopt a more serious variation of his name. Okay, McGill could live with that, but the *voice* on the recorded message, when had that shifted from tenor to baritone? Would a bass voice be next? Good God, his kids were growing up fast.

"It's just Dad, Ken," McGill said, biting off the final familiar syllable. "Give me a call when you get a minute, okay? Love you. Bye."

McGill had wanted to ask his son if he'd noticed any doppelgänger lurking nearby. If Abbie had a double, why not Ken? He didn't want to leave that question on his son's voicemail, though. It was hard enough going through life with a team of bodyguards, as it was. When Ken ... jeez, it was hard not to say Kenny.

When the lad got back to him, they'd talk. McGill would get a sense of things and respond appropriately. Try not to mislabel his son more than once or twice.

Moving on to his youngest child, he called Caitie in Santa Monica.

She was in. "Hey, Dad. I was just thinking of you."

"Favorably, I hope."

"Yeah, you're my favorite dad, no doubt."

Since Caitie had a stepfather, Lars Enquist, who was a terrific guy, McGill took his daughter's words as sincere praise.

"So what's up?" Caitie asked.

"I just talked to Abbie," he said.

"So you know. That's what I was thinking I should talk to you about."

"Wait a minute," McGill said. "What should you talk to me about?"

"Well, you're calling about our stand-ins, right?"

"Stand-ins?"

Caitie still played small parts in movies and TV, saving her pay for her film school expenses in Paris next year. McGill knew that and admired his daughter's growing sense of independence. But confusing film-work with what was going on with Abbie had left him a step behind.

Caitie clarified.

"Dad, what I mean is, my protection detail has a new member. Someone who sorta looks like me. Actually, in broad outline, the resemblance is pretty close. Good casting. Only she doesn't have my *je ne sais quoi*. Sorry if I wasn't clear, but I pretty much think in cinematic terms these days."

McGill asked, "So you know this look-alike is working with the Secret Service?"

"Sure, Sandy introduced us to each other."

Special Agent Sandra Mikaski headed up Caitie's protection detail.

"She did?"

"Of course. You know me. I *see* things. That'll be essential when I'm a director. If I saw Carrie hanging around and none of the guys —"

The Secret Service special agents, both male and female.

"— took notice of her, I might have gone over and laid some Dark Alley on her."

Dark Alley being the martial arts discipline, akin to organized street-fighting, McGill had taught all his children.

"So how do you feel about all this?"

"I'm cool with it."

But not entirely, according to McGill's acute paternal ear.

"Except for?" he said.

"Well, there is something."

"You're frightened?"

"No, that's not it."

"Really?" McGill asked.

"Really. Dad, half the people in L.A. have bodyguards. The

other half *are* bodyguards."

"That doesn't leave anybody to make threats," McGill pointed out.

"So, I'm a filmmaker, not a math geek. Yeah, there are bad guys, too. But just about anyone can be in danger anytime. I'm not special in that way. Only I have the best bodyguards in the world. I really don't worry. I'm not a kid anymore."

Yet another bulletin his children were becoming adults, McGill thought.

He asked, "Does Kenny—"

"Ken," Caitie corrected.

Restraining himself, McGill acquiesced. "Does Ken have a stand-in, too?"

"Yes."

"And since you know about that, may I assume he does, too?"

"*Oui.*"

She was teasing him now, McGill knew, but he didn't bite.

He said, "Abbie didn't."

"I wouldn't have told her either," Caitie said. "She usually has her head in the clouds. And she's more idealistic than Kenny and me."

"Ken and you," McGill said.

"*Touché.*"

Damn, if the kid hadn't set him up for that one.

He asked, "Are you planning to change your name anytime soon?"

"McGill?"

The child was merciless.

"I can have Patti yank your passport, you know," he said.

A moment of silence ensued. The threat was being taken seriously.

"Sorry, Dad. I was just teasing. A friend and I are working on a comedy script. To answer your question, I'm keeping my name the way it is. I like it, especially when it's carried by a French accent."

"Thank you. Now, tell me what's bothering you about your new double, Carrie."

"I thought I might have slipped that one past you."

"Give," he told his youngest.

"She's having trouble with her assignment. I don't think she dislikes me, but she might start soon. She's not crazy about pretending to be a teenager. Maybe the other special agents tease her or something."

"You didn't slip that one past me either," he said. "Why might Carrie start disliking you?"

"Well ... seeing how my look looks on someone else, I decided I needed a change."

Repressing a sigh, he asked, "And how did you manage that?"

Caitie told him, asked if he'd like her to text him a selfie.

Exhibiting patience more saintly than fatherly, McGill said, "Sure."

He couldn't wait to see his youngest as a blonde with spiked pink highlights.

The White House — Washington, D.C.

President Patricia Grant sat behind her desk in the Oval Office with Vice President Jean Morrissey and Chief of Staff Galia Mindel sitting in guest chairs opposite her. VP Morrissey was being included in as much of the President's decision-making process as possible. Things had been that way since the start of the year. The Vice-President was going through the run-up to Election Day in November being able to say she was the only candidate in the race for the White House who'd served a real apprenticeship to the big job.

So far, her only competition from the Democrats was Senate Minority Leader Dick Bergen of Illinois. Strictly speaking, the two candidates on the political left were not running against each other. Jean was running for the nomination of the new Cool Blue party. Dick was running for the Democratic slot. But their respective parties had held their contests on the same days. In terms of votes cast, Jean had outpolled Dick in 20 out of 33 states.

There was excitement about the new progressive party, and Jean's tough-minded, no-nonsense rhetoric had made clear that if either of the GOP candidates thought she was going to be a push-over, they'd better think twice. At a rally back home in Minnesota, held at the Xcel Energy Center, home rink of the NHL's Minnesota Wild team, Jean had spoken to a cheering capacity crowd from center ice.

Wearing her University of Minnesota uniform and holding a hockey stick.

After telling the throng what she intended to do to maintain national security, create jobs and make sure every American had a chance to earn a good living and a secure future, she asked, "What will I do to either of those guys who might stand in my way? Just watch."

The crowd cheered as it saw paper likenesses of Oren Worth and Warren Altman, dressed as hockey goalies, pushed out onto the ice, each positioned in front of a goal net at either end of the rink. The place went nuts as Jean dropped two pucks on the ice.

Using her stick to push one of the pucks forward, she rushed toward the net "Altman" was defending. At the blue line, Jean raised her stick and banged a slap shot that shredded the general's like-ness. Spurred on by a huge roar of approval, Jean wheeled, collected the other puck with her stick and similarly destroyed "Worth."

Her fiancé, FBI Deputy Director Byron DeWitt, had come up with the idea to show how hockey tough Jean Morrissey was. He'd seen a private demonstration of his sweetheart's athletic prowess and told her, "You know, you really ought to take your act public."

The Vice President ran the idea past her most trusted political adviser, the man who'd become her chief of staff if she won the election, her brother, Frank.

"Let's dress it up a bit," he said. "Throw a few more honors into the mix."

Drawing on Jean's former status as a top-rank collegiate athlete, the branding tagline became: Jean Morrissey, All-American. Honor roll smart. Hockey tough.

Both of the GOP candidates called Jean's performance on ice childish.

Their campaigns, though, started to worry big time.

Because if there was anything Americans like more than the military and self-made billionaires, it was sports heroes. The spike in mothers enrolling their daughters in pee-wee hockey leagues, alone, told the Republicans they would have trouble with the women's vote.

The Vice President's upcoming wedding to a handsome FBI man was bound to win a further multitude of female hearts and votes. A poster of Jean hitting a slap-shot, available for a $20 donation to her campaign, was proving to be a hit with a lot of male voters.

Patricia Grant, with her movie star good looks, had played her advantage subtly.

Jean Morrissey was right in your face with her athletic sex appeal.

Daring you to prove your masculinity was secure by voting for her.

The two leading politicians on the left, Jean and Dick Bergen, had already agreed to the deal that Oren Worth and Warren Altman had rejected. Whoever had a clear advantage in primary votes cast would be at the top of a combined progressive ticket, and the other would accept the Vice Presidential slot.

That way nobody's partisans would feel left out and stay at home on Election Day.

In the meantime, however, there were several important matters to be resolved on Patti Grant's watch. Chief of Staff Galia Mindel enumerated that day's list.

"We're getting closer to working out a deal with the Uruguayans to bring Tyler Busby back to the United States to stand trial."

"What does Montevideo want in return?" Patti asked.

"Military equipment?" Jean said.

Galia replied, "Not so much in terms of hardware, but personnel."

The President was clearly surprised. "They're asking us to set up a base in Uruguay?"

The U.S. was generally viewed favorably by most countries in *America del Sur,* but American military presences there were more controversial. The memory of Washington's complicity in the overthrow of the Allende government in Chile still lingered after more than forty years.

Galia shook her head. "They don't want any facilities. What they're looking for are special forces people to train local military personnel in anti-terrorism methods and strategies."

"Terrorism is a worry in Uruguay?" the President asked. "I don't remember that in any of my daily briefings."

"No, ma'am, it's not a concern at the moment."

The President looked at her number two. Jean Morrissey said, "They're doing the Boy Scout thing, being prepared. And if anything should happen they'll be more ready than they would otherwise. Also, if there was a significant aggression against their small country and American personnel are on hand —"

"We'd have a good rationale to reinforce our people and help the Uruguayans," the President said. She was glad Jean understood the subtext. It made the President feel good to know she'd be passing the baton to the right person.

"It's also a reasonable request, low key, likely to fly under the media radar and it gets us Tyler Busby in return," Jean said.

"Can we get him back before I leave office?" the President asked.

"With a little haggling between the State Department and Montevideo, I think we can," Galia responded.

Patti Grant nodded. "Good. I want to see that bastard in a federal prison cell before I leave town."

"Anything new on Representative Brock?" the Vice President asked.

"Nothing verifiable," Galia said. "There are rumors, however, that he's been killed."

"By whom?" the President asked.

"No one we can point to with certainty, but chatter intercepted by the NSA suggests that a Middle Eastern terrorist cell might be involved. The widely held inference, though, is vengeance for the death of Bahir Ben Kalil was had by his twin sister, Hasna Kalil."

The President sighed. "I don't suppose we can interview her."

"She worked for Doctors Without Borders, but our intelligence is that she's taken an abrupt leave of absence. No one knows where she is. The question now is how hard do we want to look for her."

"Let me think about that," Patricia Grant said. "What's next?"

"The bigger question of the moment is how quickly the Department of Justice should proceed with the prosecution of the representatives and senators who were looting the budget of the Department of Defense."

"Only as fast as legal prudence dictates," the President said. "We don't want any mistakes with this prosecution." She turned to Jean Morrissey, "I'm sorry if this complicates anything for your campaign, Jean, but I have no choice."

The Vice President nodded, "I'd do the same thing if I were in your position, Madam President. I do have a few questions for the chief of staff, if I may."

The President nodded. Jean turned to Galia.

"How good does the case against these … defendants look?"

Wouldn't have been polite to call them pricks in the Oval Office.

"Rock solid," Galia said. "They stole by the ton and didn't have the expertise to hide all that loot without leaving a trail."

"The American people will be able to see that when it comes out at trial?"

"Everyone who isn't willfully blind."

"Hell," the Vice President said, "it could work to my political advantage if it came out before the election, but if it doesn't, that's okay, too."

"A wise attitude, Ms. Vice President," Galia said.

Jean nodded. "Here's one thing you might pass along to the prosecution team, Galia. Tell them to let the defendants know that if they don't take any deal that's offered to them, and they're found guilty during my presidency, I'll make a public statement to the effect that anything less than a life sentence for their crimes would be inadequate punishment. I'd do that at the risk of messing with judicial prerogative. I won't worry about it screwing up a second term for me because I won't be running for one."

Galia turned to look at the President, silently asking if Patricia Grant wanted her to comply with Jean Morrissey's request. The President nodded.

"Let the bastards know that any attempt to postpone the inevitable will cost them," the President said. "Maybe we'll save the country the expense of a trial and endless appeals."

"Yes, ma'am," Galia said.

The President looked at Jean and said, "Hockey tough."

"Yes, ma'am," the Vice President agreed.

The meeting broke up a moment later, and McGill entered the Oval Office.

Once they had the room to themselves, Patti told McGill, "This must be serious, if not entirely earthshaking. I don't remember you being on my schedule today."

She gestured her husband to a sofa and sat next to him, leaving a small measure of separation as it didn't seem like a moment for cuddling.

McGill didn't waste any words. "I got a call from Abbie a little while ago. I won't say she was distraught, but she was edging that way."

He expected a show of concern, but the look he saw on his wife's face was more one of sympathy — and understanding. She had knowledge of what was going on. Had known from the start, possibly, what the situation was.

What with two of his children also being clued in before he was, McGill was starting to feel like the slow kid in class. He didn't appreciate playing that role at the moment. Before he could say a word, though, Patti took his face in her hands and kissed him.

Gently. With compassion. Not a hint of seduction to distract him.

"Abbie noticed her decoy," Patti said, lowering her hands but keeping eye contact.

McGill only nodded, fixating on the word decoy.

It sounded much more menacing than stand-in.

His heart turned to ice. "Someone is threatening our children? Again?"

Some of the more misbegotten followers of the late Reverend Burke Godfrey had made a point of menacing the McGill offspring years ago.

Allowing herself a sigh, Patti said, "Still would be a more accurate word."

"What?" McGill asked, surprised. "There have been other threats?"

Patti nodded. "Jim, there's always someone threatening you and me. Every single day. Sorry to say, most days our kids are included, too. I've told the Secret Service to let me know only of the ones that are truly credible, if you and I are the targets. The threshold for Abbie, Ken and Caitie is much lower. If any threat against them is remotely possible, I hear about it."

McGill remembered the few times over the past seven years she'd shared such information with him. He'd insisted on getting the details one more time directly from Celsus Crogher and later Elspeth Kendry. In every such case, there hadn't been anything more dangerous to deal with than someone giving voice to malignant fantasies.

That in itself was enough to make McGill's blood pressure spike.

Not that he could do a damn thing about it. If he tried to punch out every miscreant who held a vile thought against his wife or children, his arms would fall off before he got out of the states starting with the letter A.

Even so, he was still a good enough detective to ask a pertinent question.

"Do you know Kenny abbreviated his name because he called

you?"

"Ken? Yes, he asked me to do that. I said, 'Of course.'"

"He called because he spotted his decoy, too?"

Patti nodded. "He did. I'm so proud of him. I love all our children, but I think he's still with us for a special reason. He's going to do something great. I don't know what yet, but I feel it in my soul."

Hearing that sentiment made McGill's heart swell with pride. His mind, however, still focused on potential dangers.

"If there's no new threat rising above jerk-off chatter, why did the decoys pop up? Someone must have gone to a lot of trouble to find special agents who bear some resemblance."

"You know who did it," Patti said.

"Elspeth."

"Yes."

"But why?" McGill asked.

"Because she's feeling intuitive, too. She thought to herself: What would be the best time to wound me and you?"

McGill understood completely. "Right when we thought all our troubles were behind us. When we thought we were safe."

"Exactly. When there are no threats against the children on the horizon that rise above the level of being laughable. I had no way to argue with that; I certainly wasn't going to veto the idea. So I told her, yes, and with you being busy mapping out your post-White House business plans, I didn't bother telling you. You didn't need the distraction."

It was true. McGill hadn't worked a case of his own in months. He hadn't felt the impulse to do so, not with Sweetie retiring from the firm. Maybe being an executive, a delegator, would be all he was good for in the future.

He asked Patti, "Do these decoys have good enough likenesses to fool anyone who doesn't need strong reading glasses?"

"You tell me," she said.

She got up and went to her desk and opened a drawer. McGill followed along. He took the 8x10 glossies she handed him. There were two for each decoy, before and after. Before featured the special agents in their everyday appearances. Even at that point, there were strong similarities. In the after photos, with haircuts and eye colors altered, with make-up added to change the emphasis of facial bone structures, the resemblances were —

"Amazing," McGill said.

"The Secret Service, with a nudge from me, made use of some disguise artists the CIA has on staff."

"These people could work in Hollywood."

"Some of them have."

McGill took Patti's hand. "So Abbie, Ken and Caitie are as safe as they possibly can be?"

"Yes … and let's hope Elspeth's worries are just that and nothing more."

McGill felt the same way, but he was still going to talk with SAC Kendry.

Patti misinterpreted the lingering concern that showed on his face.

"Something's still wrong?" she asked.

Yielding to a rare moment of evasion, McGill said, "I was just thinking. With all this security hoo-haw, I don't even know the kids' current Secret Service code names. They do change from time to time, don't they?"

Patti nodded. She said, "Abbie is Big Sis; Ken, after he spat in death's eye, was renamed Braveheart. I told Elspeth to keep that one."

McGill beamed and nodded.

Then he asked, "What about Caitie?"

Patti said with a straight face, "She's Daddy's Girl."

That made McGill smile, too.

CHAPTER 2

Saturday, March 26, 2016
Punta de Rieles Prison — Montevideo, Uruguay

The women's prison in Montevideo was known for its "human touch" approach to incarceration. Even so, it didn't forsake traditional features like barbed wire and armed guards around the perimeter. Inside, though, the prison officers had educational backgrounds in social work, psychology and human rights.

The inmates had been convicted of a variety of crimes. The only offenses that disqualified a guilty woman from consideration for assignment to *Punta de Rieles* — Rails End —were sexually based assault and drug trafficking.

The prison featured a computer center, a bakery and a candy store.

Some people scoffed that the inmates were being pampered, but the recidivism rate for inmates confined at Rails End was 2% compared to 50% for the country's traditional prisons. As the only offense that could be documented against the Chinese woman named Ah-lam, possibly the wife of fugitive billionaire Tyler Busby, was child endangerment, flinging her infant son at an FBI agent, she'd been sent to Rails End in the hope of mending her approach to mothering.

That assumption had yet to be put to the test, but after almost a year inside the prison, Ah-lam had proved to be a model inmate. The U.S. government vigorously protested the lenient approach, and the highest authorities in Uruguayan government had been informed that Ah-lam almost certainly was a witness vital to the prosecution of Tyler Busby for attempting to assassinate the President of the United States and her extradition had been requested. Taking the American government's urgent plea into consideration, the prison authorities locked a tracking device around Ah-lam's left ankle.

If she tried to leave the prison grounds and made it past the barbed wire and the guards, an alarm would sound immediately, and she'd be captured and sent to a much less hospitable lock-up.

Ah-lam hadn't tampered with the device, but spent many of her waking hours thinking about how to defeat it, usually under the guise of pretending to meditate, an activity highly favored by the administration of Rails End.

She was deep in a session of silent scheming when one of the psychology majors employed as a guard found Ah-lam on break from her job in the candy store.

"A lawyer is here to see you," the guard said.

Ah-lam opened her eyes and asked. "Someone my husband sent?"

"No, he said he was sent by a Mr. Donald Yang of Hong Kong."

Ah-lam could only think, "*Mā de.*"

Mandarin for, "Oh, shit."

Yang had been her boss, the owner of the *Shining Dawn,* the yacht Tyler Busby had leased from the Chinese billionaire. Ah-lam had betrayed Yang and thrown in with Busby, even though she'd known she was putting a certain death sentence on herself. These days, if she had been located anywhere outside a prison, Yang wouldn't have sent a lawyer to visit her. He'd have sent thugs to kidnap her. To be presented to the boss trussed up like a sacrificial lamb.

"Is something wrong?" the psych major asked, correctly reading the distress in Ah-lam's eyes.

"No, no."

"You're sure? If you like, I can tell Mr. Kwan you don't want to see him."

Ah-lam startled visibly, and immediately hated herself for letting her emotions show. "Mr. Kwan?"

"Reginald Kwan, he said. Do you know him? He says he's here to assist you with your legal problems."

Reggie? Her youngest brother was already a lawyer. Ah-lam suddenly felt old as well as scared. It hardly seemed there was time for Reggie to go through law school, but he'd always been a smart little bugger.

Not as smart as her, though. Maybe there was a way to play things to her advantage.

Ah-lam said, "I would like to see Mr. Kwan. I am just surprised he came so far to see me."

That much was true. The guard led Ah-lam to a room that appeared to offer privacy, but who could say for sure? She'd looked at her younger brother, all dressed up and grown up. She uttered one whispered word to him.

He understood and nodded.

There were over 200 dialects of spoken Chinese. Ah-lam had just cued Reggie as to which one they'd use. The tongue of the boat people of Aberdeen Harbor. The first language both of them had learned. Ah-lam assumed their conversation would be recorded. She doubted, though, that anyone in Uruguay would understand what they were saying.

That meant they'd turn to the Americans for help. Somewhere in the U.S. population, if not in the intelligence community, were people who'd know what was being said. But finding those people might take time. If the interpreter was a civilian, striking a bargain would require haggling over a price and more time. When things dragged out, there was more room for maneuver.

If not that, then at least the drug of self-delusion.

Reggie got right to the point, showing no emotion at his sister's plight.

"Mr. Yang wants Tyler Busby to die before he reaches the United States."

Ah-lam didn't need to ask why. Busby knew something, that if revealed, would be embarrassing or, worse, damaging to Yang's patrons, the leading members of the Politburo Standing Committee. If Yang caused trouble for that hallowed body, his own head would roll.

Or he'd run and hide as Ah-lam had.

She told her brother, "The FBI also wants my help. They say I either testify against Busby or rot here in Uruguay."

Reggie smiled. "From what I've seen, conditions in this prison are much better than the ones in which you and I were born and raised."

Ah-lam couldn't argue with that. She asked, "What is the hammer?"

The threat Yang held over her.

Reggie said, "Your entire family will die, very badly, including me."

For the first time in months, Ah-lam smiled.

Reggie understood the significance. "You're right. We were never a very sentimental group. No filial piety among us."

"What else is threatened?" she asked.

"Your son Jonathan's life."

Ah-lam had had some time to consider her callous treatment of her newborn son. In the moment, she'd had no doubt that hurling him at that FBI she-devil was the right thing to do. The way that bitch slammed Ah-lam with her iron skull, Ah-lam's breastbone still ached at night. Despite everything, though, Ah-lam was glad Tyler had caught Jonathan, saved their son from any real harm.

Who was to say, maybe she would never be free again. Never have the opportunity to bear another child. Certainly not with a man as rich as Tyler, someone who in his own heart was a modern-day pirate. The combination of their genes might produce a truly exceptional young man. Someone who might become an emperor or as close to it as the modern world permitted.

"You actually care for your child?" Reggie asked.

"He means nothing to me."

They both knew that was a bargaining position, not the truth.

"Oh, well, then I will have to tell Mr. Yang there is no way for you to help him. I will await my fate with our family. You will die here alone at some distant time, perhaps after even you have forgotten who you were."

Ah-lam asked Reggie, "How do you know Tyler hasn't already told the Americans what Yang wants to hide?"

The young man shrugged. "If that was the case, all of us would be dead already."

"What is the rainbow?" Ah-lam asked.

The sun after the rain. Or in Western terms the pot of gold.

"Jonathan will be well cared for, by me, not our mother and father. He will be educated in the best schools, and he will be set free to pursue his own fortune once he is a man."

Nothing for her, Ah-lam understood. If Reggie had told a lie, it was a good one. The lack of an appeal to her own self-interest buttressed the promise of a bright future for her son. Still, she'd known very little about her brother since he was a small child. He might be a monster, though he could hardly be worse than their parents.

"All right," Ah-lam said, "I'll kill Tyler if I get the chance. But how do I get out of here?"

Reggie smiled again. "You send word to the FBI that you will cooperate, but do it immediately. The people we have watching the American embassy say that a security team from the United States has just arrived to take your dear husband back home with them."

Ah-lam understood the implication.

"They will come to ask me again if I will cooperate with their inquiries. If I say yes, they will put us on the same plane to Washington."

Reggie nodded. "If they are feeling devious, they might even put you in adjacent spaces in the aircraft, hoping the two of you will share whispers they can overhear and record."

"If we are that close to each other, I have no doubt I'll be able to kill Tyler."

Reggie gave his sister a nod and a grin, as if to say, "That's the spirit."

What he said aloud was, "Contact the prison officials as soon as I'm gone. Tell them you must speak to the Americans without delay."

Ah-lam shook her head.

Reggie was so surprised by the rejection he lapsed into English. "What? Why the hell not?"

Ah-lam only looked at him in silence until he repeated himself in Aberdeen Chinese.

"The FBI are not fools," Ah-lam said. "If I went to them, they would be suspicious. When they come to me, my change of heart will be easier for them to accept."

"What if they don't come?"

"Then, as you said, dear brother, we are all dead already."

The White House — Washington, DC

SAC Elspeth Kendry, the head of the President's protective detail, was not in her office when McGill dropped by late Saturday morning. Her secretary told McGill she didn't know when the SAC would be back. McGill said he'd wait. He could have taken the seat adjacent to the secretary's desk, but that wouldn't serve his purpose as well.

Without asking permission, he stepped into Elspeth's office. There were no file cabinets in the room, no computer or printouts on her desk. No official secrets had been left lying about. Not unless the old-fashioned looking landline phone on the desk held some classified information. Maybe a speed-dial connection to … well, whomever the Secret Service would call in a Doomsday scenario. Probably Galia, just to get a confirmation the end was near.

The secretary hadn't objected to McGill's barging in, of course.

He had rarely thrown his weight around during his tenure in the White House, but on the few occasions he had, no one ever had the nerve to tell him to buzz off. He intended to wait for Elspeth for as long as it took, right where he was.

Settling into a posture of silent determination, he was startled when Elspeth's phone rang.

Her secretary called out to him, "It's for you, sir."

Clearly, McGill thought, he'd been ratted out. He couldn't blame the secretary. She was only doing her job, and with Elspeth's devious turn of mind, she'd probably foreseen what McGill might do and had prepared her secretary for it.

McGill only hoped Elspeth hadn't called Patti and she was the one calling him.

He wanted to keep his misgivings to himself, if he could.

Nonetheless, he answered the phone before it rang a second time.

"Jim McGill."

Elspeth Kendry replied, "I was just heading out for an early lunch, sir. Since it's a nice day, I thought I'd get a hot dog on the Mall. If you'd care to join me, lunch will be my treat."

Fine, McGill thought. They could speak outdoors as easily as indoors. And now that the subject of food had been raised, he realized he was hungry. A hot dog al fresco didn't sound half bad. He said, "Where are you?"

"The West Wing entrance."

So not far from the Oval Office, McGill thought. If he'd tried to high-hand the SAC, she could have run to the President to object. Elspeth definitely knew how to seek an advantage.

McGill told her. "I'll have Leo bring my car around. If we have breathing room on the Mall, we'll walk and talk. If it's too crowded, we'll grab some dogs and take a little ride."

"Yes, sir. See you soon."

McGill and Elspeth arrived at the Mall in a matter of minutes. He told Leo and Deke to wait in the car. Leo never had any trouble with that, and Deke was in no position to object. What was he going to say? His boss couldn't protect McGill as well as he could? Not only would that hint of sexism, it would make the remainder of his career in public service miserable.

Deke, Leo and McGill weren't out the White House door quite yet.

McGill and Elspeth both donned sunglasses as they stepped out of the car. Their facial expressions and body language added to the message that they weren't interested in an approach by any member of the general public. That proved not to be a problem. The people strolling the nation's front yard were well occupied by their own companions and conversations.

Elspeth pointed in the direction of her favorite tube-steak vendor and they headed that way.

"The President told me you found out," she said to McGill.

"Yeah."

"You're still worried, even though Holly G. informed you my precautionary steps have no foundation in any credible threat." Holly G. being the President's code name.

"Uh-huh," McGill said, not looking at Elspeth.

She knew what he was doing. Giving her space to fill verbally. Explain in greater depth.

They weren't just out for a walk in the park.

McGill's experience as a big-city cop made it hard for the Secret Service to con him.

Something that had made many of its agents gnash their teeth down to the gums.

Elspeth said, "So you want to know what I'm thinking that isn't rational; something that might only be the product of professional paranoia."

McGill looked at her. "I do. In fact, I insist on it. Or I'm going to start looking around myself."

Elspeth looked back him. She didn't want that, McGill snooping.

"You wouldn't find it, what scared me."

"I can and will try."

They came to the hot dog stand before the conversation could go any further. There were two patrons ahead of them and a young couple joined the line behind them. Elspeth gave everyone nearby, including the hot dog man, a quick appraisal. Nobody needed to be shot.

Elspeth ordered a hot dog with the works; McGill, since Elspeth was buying, ordered two dogs with just mustard and tomato. He dropped a ten-spot into the tip jar. Got a warm smile from the vendor.

Then they were off again: walking, talking and eating.

Taking care not to soil their clothes with condiments.

McGill said, "Nobody asked for an autograph or even said hello."

Meaning the tourists.

"Must be the sunglasses," Elspeth said.

"Or I'm a lame-duck henchman."

"Or they got the vibe we're both armed and wanted to make tracks."

"I've been thinking it will be nice to no longer be a public figure. Just go about my business in public and attract no more attention than the next guy. Now, I'm wondering if that will make me suspicious. Will people be *pretending* if they act like they don't know me?"

"You and the President have been carrying the weight of public scrutiny for a long time. Not my place to give advice, but maybe you should go to a nice island somewhere, away from the crowd, and decompress for a while."

McGill chuckled. "Sounds good, but the missus and I aren't the idle hands type."

Elspeth nodded. "The President has her new foundation to get up and running, and you're really going to open more offices of your investigations firm?"

"Yeah," McGill said. "Once a cop always a cop, I guess."

"It'll be different for you without Holly G. being in the Oval Office."

"I know. I won't have the same clout, but I think Jean Morrissey likes me."

Elspeth laughed. "Yeah, my money says she'll beat either of the guys on the other side."

They came to an empty bench with nobody else in the immediate area.

"You want to sit while I tell you what put my nerves on edge?" Elspeth asked.

"Sure." McGill sat and devoted a bit more energy to eating.

Elspeth swallowed her last bite and took a moment to review an old memory.

"I was fourteen," she began. "My family was living in Beirut. I was a freshman in high school and my best friend was Nadine Najimy. Her father was a successful banker, but he always took the time to come to our school at dismissal time to pick up Nadine and her older brother, Philippe. Mr. Najimy never went anywhere without a bodyguard and an armed driver."

"Does that make you think of Deke and Leo?" McGill asked.

Elspeth nodded. "One day," she continued, "Nadine was absent from school. She was a great student, so I knew she wasn't pretending to be sick or anything. I figured there was some legitimate excuse. Being her friend, I thought she'd want me to get that day's homework assignments for her. My plan was to give them to Philippe to take home with him. Only he wasn't in school that day either, and he was another top-of-the-class student.

"I started to worry, but when I got home my mother told me that if there was a bug going around it was easy for family members to pass it among themselves. I pretended that I believed her, but I couldn't shake my fear that something awful had happened. I don't remember sleeping much that night, but I must've dozed a little. Long enough to have a nightmare I'll never forget. I was in some dark place. I couldn't even see what I was standing on, but it had to be small because I saw Nadine falling past me

"She had this horrible look of fear on her face. She reached a hand out and yelled, 'Save me, Elspeth!' I tried to grab her hand, but then I started to fall, too."

Elspeth cleared her throat and rubbed a tear from an eye.

"I woke up because I fell out of bed. My parents ran into my room, but they couldn't comfort me. I was sure I'd lost my friend. My parents kept me home from school that day, and when my dad came home from work he confirmed that I was right. Nadine, Philippe and Mr. Najimy had been kidnapped. Their driver and their bodyguard had been killed."

"Did all the Najimys die, too?" McGill asked quietly.

Elspeth shook her head. "Just Nadine and Philippe. The kidnappers gave Mr. Najimy a serious beating to show him what merciless bastards they were, and then they dumped him out of a car in front of his bank."

"They wanted ransom," McGill said. "Why didn't he pay it?"

"He wanted to, but his business partners were also his extended family. They didn't want their children kidnapped. They were sure that would happen if the first hostage-taking was successful."

"That and their bank would be drained of all its funds," McGill said.

"Yes, that, too. Anyway, the plan they came up with was to pay the ransom, follow the money car back to the planners, rescue Nadine and Philippe and kill all the bad guys. They managed to kill the kidnappers, all right, but those assholes were a cell of the Palestine Liberation Organization. The PLO pricks had made their plans, too. If there was a rescue attempt, the first thing they'd do was kill Nadine and Philippe. Those poor kids never had a chance."

As awful as the story up to that point was, McGill knew there was more.

He had a good idea of what it was, too.

Elspeth told him without needing to be prompted. "If Nadine and Philippe had lived that would have been their last year in school in Beirut. Their father had planned to take the family to live in France."

Just what McGill had thought. So close to being safe, but so cruelly denied.

"How about the rest of the family," he asked, "the extended

part."

"They got out of the country with most of their money. They knew they couldn't fight the PLO and win. I don't know where they went. I didn't really care. As much pain as I felt, I knew Mr. and Mrs. Najimy had it unimaginably worse. They left Beirut, too."

McGill shook his head. The vile things people could do to each other.

"Thanks for thinking of my kids," he told Elspeth.

She replied, "I don't want to see any of them reaching a hand out to me and my not being able to grab it. Don't be too hard on Holly G. for not sharing with you. I only told her I had a bad feeling. Didn't provide any details."

"Thanks for that, too," McGill said.

McGill's Hideaway — The White House

The first thing McGill did upon returning to his lair was to call his son again, the only one of his children he'd been unable to reach so far. Elspeth's story of a childhood tragedy had made it all the more urgent to reassure himself that *each* of his children was safe. SAC Kendry may have increased the security of the McGill offspring out of nothing more than a painful memory and a flash of intuition, but any good cop knew you had to trust your gut. Instinct often warned you of things your eyes and ears missed.

Ken picked up on the first ring and upon hearing his father's voice said, "Hey, Dad, I just listened to your voicemail and was about to call you."

McGill had to stifle a sigh of relief. It felt so good to hear his son's voice. Even the new, deeper register sounded right, and it held no tone of distress to signal anything was amiss.

Better yet, he was informed, "You can still call me Kenny, if you want. Caitie said you were having a little trouble with that."

"What kind of trouble, and when did the two of you talk?"

"Trouble adjusting and just a few minutes ago. I didn't let you know about the change because I made it on the fly. I just thought

Ken sounded right for being in college. With the profs and all."

"The girls, too, huh?" McGill asked, thinking he should have realized that earlier.

There was a pause on the other end of the call. Then Ken asked, "Did Caitie blab about that? I told her I wanted to tell you."

"She didn't, but is there a girl?"

"Yeah."

McGill could hear the smile in his son's voice.

"So, tell me," he said.

"Well, I was kind of moody when I got to campus and found out Cassidy Kimbrough had a boyfriend." Ms. Kimbrough being a former crush, an older woman by one year and another Stanford undergrad. "That was foolish, I know. What was she going to do? Wait and see if I got admitted to Stanford, too? The odds against anyone getting in are astronomical."

But the odds improved dramatically if you were a fantastic student, had a compelling life story by the time you were a teenager and your step-mother was the President of the United States, McGill knew.

He kept all that to himself and said, "So you were down in the dumps and then …"

"I saw a flyer on a bulletin board: Singers wanted for a comedy-slash-choral group."

"You're singing?" McGill asked.

"I know, I know. I never had much of a voice, for singing or speaking. But then it started to change, kind of late and unexpected. What really hit me was realizing I was getting to sound like you, and you sing great. I called Grandma since I know she gave you voice lessons. She gave me some tips, vocal exercises and all, and I tried out."

McGill smiled. Good old Mom. He'd have to call her soon, too.

"You were successful, I take it," he said.

"Yeah. I'm not as good as you yet, but I'm not half bad, and everyone likes my sense of humor. But the best part is I met Shay Larkin in the group. She's so great, Dad. I know it sounds strange, but she looks a lot like Patti to me. Well, what I imagine Patti looked like at nineteen."

"You're a lucky guy," McGill said.

Still, he couldn't help but wonder what Carolyn, McGill's first wife and Ken's mother, would think about her son finding a girl who looked like wife number two. Well, they'd cross that bridge if and when they came to it.

Ken said, "Our group is going to do a performance tonight and put the video on YouTube. You can watch it and see how I'm doing, get a look at Shay, too. We'll be doing a duet. Tell me if you see the resemblance to Patti or if I'm just imagining it."

"What's your group's name?" McGill asked.

"That's been our only problem so far. We haven't settled on one yet." Ken laughed. "We'll need *something* to put on the marquee real soon. I'll let you know what we come up with so you can find the video."

"Please do."

"Hey, Dad."

"Yeah?"

"Caitie said you were worried about our decoys. Mine's cool. Nothing to worry about."

"Good to know, Ken."

"I'm still keeping up with my studies, too, in case you're wondering."

"Didn't doubt it for a minute."

"Med school is still my future."

"Unless your act goes over big."

Ken laughed. "Yeah, then I'll play an MD on TV."

Father and son said goodbye, both of them happy.

The warm feeling lasted all of ten minutes before the door to McGill's Hideaway opened without the preliminary courtesy of a knock. Patti was standing there. McGill saw the look on her face. She had news and it was anything but good.

West Los Angeles, California

Secret Service Special Agent Carrie Ramsey got sent home from work that morning. Feeling like a kid scolded for not doing her homework, she fumed the whole drive back to the furnished studio apartment just east of the 405 Freeway. The federal government had provided the place as her lodgings while she worked as Caitlin McGill's diversion double. There was a bureaucratic euphemism for you, *diversion double*. Hah! All that meant was, "Shoot me, not the overprivileged little snot who wants to go study French cinema."

Carrie's instructions for that morning were clear. Wait for the hair stylist and make-up artist to arrive and recreate Carrie's appearance to match Caitie McGill's new look. Shit. She'd told SAC Mikaski that would only make Caitie want to change her look again. Too bad, so sad, Carrie was told. There was nothing the Secret Service could do about that. What they could do was rush to keep their strategy in place. Just another challenge for a special agent to roll with.

The subtext being, "Suck it up and don't whine. It'll look good on your next review."

At least Mikaski hadn't told her she'd laugh about it someday.

Then the SAC gave her some actual good news. The people who were going to provide her new appearance had been in Seattle. They wouldn't be back in L.A. for three hours. Carrie could take that time as her own. Just be back at her apartment before they got to town.

She decided the thing to do was work off some of the hard feelings. If she went to a gym to lift weights, though, she'd punch someone out if said person asked her if she was Caitie McGill. For just a moment, the idea of smacking someone amused her. Maybe she could pretend to be Caitie and get the kid in trouble that way.

Nah, she'd have to 'fess up eventually. And that wouldn't look good at review time.

What forgoing the gym left her with was taking a good, long

run. Keep her head down so no one would mistake her for the little princess. Of course, it'd be really ironic if there was some loon out there targeting the kid and he plugged her when she wasn't even on duty.

As strange as that might sound, the chances of a civilian succumbing to a criminal act were actually far greater than the jeopardy a Secret Service agent faced in the line of duty. Since the beginning of the 20th century, exactly two of its personnel had died on the job.

In 1902, William Craig perished in a road accident while riding in the presidential carriage. In 1950, Private Leslie Coffelt died protecting President Harry Truman when he shot it out with two Puerto Rican nationalists who attacked Blair House with the intention of killing the chief executive. Though fatally wounded by the would-be assassins, Coffelt managed to kill one of them and wound the other.

The only other agent to be hit by gunfire in a presidential assassination attempt was Tim McCarthy who stepped in front of a bullet meant for President Ronald Reagan. He was struck in the abdomen but he made a full recovery.

That history made Carrie want to go for a run in her Secret Service raid jacket, her employer's name emblazoned front and back. Maybe that would provide good juju for her. But SAC Mikaski wouldn't like it, and it was too warm to wear a jacket anyway.

Carrie tied her shoelaces and headed out in a Getty Museum T-shirt she'd been given upon arrival in Los Angeles and a pair of Nike running shorts. She left her duty weapon, her Secret Service ID and her fake Caitlin McGill driver's license in the studio's safe. She didn't know L.A. from personal experience, but she'd studied a street map on the flight out from Washington, DC. She was oriented to the major streets, places of interest and freeways on the Westside.

She started off heading northeast with the UCLA campus in mind. The school was a big place. She figured if she circled it and headed back to the apartment from there, that would be a good stretch of the legs. Let her work up a healthy sweat. Dissipate some anger.

And, who knew, maybe she'd spot a co-ed who looked even more like Caitie McGill than she did. Recruit the kid. Give herself the opportunity to get back to doing something worthwhile.

As she started her run, she told herself she felt nothing personal against young Ms. McGill. She'd hit town wanting to like her package, as the person to be protected was known to the Secret Service. So far, nothing about Caitie McGill had changed Carrie's preconception.

Except that the kid spoke French half the time, nearly *all* the time when she was on her phone. That made it impossible for Carrie to understand her conversations. Overhear whether she had it in mind to do something dumb that would have to be stopped before it got started. Like most practical people in high school and college, Carrie had studied Spanish as her foreign language.

That was a simple choice. Spanish was effectively the second language of the U.S., and if Carrie wanted to go somewhere outside the country on vacation, Cancun would come before Montreal. Cabo before Quebec City. Okay, if you were talking Europe, sure, she'd choose Paris over most other places, but she'd bet everyone in the tourist zones of Paris spoke English anyway.

In terms of the job she'd been assigned to do, well, even if the historical risks of working in the Presidential protective detail weren't all that great, you still had to ask yourself the one big question: Would I willingly and without hesitation lay down my life for the President?

Carrie's answer was an emphatic yes, as it had to be.

Based on that spirit of self-sacrifice, she'd also affirmed that she would do the same for anyone else whose safety was placed in her hands. The job couldn't be done on a pick-and-choose basis. That just didn't cut it.

The thing was, though, those situations called for interposing yourself between a shooter and a target who was somebody else. Nobody had ever said they would want her to pretend to *be* someone else for the express purpose of putting herself in the crosshairs. That required a different mindset.

Not that she could turn the assignment down. The ranks of the Secret Service were not meant for the faint of heart. Whatever the danger, you had to step up and be quick about it.

You couldn't dwell on the fact that the world had become a different place, even from the 1980s. These days, you could find violent assholes, foreign and domestic, at every point of the compass, and probably some from outer space for all she knew. For another thing, hardly anybody used six-shooters anymore. Didn't matter if they packed a handgun or a rifle, the magazine in the weapon would be jammed with umpteen bullets. The theory being the more lead you put in the air, the better the odds at least one round would be fatal.

And then there were the asshole bombers, suicidal or otherwise.

So, really, the job was way more dangerous now than in the old days.

The other thing Carrie just couldn't shake was the idea that by doing her best to look like Caitie McGill, she would be attracting the kid's fate to herself. And she didn't mean she'd be making a film with Vincent Cassel, a French actor Carrie had never heard of until she did the research, but one the kid went on and on about.

The fact that Caitie McGill *was* still a kid had proved to be yet another sore point for Carrie. When you did a life-and-death job, you wanted to be taken seriously. At 27, Carrie certainly took life seriously. She'd graduated summa cum laude from Northeastern University with a bachelor's degree in criminal justice. As demanded by her job, she'd done graduate work and was closing in on her master's degree in the same field, at the same stellar grade point average. She'd met all the other requirements of being a Secret Service agent, perhaps most proudly finishing in the top quartile of the physical fitness exam.

For all that, there was no denying that *she* still looked like a kid. Maybe not ten years younger than her actual age but she could pass for 20 with no sweat. She got carded at every bar she entered.

"Hey, sweetie, show me you're 21."

There were times when she wanted to whip out her federal officer's ID, but so far she'd managed to make do with her driver's license. She thought of such situations as exercises in self-control. SAC Mikaski had intuited this part of Carrie's difficulties and told her, "Be grateful for small favors. You won't always look young. Enjoy it while you can."

Sandra Mikaski was 40 but looked closer to 50.

Carrie still thought that locking in your looks at, say, 35 would be ideal.

Coping with Caitie McGill's *joie de vivre,* as the kid liked to put it, was another problem. The kid waltzed through life like she was just another teenager who had herself a real sweet deal and not a care in the world. Her step-mother's the President of the United States and her father's maybe more famous than the President. She's off to France to study movie-making in a year.

At Caitie's age, Carrie was, by her own choice, a cashier at a Foodmaster Supermarket.

Still, she couldn't say Caitie was a snob because she wasn't. She was polite, funny and considerate. SAC Mikaski had told her Caitie bought birthday presents for every member of her protection detail and at Christmas made a donation in the names of the special agents to the Fallen Warriors Fund, supporting the families of military personnel who were killed or wounded in action. Took the money out of her own pocket, too, didn't get it from Daddy or the President.

That was the kind of thing Carrie normally would have admired. Hell, she did admire it. There was a lot to like about the kid. But Caitie shouldn't think she could just glide through life. The world didn't work that way. Why the hell would the Secret Service bring Carrie in to work with Caitie's protective detail if her situation wasn't at least potentially dangerous?

And what did the kid have to say to Carrie about that?

"Well, you're all good at your jobs, aren't you?"

"Of course, we are."

"All right, then. I've got faith in you. Don't you have faith in yourself?"

Carrie had to fight from grinding her teeth. "Yes, we have faith. We have training, experience, equipment. Everything anyone could ask for to keep you safe. But we're all human, too. That means we're imperfect no matter how hard we try."

The kid had smiled at her. "I know. Sweetie taught me that a long time ago, people being fallible, I mean. So, if any bad guys get past all of my Secret Service friends, I'll just have to fall back on my Dark Alley moves."

"What?"

Caitie explained the fighting system her father had taught his children.

"You really think stuff like that will help you?" Carrie asked.

"Couldn't hurt. Bet you can't lay a hand on me. Have to warn you, though, if you try me, I'll probably leave a mark on you."

Carrie wanted to pop the kid a good one when she heard that, but she didn't think that would help with career advancement. Caitie seemed to understand the dilemma. She called in SAC Mikaski, telling her, "I'd like to show the new member of the gang that I know a thing or two about protecting myself, if all else fails. She's reluctant to do anything that might hurt me. Doesn't want to lose her job, reasonably enough. Can she and I go back to that gym we used last time?"

Last time? Carrie wondered.

She saw SAC Mikaski give Caitie a look and shake her head.

"Let's just show Special Agent Ramsey the picture I have on my phone, shall we?"

Mikaski showed Carrie a photo of a man with a battered and bandaged nose separating two black eyes. "Special Agent Godwin," Mikaski said. "He'd bet Ms. McGill he could give her a pat on the head before she could punch his nose. To make things more sporting, Godwin held one hand behind his back."

"To be honest," Caitie said, "I didn't land a punch."

Carrie was still trying to absorb the reality of the image. "How did you do all that damage then?"

"Headbutted him," she said. "He fell like a tall tree."

Carrie said, "You're about five-six, just like me. You jumped high enough to do that?"

Caitie shook her head. "He was in a crouch, making another concession to me, but he was still pretty big. My dad taught me you take what the other guy gives you. I jumped on one of his bent knees and pushed off. He wasn't expecting that. Got him with my head on the way up and the way down."

"Jesus," Carrie whispered.

"You fight as dirty as you have to; that's another thing Dad taught me."

"How did this whole thing start?" Carrie asked.

"I told Special Agent Godwin I was tough. He said, 'Show me.' So I did."

"I allowed it. The whole detail saw it," Mikaski said. "We won't be doing that again."

"Okay by me," Caitie said.

Yeah, Carrie thought, but the kid had been ready to lay out another special agent.

Carrie was sure she would have underestimated Caitie McGill, too.

After Caitie had scooted off to work on her Parisienne accent or whatever, SAC Mikaski had put a few private words into Carrie's ears. "None of what happened to Godwin was mentioned or will be mentioned to the President or Mr. McGill. Are we clear on that?"

"Yes, ma'am."

"What Caitie doesn't know and won't hear from any of us is if the angle she hit Godwin's nose on the way up had been just a bit different she would have killed him. She's more dangerous than even she knows. So let's keep her from getting too frisky with anyone, right?"

"Yes, ma'am," Carrie said.

She'd agreed wholeheartedly, but now she had another worry. Not only might the kid be targeted for death, she also might be capable of inflicting fatalities herself. Jeez, where did it all end?

For Special Agent Ramsey, it ended that day when a dark gray BMW sedan cut her off with a loud screech as she ran in the street on a quiet block of Le Conte Avenue just east of the UCLA campus. Carrie Ramsey's physical reflexes prevented her from running into the car, but by the time she got her mind oriented to her situation four guys dressed in black and wearing ski masks had jumped out of the car and two of them grabbed her arms.

She trained regularly in both Tae Kwon Do and Muay Thai, but what popped into her head first were the words she'd heard from Caitie McGill. *You fight as dirty as you have to.* She yanked the guy holding her right arm, bent over and bit down on his wrist as hard as she could. Ground her teeth into him. He howled in agony and pulled free but only after a good chunk of flesh and the structural integrity of major blood vessels had been severed.

Carrie whirled and spat the contents of her mouth into the face of the man holding her left arm. As a product of luck rather than aim, the mangled tissue and fresh blood filled the right eyehole in his mask. He recoiled and Carrie struck the left eyehole of the guy's mask with her right thumb. His yowl of pain had to be audible for blocks.

Before Carrie could make another move, she was hit from behind, tackled by someone far bigger than she was. Her spine felt like it had snapped. A wave of nausea brought up the little food she'd eaten that day. She heard a man curse in disgust and anger. His exclamations didn't sound like English to her. She was trying to sort out what language she'd heard when something sharp pierced the skin of her right arm.

Then everything went black.

Things went wrong for the attackers, too. The guy who'd had his arm chomped had gone into shock and was stumbling down the street, leaving a widening rivulet of blood behind him. He'd traveled far enough away from the others to be deemed too risky for retrieval. One of the un-maimed assailants led the partially blinded member of the cohort into the back seat of the car and closed him inside. The other able-bodied attacker opened the car's trunk lid with a key-fob and tossed Carrie inside, none too gently.

The two able-bodied men jumped into the front seats of the car. Each of them used a mirror to watch the fourth member of the crew continue to lurch the wrong way. He looked as if he wouldn't stay on his feet much longer. Perhaps not even live for more than a few more minutes. That would be for the best, his dying before the police or an ambulance arrived. But it wasn't good for the kidnappers and certainly had not been a part of their plans.

Who the hell had thought their target could *bite* one of their guys to death?

They had no more time to think about that or anything else.

The driver straightened the wheel and mashed down the accelerator.

They left with another prolonged shriek of tortured rubber.

The other thing that went wrong for the bad guys was that the tire-burning stop they'd made upon their arrival had drawn the attention of a resident in an adjacent house. That young man did what came naturally to so many people these days. He whipped out his phone and captured most of the violent episode on video. What happened next, though, went off-script.

Instead of selling the video to his favorite TV station or website, he did the socially responsible thing. He called law enforcement, and since he'd seen a kidnapping and knew who had the responsibility for investigating that crime, he didn't bother with the LAPD. He went straight to the FBI. After hearing what had happened, the special agent who took the call had the smarts to compliment the good citizen and ask him not to publicize the matter. It would be better for the victim and the Bureau if the bad guys didn't know about the video.

The young man, a theology student, said, "Of course. I'll pray for that girl. You know who she reminded me of?"

Hearing the answer, the FBI got in touch with the Secret Service and a copy of the video was screened for the President within the hour.

The White House

Patti Grant held up a hand, "First things first, Jim, our kids are all right, all of them."

McGill had gotten to his feet as soon as he'd seen the expression on his wife's face.

"What is it then?" he asked.

"There's been a kidnapping."

A roiling mixture of fear, anger and incomprehension twisted McGill's features. If not his kids, then who'd been grabbed? "Jesus," he said, "was it Carolyn or Lars?"

Patti shook her head. "No one in the family. It was Special Agent Caroline Ramsey, Caitie's double. She was taken in Los Angeles during an off-duty period. Apparently, she'd gone out for a run and was grabbed near the campus of UCLA."

So many questions popped into McGill's head, he didn't know which one to ask first. Patti filled the void by taking his hands and saying, "We should get down to the Oval Office. There may be more news by the time we get there, in any case, we'll be able to manage things better from there."

"Yeah," McGill said.

That was all he could verbalize at the moment. Patti led him to the West Wing. The pounding of his heart walled off all other sounds. He'd never felt so at odds with himself. The relief of knowing that his children were unharmed had left him near the point of physical collapse. He might not have been able to stand, much less walk, if a countervailing rage hadn't made him want to storm out of the building and rip some asshole's head from his shoulders.

His personal feelings were soon overwhelmed by empathy. Christ, even if his child wasn't taken, someone else's was. Special Agent Caroline Ramsey likely had both parents alive, as young as she must be. Looking enough like Caitie to double for her, she couldn't be more than mid-twenties.

Looking like Caitie: That thought struck McGill hard. Had the resemblance been there all along? Through Caroline Ramsey's early years. Did her parents have photo albums that mirrored his own? The very idea broke McGill's heart. Wait a minute. Had the Ramseys even heard the bad news yet? Who was going to perform the horrible task of telling them?

The weight of Patti's arm on his was all he needed for an answer.

Had she already made the call? He knew the answer to that, too. Of course, she had. She would have come to him first if the bad news had been theirs, but the Ramseys, in this case, would have been her priority.

As they neared the Oval Office, Edwina Byington, the President's longtime personal secretary, got to her feet and opened the door for them. It was unlikely she'd been given any details, but Edwina was ever sensitive to the President's mood. Seeing the expression on McGill's face only doubled her concern.

"No calls, ma'am?" she asked.

"Family only," the President replied. "Nobody else, but please ask the Vice President, Galia and her deputy to come quickly." FBI Director Haskins and SAC Kendry were already en route.

Patti and McGill embraced as soon as the door to the Oval Office closed behind them. A mutual shudder passed between them. McGill said, "So close. Too damn close."

The President nodded and kissed McGill lightly.

She went to sit behind her desk and he took a guest chair.

"You know why Special Agent Ramsey got grabbed?" McGill asked.

"She looks *too* much like Caitie."

McGill shook his head. "Because Caitie doesn't look like she used to."

He took out his phone and showed her the photo his youngest had texted to him.

"Oh, my," Patti said. "Well, that's a new look, all right. It's …"

She saw a thought had just crossed McGill's mind.

"What is it, Jim?"

"Caitie told me she decided to go for a new look once she saw how her old one looked on the special agent. But now I'm wondering…"

The First Couple had been married long enough, had shared enough intimate conversations and other moments, to know the way each other thought. Patti said, "You think Caitie regarded her increased security seriously? She took her own step to protect herself by changing her appearance?"

McGill said, "At first, I thought she was just thumbing her nose at authority."

Patti nodded. She could see that.

"But," McGill continued, "it would be even more fun if she could do that and protect herself at the same time."

Patti looked at the photo on McGill's phone again. She handed it back to McGill and said, "If all the kidnappers had were news photos of Caitie, I think her new look would fool them."

"Yeah, but Special Agent Ramsey hadn't had time to get her makeover. So, as far as the kidnappers know —"

"They have the real Caitie McGill."

"Right. Now, take that a step farther."

Never slow on the uptake, Patti saw just where her husband was going.

She said, "If the kidnappers think they have Caitie, they might have some reason to keep her alive. Using her as a trophy for a while, at the least."

McGill winced. His own thinking hadn't gone that far.

"Yeah," he said, "but if they find out all they have is a stand-in, as Caitie herself put it, what'll they do?"

The President looked grim. "Kill her as soon as they can and get rid of the remains."

Before either Patti or McGill could take things any further, the intercom buzzed.

Edwina said, "I hope I'm within your guidelines here, Madam President, but Mrs. Shady is on the line for Mr. McGill."

The President said, "Sweetie is family. Put her through."

McGill took the phone his wife extended to him. "Hello."

"Jim, I'm at the office."

Sweetie had officially retired from McGill Investigations, Inc., but she kept remembering personal belongings she'd either forgotten at the office or had paperwork she'd left unfinished. Changing the work habits of a lifetime had proved harder than she'd thought. She hadn't worked a case in a year, but she still enjoyed talking shop with McGill.

He consulted her on how he might best go about expanding the business.

"Somebody stopped by on a Saturday," McGill asked, "or did I forget to pay the rent?"

Sweetie said, "Potential clients. They're in the outer office at the moment. A couple, look like the middle of middle-age to me. Nicely dressed. Doing their level best to hold things together. I wouldn't have bothered you but they seem desperate, on the verge of losing their composure. So what do you think? Want me to tell them you'll talk to them?"

"What are their names?" McGill asked.

"Don and Sheri Ramsey. All they'll tell me is it's a missing person case."

Dumbarton Oaks, Washington DC

White House Chief of Staff Galia Mindel was taking a day off from her official duties at the White House. Filling in for her was the new deputy chief of staff, Frank Morrissey, the Vice President's brother. His hiring was decried by the opposition in Congress and criticized by right wing media as not just presumptuous but a slap in the face to the democratic process. The President, they said, was assuming her VP, her choice to be the next President, was such a sure bet that Jean Morrissey could *infiltrate* her people into the executive branch ahead of the election.

In a brief TV interview with Ellie Booker on WWN, the President was asked to respond to all the criticism coming from the political right.

Keeping a straight face, Patricia Grant said, "Golly, I hope they won't impeach me again."

After the previous attempt's failure, the considered opinion of that was: Fat chance.

In private, Galia had said much the same thing as the President, without the veneer of suitable-for-children diction: "Fuck 'em if they can't take a joke."

The Vice President and her brother felt the same way. They saw Frank's move into the deputy chief slot as a political advantage not a liability. Progressives and swing voters would see the move as a chance for Frank to get real-world White House experience. Something Jean Morrissey already had and something the candidate from the other side of the aisle wouldn't be able to claim.

So far, Frank had shown himself to be both smart and as tough as titanium. Exactly the way Galia saw herself. Her only hesitation about the move was wondering if Frank Morrissey and James J. McGill would clash. She decided both men would keep any differences they had out of the public eye.

If there were any in-house contretemps, well, Galia might enjoy seeing that.

The chief of staff's home in Dumbarton Oaks was of a piece with the elegant neighborhood. The house was large, gracious and understated. The grounds were gated and at Galia's touch of a button the wrought iron portals swung open to admit a Cadillac XTS limo. The Caddy looked right at home as it rolled sedately up the driveway and stopped opposite the front door.

A uniformed driver opened the rear door closer to the home's front door. In doing so, the driver deftly interposed his huge body between his passenger and the view anyone with a camera might have from the sidewalk outside the fence. An unseen hand admitted the visitor and closed Galia's front door behind him seconds later.

None of the behavior had looked in the least furtive.

All of it had been completely effective at blocking the visitor's identity.

Galia smiled at Augustus Wiley and hugged him. "Good to see you, old friend."

He bussed her cheek and said, "You're looking well, Galia."

She took his coat and hat. Gus had worn the same style Bor-salino since his days in law school with Galia's late husband, Nathan. He said the hat made him look like a modern-day gun-slinger. She carefully stored the chapeau and coat in the entry closet.

At the time Nate and Gus had begun their legal studies, an African American and a Jew were far from immune to the sting of exclusion by their WASP classmates. They lessened the rebuff by hitting it off from the start and becoming a study group of two. They both graduated summa cum laude, Nate going into tax law, Gus into criminal defense.

Galia said she and Gus could have a brandy in the sunroom.

He grinned and said, "You know me better than that, Galia. Let's have some Irish coffee in the kitchen. We'll spend a few minutes talking about our kids and the grandbabies and then get down to business. No better place to sort things out than a kitchen table."

Nate and Gus had always done their studying at the Mindels' kitchen table. That apartment was so small, Nate would say the three of them couldn't inhale in unison or they'd consume all the oxygen in the place, and when Gus came over they would assure the air supply by opening the kitchen window even when it was cold outside.

Galia used to claim she'd had to be thawed in the oven after a study session ran long.

"Come on, girl," Gus would say, "old Nate's gotta have a better way to warm you up than that. If he doesn't, I'll slip him a little crib sheet of the things I know."

Laughing, Galia had told Gus that he was horrible.

Truth was, Nate did learn some bedroom tricks that took her by pleasant surprise, and she couldn't imagine him learning from anyone except Gus.

So if Gus wanted Irish coffee in the kitchen, that was what he'd get.

She took his hand and led him that way, got busy making a new pot of coffee and getting out some Bushmills. They talked about family while she worked. They were caught up by the time she served the coffee and sat down opposite her dear friend.

"So how much do you know, Galia?" Gus asked.

"About what? You told me on the phone you wanted to talk about a case. That caught me by surprise. I know attorneys, especially in the criminal defense bar, are supposed to be tight-lipped."

"So we're going to play it like that, are we?"

"What are we going to play? Twenty questions?"

Gus sighed and took a sip of his coffee. Galia still knew just how he liked it. He doubted she'd ever forgotten anything that redounded to her advantage.

"Let's see if we can whittle things down to the fewest questions we can," he said. "That way neither of us will have to lie too much."

"Certainly no more than we ever have."

Until Gus's third marriage ended in court, just like the first two, Galia had sworn she'd adored each of his brides. After divorce number three, however, she'd asked, "You've learned by now, haven't you? Flashier isn't always better."

Wife number four was also a looker, but she possessed a very good mind and an even better character. That one had lasted, producing the succeeding generations Gus had always said he wanted.

"Yeah, like that," he acknowledged. "Socially acceptable lies. Now, right before I was about to tender my resignation and turn my firm over to a fine attorney who deserves to take the reins, I received a plea to take just one more case."

Galia offered a look of genuine surprise. "You're really thinking of leaving the law? My thought was you'd be in court into your 90s, giving a closing argument for some falsely accused poor soul. You'd thunder out one last compelling point to the jury, jut a finger into the air in lieu of an exclamation point and keel over dead. Sympathy for your passing would be but one more reason for an acquittal. A barrister who'd truly given his all."

Augustus Wiley looked at her with a straight face.

Then he burst into laughter. "You are so full of it."

Galia continued her riff. "Your funeral would be attended by thousands. A celestial choir of angels and bondsmen would sing hosannas as you arrived at the Pearly Gates."

"Okay, okay," Gus said. "Put the rest of the corn back in the can already. We'll try to tell each other as much of the truth as we can. I'll try not to be too pointed with my questions."

"Deal," Galia said with a straight face.

Gus nodded. "All right then. Here's what I've got. The case in question came to me courtesy of the District of Columbia Legal Defense Fund, an organization I hadn't known to exist until last month."

Galia interrupted. "Was their plea for *pro bono* representation or did it come with a retainer check?"

"Oh, there's money involved, believe me. Not quite as much as a big-bucks client would pay, but respectable."

"Good," Galia said with a nod of approval.

"But just to verify their bona fides I deposited their check and wouldn't you know it, the damn thing was good. So I gave them a call to ask how I might honestly earn their money. They said they wanted me to represent an African American client who would otherwise be unable to afford my help."

"That sounds like a worthy cause," Galia said.

"Really? Sounded a bit too scripted to be true to me. Anyway, the folks at the DC Legal Defense Fund tell me it's legit, so who am I to argue?" He laughed at the idea of a lawyer who couldn't argue any damn thing he wanted. "So there's this hardworking person of color doing domestic household management for a rich white man in Great Falls, Virginia, and he gets himself accused of stealing a valuable stamp collection. The accused has no criminal record in all his 63 years of life. He had no pressing financial needs to make him do something foolish out of desperation. His financial records show no inexplicable infusion of funds. A search of his house and car don't turn up any stolen stamps. So unless the man has an eccentric sense of humor and put the stamps on envelopes addressed to the far reaches of the world, it looks like a BS charge to me. Only the complainant is a local muckety-muck named Thomas Winston Rangel. His position is only he and Mr. Elias Roosevelt, the accused, knew the combination to the safe where the stamps were kept."

"The commonwealth attorney is going on one man's word?" Galia asked.

"Yeah, well, like I said, Rangel is prominent, and just a little bit of digging showed that he is also a serious contributor to the commonwealth attorney's election campaigns. Just a coincidence, I'm sure, but that's where things stand."

Galia took her first sip of Irish coffee. "So if you were to decide to retire, maybe go fishing, that would put you in the same boat as the prosecutor, pun intended. Screwing the little guy and deferring to the rich guy."

Gus took a good long pull on his cup. "If there's one thing I hate almost as much as injustice, it's getting played, especially by someone who's an old friend and should know better."

That wasn't a question; it was a dig at Galia.

She ignored it and said, "But hating injustice still wins?"

"By a nose, yeah."

"So you're going to help Mr. Roosevelt?"

"How could I say no? I talked to the man's wife, Mary Louise, and who does she give me as a character reference but you? Maybe my dearest friend after my wife."

Galia asked with mock innocence, "Didn't I introduce you to Mavis?"

"Galia Mindel, you make a fine cup of coffee but you are shameless."

"Comes from living in Washington too long. Maybe I'll retire soon, too. Go somewhere quiet like Manhattan."

"Be that as it may, do you know the Roosevelts?"

Galia nodded. "I do. They're fine people."

"I got the same feeling," Gus said, "but I have to ask this question: How did a houseman and his kindergarten teacher wife meet the White House chief of staff?"

Galia shrugged. "At a fried chicken picnic fundraiser for a state senate candidate."

Gus gave his old friend a probing look.

"What?" she asked. "Fried chicken can be kosher."

"I'm glad something around here is."

"Would you like the candidate's name?"

"Yes, I would."

Galia told him.

"Did he win?"

"Come on, Gus. You should know better."

He sighed. "Looks like I'm gonna have to put off my retirement a while. You sure do beat all, Galia."

"Most of the time, if I can help it," she admitted.

She'd arranged top-flight legal defense for one of her spies without leaving a fingerprint.

Maybe she'd hear a hosanna or two when her time came.

Instead, after seeing Gus off, she heard her home phone ring.

Edwina Byington was on the line.

"The President would like to see you in the Oval Office immediately, Madam Chief of Staff."

Edwina's phone voice was the epitome of professional reserve, usually.

At that moment, though, Galia thought she heard a tremor in it.

Something was scaring her, and that scared Galia.

"Lights and sirens?" the chief of staff asked.

"All due dispatch, ma'am."

J. Edgar Hoover Building, Washington, DC

Byron DeWitt addressed the Andy Warhol serigraph of Mao Tse Tung (currently transliterated as Mao Zedong) hanging on the wall of his office in FBI headquarters: "Well, Mr. Chairman, we're just about out of here, you and me."

Looking on was Special Agent Abra Benjamin, soon to be promoted to DeWitt's slot on the organizational table for her crucial role in finding and capturing Tyler Busby.

"You're talking to your artwork again," she told DeWitt. "Didn't I tell you that was one of the signs Nixon exhibited shortly before he was forced to resign?"

"I believe you did, but nobody's giving me the boot. I'm exiting of my own free will."

A rumor that Abra had heard, one she'd tried to repress, forced its way out. "Is it true your fiancée told you the directorship could be yours if she becomes President?"

DeWitt said, "You have to be careful, believing anything you hear in this town."

"But?"

"But I don't blab anything I hear in private conversations. What I can tell you is that the Great Helmsman and I will soon be lodging in Santa Barbara."

Abra had mixed feelings about that. She was sure the story about Jean Morrissey offering the top job at the FBI to her beau was true. If he accepted, he would continue to be her boss, and that would take the luster off her own promotion. It would also mean her climb to the top of the pyramid would be blocked by DeWitt. Which would gall her for as long as he held the job. So Byron's departure would be to her benefit.

Even so, she would miss him. Sure, they'd ended their physical relationship a good while ago. He'd been an exceptionally nice guy afterward. Made sure he'd treated her fairly on the job. Even found a way to keep the relationship cordial while making clear it would never go back to being what it once was: the two of them being lovers.

She'd come to accept that, mostly. What she could do, though, was indulge the memories that lingered every time they were together. And, who knew, if they continued to work with each other, she just might catch him in a moment of weakness. Of course, that'd undoubtedly cost both of them their jobs if Jean

Morrissey became President and found out.

Hell, she might beat the both of them to death with a hockey stick.

"What are you smiling about?" DeWitt asked. "Wistfully, too, I might add."

Abra pushed her fantasies aside and said, "Just regretting that I can't afford to buy Mao from you?"

"Probably wouldn't help your career advancement, hanging it in your office, without your having my linguistic and cultural background."

"I could put it in my bathroom. Hang it over the commode. See if he approves of my personal hygiene."

DeWitt laughed. "Hard to criticize that use."

DeWitt's office phone rang.

He answered by saying, "Floyd's Thirst Parlor. Thirty brands of beer on tap."

A female voice said, "*¿Como?*" Say what?

Possessing both a keen ear and a good memory, the deputy director said, "Sorry, just joking. Is this Lieutenant Reyes?"

"Captain Reyes, yes."

"You've been promoted? Congratulations."

Abra had heard enough to point at the speaker on the desk and steeple her hands in a gesture of prayerful supplication.

"Captain, Special Agent Benjamin is here with me. I'm going to put you on speaker."

"Yes, good. Hello, Special Agent."

"My congratulations, too. Is there word from Montevideo on when we can extradite Tyler Busby? I'd like to be there to bring him back to Washington, and to see you again."

Abra was all business now. Video of her bringing Busby home in chains couldn't be anything but a giant step for her career. Hasten the time when she would sit in the director's chair.

DeWitt didn't utter a peep. He had no objection to Abra's ambitions. He thought she'd be a terrific choice to run the Bureau.

"I think that decision will be coming very shortly," Silvina said.

"The news I have for the FBI will …"

Captain Reyes, though fluent in English, seemed to be searching for the right words.

DeWitt said, "Work to our countries' mutual advantage?"

"Yes, exactly. I was called to see the Chinese woman who calls herself Mr. Busby's wife, Ah-lam."

Abra asked, "Is there any doubt of her status?"

"She and Busby were married by their ship's captain using a ceremony downloaded from the Internet. I don't know if this would be recognized in your country, but in Uruguay, we have serious doubts. Not that the politicians aren't still arguing about it."

"One way or the other, how does that affect Busby's extradition?" DeWitt asked.

"It's complicated, but it goes like this. Yesterday, I went to speak with Ah-lam in prison, at her request. She told me that she'd been visited by her brother who is also an attorney."

She gave DeWitt and Abra the details.

Abra wanted to jump in immediately with questions.

Didn't only because she knew she wasn't yet the top dog in the room.

DeWitt responded in a more thoughtful fashion. "Ah-lam said her brother told her China doesn't want Busby to return to the United States alive."

"Yes, exactly."

"So, really, we don't know specifically who wants him dead."

"I took China to mean its government," Silvina said. "Don't you agree?"

"That's a possibility, but far from a certainty. It could be a mask for anyone really."

There was a moment of silence before Silvina said, "You are right. I should have seen that. What is specific is the threat for failing to cooperate: Ah-lam's entire family will die, including her son. She doesn't care about the others, but the baby, yes."

"Who's taking care of him now?" Abra said, unable to restrain herself any longer.

"I am," Silvina replied. "My family and me. My mother, my sister and me. Everyone helps, but he lives in my house."

Her voice was quiet but her tone was possessive, and she hadn't mentioned her husband.

DeWitt said, "When you spoke to Ah-lam, did she ask about her son? How well he was being cared for and by whom."

"Yes. I told her he was fine, healthy and happy. He is learning both Spanish and English."

"That bothered her, didn't it?" DeWitt asked. "Did she ask if there was anyone teaching him Mandarin?"

"How did you know?" Silvina asked.

"It's what she would teach him."

"Yes, of course, but it is a language I don't know. To get back to Ah-lam, she says she will testify against Busby instead of killing him, if she receives leniency and her son is returned to her."

Abra gritted her teeth. "Did she ask for protection, too?"

"No. I can only assume she thinks she could make her own way in the world."

Abra said, "All I can think of is how she threw that baby at me, not caring what the hell might happen to him. I don't want to see her get him back or go free."

"Nor do I," Silvina agreed. "When I spoke to my superiors, I suggested that I be allowed to keep Jonathan until he is twenty-one and can make his own choices. I also said Ah-lam should remain in prison, in my country or yours, at least until that time. I am, however, one small voice in this matter; I carry no great weight."

Abra exchanged a look with DeWitt. He nodded.

"You'll have the backing of the FBI," Abra said.

She cocked an eyebrow at DeWitt. He agreed again.

Abra said, "We'll bring all the personnel and equipment needed to bring Busby and Ah-lam to the United States safely. When Ah-lam gets here we'll tell her exactly what kind of deal she can get in return for her cooperation. It won't be a slap on the wrist, and she won't be seeing her son anytime soon."

"*Bueno,*" Silvina said. "If I may ask for one more thing, I would like to come with Jonathan, too. I've been told I can take a leave from my job and … I am not ready to leave him yet. I will go anywhere with him you care to send me."

DeWitt said, "What would you think about Santa Barbara, California? I know someone there who can teach the kid Mandarin. You, too, if you like."

"*Sí, bueno. Muchas gracias.*"

They all said their goodbyes, DeWitt promising to get in touch with the Uruguayan authorities. Before he could follow through on that, his phone rang again. The man who actually held the top job at the Bureau, Director Jeremiah Haskins, was calling.

In person, no secretary.

"Meet me at my car in five minutes. We're going to the White House."

DeWitt heard the urgency in Haskins' voice and wanted to say, "Shit." Didn't the boss know DeWitt had one foot out the door already? He didn't need to be involved in any new crisis. Damn it, why did this always happen?

Abra, who'd been close enough to overhear the director's order, gave DeWitt a cuff on the back of his head. None too gentle either.

Reflexively, he coughed up a, "Yes, sir."

As he left his office, Abra said, "Chairman Mao will understand, and I'll call Montevideo for you."

McGill Investigations, Inc. — Georgetown

Dikki Missirian, McGill's landlord, greeted him and Deke with a smile outside his building. He was sweeping an already immaculate sidewalk. "Gentlemen, it is good to see you again. May I bring some refreshments up to my favorite tenants? Margaret has already declined my offer, but …"

He shrugged as if to say opinions might differ.

McGill clapped him on the shoulder and said, "Good to see you, too, Dikki. But this isn't an occasion for niceties, I'm sorry to say."

Dikki's expression changed to a look of concern. "Please let me know if there's *anything* I might do."

McGill nodded and climbed the stairs to his office, Deke watching his back.

Sweetie was waiting for them outside the door to their suite. McGill thought he heard a woman softly sobbing. A male voice was trying to comfort her, but it was also thick with emotion, an audible if repressed fear.

"The Ramseys," Sweetie whispered.

Keeping his own voice down, McGill asked, "Did they tell you what happened?"

Sweetie nodded. "After I promised I wouldn't let it become public."

Deke kept a straight face, but he was taking in every word and note of vocalized distress coming from within the office. It was his job to keep McGill safe under any circumstance. That task was made easier by having a full understanding of any given situation.

McGill knew that and, after all their time together, Deke was more than just a bodyguard, he was a trusted friend. McGill told him, "You might hear this from Elspeth soon anyway, but there's a very bad situation going on."

He told Deke about the kidnapping of Special Agent Ramsey.

Normally stoic under the most difficult of situations, Deke flinched as if he'd been slapped.

McGill asked Sweetie, "Did the Ramseys say why they want to talk with me."

"They want to hire you, Jim. I think they're going to ask you to get their daughter back."

McGill entered his office and a well-dressed middle-aged couple, likely not more than a few years older than himself, stood to greet him. No tears showed in their eyes, but there were tracks running down their cheeks where droplets had been wiped away. McGill extended his hand to the man.

"Jim McGill."

He shook it, doing his best to firm himself up. "Don Ramsey. This is my wife —"

The woman fell into McGill's arms. Doing the only thing he could, he embraced her.

"My wife, Sheri," Don said.

Mrs. Ramsey began to cry again, quietly but with her whole body trembling. McGill held on gently, offering the silent compassion of one parent for another. He could imagine the pain he'd be feeling at that moment if Caitie had been taken instead of the Ramseys' daughter. Sheri Ramsey must have recognized his empathy.

She gathered herself and looked up at him.

After studying his face for a moment, she took a step back.

In a soft voice, she told him, "Don and I are here to ask you, to *beg* you if necessary, to find our Carrie and bring her back to us."

Just what Sweetie anticipated, McGill thought.

Finding any way to help the Ramseys, though, would be closer to impossible than just plain difficult. He said, "Please have a seat, both of you. We'll see what might be done."

McGill took his seat behind his desk, and Sweetie stood behind his right shoulder.

The better angel of his nature, to be sure.

The Ramseys retook the visitors' chairs.

Deke stood guard in the doorway, his back to the others, but his ears cocked.

"Did you speak with the President personally?" McGill asked.

Sheri Ramsey nodded with a tortured smile on her face. "My first reaction, when she introduced herself, was to think 'Who's playing a practical joke on me here?' Then I recognized her voice and I was thrilled: the President calling me. And then I turned to ice and I called for Don."

He said, "I got to where Sheri was without the intermediary steps. We both thought the President was calling us to express her regrets. The way she does when military members die in combat.

We've always known Carrie has a dangerous job. We both say a prayer for her every morning and night."

"Almost all day long for me," Sheri added. "And sometimes, for a few moments, we can forget our fears."

"Let me show you something, Mr. McGill," Don said.

He took out his wallet and withdrew a photo. He handed it to McGill, who knew what was coming. A captured moment of endearment that would last a lifetime. What he wasn't ready for was how eerily accurate his earlier thought had been: Caroline Ramsey in her Girl Scout uniform beamed at the camera holding a blue ribbon and medallion in one hand and a merit badge in the other.

Looking about twelve years old, she reminded McGill so much of his Caitie that it astounded him. The braces on Carrie's teeth even had the same decorative faux jewelry on them that Caitie's had had: rubies on top, emeralds on bottom. Handing the photo back, he looked at the Ramseys. Neither of them looked particularly like Carolyn or him. So how did their offspring come to so closely resemble his?

Actually, it was the other way around. Carrie had been born first.

Don said, "There are hundreds of pictures of my girl that make my heart skip a beat." He gave a soft laugh. "As a cardiologist, I know that's impossible, but damn if it doesn't happen. And that one I just showed you is my absolute favorite."

Sheri said, "The award was for a baking competition. Girl Scouts and cookies, you know. The mom who was leading her troop said if they were going to sell cookies they should learn how to make them. Each girl baked at home and brought the cookies to their meeting in a plain brown bag, all the same size, with the girls' names written on the bottom. Then the girls sampled the cookies and voted on the one they liked best."

"Sipping milk between each cookie to clear their palates," Don said with a wistful grin.

Despite the Ramseys' attempts to be brave, McGill could see

they were already considering the awful possibility that they were too late to help Carrie. That their daughter was already lost to them.

McGill had the sinking feeling he wasn't going to be able to give them any comfort.

"You'd like me to help find your daughter," he said.

Neither Ramsey had the nerve to vocalize their plea again. They only nodded, minimally.

"The problem with that is…" McGill noticed Deke looking at him over his shoulder. "There will be two federal agencies deeply involved in this matter. The FBI is responsible for investigating kidnappings. In this case, however, I'm sure there will be some measure of participation by the Secret Service."

Deke nodded, his face a picture of grim determination.

"As a private investigator and a private citizen, there's really no role for me to play."

McGill felt one of Sweetie's hands fall on his shoulder.

"But Jim will find one," she said. "Failing that, he'll *create* one. Because he and I are both sure that the President asked you to keep the news of Carrie's kidnapping to yourself. You made exactly the right choice in coming to him."

McGill turned to look up at Sweetie. Deke eyed her, too.

She continued, "It was right because Jim already knows. As Caitie McGill's father, he was informed of what has happened. If you had to go elsewhere in the private sector to look for help, word of what's happened would leak out and that would be bad for everyone."

Left unspoken was the reason why the story going public would be bad. If the kidnappers learned they'd grabbed a Secret Service agent instead of the President's step-daughter, they'd more likely kill Carrie and dispose of her body. Holding Caitie McGill, however, might have propaganda value or even be an attempt to extort an impossible demand out of the White House. To do either of those things, their captive had to remain alive.

Sweetie turned to look at Don Ramsey and he was sharp

enough to pick up on his cue.

"But we'd do it," he said. "Go to another investigator. We'd take that chance. We can't and we won't sit still. We need someone working for *us*. Someone with no institutional or political concerns. Someone who will bring our baby home..." His voice cracked. "Alive and well."

McGill didn't object; Deke looked like he wanted to say something, but he didn't.

There had been times in McGill's partnership with Sweetie when his conscience was taking a snooze and she came along with an alarm clock. She'd said she was going to retire from the company, but she hadn't yet, and maybe serving as the moral compass of McGill Investigations, Inc. would be reason enough to stay on.

He glanced at Sweetie and knew intuitively she was thinking the same thing.

He told the Ramseys, "I'll talk to the President. We'll work something out."

He'd be damned if he knew what that was, though.

Then he realized he had even bigger worries.

House in the Forest outside Williams, Arizona

Secret Service Special Agent Carrie Ramsey parted her eyelids a millimeter, but she was far from certain she was still alive. Her head felt as if it was stuffed with steel wool, her thin field of vision was fuzzy, and her sinuses had so narrowed it seemed as if she was breathing through pin holes. She managed to inhale just enough air to keep from gasping. Even so, she could detect the scent of ... fried onions ... and grilled beef. If her mouth wasn't so dry, it would have watered.

It took her a moment to work out the thought, but she came to the conclusion there were no fast food joints in anyone's conception of an afterlife. The only alternative left to draw was that she remained alive. With that comforting notion in mind, she drifted back into unconsciousness.

Taking with her the impression that she was chained in some fashion.

The next time she awoke her head and every muscle in her body ached but her senses had grown more functional and acute. She could see the outlines of the room where she lay. In the dim light of a single floor lamp, it looked like it belonged in a log cabin, a dated but decently maintained structure. She caught the aroma of food again: a burger *and* fries. This time, the smell did provoke a physical reaction.

A pang of hunger twisted her gut.

She caught sight of a Dairy Queen bag sitting on a nearby bentwood chair and reached for it with her right hand. It surprised her when the action brought her left hand along for the ride. She'd been handcuffed. Then she noticed a hard weight around her ankles. Shackles. She was bound hand and foot.

She was also wearing somebody else's clothes: an oversized gray sweatshirt, jeans that were a better fit but seemed cut for a male body. She still had her own socks and running shoes.

She was clearly somebody's prisoner, but that little problem was going to have to wait. Right now, all she wanted to do was eat. Get at whatever was in that DQ bag. She swung her legs off the narrow bed on which she lay and sat up. She grabbed the bag in both hands and opened it. The burger, onions and fries were cold by now but still smelled wonderful. She caught the tang of mustard, too. More taste appeal.

God, it was just like someone knew exactly what she liked. If there were tomatoes on it too, that would be perfect. There was a chocolate shake in the bag, too. Careful not to lose hold, she grabbed the burger and pulled the wrapping paper off. Cold or not, it tasted better than any burger she could remember. With a smile on her face as she chewed, she thought maybe there was fast food in heaven, only now it was good for you.

She gobbled the burger and the fries, but took her time with the milkshake. It had warmed, too, thinning on top with a heavier layer of ice cream settled on the bottom. The sugar in the drink gave her a rush, helping her head to clear, and an ache in her back to reassert itself into her consciousness. As soon as she finished the shake, she had to pee.

Looking around, she saw what looked like somebody's idea of a country commode, a wood-framed toilet, in a shadowed corner. She pushed herself upright and hobbled that way. As she moved, an overhead light came on. It wasn't especially bright, but it did banish the shadows around the toilet.

Well, if someone wanted to get his jollies watching her take a whiz, let him.

What she wasn't ready for was an unseen guy to speak to her as she lowered the jeans and her running shorts and sat.

"*Comment allez-vous, Mademoiselle McGill?*" How are you, Miss McGill?

She knew that much of the language.

The guy's French was freighted with an American accent.

By that time, Carrie remembered who she was, and how she'd fought as hard as she could — as *dirty* as she could — in L.A. So some assholes had grabbed her, thinking they'd latched on to a far bigger and more valuable prize: Caitie McGill. Someone who'd get much better treatment than she would under her own name.

The false impression wouldn't last long if they found out she didn't speak French.

Well, she had learned one special phrase just in case the kid ever truly pissed her off.

Staring at the door, as if someone might step inside the room, Carrie said, "*Va te faire foutre.*"

Go fuck yourself.

Before anyone could continue in a foreign language, Carrie added, "If you want to talk to me, speak English."

No response came as she relieved herself. Finishing her business, she pulled up her running shorts and jeans and tottered back to the bed, plopping down and trying to plan a countermove if someone came in and tried to grab or attack her. Maybe the bastards knew little Ms. McGill's foreign language skills were more polished than

Carrie's one insulting phrase.

She hadn't come up with any defensive strategy by the time the voice returned in English.

"All right. We'll speak English. Just so there's no doubt what we're saying. The first thing we want to know is what your life is worth. What should we ask for your safe return? What would your father do to get you back? But more important, what would your step-mother, President Grant, do to get you back?"

Carrie was tempted to respond immediately with more vulgarity.

But she wasn't some gullible citizen who didn't have any training.

If these pricks wanted to get her talking, they had to be planning to use her own words against her. They could be recording everything she'd said. Maybe they'd even gotten video of her going potty. Well, tough darts for her if they had. If that was the worst thing she had to worry about, she'd be home free.

"What's the problem, Miss McGill? Nothing to say? If you're not worth anything to us, we might as well kill you now."

Carrie said, "As long as you're ready to die for your shit-ass cause, too, whatever it is."

She heard more than one male laugh.

There were two or three of them, she thought. Nearby at least. There might be more elsewhere.

"We were told you think you're tough."

"*Think?* That guy I bit, how's he doing? Or the one I got in the eye with my thumb?"

The asshole had just clued Carrie to the fact that they expected resistance from Caitie, but now she wondered how carefully she would have to calibrate her attitude. Give them too much lip and they might suspect something.

Even so, she couldn't help herself. "The price of my life? More than all of yours. You kill me and the gloves come off. You got that? It means payback times ten. Or a hundred. You keep tacking on zeros, you'll know what I mean."

There was no response. Maybe she had gone too far or given

them an answer they couldn't use to squeeze the President or Mr. McGill. They might be coming in to put a bullet into her head right now. She gathered her legs under her as she sat on the edge of the bed.

If somebody opened the door and had a gun in hand, she'd launch herself at him.

Get him with her head like Caitie McGill got Special Agent Godwin. Only maybe she'd manage to get a little better aim than Caitie. Drive nasal cartilage into the prick's brain and kill him.

The confrontation didn't come to pass, though.

Carrie felt her eyelids grow heavy and her tense muscles become slack.

The bastards had drugged her food. Whatever happened next was their move.

The Oval Office

Edwina Byington saw McGill approaching the Oval Office under a full head of steam. Not quite at a run. That might have alarmed the Secret Service and panicked everyone else in the building. Nonetheless, it was clear that he wasn't going to tolerate a moment's delay in getting to see the President.

Edwina popped up and swung the door open just in time to admit him and say, "Mr. McGill to see you, Madam President."

She closed the door to the Oval Office and couldn't help but wonder what would happen inside that room.

McGill noticed — recognized — all the others who had gathered at his wife's beck and call. But he didn't have time for them right now. He came to such an abrupt stop in front of the President's desk he almost vibrated like a tuning fork.

"The kids," he said to her. "Our kids. The other ones, Abbie and Ken. If someone made a grab for Caitie, why not the other two?"

Patricia Grant came around her desk and clasped McGill's hands in hers.

"Elspeth raised that possibility a few moments ago. Everyone protecting all three of our children has been placed on high alert. Additional personnel are en route. We're not going to let anyone hurt them, Jim."

A shudder of relief passed through McGill. He took a deep breath and let it out slowly.

"Good … what about Carolyn and Lars? Has anyone told them?"

The President shook her head. "I thought you'd want to do that."

McGill nodded. "I do. It'll be best that way." He looked at the others sharing the moment and the room with him and Patti.

Jean Morrissey and her brother Frank were there. So were Galia and Elspeth. FBI director Jeremiah Haskins and Deputy Director Byron DeWitt. The last two were going to be especially important to him.

He said, "I'm sorry to burst in on everyone, but …" He shrugged. Getting no objections, he continued, "If you'll give me just a few minutes to speak with Carolyn and Lars Enquist, I'd like to join you for the discussion of this problem."

The President asked, "You reassured the Ramseys we'll do everything we can?"

"Yeah," McGill said. *"Everything."*

His last word, loaded with subtext, begged for explanation.

But Galia told McGill, "Use my office to make your call, if you like."

The chief of staff's workspace was adjacent to the Oval Office. McGill nodded his thanks. Before he could leave, though, Elspeth added, "Sir, you might mention to Mr. and Mrs. Enquist that I've detailed Secret Service personnel to back up their security officers from the Evanston Police Department."

McGill said, "Thank you."

When McGill returned to the Oval Office the President asked him, "Are Carolyn and Lars coping?"

He nodded. "As best they can. They want to gather all the kids and hunker down at a country place they bought in Minnesota."

"Not a bad idea," Elspeth said. "Might be easier to defend. Wouldn't have to be for long." She looked at the FBI's representatives, Haskins and DeWitt. "We're going to get these guys, right, gentlemen?"

Director Haskins said, "Yes."

Deputy Director DeWitt was more equivocal. He looked at the President. "We'll end the near term threat. Put the perpetrators on the run. That should be doable, Madam President. Whether we get the individuals responsible for Special Agent Ramsey's kidnapping, maybe is the most honest answer."

Spoken like a man about to leave his career in government behind, McGill thought, undercutting his boss's reflexive optimism.

The President gave the contrary opinion a moment's thought and turned to the Vice President. "Jean?"

"To be blunt, Madam President, we shouldn't give a damn about political considerations here. If Special Agent Ramsey is still alive, we have to take any and all measures to get her back. I understand the deputy director's reluctance to make any promises, but we have to put all available resources to work on this threat. We might well have to pull people off other jobs to do it. This is a threat to both the presidency and our nation's children."

McGill gave the VP a look, wondering if she'd somehow intuited what he had in mind.

"Galia," the President said to her chief of staff.

"I agree with the Vice President. Before joining everyone here, I had word from Los Angeles that the wound Special Agent Ramsey inflicted on one of the kidnappers was fatal. With a bite, the special agent, in the term I was given, grossly severed the kidnapper's radial artery. The result was the same as if the individual had sliced his wrist in a suicide attempt. He bled out before medical help reached him. I know it sounds vicious, but anyone who fights that hard to defend herself deserves our most intense efforts to bring her home safely. This is an all-hands-on-deck moment, and if we need more help, we draft it."

The chief of staff spared a glance at McGill.

He thought she knew *exactly* what he had in mind.

"Jim," the President said, catching McGill a little off guard.

He still got right to it. "The Ramseys want to hire me to find their daughter. Mr. Ramsey showed me a picture he carries in his wallet: Carrie in a Girl Scout uniform. It looks so much like Caitie, I'd think they were sisters, if I didn't know otherwise." McGill paused to reflect, finishing with a sigh. "My heart was breaking for the Ramseys, but I was trying to think of a way to tell them that there was no room in this matter for a private investigator."

Director Haskins looked as if he'd just dodged a migraine.

Deputy Director DeWitt's expression said he'd just had an epiphany.

One he could hardly believe.

"So what did you do, Jim?" the President asked.

"Before I could crush the Ramseys' hope, Sweetie saved me. She said I'd help. Do whatever I could. I've never argued a moral choice with Sweetie, and I wasn't about to start. I told Don and Sheri Ramsey I'd find a way to lend a hand. Do whatever I could."

Patricia Grant also saw what was coming now, but she still wanted to hear it.

"And what do you have in mind?"

"You remember how after you were first elected to the presidency you jokingly asked me if I wanted to run the FBI?"

The President nodded. "I do. You said no."

"I still don't want the director's job." He turned to Haskins. "No offense." Looking back at his wife, he said, "I think the only way I can honor the Ramseys' request is to become one of the team, officially."

The President said, "You want me to give you a job with the FBI."

"I don't expect a pension," McGill replied.

Destry Theatre Centre — Palo Alto, California

McGill and Caitie sat in the top row, the last two seats, stage right. They were the only theater-goers seated at the moment, but a placard inscribed RESERVED rested on the seat next to Caitie in anticipation of a full house. There was an exit adjacent to McGill with a cluster of Secret Service agents standing just outside. Deke Ky had McGill and Caitie's backs covered. McGill was also armed. More agents lurked backstage doing their best both to maintain a razor sharp vigilance and not to freak out the students who'd come to put on a show that night.

Ken McGill was behind the curtain with the other members of the troupe that would perform that night. He was doing his best to keep things loose. Telling stories of how his life had been filled with bodyguards since middle school, and how so many Secret Service agents had stepped forward to offer their bone marrow to him when he got sick. "With these guys around," he told the others, "the only ones who have to worry are the creeps."

He turned to face a nearby knot of agents and applauded them. The other student-actors and stagehands caught the spirit and joined him. The men and women who were willing to take a bullet for their packages proved far less stoic in the face of heartfelt appreciation.

Most of them had to look away before their emotions gave away their softer sides.

A couple, though, grinned and gave Ken a thumbs-up.

One even cracked wise. "Leave any leg-breaking to us."

At the opposite end of the theater, Caitie McGill was having anything but a good time.

She glanced at her father, but didn't utter a peep.

Even so, McGill knew a telling glance when he saw one.

"Say whatever's on your mind," he said. "I'm not in a mood to scold."

Despite being given *carte blanche*, Caitie leaned in close and whispered, "If I had the chance, I'd kill the bastards who kidnapped Carrie."

Strong stuff to hear from a teenage daughter, McGill thought. He was sure Caitie wasn't simply being dramatic. "At your age, I'd have felt the same way. Being quite a bit older now, I'd be content to let them rot in prison and expire on their own schedule."

Looking not in the least as if she was joking, Caitie asked, "Where's the fun in that?"

Caitie had been flown up to Palo Alto in a government aircraft with twice the usual number of agents surrounding her. She'd been protected against everything but the San Andreas Fault. McGill had thought she'd resent the disruption of her personal and professional obligations. There hadn't been a complaint on either of those counts.

Instead, she was furious with herself for having gotten her new look.

"I didn't have to do that," she'd told McGill. "I just had my nose out of joint and felt I should be a pain in the ass to get even. The whole thing wasn't Carrie's fault but I took it out on her." She shook her head. "That wasn't fair at all. Goddamnit, Dad, what if she's …"

She locked her jaw before she could say "dead."

At the risk of being rebuffed, McGill put an arm around his youngest's shoulders.

She let it lie in place, even burrowed into him as far as the arm rest would allow.

What she didn't do was cry. McGill would bet she was scheming to find a way to save the day. Failing that, a means to make the bad guys pay. Being a devoted father, McGill had flown west not just to see his son perform and temporarily pull him out of school, but also to see if his daughter might find absolution for a misplaced sense of guilt by helping him with the case.

"You haven't hired a casting director yet, have you?" he asked.

The question was so out of left field Caitie had to look up. "What?"

"Well, you told me you're working on a script with a friend, right?"

"Yeah."

"Okay, so knowing you, there must be a plan to shoot what you write."

Caitie nodded.

"So who's going to do your casting?"

By now, Caitie had figured out her father wasn't simply trying to distract her. He had a point to make and would get to it in his own way. She sat up straight and he withdrew his arm.

"I am. Well, Ben and me. My co-writer and co-producer."

McGill was tempted to ask: Boyfriend? But he decided to save that for another time.

Instead, he said, "Am I right in thinking you and Ben are looking for newcomers, as that's all your budget will allow."

"Well, we do have *some* money, but yeah."

"So, you keep a sharp eye out for talent. Faces you find interesting, at a minimum."

"Of course, that's how …" She got it now. What her father was getting at. "You want to know if I've noticed anyone who stuck out as, what, unusual lately."

McGill nodded. "Unusual and no-good, if you don't mind that characterization."

Caitie grinned. "I kind of like it. No-good is so old fashioned and corny it's almost hip."

"Okay, here's a bit of elaboration. Someone doesn't have to be brawny to be threatening. A person might look quite ordinary physically, but he might be missing a lesser or greater degree of empathy. Someone who looks like he'd let a door slam in your face rather than catch it. Or let you step in front of oncoming traffic without saying, 'Look out.' You can see things like that in some people's faces, if you look."

Caitie made a leap and said, "There have to be people who'd *push* you into traffic, too."

"Yes, there are. I don't want you to force things, but when you have some quiet time, let your memory roam and see if you can come up with anyone you've seen anywhere near you in the past month or so who looked no-good."

McGill saw his daughter was buying into his idea, nodding her head and already searching her memory even though he'd said not to press. Still, it was good to have her invested. It would make her feel useful and, you never knew, a break in a case might come from any direction.

She snapped out of her reverie and asked, "Can I talk about this with Ben?"

"Sure, if you think that might help."

"I think it could. He has a great eye. He's a cinematography student."

"Then, by all means, yes."

Caitie kissed her father's cheek. She'd never really been all that interested in either police work or private investigations. Mostly, it seemed like a lot of straining at the gnats of everyday life, looking for the one thing that was out of place. *Quel ennui.*

How boring.

Looking for a kidnapper — maybe more than one — who'd grabbed a Secret Service agent — someone who looked a lot like you — that was … well, *cinematic.* Couldn't possibly be more on point for her interests.

Following the flow of her imagination, Caitie decided not to tell her father that Ben had more than a great eye, he often shot photos of people he found interesting in one way or another. Wouldn't it be great if she and Ben were the ones who nailed those kidnapping pricks? Brought the Secret Service, the FBI and wrath of God crashing down on them.

"You okay, honey?" McGill asked. "Your face is getting a bit red."

She smiled and said, "I'm just glad I might be able to help."

Having said that, Caitie thought it was going to be a real buzz-kill if she and Ben came up empty. That might mean … No, she wouldn't let herself think what that might mean for Carrie.

So she changed the subject. "Mom told me you joined the FBI. I laughed. She had to be kidding me, right?"

"Yes and no. I've made an official connection to the Bureau, but I'm not a special agent."

"What are you then?"

"A presidential consultant to the Department of Justice."

"What the heck is that?"

"That's a one-time-only job classification that pays a dollar per year but allows me to carry FBI credentials and hold a federal officer's firearms permit. It also means nobody can boss me around except Patti."

Before Caitie could comment, a familiar voice asked, "Is this my seat?"

Both McGills looked up and saw a familiar face wearing an unfamiliar color.

"What?" Celsus Crogher asked. "A guy can't get a little sun?"

Neither McGill nor Caitie would have thought a tan Celsus was even possible.

He told them both, "Merilee thought some color would look good on me." He turned his focus to McGill. "You hurt my feelings and you'll have to find someone else to keep your kids safe."

Celsus had been hired to manage the security for the assembled McGill clan at Carolyn and Lars' Minnesota country place.

The idea that the former Secret Service SAC had feelings that might be bruised was yet another revelation.

"Hey," McGill told Celsus, "you've never looked better to me."

CHAPTER 3

Sunday, March 27, 2016
SNAM TV Studio — Washington, DC

S atellite News America, nicknamed SNAM, called its Sunday
morning news and politics show "Wake Up, America." The
double entendre was obvious and intentional. Get out of bed, sure,
but also get a clue. To furnish the details of those clues, SNAM
provided what amounted to a political catechism for right-thinking
Americans.

The irony being that SNAM was a British-owned company.

Sometimes referred to as "King George's Revenge."

Monty Kipp, the show's host, had been a subject of the Queen
before becoming a naturalized citizen of the United States. While
nobody had ever asked to see Kipp's Certificate of Naturalization —
yet — he could have produced it if asked. Despite the camouflage of
that shield, in his heart, Kipp thought of himself as an Englishman.

His Cockney accent had migrated before the rest of him,
shifting in tone from the East End to Chelsea. The one in London,
not New York. Kipp often thought of going home to die, but he
wanted to die rich. Wealthy enough to have his point of departure
be Sloane Street.

He wasn't there yet, but the way American yahoos loved his
upper-class British tones, it shouldn't be too long. If only he could

moderate his drinking enough not to have his liver quit on him prematurely. The problem with that was he saw the world as increasingly becoming a place best traversed inebriated.

He had his wits about him, though, as he greeted his guest that morning, Senate Majority Leader Oren Worth, Republican of Utah, and the certain nominee of the Republican Party to be the next President. Well, probably so, if things went according to form.

Kipp stood and greeted Worth with a firm handshake and a smile.

"Good Sunday morning to you, Mr. Majority Leader. Welcome to the show."

Worth nodded, offered a measured smile and said, "Glad to be here."

The two men sat in facing chairs that allowed a respectable bit of leg room.

None of that bumping knees bilge for Monty.

Before starting his interview, the show's host looked into the camera and told his audience, "General Warren Altman, currently running second for the GOP nomination to be its Presidential candidate, was also asked to appear with us this morning. His campaign told us that a scheduling conflict made that impossible. So here we are, *tête à tête,* with Senator Worth. Let me start, sir, by asking you for your evaluation of the current status of both your competition with General Altman and how you stand in the voters' minds versus Vice President Morrissey."

Worth summoned a broader version of his earlier smile. "I'm beating the general right now, and I will beat the Vice President in November. I don't know anyone who's doing better with the American people than I am. My plan is to show even more of my fellow citizens that I'm worthy of their trust and support."

"I see," Kipp said. He'd heard those exact words in several of Worth's recent campaign speeches, and was ready with a riposte. "In 1984, Ronald Reagan won 49 out of 50 states running against Walter Mondale. Do you think you can go the Gipper one better and run the board, win all 50 states?"

Worth laughed, showing faux but plausible good humor. "I'm sure Vice President Morrissey will get *some* votes. From family and friends, some of the people working on her campaign and so forth. And let's remember Walter Mondale carried his home state of Minnesota, where the Vice President also hails from, so winning every state would be tough. But I promise that my margin of victory will be one of the most impressive in our history."

Kipp said, "Well then, given how formidable an opponent you'd be for Vice President Morrissey, do you consider her upcoming marriage to FBI Deputy Director Byron DeWitt to be a union of convenience, something done to mitigate a political disadvantage?"

Worth bit his lower lip, presenting the image of a man being thoughtful.

Or at least one doing his best not to put a foot in his mouth.

"You know, I can't say I think any two people would get married for any reason except that being together makes them happy. So, no, I would not say any political calculation was involved."

Kipp kept a straight face. Of course, Worth thought politics were behind the wedding, at least in its timing. The senator surely knew the only bachelors ever to be elected President were James Buchanan and Grover Cleveland, the latter in 1885. After a 131-year run of married Presidents, it was more likely a same-sex marriage candidate would be elected before a bachelor.

Which meant Worth was as much a straight-faced liar as any other politician.

An easy assumption to make but always good to know for certain.

Kipp's next question touched on an even more sensitive possibility.

"Let's assume, Senator, that President Grant is watching our conversation this morning. She takes your prediction of a historic general election victory to heart. She was impeached last year. She has to be fed up with an obstructionist Congress, knows she won't see any legislation that's important to her passed in the remainder of her second term. So she thinks 'To hell with this. I'm going to resign. I'll let my Vice President have the job, get hands-on experience in the Oval Office and as the commander-in-chief. If a crisis comes up and Jean Morrissey handles it well, let's see any Republican or True South candidate top that. Let's see them beat a battle-tested sitting President.' How would you react to that, Senator?"

It lasted only a single heartbeat, but Oren Worth's mouth fell open.

He always did his homework. He was a grinder. What he owed his success to, in business and politics, was that he could grind faster than anyone else. Get the answers before the competition did. But this limey sack of shit staring at him had caught him flat-footed. Asked him a question neither he nor any of his people had ever anticipated.

He knew he had to answer it before the silence grew too long. But the best he could come up with was: "That would be unfair."

Kipp couldn't help himself. He laughed, moderately but aloud.

"Come now, Senator. Who expects fairness in politics?"

Worth couldn't stop a flush of both embarrassment and anger from staining his face.

"That would never happen, what you just suggested," he said.

But the look in Worth's eyes said he was worried that it just might.

His situation was becoming a debacle. He made another stab at righting it.

"If something like that was planned, you couldn't keep it secret. Patti Grant couldn't. Everything leaks in Washington. It would have become news by now."

And that was when things got dangerous for people other than Oren Worth.

Kipp said, "There are always exceptions, Senator. SNAM likes to keep a close watch on newsmakers in our country. As of this moment, the President has closeted herself at the White House, receiving no visitors, and her husband, James J. McGill, and their three children have left Washington and their other respective homes for destinations unknown."

"Camp David," Worth said, a note of hopeful desperation in his voice.

Kipp shook his head. "Marine One, the President's helicopter, is at its base. No traffic, either on the road or in the air, has been seen arriving at Camp David. If the President's blended family is gathering in private somewhere, she might have cleared her schedule to facilitate a matter of discussion serious to all of them, wouldn't you say? Is it now too hard for you to believe that President Grant might resign and you might have to run against President Morrissey? And who knows if our new President might be welcomed into office with a baptism of fire to test her mettle if nothing more? Something to conjure with, wouldn't you say?"

Obviously, it was. But Worth was at a loss for words.

As "Wake up, America" went to a commercial break, the people behind the kidnapping of Special Agent Carrie Ramsey — Caitie McGill to them — had been watching and had taken note of the news that the President's family had gathered in an unknown location. If they were lucky, that could dovetail with their plans beautifully.

Departing Montevideo, Uruguay

The Gulfstream G550 lifted into the air with the smooth surge of power most often enjoyed by the elite of business, entertainment and government. Its flight capabilities and creature comforts made it worth every penny of its $53.5 million price tag, assuming you had such a sum to spare. The aircraft, in its most common configuration, could seat 19 and sleep eight.

The iteration of the G550 that FBI Special Agent Abra Benjamin had borrowed from the United States Air Force had a smaller capacity for both seating and sleeping. That was due to the two secure cabins, i.e. cells, that faced each other at the rear of the plane. Each cell could hold two prisoners no larger than 150% of average U.S. male dimensions: five feet nine inches and 195.5

pounds.

Each cell had a two-way mirror viewport: Captors could look in; captives could see only their own reflections. Prisoners could be hand-cuffed and shackled to either a bed or chair, both pieces of furniture were fixed to the cabin floor. An aircraft-sized commode took care of nature's necessities in each space. Toilet paper, which might have been used in an attempt to gum up the plumbing and interfere with the aircraft's operation, was unavailable.

This type of plane was known as a rendition aircraft. An earlier model was called "The Guantanamo Express" for its frequent trips to Cuba. Even before that, such flights were used by the CIA to repatriate South American dictators to their homelands to face trial and/or execution.

Tyler Busby, fugitive billionaire, was secured in one cell of the G550; his putative wife, Ah-lam, was cuffed to the chair in the other cell. Each was within reach of a call button that would summon Abra, if they felt like talking meaningfully. Providing the FBI with testimony that could be used in court against each other or third parties.

Prior to takeoff, Busby had said only, "I'll talk, all right, but only after I confer with my lawyer. You can bet I'm going to get the best plea deal in history."

"You think that'll include a lifetime supply of Viagra?" Abra asked.

That had made the two U.S. Marshals aboard laugh. Marshals had the responsibility of bringing in fugitives. Even crazy rich ones from abroad. Exercising her legal training and an overabundance of caution, Abra had dragooned the marshals so no defense attorney for Busby could say she'd cut any corners.

There was also a video of Busby being read his Miranda rights.

One of the marshals who'd enjoyed Abra's joke was kind of cute and wore a cowboy hat. The guy watched too much TV, trying to look like that actor on the cable show Abra had seen once or twice. He tried coming on to her during an idle moment, but she told him, "You've got the look, but your voice is all wrong."

He had a Brooklyn accent. The marshal grinned. "You mean it's not country like the guy on TV? Listen, he was born in Hawaii, grew up in California and started his acting career in … New York. And I dressed like this before that show came on."

Then in a perfect knockoff of the country accent the actor on TV used, the marshal said, "I don't pull my sidearm unless I'm gonna shoot to kill."

His partner rolled his eyes, no doubt having heard the come-on many times before. Even so, Abra let him give her his business card: Matthew Bascom. Somewhat of a country name, she thought, maybe more an Old West moniker. She stuck the card in a pocket and thought a cowboy might make a good change from Byron DeWitt.

By the time the G550 reached cruising altitude, both marshals were dozing, Bascom with his hat over his face. Abra might have napped, too, only Tyler Busby buzzed. The cabin attendants, armed though they were, had been instructed not to attend to the prisoners. Abra was the only one who would talk to the fugitive billionaire until they reached Washington.

She walked to the rear of the aircraft and looked in at Ah-lam first. She was slouched in her chair and appeared to be sleeping. Accepting if not content with her fate. Abra had told her that Jonathan, her infant son, was safe. No thanks to her. Abra still wanted to beat the woman with a stick for using the child as a throw toy.

Abra turned to look in on Busby. He, too, sat on his cell's chair, tapping one foot rapidly. Like he was waiting for a shoe-shine boy who was keeping him from more important things. Abra unlocked the door and stepped inside.

"What do you want?" she asked. "You said you weren't going to talk without seeing your lawyer first."

His gaze started at her face and worked its way down, stopping at all the obvious places.

The special agent sighed. "Your head's on the chopping block, and you're thinking about sex?"

Busby lifted his eyes. "We're all motivated by something."

"Like money, power and assassinating the President? Before you answer, be advised that this conversation like any other we might have on board is being recorded and transmitted in real time to Washington."

A precaution taken in case any mid-flight misfortune befell those aboard.

Busby smiled. "I'm glad to hear that."

"You should also remember that anything you say may be used against you in court."

"Oh, I would never do anything to harm my own cause."

"Then what do you want?" Abra asked.

"I want to position myself for an early release, of course."

"Fat chance." If not for the recorder, it would have been fat fucking chance.

"I can understand your hostility toward me. Your opportunities for professional advancement are much better if I spend the rest of my life in prison."

Or on federal death row in Terre Haute, Indiana, she thought. I'd come to see you get the needle. Two more things she'd have liked to say.

She contented herself with, "We'll discuss my career prospects some other time. If you have anything of significance to say, now's the time. If you press the call button again, I'll have one of the marshals answer it."

Busby didn't like that idea. "Have you spoken with Ah-lam yet?"

"You answer the questions, not me."

"Just this one thing, at least. Is Jonathan safe?"

Abra knew that among all his other character deficits Busby was a con-man, but he did seem honestly concerned about his son's welfare.

"Yes," Abra said.

"There are people who would like to wound Ah-lam and me by hurting or even killing Jonathan. You know that, don't you?"

Abra didn't respond.

Busby looked at her a moment longer and nodded his head.

"You do know it. Very well, here's why I buzzed you. Whatever else you might think of me, I'm sure you've learned that I'm actually quite the good businessman. So ask yourself: If I had been thinking of killing President Grant, wouldn't I have done a thorough survey of all the other people who might be thinking the same thing and stood a good chance of succeeding? If I had found someone who might save me the trouble, why would I even bother?"

"Personal satisfaction?" Abra said.

Busby laughed. "Yes, well, I can see where you might think that, but with me, the result is always more important than the process."

"So stop trying to show me how smart you are and cut to the chase."

"Very well. Arrange to have someone with serious political weight standing by when we land in Washington. The attorney general, say. If he and I, and my lawyer, of course, can agree on adequate leniency for me, I might be able to provide you with the names, means and methods of groups planning to do in the President. A couple of years ago, their plans might have been still in the formative stages, but by now I suspect they could have matured considerably."

Abra did her best to keep a straight face, but she couldn't help but think that a plan to kill the President might be initiated by kidnapping one of her husband's kids. Get the Secret Service and everyone else looking the wrong way and —

Abra's silence, not her eyes, gave her away.

"A scheme is already in motion," Busby said with a smile. "Ah, well. That strengthens my bargaining position, doesn't it?"

Chief of Staff's Office — The White House

Galia Mindel didn't play chess, not the board-game kind. The pieces had insufficient utility. The board offered too little room for maneuver. If there was a clock involved to keep the game moving, she found the pace too rigid and arbitrary.

What she loved about chess, though, was the idea of thinking several moves ahead. Pressuring your opponent to shape the battlefield the way you wanted it. Then being ready to pounce once the other guy fell into a trap he never saw coming.

On the other hand, if *you* were lulled or spurred into making the wrong move, you must have prepared, in advance, a way to escape or better yet turn things around on your opponent. No victory was sweeter than one that began an inch from disaster. She'd loved doing that when she was younger. But now Galia had started to think she'd gotten too old for that shit.

She'd recently confided her growing self-doubt, though no specific details, to an old friend outside of politics who was a chess grandmaster. He'd clarified things wonderfully for her. "Each of us plays our own games, Galia. But in our minds we are fighting wars. A person can take only so much of that."

Maybe so, but Galia wasn't about to see a shrink with a claim of PTSD. That would be an insult to everyone who'd experienced real trauma. Of course, now that she thought about it, New Hampshire Secretary of State John Patrick Granby had tried to garrote her in the White House Press Room. Would have succeeded in killing her, if not for James J. McGill's intervention.

She hadn't had a nightmare about that for quite a while. So she must have retained some degree of both mental and physical toughness. Be that as it may, she was getting tired of the struggle. Her friend was right: A person could take only so much.

She'd no sooner concluded that fatigue was her problem than her phone rang.

Not many people could get through to her at the White House on a Sunday.

Augustus Wiley could. He asked, "You sitting down, Galia?"

"I work best from my backside, Gus. What's up?"

"I'm hoping you can tell me. I just got off the phone with the commonwealth attorney for Fairfax County, Virginia. He apologized for intruding on my Sunday, but he said he'd be making my

Monday easier."

Galia knew intuitively what had happened. "He dropped the larceny charge against Elias Roosevelt."

"Nobody likes a smarty-pants, Galia."

"You get to keep your retainer, Gus."

"That helps ease the hurt. What else you gonna tell me you already figured out?"

That didn't take long for Galia either. "T.W. Rangel called the prosecutor. Apologized profusely, telling him he found the missing stamp collection. He's dismayed that he ever thought a loyal servant —"

"Employee," Gus said.

"Right. He'd have been politically correct about it. Anyway, he'd misjudged someone who deserved better, and he promised to make amends."

"He did. A tidy sum was promised, according to the commonwealth attorney. Galia, I'd like to think my very appearance on Mr. Roosevelt's behalf put the fear of God into the other side, but I know better than that. So why don't you tell me what really happened?"

Galia said, "It *was* the fact that you showed up that mattered. I had thought things would proceed farther, legally, maybe even going to a verdict. But T.W. Rangel decided he had seen enough when a lawyer billing your hourly fee showed up to defend a man of modest means."

"So this was all a game," Gus said.

"Just the start of one," Galia replied.

"Do I want to know the details?"

"Better that you don't for now."

"Meaning that you might need your own lawyer by and by."

"Maybe not even that long," Galia admitted.

"So I shouldn't go on any fishing trips?"

"Sure, go. Just leave a phone number where I can reach you."

"Galia, I'd be deeply disappointed if you used any other attorney."

"I won't," she said, "but I will try to keep things from reaching that point. Thank you for calling, Gus."

"Anything for my old friend Nate's best girl."
That brought a tear to Galia's eye. She said goodbye.
Then she made a move to get T.W. Rangel's attention.
Show him he was trying to punch above his weight class.
And it wasn't going to work.

SNAM Offices — Washington, DC

Monty Kipp's personal assistant, Esme Thrice, buzzed him.
"A gentleman named Rangel would like to speak with you, Monty."
Esme had begun her duties with Kipp by addressing him as sir. That made him feel he was far too old for her, even though from the moment they'd been introduced he'd thought of her as Do-Me Thrice. That, of course, was wishful thinking. Twice would have been a monumental achievement. Once would have been worth the price of his tattered soul. Only Old Nick didn't seem to be in the market for his spark of the divine. Nonetheless, a bloke could still dream.
Then he found out Esme was married, to another woman. And, good Lord, wasn't the missus every inch a beauty, too? To think of the two of them together with him was such a cornucopia of fantasies that Kipp could do nothing but be entirely proper with Esme.
So she would stay on and continue to fire his imagination if nothing else.
"Does Mr. Rangel have a first name, Esme?"
"He offered only two initials: T and W. He sounded as if you should know him."
It took him a moment, going back to the farthest reaches of his memory. "Thomas Winston Rangel. Bloke with an academic background. Georgetown, I believe. Did some strategy work with the GOP grandees in the House and Senate."
"You never cease to amaze, Monty. Shall I put him through?"
Operating on the principle that the oldest dogs knew where

the most bones were buried, and who knew what T.W. Rangel might have dug up, Kipp said, "Yes, please, Esme. Let's see what Mr. Rangel has to say." The connection was made. "Monty Kipp here."

"T. W. Rangel. I saw your show this morning, Mr. Kipp. You flustered Senator Worth in a way I'd never seen before."

"You haven't called to complain, have you, sir?" Monty had no time for gripes.

"Not at all. I meant my observation as a compliment. I have a story you might like to pursue."

People had ideas for Monty all the time. He couldn't walk down the street in Washington, New York or London without barrages of rubbish being launched at him. Occasionally, there was some mad notion that he might have found worth pursuing when he was starting out. Within the past five years, though, he couldn't recall a single unsolicited idea that he'd pursued.

A mature man had only so much time he could afford to waste.

Still, as he recalled with increasing clarity, Winston had kept important company. So why not afford the blighter a moment of ear-time? But one thing had to be clear from the start.

"You'd like me to knife someone for you, sir, is that it?"

Rangel had the wit and the spine to laugh and say, "Of course, I do. That's been your life's work, hasn't it?"

"I tend to work more often with a scalpel than a dagger these days, but yes. You are correct."

"I trust you've read enough about your adopted country to know who the greatest political blackmailer in American history was," Rangel said.

"The late Mr. J. Edgar Hoover, iconic first director of the Federal Bureau of Investigation. No one crossed the man, not even Presidents."

"Because he knew all their secrets and could destroy them," Rangel said.

"This is schoolboy stuff, sir. I hope you wish me to work on something more contemporary. Not a topic fit for Ken Burns."

"What if I told you that an even greater blackmailer is still at work within our government. Someone who is far shrewder than Hoover was and whose hold on political figures has a more sizable reach? Someone who's much closer to the pinnacle of power than a glorified law enforcement bureaucrat was. Would that interest you, bringing such a story to light?"

Monty Kipp's appetites extended beyond sexual matters.

Given the rigid class structure of his homeland, there was little sweeter in life than bringing down the high and mighty. Doing so in the United States just before absconding to London, retirement and leaving a larger-than-life legend behind ... well, that did have its appeal.

Perhaps he'd even be able to persuade Esme and Lara to accompany him home.

"You have my undivided attention, Mr. Rangel. Pray continue."

"Begin your inquiries with how a domestic worker named Elias Roosevelt, accused of theft in Virginia, came to be represented by an attorney named Augustus Wiley who charges $2,000 per hour. See how conveniently the DC Legal Defense Fund sprang into being just in time to help Mr. Roosevelt. Once you've done that, look for a connection to the disappearance of Senator Randall Pennyman of Georgia."

"The bloke who's accused of setting up false charities and swindling churches throughout the country?" Kipp asked.

"Fraud is just the start of the list of crimes you might uncover. Hijacking the government of the United States will be where the trail ultimately leads, and it won't stop until you're inside the Oval Office."

A chill ran down Monty Kipp's spine.

But not for any reason T.W. Rangel might have guessed.

Olmsted County, Minnesota

Carolyn and Lars Enquist, the McGill children's mother and step-father, had bought a 150-acre parcel 20 miles outside of

Rochester. The land came with a six-bedroom farmhouse that had been completely updated five years earlier. It was heated, cooled, and electrified by solar, geothermal and wind power. The surplus energy it sold to the municipal power agency paid the real estate taxes.

Stands of apple, pear and cherry trees grew on the land. Gardens of tomatoes, lettuce, cucumber, cabbage, potatoes, beets, barley, hops, kale, parsley, caraway, dill and onion were planned by Carolyn for the coming spring. Lars intended to both brew his own beer and distill his own aquavit.

A three-acre bean-shaped pond graced the back of the house, the shoulders of the body of water were draped by a scarf of evergreens. Carolyn and Lars were discussing the idea of stocking the pond with largemouth bass, and joking that piranha might be a better choice if they were bothered by any unwelcome guests.

A former barn had been redone into a workshop and space for eight motor vehicles. The one-time hay loft had room for a Piper Cub, but not the length to make a takeoff.

The couple had financed the purchase of the property with the sale of three of Lars' four drugstores in Evanston, Illinois. In case a Minnesota winter ever got to be too much for them, the funds from the sale of the last store, Lars' original place of business, had gone to cover a three-bedroom condo in Sarasota, Florida.

The Enquists had their retirement planned to a fare-thee-well.

Never expecting their northern home might need to be used for a hideout.

McGill was the first one out of the black, armored Suburban that had just completed the drive from the Rochester airport. He shook Lars' hand and said, "Great place you've got here. That driveway of yours has to be a half-mile long. A lot of snow to clear in winter."

Lars smiled and said, "We've got a plow blade to put on the Land Rover."

McGill hugged his ex. "You look happy. I thought you might be —"

"Worried sick?"

Before Carolyn could respond to her own question, Ken and Caitie joined their parents, after sharing embraces with Lars. Carolyn put an arm around each child and kissed them both, refraining from commenting on Caitie's new look.

Looking back at McGill, she said, "You're going to do your best to find that poor girl from the Secret Service, aren't you?"

McGill got the impression his ex was no longer as fearful about any possible misfortune that might befall him as she once was. Ah, well, the passage of time and the love of a new mate could alter old feelings. He could identify with both halves of that equation himself.

He reached into a pocket and took out his new FBI badge, showed it to Carolyn and Lars. "As I've already told Caitie and Ken, I've been deputized, if only temporarily. I've also been hired by Carrie Ramsey's parents. In each capacity, I'm taking only a dollar for my time." Changing the subject, he asked, "Is Abbie inside?"

Lars nodded.

Carolyn said, "Working on a school paper. Trying to keep her mind off what's happening."

Celsus stepped forward. "The Secret Service has the perimeter covered, but I'd be happier if everyone went inside. Paranoia never rests."

Lars led the way to the front door. Carolyn said, "My safe-house is your safe-house."

Ken took his mother's arm and walked inside.

Caitie hung back, and McGill waited with her. Celsus cooled his heels behind them. Once Carolyn was inside, Caitie took McGill's hand and started walking slowly toward the house.

"Is there any way you'd take me with you?" she asked her father.

"What, on my investigation?"

"Yes."

"No."

"I'm so angry I think my head will explode. Blow right off and leave a mushroom cloud."

"You still think what happened to Special Agent Ramsey is all your fault?"

"No, not all of it, but some of it is."

McGill couldn't argue with that. Didn't try. He pursued a line of reasoning he hoped would be persuasive. "Do you think the special agent has a better chance of coming home if I help look for her?"

Caitie looked up at her father. She was fighting back tears as she nodded.

"I do, too. But there's no question in my mind, if you came along, your welfare would be my first concern and nothing else would come close."

Caitie lowered her head as tears now rolled down her cheeks.

McGill put an arm around her shoulders. "I'll do better work if I'm not distracted, if I know you, Abbie and Ken are safe. Tell you what, though …"

Caitie looked up at him. "What?"

"I promise to listen to any ideas you or your brother and sister might have, things that could be helpful. You can help in that way."

Caitie took a thumb drive out of a jacket pocket and handed it over.

"What's this?" McGill asked.

"Copies of photos Ben sent me. I wasn't going to give them to you right away. But I do want to help in any way I can."

"Ben's your collaborator back in California?"

She nodded. "He likes to shoot pictures of people he thinks stand out. Casting possibilities. Or just people who are … unusual."

"Were you with Ben when he took some of these pictures?"

"All of them. I had him sort them that way."

McGill kissed the top of his daughter's head. "You know, not to disrupt any of your career plans, but you might make a good detective."

They stopped at the doorway to the house.

"Still won't take me with you, though, right?"

"Right."

"It's going to be hard, waiting here."

"I know," McGill said, "and I'm sorry to say it might get even harder."

McGill gathered the blended family in the house's library. He was pleased to see a home that had a room filled with books. The space wasn't a complete rebuff to an increasingly digital world, though. A 50-inch flat screen TV, high-definition no doubt, occupied a corner of the room. An e-reader rested on a table next to an armchair. Modern and traditional means of transmitting information seemed to co-exist peacefully.

How well mankind's original means of communication, word of mouth, went over, McGill was about to see. His kids, Carolyn and Lars were all seated and awaiting his spiel. Celsus leaned in and whispered to McGill, "The secure communication link is in place. Just use the remote to turn on the TV."

McGill nodded. "Thanks, Celsus. Give us a little breathing room, will you?"

"As much as we can."

He stepped out of the room.

McGill got right to it. "You all know why we're here, right?"

Abbie said, "Because the kidnappers might want all of us: Ken, Caitie and me."

"That's right. Possibly even your mom and Lars as well."

Mr. and Mrs. Enquist looked at each other. Clearly, they hadn't been informed. Carolyn looked at her ex-husband and said, "Wait a minute. What value could we have to anybody? You and I split up years ago."

"Yes, we did. It was just your bad luck, though, that the parting was amicable. That the two of us, and Lars, have done our best to keep our family as functional as possible."

Ken said, "So has Patti. I wouldn't be here without her."

Patti had been the bone marrow donor for Ken, at no small risk to her own health as it turned out.

"Right," McGill said. "That's why she's going to join us now. The point is, we all have skin in this game."

He picked up the remote control and turned on the TV.

Patti came into view, sitting on an easy chair in the Residence at the White House, dressed and groomed casually. Looking as much as was possible for her just like an ordinary step-parent.

"Hello, everybody. I'm sorry I can't be with you right now. I wish I could give you all a hug."

Everyone said hello in return. Expressed the desire to see Patti in person, too. But the casual conversation was kept short. Family gathering or not, they all knew this was a business call.

"You want to tell them, Jim, or should I?"

"You start, I'll finish," McGill said.

"Okay. It's only natural that all of you will want to know every small measure of progress we make in bringing Special Agent Ramsey safely home. Other than her mother and father, I can't think of anyone who might have more of an interest than us."

"I'm especially interested," Caitie said.

"Yes, you are, Caitie. That's why your dad and I hope you can set the tone for the rest of your family."

"What do you mean?" Caitie asked.

"Jim, you want to take it from here?"

"Yeah," he said. He looked at everyone in the room, finishing with his youngest child. "When a person is kidnapped rather than killed outright, that implies the kidnappers have a reason for keeping their victim alive. There might be a quid pro quo for the victim's release. It might be a monetary ransom or in this case, it might be a political demand.

"In either of those situations, the bad guys have to provide a proof of life. It could be a still photo with the victim holding that day's newspaper or a video with the victim speaking of an event that happened that day and is public knowledge. A sports score, say."

"Wouldn't that be good?" Abbie asked. "Seeing that the special agent hasn't been killed."

McGill said, "Yes, that part is good. What might come next is not. To demonstrate their ruthlessness, the kidnappers might harm, maim in some vicious way, Special Agent Ramsey."

"Good Lord," Lars said.

Patti said, "That's what might happen in a more normal case, if anything about a crime like this can be called normal. The FBI pro-filers I've spoken with feel that as long as the kidnappers think they have Caitie, they'll be more reluctant to disfigure Special Agent Ramsey."

"Why?" Caitie asked.

Looking at his daughter now, McGill had no doubt she'd attempt mortal vengeance on the bastards who grabbed Carrie Ramsey. Then again, he might do the same.

He said, "Because, honey, someone with your prominence is more valuable to them if she remains unhurt, at least physically. That's not to say something awful, though short of death, might not happen if these people think their demands won't be met. Committing some type of atrocity might be what they see as their last means of leverage."

Carolyn said, "But we don't even know who they are, right? How can we know what they might want?"

Lars had a point that pre-empted Carolyn's questions. "Isn't it true that our government never pays *any* ransom? Won't even negotiate about it."

McGill said, "That's our government's standing policy, yes. It has been since the Nixon Administration."

"What happened back then?" Abbie asked.

Patti said, "In 1973 two American diplomats in Sudan were kidnapped by the Black September terrorist group. They demanded the release of Palestinian terrorists being held in Israel, members of the Baader-Meinhof Gang in Germany and even Sirhan Sirhan, the assassin of Robert F. Kennedy. President Nixon said no, and it's been no ever since."

Ken asked, "Were our diplomats killed?"

"Yes, they were," Patti said.

Carolyn had the next question. "If everyone knows this policy, why would anyone bother with kidnapping? Doesn't it make more sense just to kill a targeted person?"

"Jim," Patti said.

McGill sighed. "If you simply kill someone, there's no room for hope. Anger and the desire for revenge are the most likely responses. If you kidnap someone, there is room for hope, desperate and unrealistic though it might be. Beyond that, there's much more room for blame if the victim does die. Vengeance might still be had but the cost will be far higher and leave behind abiding social and political division."

"That's why there was a kidnapping not a killing," Abbie said. "One divides, the other unifies."

"Yeah," McGill said.

"I still can't get past the kidnapping thing," Carolyn said. "There are other ways to hurt society. *Mass* shootings. So why *this* kidnapping?"

"Because somebody is trying to break new ground," McGill said. "Nobody has ever tried to kidnap a member of the President's family before. Having a hostage like that might be just the thing to change our policy. But the price to pay would be horrible."

Patti agreed. "Not just in money paid or terrorists set free. The real cost would be to our society. By making an exception, the government would be saying some people are worth ransoming while most others aren't. There's no way something like that would be acceptable to most Americans. Even attempting to formulate a rationale for paying ransoms selectively would destroy the pillars of our democracy as a society based on equality."

McGill said, "If exceptions were made, it would also have the ironic effect of making the rich, famous and powerful the exclusive targets of kidnappers. Why bother with anyone who won't get you what you want?"

"That isn't funny," Caitie said.

"Didn't mean it to be, my dear," McGill told her. "Patti and I are just trying to lay things out for all of you here. The way these things tend to play out, the bad guys try to put pressure on the family of the victim. Make them eager to meet any ultimatum. We expect that these scumbags, whoever they are, will try to reach Patti or me. Make their demands.

"If they don't like our reactions, they'll take their crime public. Try to get people's opinions, yea or nay, to add to the pressure we're feeling. So if you turn on the television here or go online, you might see that story play out. It will be ugly and painful. Whether you follow the story or choose to ignore it, that's up to each of you. We just felt you had to be informed before you decide."

Abbie said, "Everything you've just told us means you can't negotiate and won't pay for Special Agent Ramsey's release."

"That's right."

Ken said, "But you'll do everything you can to get her back."

"We all will," McGill said. "Patti and me in particular."

Nobody had another word to say.

But they all wondered the same thing.

Would the no-deals policy have held up if Caitie really had been kidnapped?

Angel Fire, New Mexico

The town was a ski resort on the Enchanted Circle Scenic Byway. Its base elevation was 8,600 feet rising to a peak of 10,167 in the Sangre de Cristo Mountains. There was still snow on the slopes but after two weeks of rising temperatures, it was patchy and slushy. The skiers had all gone home, leaving the permanent population of little more than a thousand souls happy that they'd had a good season up until the warm front had moved in. Damn global warming.

A good many of the year-rounders had decided to take their early off-season vacations to places where it was *really* warm: Palm Springs, Cabo San Lucas and Hawaii. The skeleton crew left in the village paid little attention to the weathered white Ford Econoline vans with the familiar logos front and back that pulled into a home that had been rented on Back Basin Road.

The windowless utility room in the house, between the two-car garage and the living area, had two steel doors opening on the adjacent spaces. Opening when they weren't locked, that was. Special Agent Carrie Ramsey had tried both doors and given each of them a good kick when it refused to open.

The physical efforts made her head spin. She walked a crooked path back to the cot on which she'd awoken. Thinking someone was probably watching her via a hidden camera, she pulled the blanket up over her head. Damn thing smelled bad. Not because it was old; more like it was new and hadn't been washed yet. Some kind of chemical stink.

That analysis made her wonder if she was inhaling some sort of disabling agent. A chemical whose fumes would render her physically incapacitated, if not unconscious. Was that why she'd felt dizzy? She flung the blanket off her and across the room.

Her breathing improved immediately. The air was cool and fresh. But she missed the cover and the sense of privacy the blanket had given her. The best she could do to get a measure of her own space back was to lie on her right side and face the wall.

As her mind cleared and her memory came back into focus, a battle of emotions took shape: despair versus rage. The sense of hopelessness told her she was fucked; the fury said maybe so but she would still rip somebody's head off the first chance she got. Make them pay for what they'd done to her. If they were going to kill her, she'd do her best to even the score as much as possible.

Given its superior energy, her wrath got the better of the fatalism. Then reason made an unexpected appearance, suggesting that the way out was to survive until the good guys arrived. Sure, hope the cavalry would ride over the hill with its flags flying and a bugle sounding the charge. Hell, that was movie stuff ... but, hey, wasn't she supposed to be passing for a kid who was an actress?

That's right, she was. She had to keep that in mind: Caitie McGill was the target. Right? Had to be. What sane people would intentionally grab a Secret Service special agent? Well, there might be some crazies who'd do that, but they'd have to expect a much smaller return on their effort. You grabbed a headliner, that was where you got the fame. You put a bit player in a sack and hauled her off, you couldn't expect any real payoff.

After disappointment set in, you just dropped her in the nearest body of water and made a bigger and better plan.

One the good people who'd refused to negotiate with creeps like you couldn't shrug off.

Thinking about being dumped like garbage ratcheted up Carrie's temper further, but reason wouldn't give up yet. Who has to be looking for me, she asked herself. Her brothers and sisters in the Secret Service, surely. The FBI, too. Kidnappings were their thing. Anybody else?

The entire armed forces of the United States would be nice.

Maybe the commander in chief, too. Yeah, the President.

Thinking of Patricia Grant brought another name to mind: James J. McGill. The President's henchman. He was some kind of tough-ass; everybody in the Presidential security detail knew about him, even the newbies like her. The guy was a detective, too.

Only he worked in the private sector. Had no official capacity. How could he get involved in the hunt? Short answer, he couldn't. But maybe there was a longer answer. She'd probably been snatched because she looked like Caitie McGill. Wouldn't that mean something to him?

Had to, she thought.

Yeah, no doubt about it. And being married to the President, he could find a way to get some kind of official standing and be involved. Or she was just spinning gossamer webs of fantasy, but it made Carrie better to think McGill was looking for her. It put a face on the idea that her rescue was important to a lot of people.

Especially Mom and Dad.

Her eyes filled with tears. She couldn't let them down. Break their hearts by not surviving.

Goddamnit, she was going to get out of this mess if she had to kill more people than a natural disaster. So what did she have to do? Make sure the assholes holding her continued to think she was Caitie McGill for starters. With her tears drying on her face, Carrie had to smile.

What did that overprivileged little wannabe *auteur* think about her stand-in disappearing? Had she even noticed? Probably, yeah. Whatever else Caitie was, she was sharp. Did Caitie care that she was gone? Maybe in the abstract. Otherwise, she was probably glad.

So Carrie thought it would be a hoot to return and tell her, "I'm *back.*"

Yet another reason to stay alive.

Having decided she'd give her all to having a future, Carrie knew it was time to do a mental survey of her physical well-being. Her head was still a little fuzzy from whatever drug they'd used to knock her out. Her neck was a bit stiff, but she could work that out. Her arms felt good and her hands clenched and opened with ease. Very important, that, if she needed to come out fighting.

Her stomach felt empty enough to make her realize she was hungry. That presented a dilemma. She had to eat, but how could she trust any food they gave her. It might knock her out again. If they wanted to do her in without risking damage to themselves, they might even put a dose of something toxic in a meal.

She couldn't think of a damn thing to do about the situation at the moment.

So she went back to her no-hands-on physical examination. Her hips felt good, an important consideration if she felt the need to kick someone's teeth down his throat. Her next point of concern stopped her cold. Jesus, how could she *not* have felt this sooner?

As far as physical sensations went, it was unlike any other in her experience. She felt as if someone had given her a pelvic exam. Used a speculum to see what they could see. Being as subtle about it as she could — in case there was a camera on her, and she'd bet there was — she gently felt her genitals. There was no pain in response.

She didn't get the impression she'd been raped while unconscious, but somebody had gotten a very close look at her. But why the hell would —

Damn! Whoever had grabbed her wanted to see if she was a virgin.

Thinking what? That Caitie McGill might be chaste? Which forced Carrie to wonder: *Well, was she?* Carrie couldn't imagine that any of the bosses in the Secret Service had ever imagined her resemblance to Caitie would have to go that far. Carrie had her first time when she was twenty. From there, she hadn't kept a tally, but no way was she virginal. What if Caitie had become sexually active but only recently? Would there be any way an exam could tell the difference?

Before her pulse shot up too far, Carrie thought to ask herself if there was any way the kidnappers could know what Caitie McGill's sexual experience, if any, was. She didn't *think* so. How could they? Kids didn't brag about keeping their virginity on Facebook, did they? Okay, maybe some of them did.

But a kid who was fluent in French and was going to Paris to learn film-making?

Nah. So if the bad guys wanted to accuse Caitie of being a slut, based on the exam they'd given to Carrie, well, she'd have to go with it. Say, "Yeah, what's it to you?"

If they tried to take carnal advantage of her, she'd remind them she'd almost bitten a guy's *arm* off. She'd bet there wasn't a Romeo in the world who'd get into bed with her once she'd flashed her teeth at him. Made it plain she was willing to chomp *anything* off.

CHAPTER 4

Monday, March 28, 2016
RFK Department of Justice Building — Washington, DC

M cGill said to no one in particular, "I think I'm going to need my own airplane."

He was sitting in the office of U.S. Attorney General Michael Jaworsky. Seated beside the AG on one of the two facing sofas in the suite were FBI Director Jeremiah Haskins and SAC Elspeth Kendry of the Secret Service. On the opposite sofa sat McGill and to his right FBI Deputy Director Byron DeWitt.

It was not yet eight a.m. and McGill had been up most of the night before talking with his children, his ex-wife, Carolyn, and Lars Enquist. They'd discussed the ramifications of being active targets of unidentified but truly dangerous malefactors. Carolyn had surprised him and the kids with her initial statement.

"I've kept up with my marksmanship practice," she said.

McGill said, "What?"

"After the last time, when we all felt threatened and Sweetie showed me how to shoot, I've continued to go to the firing range. I have to say, I'm really good."

"Did Sweetie recommend another instructor?" McGill asked.

"Yes, another woman. She's with the Evanston PD."

Sweetie hadn't said a word to him about any of that.

As if reading McGill's mind, Carolyn said, "I asked Sweetie not to say anything."

"She hasn't." McGill looked at Lars. "Do you know about all this?"

"Yes. Carolyn brought me along to see how proficient she is." Looking sheepish, he added, "I felt it would be only fair to share the burden. I've started to shoot, too."

The McGill children gaped at two of the most important adults in their lives as if they'd revealed themselves to be space aliens of a type drawn by Gahan Wilson. McGill felt nearly the same way.

"You bought your own gun, Lars?" he asked.

"Oh, no. No need for that. I use Carolyn's. I just thought, you know, it should be like sharing the driving when we take a road trip."

"He's almost as good a shot as me, though," Carolyn said with a proud, proprietary pat on her husband's leg.

McGill didn't know whether to laugh or cry. He could see Abbie and Ken felt the same way. Caitie, on the other hand, looked fascinated. Like she might ask Mom and Stepdad to take her to the nearest range and let her try her hand. Hoping that putting a round in the center ring was a family talent.

Given his youngest's spoken desire to avenge the kidnapping of Carrie Ramsey, he felt more than a little uneasy. Well, he could tell Carolyn what Caitie had said, and let her deal with it. He had too much on his plate at the moment to play father knows best.

That was just what he did, and was pleased when Carolyn didn't express the feeling that she was being dumped on, saying, "Okay, you're right, but especially in her case, she has a right to defend herself. Dark Alley goes only so far."

McGill winced.

Looking at both Carolyn and Lars, he said, "Dark Alley goes *plenty* far. If you knew what Caitie can do with her hands, feet and other anatomical points, you'd be as shocked as I am about your shooting skills. Just be careful, all right? And listen to what Celsus has to say about using a firearm in the presence of armed security personnel."

"Why would Celsus say anything?" Carolyn asked.

"Because I'm going to tell him you've got a gun and both of you know how to use it."

Carolyn wasn't thrilled about that. Lars took it better. The discrepancy of opinions caused friction between them. Great, McGill thought. He was tempted to tell them the statistics on how often domestic disputes were resolved with a fatality when there was a gun in the house.

He didn't only because he thought it would pour fuel on the fire.

Before leaving for Washington, McGill did inform Celsus about Carolyn having a gun in the house. The former Secret Service agent was grateful to learn of that. If a firefight were to start on or near the premises, Celsus didn't want anyone to succumb to friendly fire.

He wasn't, however, looking forward to his chat with Carolyn.

McGill sneaked into each of his children's rooms before leaving Minnesota to fly back to Washington in the wee hours before dawn. He actually managed to lightly buss both Abbie and Ken on the forehead without waking them. Caitie was wide-eyed and waiting for him.

"You don't have to say it," she said.

"Goodbye?"

She wasn't amused. "Not to ask Mom to teach me to shoot."

"You already know how to defend yourself."

"If I was staying home, in the U.S., I would ask her, but the French police would never let me have a gun when I go over there."

"Good for them. We should all be so smart."

"But I want you to teach me The Lord Shall Provide."

Dark Alley was divided into two parts: Biologicals, i.e. body parts, and The Lord Shall Provide, i.e. any object that came to hand.

"Knives in particular," she said.

McGill asked, "Not explosives or motor vehicles?"

"I'm not kidding."

"I know. That's what scares me."

He told her they'd talk about it after he got Carrie back.

That notion was good enough for Caitie to kiss him hard on the cheek.

The intensity of that scared him, too.

Byron DeWitt gave McGill a gentle nudge, bringing him back into the present moment.

"What kind of range do you want your plane to have and do you want it to come from Justice, Treasury or the military?" DeWitt asked.

McGill hoped he'd been daydreaming not dozing. He hadn't thought about the specifics of his requirement, but he said, "Say something that can make good time from Miami to Seattle or maybe even Juneau. My feeling is whatever we're looking at is domestic. I don't think Europe, Africa or Asia are in the picture."

DeWitt asked, "What about South America? That's where we found Busby."

As if DeWitt had been speaking of the devil, the AG's secretary buzzed in on the intercom and said, "Special Agent Benjamin is here with her prisoner, sir."

Busby.

Jaworsky told her, "Send them in, please."

Abra Benjamin had two U.S. marshals with her, one wearing a cowboy hat. They brought Busby in wearing handcuffs and shackles. They sat him down in a sturdy wooden chair brought in just for Busby. The marshals secured Busby's arms and legs to the chair.

Benjamin told Haskins and Jaworsky, "Gentlemen, the FBI has formally accepted transfer of custody for this prisoner."

"Where's my lawyer?" Busby demanded.

Not liking his tone, the marshal in the hat raised a hand to smack Busby's head.

The AG stopped that with a shake of his head and said, "Thank you, gentlemen. Unless you have some obligation that can't wait, take the rest of the day off."

The marshals said thank you and left. The cowboy, DeWitt

saw, gave Abra a wink as he departed. Everyone else had to see it, too. Cheeky bastard. Abra seemed to think nothing of it and sat on McGill's left.

"What's he doing here?" Busby nodded in McGill's direction. With a sneer in his voice, Busby added, "He's a *private eye*. He shouldn't be here."

McGill thought, I'm here to throw you out a window if you really annoy me.

But he deferred to Jaworsky to give voice to the situation.

The AG said, "Mr. Busby, you may have been important to some people once upon a time, but that is no longer the case. From what Special Agent Benjamin has told us, you think you have some leverage to improve your circumstances. You don't. Put that thought out of your mind. You are going to die in confinement. The only question left to determine is just how vile your durance will be. Moderation of the conditions you'll experience will be considered only if your cooperation is complete, timely and absolutely true."

Busby let a moment pass in silence and then he laughed. "That's all you've got for me? Extra gruel at breakfast? No, thanks. I want my lawyer now."

None of the others said a word, but Busby flinched when McGill leaned forward.

He didn't get to his feet, only rested his elbows on his thighs and steepled his hands under his chin. He looked at Busby as if he was a bug. Maybe the kind to impale with a pin and study at length or simply something to be ground to pulp under a shoe. In either case, the outcome for Busby would be painful and terminal.

Busby tried to object to the prolonged scrutiny but his throat was too dry to speak.

Then McGill had an idea and it brought a wicked smile to his face.

"What?" Busby croaked. "What are you thinking?"

McGill didn't answer. He turned to DeWitt and whispered into his ear. A look of surprise appeared on the deputy director's face and he smiled, too, and nodded. The other law enforcement officials in the room said nothing but Busby could see that they were all getting excited about something.

That fucker McGill had come up with something they'd like when they heard it.

Busby wanted to think they were all putting on an act, but he knew that all of these shits couldn't have that much acting talent. They'd be on Broadway, not in Washington, if that was the case. "You can't pull any BS on me," he said. "I'll get to see my lawyer eventually; I've got rights."

McGill came to his feet, making Busby try to retreat into the unyielding chair.

Here was the man whose wife he'd tried to have killed.

Payback was a personal matter to him.

But McGill turned to the attorney general and said, "By all means let him see his lawyer …" Then he looked back to Busby and completed his thought. "… for all the good it will do him."

After Busby had been taken away, McGill gave DeWitt the thumb drive Caitie had given him, explained what was on it.

"Sharp young lady," DeWitt said with a smile.

McGill said, "Probably sharper than I know; one of many traits that scares me."

Georgetown

Don and Sheri Ramsey had sublet a one-bedroom condo just off Wisconsin Avenue, within walking distance of the offices of McGill Investigations, Inc. If the occasion demanded, they'd *run* to hear what McGill had to tell them. Anxiety over their daughter's plight was eating them alive. They were willing to grasp at any straw that might suggest a favorable outcome.

They visited Grace Episcopal Church daily, prayed silently and aloud several times each day, beseeching the Divine for their child's deliverance. There were also the silent, aching moments of despair when they felt certain Carrie was lost to them. Never to be held or even seen again.

So when Sweetie called, at McGill's request, they were only too glad to have her stop in. They greeted her with handshakes and hugs. From Sweetie's point of view, the Ramseys reminded her of the terrible night she'd had to hold and console Patti Grant after the murder of her first husband, Andy.

Sweetie accepted a glass of water but not the offer of anything more. She sat in an easy chair facing the Ramseys, saw their desperate yearning for good news and their fear that there wasn't any.

McGill had given Sweetie one hopeful tidbit to offer.

Sweetie prefaced it with caveats. She said, "The two of you need to keep the lowest profile possible. Jim has arranged a cover story for you. Don is in town to confer with another cardiologist, Dr. Henry Coulter, on a research paper the two of you are writing."

Don said, "I don't know any Dr. Coulter."

"Check your iPad. We sent you a photo and a bio for him."

Sheri said, "He's someone you trust?"

Sweetie nodded. "The good doctor is also a Jesuit priest. He knows all about keeping a secret. He also said if either of you needs to talk about how you're feeling, he'd be happy to listen to you. On top of all his other accomplishments, Doc Coulter served in the army. He knows about people going through difficult situations."

The Ramseys shared a pained smile and nodded, pleased by the offer.

"Okay, Jim said to let you know about any progress he might be making in the case."

The mere mention of the word progress made the couple sit taller.

Sweetie held up a hand like a traffic cop. "You can't tell anyone, not even Doc Coulter if you talk with him, about any details I give to you. The warning here is, what might seem like a lead in a case doesn't always prove to be conclusive. You understand what I'm saying?"

Slumping a bit, they nodded.

"Okay, this is what Jim's going to follow up on."

She told them about the photos that Caitie's friend Ben had taken.

"These images will be run through the FBI's database of individuals with criminal records or known associates of people with criminal records. Your daughter's abduction wasn't a spur of the moment thing. Somebody planned it and somebody carried it out. If one or more photographs we have is of a person with a relevant criminal record, that would be our best lead. But it's possible a match won't be found. So you have to be ready for that, too."

"How many faces are there in the photos you have?" Don asked.

"Over 500 is what Jim told me. A number of the pictures were taken in the vicinity of film shoots. So most of the onlookers were probably just curious or star-struck, but that would also be a pretty good cover for someone with a darker purpose in mind."

"What do you think, Margaret?" Sheri asked. "Will anything come of this?"

An unqualified yes was the answer both Ramseys wanted. Sweetie could see that. But she couldn't give it to them.

"I don't think there's any way to say right now how helpful this might be. What I do know is I'd rather have the possibility that something good might come from it than not have anything at all."

Before the couple could come out and ask if there was nothing else in the way of a lead, Sweetie turned things around on them.

"If you're up to to answering some questions, I'd like to know what kind of a child Carrie was growing up. How she handled her teen years. What her time in college was like. What kind of failures and triumphs she experienced along the way. How she came to choose a career with the Secret Service. Anything and everything you can think of that would paint a clear portrait of who your daughter is."

Don and Sheri looked at each other, didn't say a word. Just nodded and exchanged a hug.

Sheri started, "Carrie was a joy from day one."

"And feisty as hell, too," Don added.

Sweetie listened closely, a picture of the woman taking shape in her mind. Jim would compare Sweetie's notes to what he found in Special Agent Ramsey's Secret Service personnel file. Get an idea of what the captors would have to deal with … and Jim would have to decide how similarly Carrie would behave to Caitie, had his child actually been grabbed.

That would give him an idea of whether the special agent would be up to pulling off a continuing deception, fooling the people who had her. It might also be useful in devising a rescue attempt, should that possibility arise.

Recounting episodes of how their daughter had exhibited her intelligence, creativity, strength and courage began to buoy the Ramseys. How could such a magnificent young woman fail to rise above even this dreadful set of circumstances?

Sweetie offered a silent prayer that they were right.

McGill Investigations, Inc. — Georgetown

"Carrie Ramsey was one of those kids who stood up to bullies," Sweetie said.

"Yeah?" A smile of approval formed on McGill's face.

He and Sweetie were sitting in his office, sipping White House ice tea McGill brought over from the Executive Mansion.

"Yeah, from an early age. Second grade from what both her parents remember. She absolutely would not allow any of her classmates or younger children to be picked on. Stood right up to boys who were bigger than her. Fought them when she had to."

"How'd that work out?" McGill asked.

"She didn't always come out on top, but she 'got her licks in,' as Don told it."

McGill was liking the young woman more and more. "Being a doctor, her father patched her up?"

"That usually fell to Sheri. Don worked long hours."

"How'd the school take it?"

"Meetings with the parents. Both sets were firmly informed the fighting had to stop. Blame equally apportioned, until the parents of the kids Carrie had stood up for involved themselves. Backed up the girl who'd protected their kids. Then the scales of justice were rebalanced. Two of the bullies were taken out of school by their parents when the finger of guilt was pointed at them."

"That settled things down?" McGill asked.

"For the most part, for a time. But there were new kids who transferred in and didn't know the lay of the land. A couple of confrontations ended with nothing more than verbal abuse and a steely-eyed determination not to be intimidated on Carrie's part. But there was one last physical dust-up in the seventh grade. A new kid, a relatively big one, took an interest in one of Carrie's friends. The girl didn't reciprocate. The boy kept pushing."

McGill asked, "The girl and her parents didn't go to the school, talk to the principal?"

"They did, and things improved, as far as conduct on school grounds went. So the creepy kid decided the thing to do was press his case on the way home. That'd be none of the school authorities' business, he thought. So one Friday after school, he made his move. Started walking behind the girl, telling her she was going to be his girlfriend, like it or not."

"Carrie was with the girl?" McGill asked.

"Yeah. The boy told her to get lost. Carrie ignored him. He put a hand on Carrie's shoulder and that was it. All the justification she needed."

McGill said, "She knew how to do more than scrap by that point."

"Yeah," Sweetie said, "she had three years of tae kwon do classes by then, courtesy of Mom and Dad, and she put the aggressive kid in the hospital with one kick that ruptured his spleen. The cops came, got the details, refused to press any charges against Carrie, told the Ramseys they could file a charge against the boy for laying a hand on their daughter, if they wanted.

"They declined but when the boy's parents sued them, they countersued and won: thirty grand. They told Carrie they'd invest the money for her college fund. She said give it to a charity that helped bullied kids. So that's what they did.

"A counselor in high school who heard through the grapevine about Carrie's exploits suggested she might want to look at a career in the Secret Service as they had the job of protecting people. She followed up and that was that.

"Except that she worked her way through school when she didn't have to, not with Don knocking down a cardiologist's salary. She also received an admission letter from Amherst, after applying at Mom and Dad's request, but she went to Northeastern because its criminal justice curriculum was more on point for her professional goals."

Sweetie opened her hands wide in a there-you-have-it gesture.

"Great kid, fine young woman," McGill said.

Sweetie agreed. "She's all that, but I bet you're worried now about the same thing I am."

"Yeah," McGill said. "Assuming she's still alive, she's going to make a move against the people who took her."

"Probably sooner rather than later," Sweetie added.

Olmsted County, Minnesota

"When did you get married?" Caitie McGill asked.

Celsus Crogher said, "What?"

The two of them were sitting on the terrace overlooking the pond at the rear of Carolyn and Lars' house. The temperature hovered in the mid-40s, but a crisp breeze out of the north made it feel colder. A pale sun in a clear sky provided more artistic ornamentation than warmth. Caitie wore a UCSB hoodie, jeans and sneakers. Celsus wore a dark brown leather jacket, khakis and black shoes with rubber soles.

"You're wearing a wedding ring," Caitie said. "I don't remember seeing that before."

"Your memory's that good?"

"Has to be. Can't act if you can't remember your lines."

Celsus nodded. He could admire just about any professional who worked at her craft.

"How about remembering your wardrobe?" he asked.

"What's that mean?"

"You're supposed to wear sunglasses when you're outside. Both for your protection and Special Agent Ramsey's."

Caitie was about to ask, "What, here in the middle of nowhere?"

But she knew the sunglasses had been Celsus' idea. He said it wouldn't be good for the special agent if the real Caitie McGill was spotted out in public. Even with Caitie's new look, some sharp-eyed, quick-witted bad guy might recognize her. And there was no saying that whoever had grabbed Carrie Ramsey might not still be looking for the other McGill kids.

After all, that was why they'd all gone into hiding.

From a personal point of view, Caitie didn't want to do *anything* that might cause further harm.

She said to Celsus, "Stay here, okay? I'll be right back."

Celsus nodded.

Caitie was back quickly wearing sunglasses with round blue lenses.

Celsus laughed.

"What?" Caitie asked. "These aren't good enough?"

"They're fine. They just remind me of hippie glasses from the '60s."

"You're not that old."

"No, I'm not, but I know people who are. One of those fogies gave me a pair of shades that look pretty much like those you have. Never wore them. I'm more of an aviator-style guy."

Caitie said, "You're a guy whose style is changing; anyone can see that."

Celsus nodded. "I know. Sometimes *I* don't recognize myself."

"You're happier."

"Yes, I am."

"You're married, too."

"Right again."

"Anyone I know?"

"Don't think so. Her name is Merilee Parker."

"She must be something."

"That and more."

Caitie changed the subject. "You never liked my dad, did you?"

"Not much. Not at all, really."

"Because he wouldn't do what you wanted him to do, right?"

"Right."

"I'm like that, too."

Celsus had been scanning the threat horizon. Some things never changed. Now, he looked at Caitie. "What do you mean?"

"I like to go my own way, too, whenever possible."

"Let me see your eyes."

Caitie lowered her glasses to the tip of her nose. "No drugs, no alcohol, no intent to cause trouble." She put the shades back in place. "I just wanted to let you know who I am."

"The answer is no," Celsus said.

"What's the question?" Caitie asked.

"Whatever you have in mind. It's a blanket no."

Caitie sighed and said, "Okay."

"False assent," Celsus told her.

"What?"

"You're trying to fake me out, pretending to be agreeable."

"You're right, I am. But I won't bug you for a while."

"Thanks."

Caitie looked out at the pond and the stand of trees beyond it. "If they come, I think it'll be from that direction."

Celsus was tempted to say, "Who?" Only he didn't want to insult the kid.

She was too smart not to think he didn't know what they were talking about now.

She meant the direction from which an attack on the house might come. Hiding out had its advantages, but putting all your eggs in one basket only made for a bigger prize. Harder for the bad guys to resist.

"Me, too," he told Caitie. Adding, "I want to cut down all those trees, but your mother and Lars won't let me."

For just that brief moment, Celsus sounded like his old self.

Florida Avenue, Washington, DC

Sweetie smelled eggs and onions when she returned to the townhouse where she lived with her husband, Putnam Shady, and their adopted daughter, Maxine. Taking a seat at the breakfast bar, she said to Putnam, "Pretty late for breakfast."

He looked over his shoulder from the pan in which he was scrambling eggs and smiled. "But only a little late for brunch. You want some? I made plenty, and I've got to watch my boyish figure."

Putnam had been soft around the edges when he first met Sweetie. These days, he could be a cover model for *Men's Health.* He'd always said he had to catch up with her physically; now, Sweetie was in pursuit of the example her mate had set. Since she'd decided to eschew any form of police work, even the private kind, she'd let her fitness slip.

"Yeah, I'll have some, thanks," she told Putnam.

"Yes, ma'am."

He set out two plates and poured two cups of coffee, black. He eschewed sugar but put a bowl and spoon out for Sweetie. She pushed them away. If he could handle his liquid caffeine unsweetened, so could she. It helped, though, that Putnam always used the most exotically tasty beans. She could never remember the names, but she always liked the taste.

The eggs were great, too.

"Maxi got off to school, okay?" Sweetie asked.

"Well, she wanted to drop out and go to work for me so she could get a jump on becoming the first female President of color, but I told her you pretty much had to have a college degree these days to run for President, and that usually required that you make it through elementary and high school first. She said, okay, she'll start attending classes year 'round to speed things up."

Sweetie rolled her eyes. "How's the rest of politics?"

Putnam was keeping an eye on the nationwide slate of candidates fielded by Cool Blue, the new progressive party he and billionaire Darren Drucker had started. They had an even hundred people running for seats in the House of Representatives, a dozen more running for Senate seats and Vice President Jean Morrissey running for the presidency.

Besides making sure everyone was hewing to Cool Blue's political ethos of friendly, stylish liberalism, Putnam watched over the campaign budget for each race, the tenor of the political ads being used and, of course, how their people were faring in the polls against the opposition.

"You know what," he said, "we're going to do very well. We'll be a force in both houses of Congress and I think we're better than even money for Jean to win the White House."

On that happy note, Putnam kissed Sweetie and gathered the plates, cups and flatware to rinse and put in the dishwasher.

He had his back to Sweetie when she said, "You never asked me why I never circulated a petition to get my name on the ballot for our local city council seat."

Putnam dried his hands and looked at her. "What, you want me to nag?"

"No, but I'm surprised you didn't say anything."

"Margaret, I know this about you. When you want something, you go after it hard. You didn't do that when it came to running for city council. You never even talked about it after the first week you came up with the idea. I thought the best thing I could do was wait, watch and support whatever came next. Only next didn't come."

Putnam shrugged. "That's fine; I'm involved enough in politics for all of us."

"And now Maxi wants to go to school full time so she can do it, too."

Putnam retook his seat at the breakfast bar. He gathered his wife's hands in his.

"Are you at a loss for what to do with your time?" he asked.

"For a purpose-driven woman, that would be a terrible thing."

"I like what I did today. I like what I did that led up to today."

She told him about talking Jim McGill into seeing the Ramseys; told him about getting the couple to speak about their daughter; told him she feared the special agent might make a dangerous move that wouldn't turn out well.

Putnam listened carefully, as he always did with Sweetie.

Then he asked, "Did I ever tell you about Steve Bidwell?"

Sweetie shook her head. "Who's he?"

"He went to law school with me. An older guy and originally a Quaker. Pacifist to the core, but he accepted being drafted into the Army and serving in Vietnam — on the condition that he wouldn't carry a weapon and certainly wouldn't take anyone's life. The army could live with that. He became a combat medic. Saw some really horrible action. Saved more than a few GIs' lives. But he was eaten alive by guilt that he came through all that hell without a nick. Asked himself and a few close friends why he should have been spared. He was nobody special. Certainly no better than the next guy, and plenty of those guys got killed or maimed."

"Survivor's guilt?" Sweetie asked.

"That and a crisis of faith. He admitted to himself and a few of us that when he saw guys he'd come to care for die and get wounded, he wanted to know where the hell God was. More than that, he wanted to strike back. He wanted to kill those bastards on the other side. He was just about to ask for permission to carry a weapon when he got rotated home. Early. Another medic thought he was cracking up, and passed the word to their commanding officer."

"So he came home in one piece because he was lucky in more ways than one," Sweetie said.

"Yeah, but things could have gone the other way. He could have hit his limit sooner without anyone noticing, and, who knows, he really might have picked up a rifle and killed somebody. Maybe a lot of people."

"And your point is?" Sweetie asked.

"My point is people can go into situations with the best of intentions and still have things come out wrong. Steve submitted to the draft to save lives but came close to taking them. Only luck, as you say, saved him from that. You went into police work to help people, not kill them. It was nothing more than *bad* luck that an idea you had led, indirectly, to someone's death."

As Sweetie thought about that, Putnam gave her something else to mull. "On the other hand, it was good luck that the bullet you took for Jim McGill didn't kill you. Where would Maxi and I be right now if it had?"

That thought rocked Sweetie. Brought tears to her eyes.

Putnam said, "Maybe I just talked you out of going back to the work you really want to do, but I think you could set guidelines for yourself that would keep you from even an inadvertent loss of life, especially your own. You might give it a try, if you think your old boss would want you back on such terms."

Sweetie smiled through her tears and kissed Putnam.

"What happened to Steve Bidwell?" she asked.

"A good woman got him past his troubles."

McGill Investigations, Inc. — Georgetown

"Caitie's up to something," Celsus Crogher told McGill.

Celsus had called from Minnesota to rehash his conversation with Caitie just minutes after Sweetie had left McGill's office. She had left McGill with one of life's great clichés regarding old friends running through his mind.

The place just isn't the same without you.

The call from Celsus displaced his pining for Sweetie.

Trying to guess what manner of mischief his youngest might have in mind at any given moment was one of McGill's toughest continuing challenges. His usual inclination was to imagine the most outrageous possibility he could, but that was inhibited, usually, by the paternal injunction that said, "Nah, she'd never do *that*."

Would she?

Before he could attempt to answer that awful question, Celsus veered off-topic and truly shocked McGill.

He said, "Merilee wants to have a child."

McGill almost replied, "With you?"

Instead, he limited himself to: "And?"

"I thought I should ask you," Celsus said. "You know, I thought you could give me a straight answer whether it would be a good idea. Especially for a guy like me."

McGill said, "A father's first job is to always be there when his child needs him. You think you'd have any trouble with that?"

"No."

"How would you feel about seeing a daughter or a son who reminds you of Merilee every time you see her or him?"

"Great."

"You'll be just fine."

"It can't be that easy."

"It isn't. The thing about kids is they have their own plans."

"Like yours does right now. The one she hasn't told me about yet but has me worried anyway."

McGill laughed. "See. You're already gaining valuable experience."

"Yeah." Celsus said he'd report back when he found out what Caitie wanted.

McGill had no sooner put the phone down than Deke knocked on his office door.

"Visitor," he said in a flat voice.

"I'm not taking any new clients at the moment."

"It's not like that. He says he has information you should hear."

McGill caught the tone in Deke's voice. "This is someone we don't like?"

Deke nodded. "Monty Kipp."

McGill thought about that. He'd once scared the tabloid newsman shitless. It was barely possible Kipp had some trick up his sleeve to play on him. Say, if he'd just learned he had a week to live and wanted to get even. On the other hand, it might serve a twisted purpose on Kipp's part to provide a piece of information he'd find useful.

"Send him in," McGill said.

Kipp stepped into McGill's office as if he was entering a lion's den; he could only hope that he wouldn't be eaten alive. Forcing a nervous smile onto his face, Kipp asked, "You're not about to clean your sidearm again, are you?"

McGill had been doing just that when he'd lectured Kipp that he'd better not even fantasize about shooting and publishing *au naturel* pictures of the President. Kipp had sworn he'd never let such an idea ever cross his mind again. The two men hadn't spoken since.

McGill said, "No, but depending on what you have to say, I might clean my cuticles with a Bowie knife."

The joke should have been obvious, but Kipp had memories of their prior encounter that still made him tremble. He took a half-step back and looked as if he might bolt. McGill held up a hand.

"Just kidding, Monty. I'm not feeling homicidal at the moment. Have a seat."

Kipp did, sitting at the edge of a guest chair in case McGill's mood changed.

"What brings you here, Monty?"

"I was approached yesterday by T.W. Rangel. Do you know who he is?"

"I do. Does Mr. Rangel have any expectation of privacy regarding your conversation with him?"

Kipp laughed, sat back in his chair now. "Anyone familiar with me and my professional reputation should know better than that."

He was, after all, a tabloid reporter for the ages.

Then Kipp caught McGill's flat stare, interpreted it correctly and all merriment drained from his face. He said, "I've never spoken a word about *our* private conversation."

"Neither have I," McGill said.

"I can't even think of a way to have it published posthumously in my memoirs without making myself look like a squish. I could lie, of course, pretend I'm the one bloke who stood up to you and came out on top. Only, with your continuing exploits, no one would believe that."

"Some things are best left alone," McGill said. "Meanwhile ..."

"Yes, well, Rangel came to me and suggested it would be worth my while to look into how a man-servant named Elias Roosevelt was accused of theft and was able to gain legal representation by a bloke called Augustus Wiley who usually toils for $2,000 per hour. Presumably, Wiley was paid that amount by a recently established entity calling itself the DC Legal Defense Fund."

Kipp watched to see if any of his information was familiar to McGill.

He only shrugged and said, "Go on."

"I went only so far as to check on these facts. Augustus Wiley, Esquire, does in fact charge the exact toll Rangel mentioned for his time, and the DCLDF was established *after* Mr. Roosevelt was charged with a crime. Convenient for him and certainly not a coincidence."

McGill nodded. "I agree. What else?"

"Rangel suggested I look for a connection between Mr. Roosevelt's good fortune and the sudden disappearance of Senator Randall Pennyman of Georgia."

McGill didn't pay particular attention to the misfortunes of run-of-mill pols. So many of them were ticking time-bombs, their careers self-manufactured to explode. But when a member of the Senate took it on the lam with the FBI in hot pursuit, well, that was more his kind of story.

If there was a link between the Roosevelt and Pennyman situations, that was truly intriguing.

"You've got my attention, Monty. But I think the big reveal is still out there."

Kipp nodded. "Rangel told me there's a blackmailer at the center of these matters and many more, someone who makes J. Edgar Hoover look like a small-timer. That and the trail leads to the Oval Office."

Galia, McGill thought.

He kept his expression neutral. Kipp had to know of the chief of staff's reputation. She got things done. Sometimes apparently by magic. Only none of the hard-asses in DC really believed in wizardry. They knew only too well, though, how having the goods on someone made them wonderfully malleable.

Kipp went on, a look of regret in his eyes, "I'm unable to express how much I want to pursue this story. It would be a brilliant capstone to my career."

"Only you're too afraid of me."

"Yes."

McGill said, "Good."

"Would you really do me harm?" Kipp asked. "Possibly even do me in?"

McGill didn't say a word, only let Kipp look him in the eye.

Interpret for himself what he saw.

"Yes, well," the old sleaze-monger said, "I can't promise Rangel won't go to someone else with his tales, but I can assure you, much to my regret, that I won't be the one to tell this story."

He got to his feet and gave McGill the slightest of bows.

"Hold on, Monty. I appreciate your coming by."

"A necessity, nothing more, I assure you."

"There is more," McGill told him.

"And what might that be?"

"As terrified as you might be of me, you're still hoping for a token of gratitude."

The two men exchanged a look, and Kipp chuckled and nodded.

"The President is well served by you, sir," he said.

McGill said, "I do my best. I also don't let favors go unreturned. Give me a number where I can reach you at any time. I might have something good for you before long."

Kipp provided a number and asked, "Does this mean we're chums?"

"Not even close," McGill replied.

Kipp respected McGill's honesty, and left with a click of his heels.

J. Edgar Hoover Building — Washington, DC

Ah-lam was brought into Byron DeWitt's office wearing handcuffs, shackles and an orange jumpsuit. Despite the jail-bird jewelry and garb, and smudges of fatigue under her eyes, DeWitt thought she was a looker. He gestured to the special agents who brought Ah-lam in to seat her in the visitor's chair opposite him.

"You guys can go," he told the special agents. "I'll yell for help, if I need it."

The prisoner paid no attention to any of the FBI personnel.

Her attention pinned itself to DeWitt's serigraph of Chairman Mao.

"They don't make helmsmen like him anymore, huh?" DeWitt said.

Ah-lam faced him, offering a look of incomprehension.

He switched to Mandarin. "We can speak your language, if you like."

Her head jerked back and she looked affronted by the fact that conversing in Chinese was even a possibility. Then she said, "English."

"Okay. You have a question about my taste in art?"

"How is it possible you can have that here?" She looked up at the portrait again.

"The answer, I'm afraid, is ironic. Mao is here as a result of capitalism. It was part of the price the FBI had to pay to hire me."

Turning her gaze to DeWitt, she asked, "You are very important then?"

"Depends on whom you ask. Sometimes, yes. Other times, not so much."

"What can you do for me?" she asked in an imperious tone.

Especially for someone bound hand and foot.

"I'd offer you a cigarette, only this is a non-smoking building."

"You are not funny."

"No?" DeWitt asked. "What would you find amusing?"

"Being free. Having my funds returned to me. Regaining custody of my son."

A clearly defined value hierarchy, DeWitt thought. The kid came in third.

"What about your husband?" he asked. "Want him back, too?"

The look of distaste on Ah-lam's face said it all: Tyler Busby could rot for all she cared.

"Good answer," he said, "because he's not going anywhere."

"I only wish you had re-education camps in this country. That is where I would send him."

DeWitt said, "He'll learn many lessons where he's going, few of them pleasant. That's the best we can do."

Ah-lam studied DeWitt, trying find an angle of approach. The man seated opposite her affected a relaxed posture and manner. She might have arrived at his office for a job interview, not an interrogation that could send her to prison for life ... or even to her death? She knew that the United States had capital punishment. Was the only country in the Americas that did. Just her luck. She wondered if ...

Her eyes widened, her mouth softened. Her shoulders spread and her chest lifted. Her thighs fell open. She was just about to smile when DeWitt responded non-verbally to all her silent cues. He held up a hand and shook his head.

"Let's leave it at that, shall we?"

"You do not like women?" she taunted.

"Women, sure. You, not at all."

Harsh, but sometimes you had to be direct. Before she could withdraw or even pout, DeWitt said, "Let's get back to the things you want and remember we're all good capitalists around here, including you. The things you want are freedom, money and your son. I'll tell you right now the boy is off the table. You tried to use him as a distraction when you attacked an FBI special agent. He might have been hurt or even killed. You're not getting him back. Ever."

Bound hand and foot or not, DeWitt thought she just might launch herself at him.

Before that could happen, he added, "That still leaves freedom and money to be discussed."

Two considerations not to be sneezed at, obviously. Ah-lam relaxed and sat back.

"You have such power?" The note of doubt in her voice was clear.

"I have the power to recommend, but people around here tend to take my advice about China and its people."

Ah-lam looked up to Chairman Mao again and then back at DeWitt.

"What would you want in return for my freedom and money?"

DeWitt said, "Your testimony against Tyler Busby. Everything you know about him directly, that is from his mouth to your ears."

Ah-lam laughed. "That would be my pleasure."

"Yeah, that's the easy part. Here's the hard part. We also want to know all about Donald Yang, your old boss in Hong Kong. We want to know who Mr. Yang's patrons in the Politburo Standing Committee are."

The ultimate center of power in China.

Ah-lam went pale when she heard that.

"I said it would be hard," DeWitt reminded her. "Now, here's the toughest part of all. We want to know if Mr. Yang or any of his superiors were involved in or had knowledge of the plan to kill President Patricia Grant. The United States is going to have a serious bone to pick with China, if they did."

DeWitt repeated his final thought in Mandarin, in a culturally equivalent phrase, in case Ah-lam was unfamiliar with the American idiom.

The fact that he could do so unnerved her almost as much as what he wanted her to do.

DeWitt shrugged, indicating it was her choice to make.

"Life can be a bitch, can't it?" he asked.

He was sure she'd understand that even if she'd never heard it before.

McGill's Hideaway — The White House

Blessing, the White House head butler, gently roused McGill from the nap he'd been taking on the leather sofa in his personal retreat. After speaking with Monty Kipp at his office, a wave of fatigue had overtaken McGill. Apparently, he couldn't get by sleeping only two hours out of the past thirty anymore. Yet another regret of getting older.

Blessing told him, "Deputy Director DeWitt is at the West Entrance, sir. He should be here directly. If you wish to freshen up first, I can bring him a drink while he's waiting."

McGill nodded, clearing some of the cobwebs from his mind.

"What time is it?" he asked.

"Two in the afternoon, sir."

McGill had lain down at noon, telling himself he'd take a fifteen-minute doze before having lunch. No telling how long he might have slept if left undisturbed. Maybe after Jean Morrissey was sworn in next January he could sleep for a month or two with only occasional interludes of consciousness.

He and Patti could set up adjacent hammocks on some tropical isle.

He got to his feet and told Blessing, "Please ask the deputy director to give me ten minutes. Then he can meet me in the family dining room. I need a quick shower and I need some food: lean corned beef piled high on caraway rye, a small bowl of kettle chips and an ice tea. Ask the deputy director if he needs something to eat. The way things are going, he may have missed lunch, too."

Blessing nodded and left to set the wheels in motion.

The head butler had informed the President and McGill that he was going to retire from the White House staff at the end of the President's second term. McGill had wondered if Blessing wanted to take it easy or if he might be agreeable to continue working for him and the missus when they were private citizens again.

That was rich. Having a butler on his own dime. Showed how much a man could change just by being close to real power and privilege.

Then again, if Blessing went along with the idea, it would no doubt be because Patti was the big attraction not him. Well, maybe it'd be a little because of him. He was a fun guy, wasn't he? In any case, he felt a lot more human and close to functional after he had showered and dressed in fresh clothes.

Blessing had the table set for two and DeWitt was already in place, chopsticks in hand.

McGill's order was filled to perfection, as always. DeWitt was having hibachi chicken, grilled veggies, brown rice and hot green tea. He was hungry, too, evidently.

The deputy director got up from his place at the table and said, "Blessing told me it'd be okay if I started without you. I didn't think I should doubt him."

"I never do," McGill said, gesturing DeWitt back into his seat.

He sat and took a bite of his sandwich. A look of bliss filled his face. He chewed, swallowed and said, "How's your lunch?"

"Terrific."

McGill nodded. "You can't beat the White House kitchen. Anything you want, anytime you want it, and it's all good. So you've got to watch yourself. Gluttony might be lurking just around the corner."

DeWitt got the impression McGill's warning was for him personally.

"You're assuming Jean is going to win the election?" he asked.

"You're not?"

DeWitt sighed. "I am … and sometimes I regret the idea. I seriously miss California. I think of the life the two of us could have there."

McGill paused in the consumption of his sandwich. "But you will be there at least part time, right? You're going to be the guy running my L.A. office."

"I am. Jean and I have agreed on that. It's just …"

"You have reservations, but not about your fiancée, I hope."

"Not in the usual way. No cold feet about Jean and me, except I can't help but wonder if she does well in her first term, and is in the middle of some important effort, will she be able to walk away from the job?"

McGill asked, "You think Cool Blue will rescind its one-and-done term limit for the presidency?"

DeWitt shrugged. "I don't know. Maybe. If you think about a political party, especially a new one, having a President who's doing a great job and looking like she could be a shoo-in for a second term, would they really want to turn to someone else? Even if they did, though, I believe we've seen a President switch parties and still win."

McGill nodded. Patti had done just that.

Now, he sighed and told DeWitt, "Well, maybe you can hope Congress will be even more of a pain in the ass than it already is."

DeWitt grinned and asked, "You think I might get to beat up a senator, too?"

McGill laughed and said, "You can always hope."

The two men finished their meals and got down to the matters at hand.

DeWitt took two iPads out of his bag. No fancy leather attaché case for him. An olive drab canvas messenger bag, frayed around the edges. McGill asked, "Is that standard issue from the People's Liberation Army?"

DeWitt smiled and shook his head. "Not Chinese at all." He flipped it over and showed McGill its logo. A bald eagle fronted by a shield with a *fleur de lis* in the background. "This thing's so old it was made in the USA."

"Patriotic," McGill said.

DeWitt handed an iPad to McGill. "As a colleague in the Department of Justice, that's your personal, if temporary, data device. The unit's password numbers are 01202017."

McGill said, "My civilian iPad needs only four numbers; the government doubled that?"

"Makes it harder to crack the code by quite a bit. All sort of self-destruction takes place inside if anybody tries to open the shell the wrong way. Nothing's foolproof but our alterations stack the deck in our favor."

McGill nodded. "Good to know."

"You need that number again?"

"Unh-uh. Recognized it the first time. Inauguration Day next January."

McGill tapped in the number and was greeted by a crime scene photograph of a man's face. A man who had died badly. His pain and the awareness of an onrushing death had been intense.

"That's the guy Special Agent Ramsey took down when she was grabbed. She severed the radial artery in his arm with her teeth. The damage was too great for the exsanguination to be stanched by his other hand. He was dead at the scene by the time the first responders arrived."

"You have a picture of the bite wound?" McGill asked.

"On my machine, not yours." The deputy director swiped to it and showed McGill.

The man's flesh and blood vessels hadn't just been cut, they'd been mangled.

"She put a lot of effort into that," McGill said.

"Yeah. Now, look at the next photo on your machine."

There he was again, the guy who'd met the very bad end. This time, he was alive, well and sneering. Something had struck the guy as contemptible. Something he was staring at, the way his eyes were focused.

DeWitt told him what. "That's a photo from your daughter's thumb drive. She told you her friend shot people who watched Caitlin's film shoots around L.A., right?"

McGill nodded. The idea that anyone might hate his daughter that much stunned him. Caused his blood pressure and adrenaline to rise, too. The fight-or-flight response. And McGill wasn't thinking of running. If the guy wasn't already dead —

"The body in L.A. had no identification on it," DeWitt said, "and the first pass of the man's likeness through the facial recognition software in the Bureau's image databases hasn't turned up a match. So the bastard doesn't have a criminal record in this country. He's not on any terrorist watch list. And Interpol hasn't found a match either."

"You're running all the other photos from Caitie's thumb drive through your systems, here and abroad?"

"Yes. So far no word on any positive results. Most of the people on the thumb drive were probably just citizens watching scenes from a movie being filmed. One thing that's in our favor, though, this kid, Ben, has a good eye for people who stand out. That's how he got the picture of our dead kidnapper. What we'd like to do is get copies of his other photo files. We can get a subpoena if we need to, but artists can get contrary. If Ben feels he's being pushed, he might push back. Get a lawyer involved and waste time."

McGill said, "You have a law degree, right?"

"Yes, that's how I know these things can get unnecessarily complicated."

"I'll talk to Caitie," McGill said, "ask her to talk to her friend."

"That'd be great. There's one more thing about this, though."

"What?"

"Do you think your daughter might be up to looking at the guy's picture? The one where he's still alive. She might have noticed him and, maybe, if he was with someone."

McGill nodded. "Yeah, I'll ask that, too."

He told himself he should have thought of that. Probably would have if his own child wasn't the one involved. The person the assholes had intended to kidnap.

McGill said, "She'll probably be only too glad to help. Get her friend to go along with your request, too."

"Good," DeWitt said. "You want to tell me the idea you had in our meeting with the attorney general this morning?"

That question actually perked up McGill. Made him think he wasn't losing his game entirely. He swiped his iPad back to the grimacing death's head shot of the kidnapper. DeWitt did the same.

"What I was thinking is Philip Brock is probably dead by now. Is that how you feel?"

DeWitt agreed. "Him and the Uruguayan jailer who let him go. That guy's now missing, too."

"Okay," McGill said. "Well, the way the world works now, we've seen even the most brutal killers make videos of their butchery. What's to say someone didn't record Brock's awful final moments? If they did, maybe they're holding on to the video file for a specific release date. Or they could have circulated it where most people would never see it."

"The Dark Net," DeWitt said with a nod. "Internet sites most people never see. The Bureau hasn't looked there yet."

"Give it a try," McGill said. "If you find it, and it's gruesome, we can show it to Tyler Busby. Let him know what could be waiting for him, too, if he so much as makes bail while awaiting his trial."

"Bail in a case of attempted Presidential assassination?" DeWitt asked.

McGill said, "I'd be surprised, too, but with a multi-billionaire and a bonehead judge, who knows? Why take a chance? If we can scare Busby badly enough, maybe he'll own up to what he did. Prefer a slow death behind bars to a far more ghastly one outside the prison walls."

"Yeah, okay, I'll check it out. See if anyone videoed Philip Brock's last moments."

For the first time, DeWitt saw just how ruthless McGill could be.

At least when acting in defense of his wife and children.

Then McGill had another suggestion. "As long as your snooping is going to extraordinary lengths, why not see if our surly stiff …" McGill pointed to the image of the guy Carrie Ramsey had mauled to death. "… has a driver's license or some other state-issued photo ID?"

DeWitt said, "Good idea. He might be a first-timer, recently radicalized."

"Scary idea, really, Americans turning on each other," McGill said. "Maybe the CDC can come up with a vaccine for that."

The West Wing — the White House

McGill's body temperature, as measured by White House physician, Artemus Nicolaides, was 98.7, then again he always ran just a touch hot. As he sat in a guest chair next to Edwina Byington's desk just outside the Oval Office, Nick checked his eyes, ears, nose and throat for any sign something might be wrong. Nothing was. His heart rhythm was steady and within normal range. His blood pressure was up just a tick.

"Must be the salt in the corned beef," McGill said.

"Have you been keeping up with your cardio exercise?" Nick asked.

"Not as much as I should. I could use a good, long run."

"Not too long or too fast."

"Right." McGill smiled. "I'll ask Sweetie to pace me."

He'd requested the cursory physical exam because Patti was talking with Jean Morrissey and Edwina said they shouldn't be interrupted unless the matter was urgent. McGill thought what he had to say could wait a little while. Then it occurred to him to have Nick give him a quick once-over. He didn't have any overt physical complaints, no aches or pains, he just felt *compressed*. He thought that would be the best description.

He was keeping himself under control in a situation that begged for an urgent, highly physical response. Some soulless shits had kidnapped a young woman they thought was his daughter. The feeling of relief that the pricks had made a mistake had worn off. He was coming to feel they'd grabbed a daughter he didn't even know he had.

Even so, he knew the distress Don and Sheri Ramsey were feeling was infinitely greater. Thinking about that made him want to charge off and … come up with an idea that would be helpful. Bring matters to an appropriate resolution. Carrie Ramsey would be restored to freedom, and the bad guys would get it in the head.

If it turned out Carrie was already dead, he might not be responsible for what he did.

"Mr. McGill."

He refocused on the person addressing him: Edwina.

"You can go in now, sir."

McGill summoned a smile unsupported by real feeling and said, "Thanks, Edwina."

McGill leaned over the President's desk, met his wife leaning the other way, and shared a kiss. She squeezed his arm as their lips lingered. The combination lifted his spirits.

As they took their seats, Patti asked, "Any news?"

He told her about the photographic match the FBI had made but the lack of identification of the guy in the picture.

That and his suggestion to search hundreds of millions of ID cards belonging to innocent citizens. "You think anyone's going to complain about that?" he asked.

"You mean in Congress or the media? Certainly. No doubt about it."

"You could put a stop to it before DeWitt moves on it," McGill said.

Patti shook her head. "We wouldn't do that if it was really Caitie who'd been taken; we won't do it now either."

"Might be used against Jean Morrissey."

"Might be, but Jean is tough. She'll punch back."

McGill smiled. "Maybe you should have played hockey at Yale."

"I'm not sure the Bulldogs had a women's team when I was there. We weren't as athletically *avant-garde* as the University of Minnesota."

"Moving right along," McGill said. He told Patti that Monty Kipp had come to see him.

"Really? He thinks I'm still cheesecake photo material?"

"Of course you are, but I won't tell. No, he came to tell me that T.W. Rangel is trying to get some tabloid titan, starting with himself, to track down the biggest political spymaster and blackmailer this town has ever seen. Someone with an open door to this very office."

They both knew who they were talking about but neither mentioned the name.

"My thinking is," McGill said, "with all the trouble the Republicans are in with their members in the House and Senate dipping into the Pentagon budget like it was their personal piggy bank, it would go a long way to balancing the scales of justice if they could make your entire administration look like one big crime scene."

With a grim note in her voice, Patti said, "They'd love that, all right."

"Kipp admitted that he's too afraid of me, much to his regret, to pursue the story, but he's sure one of his slimy colleagues will take up the challenge."

"I have no doubt about that," Patti said. "This could end Jean's chances of being elected. God, I'd hate to see Oren Worth succeed me."

McGill said, "I have an idea, as any good henchman should."

"What is it?"

"Rangel wasn't arrested for stealing Edmond Whelan's 'Permanent Power' manuscript because it wasn't found in his house. If he was smart, he'd have burned the damn thing, but guys like him, they can obsess about anything that might diminish their self-images. With something like a book, he'd likely insist that a correct reading of his criticisms of Whelan's work would prove he was right all along. If his contemporaries can't see that, surely enlightened future readers will."

"You're some psychologist, Jim."

"Show me a good detective, or even a decent street cop, who isn't."

"So you think Whelan's manuscript with Rangel's annotations still exists somewhere."

"Yes, and the guy to talk to about where it might be hidden is

Whelan. He'd have a better idea than anyone else."

"But you're far too busy to take on this chore," Patti said.

"I am, but Frank Morrissey is a tough, smart guy. He should be able to find a way to cut a deal with Whelan to help. Then you get Rangel indicted, put him on the hot seat and any claims he makes about a certain person we won't name here will look dubious."

"You are some henchman, James J. McGill."

"You gonna be happy with me when I'm just your husband?"

Patti smiled. "The way you kiss, sure."

Cheyenne, Wyoming

At 146 feet in height, the State Capitol was the tallest building in Wyoming. In bigger, more densely populated U.S. cities, there were parking structures that climbed closer to the clouds. Still, the center of state government had more than sufficient stature to look down into a window of a nearby medical office building in which a man calling himself Lewis Addison Armistead spoke with a physician whose real name was Tom Kirby.

The two of them sat in front of a window to avail themselves of the bright sunlight entering the room. Armistead was hoping natural illumination would prove more revealing than the over-head fluorescents. The men were peering at a grainy close-up photograph of a vagina.

Armistead hadn't said whose nether region it was, and Kirby hadn't asked.

The doctor and his visitor didn't know each other but had compatible political leanings and an acquaintance in common: reasons enough for Kirby to be of unpaid and unacknowledged assistance to Armistead without asking any questions.

"There's no real way to determine whether this person is a virgin," Kirby said.

"Not even for a doctor?" Armistead asked, sounding doubtful.

"Well, if she had a tattoo on the inside of her thigh that said, 'Good times straight ahead,' that might be a clue."

Armistead frowned and asked, "What about the hymen? I thought if it was unbroken then, yeah, she hasn't had sex yet. That's what I've read, anyway."

Kirby exhaled softly. "You've been reading the wrong materials. Yes, a hymen might be torn by intercourse, but riding a bike, doing gymnastics or using tampons might produce the same result."

"But one of those things must have done the job, right? In this case, I mean." He tapped the photo.

"Yes, one of those things or something else. The hymen is not intact."

"So, let's say it was sex. Can you tell how experienced she is?"

With anyone else, Kirby would have rolled his eyes. He got the impression, though, that Armistead was the kind of guy who wouldn't appreciate even silent criticism. "No, you can't tell if she's experienced any sort of penetration at all, other than to say that in this photo there are no signs of the tearing and bruising often associated with a rape."

Armistead was getting frustrated. "Why not? Why can't you tell?"

Kirby lost his patience and professional demeanor. This guy was making him think being a liberal might not be so bad. They had to be smarter, on average, than this dummy.

He told Armistead, "A woman is not like a tree. She doesn't get a ring around her labia every time she has sex."

Armistead stood up, photo in hand, unhappy and ready to leave, his jaw muscles bulging.

"Can you tell me, at least, how the hell old she is?" he asked.

Kirby was an ear-nose-and-throat specialist, and he believed in treating women with an old-fashioned courtesy. He found the whole session with Armistead distasteful and even alarming. While the man had been referred to him by a friend, there were limits to any favor.

In order to get rid of Armistead, though, Kirby gave him a reasonable guess.

"Late teens to mid-twenties."

From Kirby's point of view, his answer produced the best possible result.

Armistead left immediately, highly frustrated.

Russell Senate Office Building — Washington, DC

Majority Leader Oren Worth's chief of staff, Devra Tomkins, a BYU Law School grad, told her boss, "They're cooked, all of them."

The metaphor made Worth wince. He had been thinking, obsessing, about how big a wienie he'd looked on television yesterday, fumbling for an answer to the question from that grinning Brit hyena Monty Kipp. Oh, Kipp had been polite enough verbally. In terms of substance, though, Kipp had reamed him but good.

His subtext being, "Tell me, Mr. Majority Leader, are you man enough to displace a woman who might have no more than six months experience as President? Because, you know, Patti Grant might think it would be great fun to do something that underhanded."

That was what the hell Kipp had really meant.

And Worth couldn't help but think that Kipp might have just planted that seed in Patti Grant's mind. Sure, why not do exactly that? What would the downside be for the President? She'd be free from dealing with all the bastards in Congress who'd had impeached her and tried to convict her. Worth had voted with all his colleagues on the right to end the Grant presidency.

Now, maybe she'd leave office on her own terms. Give everyone the finger as she went. Leaving them with Jean Morrissey in the Oval Office to boot.

And what had the majority leader of the Senate had to say about all that to Kipp?

It would be *unfair.* Wah-wah-wah. I'll pout and cry and hold my breath until I turn blue.

The only good thing that might have come of his pathetic response would be if his one serious opponent on the right, General Warren Altman, had laughed himself to death. So far, though, no reports of Altman's demise had surfaced.

"Mr. Majority Leader," Devra said. "Senator? *Boss!*"

Worth snapped out of his exercise in self-pity. "Yes, Devra, what is it?"

"I think it's time for our party to cut its losses."

Worth's jaw dropped. Was she suggesting he resign? Forget about ever being President? That there was no way to make a comeback from yesterday's show of weakness?

Devra answered his unspoken questions by addressing targets other than himself.

"I think every last one of those lunkhead thieves in the Senate and House has to own up to what he did, say he's sorrier than he's ever been before and take his medicine. March off to prison without complaint. Just like he's truly penitent. If you can get all of them to do that, we can turn a political loss into a big gain."

Worth looked at her as if she was speaking in tongues.

Glossolalia being an evangelical thing not something Mormons did.

Devra saw his doubt, but didn't yield to it. "Think about it, sir. What's more noble than repentance and redemption? Our party admits the obvious: There are sinners amongst us. But our people's faith is strong enough to overcome our faults. Even though the weight of our failings has driven us to our knees, our moral core will lift us up to stand tall in righteousness again."

Devra's suggestion made Worth think any number of things, among them: She missed her calling choosing the law over the clergy; being a lawyer, though, he'd want her to deliver the closing argument in any criminal trial he might ever face; and no way in hell would those bastards who had looted the treasury ever willingly walk into prison.

They'd fight that outcome 'til their last breath, possibly even choosing suicide over incarceration. Just suggesting that they do the right thing for the good of the party would make them sneer in unison. Maybe even spit in your eye. His eye if he was the one who brought up the subject.

Devra saw she hadn't prevailed with her strategy.

Maybe had even jeopardized her job.

So she proved she could and would think like a shyster when necessary.

"Of course, our senators and representatives wouldn't have to endure either harsh conditions or lengthy sentences. Once you enter the Oval Office, you could see to it that the Bureau of Prisons assigned them all to the least objectionable minimum security facility, *en masse* if you like, and then, say six months before the mid-term elections, you offer them clemency, full pardons. You become a hero to our party, to our religious-right voters and to conservative-leaning independents. It's win-win for everyone."

Worth understood the rationale and benefits of the scheme. You used the rich person's justification for leniency: *He, she, they have suffered enough.* This inclination to mercy, of course, applied only to the well-off and the well-connected. Any nay-sayers — liberals that was — would be seen as hard-hearted, people you really didn't want to send to the halls of power and have them come after you if you made one or two little mistakes.

Politically, clearing the decks of right-wing malefactors would give Worth free rein to go after the Democrats and Cool Blue, stick it to the crooks, creeps and connivers on their side of the aisle. Not that he was sure he'd be able to find anything on Cool Blue; they were still too new. But there were legislators who played fast and loose among the Democrats, putting stacks of ill-gotten cash in their kitchen fridges among other things.

Best of all, sweeping all the scoundrels on the right off to the hoosegow would leave the spotlight of public wrath focused solely on Galia Mindel's coming comeuppance. That would taint the whole political left from Patti Grant on down. Worth would be able to literally waltz into the White House, if he so desired.

So Devra was right. Her plan was both solid and politically astute, assuming Worth could get the kleptomaniacs in Congress to go along with the scheme. He thought maybe that wouldn't be as hard to accomplish as he'd first imagined. All he'd have to do would be to ask them who they thought would keep them behind bars longer, President Worth or President Morrissey.

There was only one problem. Monty Kipp had just made Worth look like a wuss on national television. He couldn't magnify that perception by working to get members of his own party to march themselves off to the clink like a chain-gang gospel choir singing "Nobody Knows the Trouble I've Seen."

Wimp would be the least of the things they'd call him.

Besides that, Worth liked to think of himself as a strong individual. He hadn't gotten to where he was by being weak. He'd become wealthy and politically prominent by being smart and tough. What happened with Kipp yesterday had been an aberration. Maybe he'd even suffered a small stroke. Not that he'd ever inject a personal health concern into his campaign.

No, what he had to do was lead the charge to save his colleagues who were facing what looked like a certain future as jailbirds. If he could pull that off, he'd make Altman look like the nonentity he was. He'd been a bomber pilot? So what? Oren Worth was the one who'd saved the professional lives of his fellow lawmakers and the political fortunes of his party.

There'd be no one who could top that.

He told Devra, "Thank you for your suggestion, but I think we'll go with a different idea."

She nodded and said, "Of course."

When Worth told her he was giving her a raise, she added, "Thank you."

But he'd been out in the ozone so long, just about half-an-hour by her watch, that she knew Oren Worth was losing his grip. Possibly, the executive functioning of his brain was slipping. Certainly, his view of the political reality he faced in running for the presidency was askew. If he couldn't show the voting public he could be tougher and more ruthless than Jean Morrissey, he was toast.

If he'd proven he could stand up to the thieves in his own party, the public would have eaten that up like free hot dogs. But apparently Oren Worth had other plans.

So Devra Tomkins decided to make a few of her own.

Starting with quietly looking for a new job.

Olmsted County, Minnesota

Celsus Crogher found Ken and Caitie McGill out in a meadow beyond the stand of trees and the pond behind their mother and step-father's house. Celsus had been alerted by the two Secret Service agents detailed to the two McGill children. Celsus watched them go about what seemed to be a game.

They'd stacked two mismatched chairs; the smaller atop the larger. Three metal cans holding green beans, prunes and peas were the other props in the game. The smallest can, the peas, was placed on the seat of the upper chair; the mid-size can, the prunes, sat on the seat of the lower chair, between the legs of the upper chair; the largest can, the beans, rested on the ground between the legs of the bottom chair.

The two McGill kids stood maybe thirty feet distant with a pile of stones, large and small, they had gathered. Ken and Caitie would each take three stones in hand at a time. They'd call out a sequence of cans they'd targeted — top to bottom or the reverse — and then hurl their stones. They kept tallies of hits and misses in their heads.

They'd been at it for fifteen minutes by the time Celsus showed up.

He watched a round of throws and thought both kids had pretty good hand-eye coordination. They hit their marks maybe 50% of the time. Celsus spoke quietly to the two special agents on hand.

"Mom and Step-Dad know about this?" Celsus asked.

"Yeah," Special Agent Arlene Coyle said.

"And they're good with it?"

Special Agent Rick Dexter said, "They're having a discussion, but said to let the offspring proceed until further notice. You have any objections, sir?"

Celsus watched Ken and Caitie go at it. Both of them throwing at the same time. One would call out the target and they'd both fling their stones. It looked to Celsus like Ken had the stronger arm, but Caitie had the quicker release. They both had pretty good eyes.

"Did they say how long they're going to keep this up?"

Coyle said, "Yeah, until they bust the cans."

Dexter added, "They picked stuff they don't like to eat."

Celsus hated peas and prunes himself. Beans didn't do much for him either.

"Are they getting any better with their aim?"

Both special agents nodded.

"Could do some real damage with the right rocks," Coyle said.

"Up to a certain range," Dexter added.

"With stationary targets," Coyle suggested.

Dexter nodded. "Providing they weren't taking fire. You know, from real weapons."

"That's what you're here for, to see that doesn't happen," Celsus said.

Both agents said, "Right."

"Abbie didn't want to play?" Celsus asked.

"She said she has a Filipino friend at school," Coyle said.

"What's that mean?" Celsus asked.

Dexter said, "The Filipinos have a knife culture or so we were told."

Coyle added, "Abbie told her shadow, Special Agent Kearny, she's learned some things about knife-fighting even her father never taught her."

With a straight face, Dexter said, "So what Abbie's doing, she's keeping her blade skills sharp."

Celsus had to conclude all three McGill kids were sending him a message.

Anybody came after them, they'd be in on the fight.

The only thing to do with that was to relay it to Holmes.

James J. McGill's Secret Service code name.

GCDC — *Washington, DC*

The restaurant, specializing in grilled cheese sandwiches from the classic to the elaborate, e.g. lobster toppings, was located on Pennsylvania Avenue just a big burp away from the White House. Ellie Booker and Didi DiMarco had a corner table to themselves. Each of them wore a baseball cap and sunglasses to avoid members of the public who were starstruck and preferred TV newswomen to glam Hollywood faces.

They also kept their publicly recognizable voices down. The adjacent tables were empty but lots of people in Washington were born eavesdroppers and had acute hearing. They sometimes listened in to nearby conversations just to keep in practice.

Ellie and Didi were two of that type.

The conversations they overheard were mundane: tourist chatter and workday gripes.

When Ellie felt the coast was clear, she got down to business. "I won't ask you to say so, but I'm sure you're working on the 'Where's Phil Brock?' story just like I am."

Didi didn't say a word about that notion.

"That's okay," Ellie said. "I'm going to tell you what I've got anyway."

Being professional rivals with no personal love lost between them, Didi asked, "Why would you do that?"

Ellie said, "Only one reason: This story just might get me killed."

Didi slid her sunglasses down to the tip of her nose. Ellie did, too. Didi saw no hint of deceit in Ellie's eyes. No BS and no fear. Both women put their shades back in place.

Didi said, "So what are you doing here, setting me up to be the next one to get it in the head after you get bumped off?"

Ellie shrugged. "Only if you don't want to get the biggest story of your career. Still, I wouldn't blame you if you walked away.

Lunch is on me either way."

Didi had the uneasy feeling she was being taken for a sucker. Even so, *if* Ellie was playing things straight, *and* Ellie did get killed pursuing the story of a fugitive congressman, *and* Didi broke the story while preserving her own precious derriere, that would mean …

Well, she didn't know how the fame she'd accrue would translate into money, airtime and ancillary media exposure — she'd have to leave that to her agent — but the haul would be enormous. As to the risk of her own well-being, that would only add to her legend.

"Okay," Didi said, "I'm in. What have you got?"

"The estranged wife."

Didi said, "Wait a minute. Phil Brock was never married."

"Not Brock's wife. The wife of the Uruguayan jailer who let Brock go."

The media had long speculated that Brock must have had inside help to escape from his jail cell. The Uruguayan government had steadfastly refused to comment on that possibility. Which could only mean, of course, someone crooked inside the jail had aided and abetted Brock's getaway.

The problem for the media was figuring out who.

Ellie Booker had apparently cracked that nut.

"What jailer?" Didi asked.

"The head jailer, who else?"

"How do you know it was him? Just because he disappeared, too?"

"Duh," Ellie said.

"Everybody thinks he *might* have been the one, but nobody can *prove* it."

Ellie sighed. "What are the two reasons a man might risk his job or his life?"

"Money and/or sex."

"Right. In most cases. Personally, I don't think the jailhouse chief would be willing to risk his own freedom just to get his wienie cleaned. Do you?"

"Eew." Didi's face scrunched up in disgust. "You mean getting oral sex from Brock while he was in jail? No, I don't see that at all. But Brock did have money. He could have *bought* his way out."

Ellie said, "Lots of people, including both of us, have thought of that. But there's no record of Brock moving any funds right before or after he disappeared."

"Yes, but nobody's sure Brock didn't have hidden funds and used them."

"That's true, but that idea is a dead end. There's no way for you, me or any newsie to discover whether that's true. So I thought: What if Brock did offer a bribe to the jailer and somebody else topped it?"

"Who would do that and why?" Didi asked.

"I don't know. At first, who would put up the money didn't matter. I just wanted to see if that possibility might explain a few things."

Didi said, "And it led you to the jailer's wife, who you say is estranged."

"*Was* estranged."

It took Didi a beat to catch up. She didn't think Ellie was saying there had been a reconciliation. How could there be if the jailer had disappeared? The only thing that left was …

"Jesus, the jailer's *wife* has vanished, too?"

Ellie nodded. "But not before she talked to me, and the only reason she did talk was because I paid her on the spot. A nice chunk of cash, but not enough to start a new life somewhere else. She told me she got a call from her ex-husband. He said he'd done something risky. She said doing stupid stuff all the time was why she was leaving him. He'd blown every *centavo* they had and would never change."

"Did he confess to letting Brock go?" Didi asked.

"No, but she figured it out pretty fast when the news broke. What he gave her was the license plate number of a car. He said if anything bad happened to him, she should tell the police that the people who owned the car had double-crossed him."

"Killed him."

"Yeah," Ellie said. "He told his wife he would send her as much money as he could right away, but she wasn't going to get his pension after what he did."

Didi shook her head. "And she didn't get a dime, right?"

"Right. So when I came along, cash in hand, she was only too happy to talk to me. I got the license plate number from her and checked it out."

"And the big reveal is?" Didi asked.

"It was a diplomatic plate belonging to the Hashemite Kingdom of Jordan."

Didi sat back in her chair. "No shit?"

"No shit. I checked for any kind of political hoo-haw Brock might have raised against Jordan when he was in Congress, but I couldn't find any reason for an Arab king to be pissed off at him. What I did find out was Brock had been a friend of Bahir Ben Kalil."

"Who's he? Wait a minute. Didn't I hear about that guy being killed locally a while back?"

Ellie nodded. "BBK was the personal physician to Jordan's ambassador to the U.S."

Didi ran that data through her mind. "Are you saying Brock had something to do with the death of his friend and the Jordanians grabbed him as payback?"

"I couldn't find anything to suggest the government of Jordan itself was involved, but diplomats in foreign countries don't usually drive their own cars, do they? Jordan does have its own radical groups, and I thought maybe one of the working stiffs at the Jordanian embassy in Montevideo, say a chauffeur, had been converted or coerced by the jihadis. I was just spitballing but that's how I'd gotten as far as I had."

Didi was pretty much up to speed now. "So you called on the estranged wife again to see if she'd heard anything further from her husband. Only by then she'd been grabbed, too."

Ellie said, "Yeah, but I did get hold of her sister. When I told her who I was, she thanked me for the money I'd provided the missing wife. The cash had been left behind — another sign that the wife had been snatched and hadn't just run away. The sister said the remainder of the extended family was going on the run."

"And now you think someone might be coming for you, too?" Didi asked.

"I gave the missing wife my name. My guess is she passed it along to the bad guys, you know, once they started questioning her."

"Jesus, woman, you're handing me a live grenade," Didi said. Unable to stop herself, though, she asked, "Do you have anything else?"

"I couldn't find anyone directly connected with the jailer's kidnapping in Uruguay, but I did discover Bahir Ben Kalil had a twin sister, Hasna Kalil. Who knows, maybe the two of them were close."

"Did you tell anyone in federal law enforcement about all this?" Didi asked.

"Not yet. I don't think I'm going to do that directly, either."

"And indirectly?"

Ellie said, "I'm thinking I'll try to have a chat with Jim McGill."

McGill's Hideaway — The White House

McGill and Patti were having a *digestif* after dinner. They sipped the Italian brandy McGill had come to favor and watched the flames dance in the Executive Mansion's last wood-burning fireplace. They knew the respite from their troubles, personal and political, would be short lived but were content to enjoy it in companionable silence.

Then McGill asked, "How long do you think it will take?"

"What?"

"The time necessary for us to decompress after leaving this place."

"I thought you liked your hideaway," Patti said.

"I do. I've been saving my nickels and dimes. Wherever we go, I'm going to build a room just like this one."

"Better be somewhere that still allows you to put woodsmoke into the air then."

McGill hadn't thought of that. He began to factor it into his thinking.

For the moment, though, he said, "I meant, really, how long do you think it'll be before you and I and our kids are irrelevant to the creeps and crazies of the world and no longer worth threatening?"

Patti knew that her husband's question wasn't an idle one. He wanted to know what his responsibilities to the people he loved would be. So she gave his inquiry serious thought.

At length, she said, "I think it will depend on two sliding scales moving on parallel tracks but in opposing directions. The first is how fast and how high Jean Morrissey's profile as President — or Oren Worth's or Warren Altman's, heaven help us — rise in the public eye and how quickly our public profiles descend."

Patti gave her assessment a bit more consideration and decided she had it right.

"After all, what's the point of bothering with someone who's yesterday's news?"

McGill had reservations. "Well, it's not like we're going to become recluses. You'll have Committed Capital to run and I'll be presiding over my own little empire."

Patti grinned. "I think you're confusing your titular roles. Presiding is what presidents do; empires are ruled by emperors."

"Maybe I'll wear different hats on alternate days," McGill said.

"Highly innovative, and you're right about the two of us not running off to a dank retreat on distant moors, but I think the equation still holds. If we lower our public profiles only by half, I'm sure the problems faced by the next resident of this house will eclipse notice of whatever you and I are up to."

"A year, you think, before we can let our guard down just a little?" McGill asked.

"Maybe two years. By the next mid-term elections, we'll be old hat."

Before the conversation could go any further, a polite knock sounded at the door, and after permission was given, Blessing entered with a portable phone in hand. He asked the First Couple if they might need anything. When he was told things were hunky-dory, in McGill's phrasing, he gave the phone to him.

"Mr. Celsus Crogher called from Minnesota. I asked if the matter was urgent or if it could wait until after dinner. He said it could wait that long but not much longer. Also, Ms. Ellie Booker called, saying she had an urgent matter, possibly life or death, to discuss with you."

"Nothing to do with our children?" McGill asked.

He wondered if Ellie had somehow found out about Carrie Ramsey's kidnapping and thought Caitie had been the one who was grabbed.

"She didn't specify, sir, and I didn't think it was my place to ask for clarification."

McGill realized that *he'd* just spoken out of place.

Blessing had no knowledge of what had happened in Los Angeles. Bringing up his kids had been a mistake. His consolation was Blessing would never talk about anything he'd heard at the White House to anyone.

Blessing said, "Return calls to Mr. Crogher and Ms. Booker are queued up, sir, if you care to make them."

As Blessing departed, McGill made the first call.

Patti remained seated at McGill's side. As he'd told her many times, and she'd come to accept, his kids were her kids, too. She couldn't imagine loving them any more than if she'd given birth to them. As for her relationship to Ken, well, there was nobody who'd meant as much to him as she had in his hour of greatest need.

When McGill reached Celsus, he said, "You're on speaker and

the President is with me."

"I'm honored."

"Me, too, Celsus," Patti said.

The former SAC got down to business. He asked McGill, "Have you ever seen the movie *Straw Dogs?*"

McGill thought he might have, and was reaching to recall the details when Patti said, "I have. Dustin Hoffman and Susan George. An American husband and English wife. They buy a home in a rural part of England."

"Cornwall," Celsus said.

The memory clicked in for McGill. "Yeah, there are hassles with the locals. Some personal, some tribal. And —"

Patti said, "The villagers attack the couple's home, and they defend themselves, viciously."

McGill added, "It was a Sam Peckinpah movie, wasn't it?"

"Yes," Celsus said.

"Are the kids watching it?" Patti asked.

"Yes. Tonight's feature film, as selected by Caitie."

McGill said, "She's probably the only one of them who knows about it, and only because of her own film background."

"Are Carolyn and Lars watching it, too?" Patti asked.

Implicit in her question was whether the other parents in the blended family thought the movie was appropriate for … Oh, hell. Even Caitie was old enough to make her own choices about what movies to watch now.

Even so, Celsus answered the question. "They're in another room, reading."

McGill said, "You called about more than an old movie, Celsus."

"Yeah, I did," He told them about Caitie and Ken throwing rocks at cans, and Abbie practicing her knife-fighting moves.

Patti was shocked by Abbie's activity more than the rock-throwing of the younger children. "Abbie has a knife?"

"We don't know that, ma'am. She was using kitchen knives, according to what I was told."

McGill found that intriguing. "How did she respond when she

was questioned? I assume somebody asked her what she was doing."

"She said she learned the techniques from a Filipino friend at school. She was filling in the gaps you overlooked when you taught her how to use a knife."

Celsus's tone had been deadpan, but the content got Patti's attention.

She looked at McGill and asked, "You taught Abbie how to knife-fight?"

McGill nodded. "Only after she asked me. She said she didn't like guns."

Seeing his wife was still grasping for comprehension, he added, "If you'll recall, you asked me for a bit of instruction in Dark Alley and used what I taught you to discreetly beat up the prime minister of the United Kingdom. How could I do less for our daughter?"

The memory of that satisfying moment brought with it inevitable acceptance.

"I don't see how you could," Patti said.

"Well, let's hope she doesn't stick anybody important in the gizzard," Celsus offered.

McGill and Patti looked at each other in surprise. Celsus had made a joke. Yet another sign of his steadily increasing humanity.

"I'm hoping you won't let anything like that happen, Celsus," McGill said.

"My people are working hard to see that it doesn't come to that, but that's beside the point."

"The point being?" McGill asked.

"You know."

McGill said, "All of this is the kids' way of saying that if the bad guys come charging over the hill, they're going to join the fight in any way they can. They won't hide and hope for the best."

"Right," Celsus said. "Got to admire them for that."

McGill was tempted to tell Celsus to ask Merilee how she'd feel about her hoped-for child entering the fray, but he decided to save that one for another time.

He said, "It's also Caitie's way to tell us it makes more sense to let her siblings and herself take some practice at the firing range."

"She's the instigator, no question," Celsus said, "but if you're right about Abbie, it'll be only the younger two-thirds at the range. What do you want me to do? I mean, tomorrow they might start making Molotov cocktails."

"Let Ken and Caitie go to a well-run range, on one condition."

"What?"

"They get Carolyn's permission, too, and she goes with you and them and helps to supervise the kids."

If there was anything to take the thrill out of shooting a handgun, McGill figured, it would be having Mom hover over your shoulder nitpicking your technique and reminding you of the moral consequences of ever discharging a round.

Celsus understood, even chuckled. "Good one."

Patti dispelled any levity with a single question. "Celsus, what are the chances *any* kind of defensive action will even be necessary?"

"One in a million, ma'am. But as long as there's that one possibility we have to ignore the rest of the arithmetic and consider it to be a hundred percent."

After he ended the call, McGill told Patti, "Practical paranoia is a necessary part of Celsus's mindset."

"You're telling me about paranoia?" Patti asked, arching an eyebrow.

McGill said, "That's right, you know a thing or two about the worries of the world."

Patti said, "Like nobody other than another modern-day President could even guess."

"Would you like a foot rub, my dear?"

"I would, later. I'll skip listening in on your call with Ms. Booker. You don't even have to tell me about it, unless it's something I absolutely need to know. Even then, break it to me gently."

She gave McGill a kiss and left for another part of the White House. He hoped it was for a hot bath, but more likely it was a return to the Oval Office. On a slow day, the President was busier than Santa on Christmas Eve.

When the door clicked shut behind Patti, McGill made the call.

Without bothering about a hello, he asked, "Have you really stepped in it this time, Ellie?"

"I might have, no BS."

"Is the problem foreign or domestic?" McGill asked.

"Foreign but with a good chance of coming home to roost."

McGill said, "Have you thought of contacting someone who has an actual badge? Real police powers. Available to work 'round-the-clock work shifts."

"If I did that, I'd have to start at the bottom of a bureaucracy, and by the time it got to someone who could make a decision, if it ever made it that far, I might be dead already."

Ellie's voice was even in tone, but McGill recognized she was being completely serious. Her life was in jeopardy. Maybe hers *and* someone else's.

"Okay," McGill said. "You've got my attention."

Ellie repeated the narrative she'd shared with Didi DiMarco.

"Huh," McGill said. "Did this missing jailer's wife give you the impression that no one from the FBI or anyone else in our government had been in touch with her?"

"It wasn't a question of gleaning an impression. She told me exactly that. She was frustrated as hell about it. I have no doubt she was telling the truth."

"So she cared about her husband?"

"No, she wanted the money he promised her."

"Yeah, that works as motivation, too," McGill said, "but why didn't someone from our embassy think to talk with the woman. There had to be someone there or here in Washington who could have come up with the idea."

Ellie said, "I'm sure there was, but the diplomats at the State Department had to negotiate with the Uruguayans about extraditing Tyler Busby. He was a bigger fish than Philip Brock, right?"

McGill agreed with that.

"So," Ellie said, "they wouldn't want to mess that up by sneaking around in someone else's back yard, questioning one, and maybe more, of their nationals about a situation that was clearly embarrassing to them. Letting a foreign prisoner waltz out of one of your prisons has to leave egg on your face. Reminding the locals of the fact probably wouldn't go over well."

McGill laughed. "That didn't stop you."

"Well, hell, I don't work for the government, and I'm incorrigible."

"All a part of your charm," McGill said. Hearing about how Ellie had boldly seized this opportunity gave McGill an idea.

Before he could mention it, Ellie told him what she had on her mind.

"I don't think it's just me puffing up my ego to think somebody might try to grab me."

After what had happened to Carrie Ramsey, McGill wasn't about to downplay anyone's suspicion of being kidnapped.

"I do think you should be careful," he said.

"I want to do better than that. I want a couple of federal agents with me around the clock for at least a month. A man and a woman. You know what, maybe it'd be better with two women and forget the guy."

"Make the bad guys think you're an easier target?" McGill asked.

"Exactly. Listen, I'm licensed to carry. I'm pretty sure I can handle things myself, but that probably wouldn't leave me any margin for discretion. I'd have to go for the kill."

The blasé note in Ellie's declaration that she'd be ready to take a life caught McGill by surprise. *Shoot someone dead? No big deal.* The thing was, it hadn't sounded like empty braggadocio or even an unexamined possibility.

Hell, it came across like something she'd actually *done* before.

And hadn't been bothered by it.

"You still there?" Ellie asked.

"Yeah," McGill said. He took the discussion in another direction. "If someone were to make an attempt at kidnapping or killing you and they were taken alive, that might provide a big lead on actually finding out what happened to Congressman Brock."

"Just what I was thinking," Ellie said.

"Could also make a helluva first-person report for you to do on TV."

"I was thinking of that, too. So can you help me?"

McGill had thought, just moments ago, that he might ask Ellie if she'd like to go to work for him if she ever grew tired of TV work. She was a first class detective, no question. Now, though, having imagined that Ellie might have blood on her hands, he decided to hold off.

Big media might be a better fit for her.

McGill said, "Yeah, I'll make a call."

J. Edgar Hoover Building — Washington, DC

"One hundred and forty-nine possible matches spread across thirty-seven states," Deputy Director Byron DeWitt said.

The names and driver's license images of motorists from coast to coast and Alaska and Hawaii were cached on his iMac. The file had arrived an hour ago from the FBI's Computer Intrusion Section, the group of federal techies originally conceived to investigate cyber crimes and protect the Bureau from black-hat hackers. A heartbeat after the section's initial mandate was laid down, the people in the room looked at each other and thought: *Wouldn't it be fun and, of course, necessary to hack the bad guys' computers.*

Sure it would, and thus the section's authorization was expanded.

Though never written down.

The federal government would never admit publicly that it was right up there with the Chinese, the Russians, the Israelis and dozens of other countries who loved nothing better than poking their noses into someone else's digital data.

In terms of the matter at hand, the FBI didn't notify any of the states whose DMVs they'd snooped. That was understandable, really. If the feds had informed bureaucrats throughout the nation of what they needed and the reason why, the story would be on Facebook, BuzzFeed and the *New York Times* before you could blink twice, and then where would Special Agent Carrie Ramsey be?

"Possible matches but not one that's definitive," DeWitt said as he scrolled through the photos, hoping his eyes could see what the facial recognition software had missed.

A conclusive match for the guy Special Agent Ramsey had fatally chomped in L.A.

Special Agent Abra Benjamin was looking through the same file on her iPad.

She said, "I never noticed before how similar driver's license photos are to crime scene pictures. Dead eyes everywhere. All you'd have to do is add chalk lines and they'd be indistinguishable."

DeWitt chuckled. He'd always liked Abra's morbid sense of humor.

For two people who might have come to a bad end, personally and professionally, they still got along well. Abra had invited him over to her place for dinner that night. She said, "Even if they expect us to work around the clock, that doesn't mean we have to do it in the office."

Abra didn't intend to cook for him, of course. She never had, even in the old days, pleading an allergy to stoves. Kitchen sinks, too. The farthest she would go was a dishwasher.

She was far less inhibited in the bedroom. Almost anything went there. That was a point DeWitt had not forgotten, but chose not to remember in detail. He was now mindful that just being at Abra's place for carry-out Chinese wouldn't look good to his fiancée, Vice President Jean Morrissey.

Abra knew that, too. She might have said she was just kidding if DeWitt had accepted the invitation. Then, again, she might have brazened it out. It was always a close question with her as to what she valued more, personal satisfaction or professional status.

Seeing that DeWitt wasn't about to put a foot in her snare, though, she opted to keep climbing the organizational ladder. They had their dinner orders from The Sichuan Garden sent to the office. Nobody in Washington, other than neglected spouses, objected to public servants burning the midnight oil.

At least if they did so with the office door open and refrained from making any guttural sounds that might be misinterpreted. DeWitt and Abra were careful to observe both points of etiquette. That and not drip any soy sauce on their clothing.

"We couldn't even find a DNA match in the system," DeWitt groused. "Who the hell was this SOB Carrie Ramsey sank her teeth into? The Phantom?"

Abra said, "Maybe he started out Amish and moved on to Christian Science. How could we ever catch someone like that?"

"Start licensing horse-drawn carriages," DeWitt said.

The two of them looked at each other, wondering the same thing: Did states license carriages? The question had never occurred to either of them before. *If states did license carriage drivers, did such documents bear the licensee's photograph?*

They agreed on the answer to the last question.

Definitely. Any license worthy of its name these days would include a photo. Images that showed up under ultraviolet light and bore laser perforations, too, most likely. Maybe there were more security features they hadn't even heard about yet.

Getting enthused about the idea, even if it was a bit farfetched, DeWitt and Abra acted like good executives and delegated the grunt work to underlings: Run the face of the dead kidnapper against the licenses of any carriage driver in the country.

They didn't know whether to feel good or foolish about what they'd just done.

It was a fact that the bastards who had grabbed Ramsey hadn't made their getaway in a buggy; they'd used a BMW. A far faster and, on the Westside of L.A., less conspicuous means of escape. Of course, maybe that was point: blend in with the local environment.

DeWitt suggested as much to Abra.

She nodded. "When in the city, be a city mouse. In the country …"

She paused to let DeWitt complete the thought."

"Be the rat you really are," he said. "I like it."

"You think Ramsey's out in a wilderness somewhere?"

DeWitt considered the question. "Depends on who the bad guys are. We've got one guy who, so far, looks like he's lived his life without a hint of binary code. No ones, just zeros. On the other hand, we know there's a wheelman with a powerful German import. That says city boy to me."

"Me, too," Abra said. "So what do we say? They're part of a conspiracy big enough to embody both urban and backwoods bastards?"

"That and both sides have a grudge against the President and her family."

Abra nodded. "Right."

DeWitt took his thought a step further. "Or maybe it's the other way around."

"What do you mean?"

"Maybe hurting the President isn't the main goal here."

Abra's first thought was: *Then who?*

She arrived at the answer before needing to voice the question. "McGill."

The word was no sooner out of her mouth than DeWitt's cell phone chimed.

The deputy director showed the special agent the caller ID screen: JJ McG.

Sturgis, South Dakota

Special Agent Carrie Ramsey woke up knowing she'd been drugged again. She didn't know how that had happened. As the gnawing pain in her gut told her, she hadn't eaten in a longer time than she could remember. But by then she'd been rendered unconscious more times than she could accurately recount, and time was a slippery concept. She couldn't say if she'd been held days or weeks.

Feeling her arms and legs, though, she knew she still possessed a decent muscle tone and guessed her captivity had to be of relatively short duration. She'd have no muscular definition left if she'd been held even a month. Hell, from lack of proper nutrition and hygiene, her teeth might be coming loose, if she'd been chained up a prolonged time.

One thing was certain, she'd been a prisoner long enough to smell bad. B.O. plenty. Maybe that was a part of the plan. Make her choke on her own fumes. Her breath reeked, too. The last thing she could remember eating was a bag of fast-food fries. She still had the taste of potato, grease and salt on her tongue. She would have spat, if she could have summoned enough saliva.

Something else continued to register on her taste buds: the flesh and blood of the arm she'd chewed. Rank as hell. Or maybe she was just imagining that. She didn't think the pricks who were holding her would ever be able to beat the truth out of her, but she might sell her mother for a toothbrush.

That thought had no sooner occurred than tears of regret appeared in Carrie's eyes. No, hell no, she'd never do anything to dishonor her mom or dad. They could kill her first. All she'd ask was the chance to take another of them with her. Make *them* rue kidnapping her.

Her tears flowed but she made no sound. Wouldn't give them that satisfaction. She blinked her eyes clear and looked around. She was in another windowless room. Much like the last one she could remember. Only the shade of gray paint on the walls was a touch darker.

Carrie thought she had to be in a private home or commercial structure. You couldn't drag someone bound hand and foot into even the sleaziest motel without the front desk getting nervous enough to call the cops. The fact that she'd been locked up in at least two nearly identical rooms suggested that there might be others: a series of informal but effective holding cells.

That made her think that she hadn't been grabbed by a solitary group of loons. There had to be some kind of organization behind the crime. It didn't have the feel of a drug operation to her. Her place of confinement wasn't a stash house for bank robbers or a hide-out for auto thieves either. It certainly didn't have the feeling of a lair for cybercriminals.

A more apt criminal activity for the space came to her with a jolt: human trafficking.

Modern day slavery, sexual or otherwise. A place where free will went to die and unquestioning submission became the only way to survive. To hell with that, Carrie decided. She would die fighting rather than submit.

But there had to be more involved. The shit-heads who'd taken her had to think they were snatching Caitie McGill. Didn't they? She thought about that for a minute. Yeah, of course, they did. There was no way this was a random event.

Sexual predators didn't travel in a pack. If there had been one or even two of them, maybe it could have been psychos. But not four guys. This had to be ... what? Taking a prized individual for some kind of prisoner swap. She could see that, if the kidnappers were foreigners.

She hadn't gotten that impression, though. She couldn't remember the faces of the creeps who'd grabbed her in L.A. She knew she'd seen them, but having been drugged more than once maybe her brain cells were getting scrambled.

There was a cheerful thought: *Yeah, the special agent made it out alive, but she was never quite the same. That's her sitting over there in the corner drooling, doesn't really have much to say for herself anymore.* Another outcome where she'd rather die.

That thought had no sooner entered her mind than she heard footsteps approach.

She'd yet to see or speak with any of her captors after she'd been taken.

But then the door to the room opened.

J. Edgar Hoover Building — Washington, DC

McGill called DeWitt and told him and Abra of his conversation with Ellie Booker.

The two FBI colleagues looked at each other. DeWitt saw Abra had something she wanted to say. He didn't worry about being pre-empted. He nodded and gave her the go-ahead.

"Mr. McGill, this is Special Agent Benjamin. Is it possible Ms. Booker is over-dramatizing here? Trying to rope both you and the Bureau in to punch up a story idea she has in mind."

"I asked myself the same thing," McGill said. "I've worked informally with Ms. Booker before. She played it straight with me because she knows it's in her own interest. Of course, now I'm nearly out the White House door. So, maybe I'm not as valuable as I used to be. Then again, Special Agent, I assume you made a few good contacts when you were in Uruguay. If I'm right, you could use them to see if the jailer's wife has disappeared. If that's the case, Ellie Booker's story would seem credible to me."

DeWitt said, "Certainly a reason for Ms. Booker to be careful, if people are disappearing, and a chance for us to make an interesting arrest if someone does come after her."

"Maybe a chance to find out where Philip Brock is," McGill said.

"Assuming he's still alive," Abra replied.

"Right," McGill agreed, "and if he's not, maybe it's a way to find the killers."

DeWitt asked, "So Ms. Booker is asking, through you, for FBI protection?"

"She thinks two able female special agents would be the best way to do it."

"One close, one more distant but not too far away," DeWitt said, getting a feel for the idea.

"With lots more ready to hit the gas and make a fast arrival," Abra added.

McGill said, "You can work out the details as you think best."

Abra tried one more time. "You're *sure* this isn't just an exercise in self-promotion, sir?"

McGill laughed. "Ms. Booker made it clear to me that she hopes to get a big story out of this situation. But I feel she's telling the truth. She's in danger, and this is probably our best chance to bag whoever took Philip Brock."

"I agree," DeWitt said. "How can we reach Ms. Booker?"

McGill gave him the number.

Abra had one more question to ask. "I've seen the woman on TV, but what's she like to work with?"

McGill said, "She's smart, tough and opinionated. She's also licensed to carry a concealed weapon. My overall impression, Special Agent, is she's a lot like you."

Sturgis, South Dakota

Carrie Ramsey thought the guy who entered the room where she was being held looked to be in his early-to-mid thirties. Might be as old as forty, though. It was hard to tell with the get-up he was wearing: A Smokey Bear-style hat, an olive-drab short sleeved shirt with epaulettes and matching shorts. Calf-high tan socks and hiking boots completed the ensemble.

In Cheyenne, he'd called himself Lewis Addison Armistead.

He looked at her for a moment without saying a word. Satisfied with what he saw, he smiled at her. Looked as if he brushed his teeth after every meal but hadn't had the needed attention of an orthodontist.

"You're not eating much, Caitie," he said. "You're starting to lose weight."

Carrie didn't like the fact that the guy was letting her see his face. Probably meant he didn't expect that she'd ever to be able to testify against him in court. She entered that fact into her calculations for survival.

Hewing to the pretense that she was Caitie McGill, she replied in French, "*Va te faire foutre.*" Go fuck yourself.

She'd heard Caitie say it often enough, often in jest to her friend with the camera, that she'd recorded the phrase and obtained a translation.

The guy in the Smokey hat took the insult well. Probably because he hadn't understood her, not that she would count on that. In any case, he only smiled with some apparent warmth. As if he bore her no hard feelings. He was just a guy doing his job.

"Sorry," he told her, "the best I can do is English and some Spanish."

Carrie still wasn't going to bet that was the truth.

This time, though, she could reply through her own study of Spanish.

"Come mierda." Eat shit.

"Now, that one I know, and it's not nice."

"Yeah? Take this hardware off me and let's see if you want to fight about it."

This time he laughed, not cruelly, but with interest.

"You know, I'd love to do just that. Scrap with you some, settle you down. Then maybe we could enjoy ourselves a while."

Feigning incredulity, Carrie said, *"That's* what you want?"

"Honey, that's what everybody wants, one way or another."

"Okay, okay. So fight me. Take me, too, if you can. But I'll tell you right now, you let me out of these chains, I'll wrap them around your neck and squeeze 'til your head pops like a pimple."

A new light came into the guy's eyes. He was no longer friendly, but he was far more interested. The SOB was a predator and a sadist. He thought she was talking a far better game than she could play. He wanted to *show* her who'd be the boss.

Carrie didn't know if the prick had reinforcements nearby. That really didn't matter. The longer she was held, bound hand and foot, the weaker she would become. If she could con this simpleton into removing her handcuffs and leg shackles right now, she'd collapse his windpipe with a first strike and worry about any other shit-heads later.

This time she insulted him in English: "Chickenshit."

He took a step forward but then caught himself and stopped.

Carrie imitated chicken sounds. *"Bawk, bawk, bawk."*

The guy's face went red; his eyes narrowed to pinpoints. She almost had him, but then he looked over his shoulder. Someone else was nearby, someone this prick didn't dare cross. A superior both in rank and strength. That didn't stop him from looking back at her, though, giving her his best evil eye and shaking a finger at her, warning of horrors to come.

Carrie produced a sneering laugh and said, "Pussy."

That got him. He started her way, his hands opening and closing like talons.

Until a deep voice came over a hidden speaker, saying, "Not now."

Smokey looked back toward the open doorway, as if someone might be coming to enforce the order. Before there could be any doubt of how to proceed, the deep voice added, "You can have your fun later."

The bastard turned back to look at Carrie. "I will be back, and you and I are gonna have a *real* good time, I promise."

"Yeah, sure. Get your teeth fixed first, okay?"

The asshole went stiff, looked like he'd just been electrocuted.

Carrie gave it one last try. "Be sure to bring a note from Daddy, too, saying you have permission."

Smokey clenched his fists again, turned and stomped out of the room, slamming the door behind him. Carrie waited, watching, in case the exit was just a head-fake and the prick intended to burst back in as soon as she relaxed. But neither he nor anyone else appeared.

Well, she now knew there were at least two of them holding her.

And Mr. Basso Profundo was running the show.

She didn't know if any of that would be helpful, but gathering as much knowledge as you could was usually a good idea. You never knew when some tidbit might come in handy.

Before long, Carrie curled into the most comfortable position she could manage. She didn't know whether it was day or night, but her adrenaline rush was receding and she was tired. She tried to doze while leaving her eyelids slitted open, but they soon became too heavy to keep from closing.

As she started to drift off, Carrie comforted herself with the verbal victory over the dweeb in the Smokey hat. Jeez, just how inbred was that geek, anyway? The others, whoever they were, had to be smarter or they'd never have managed to kidnap her.

Well, at least the bad guys still thought they had Caitie McGill.

That made Carrie wonder how well the real Caitie would be handling this situation. Probably not too badly. She was a tough nut, that kid, even if she was privileged as hell. She'd probably have cheered Carrie on if she'd seen how the special agent had handled that creep.

That comforting thought accompanied Carrie down to another night of sleep in captivity.

The White House — Washington, DC

McGill had just completed his evening ablutions, which seemed to grow longer and more tedious with every passing year, and was about to climb into bed when his cell phone on the nightstand rang. He looked upon the instrument with suspicion. Patti was still up burning the midnight oil, but when he went to bed first with no expectation that she'd be joining him soon, she usually sent him a text, a line or two from a Shakespearean sonnet.

"In black ink my love may still shine bright."

Worked in pixels, too. At least when Patti sent the text.

This, however, was a call, and it didn't come from his wife.

The caller ID said: Ramsey, Donald.

McGill's heart sank. Had the Ramseys been the recipients of the worst news a parent might ever hear? *"Sir, this is the police. We're sorry to inform you that your child ..."*

He didn't even want to complete the thought. He'd been the bearer of such messages during his years with the Chicago Police

Department. Doing so had always made him rush home to make sure his own children were alive, well and likely to remain so.

By the second ring, McGill's thoughts had shifted. How had the Ramseys gotten his cell phone number? The answer was swift in coming. Sweetie had given it to them. They'd had her number because she'd also provided that.

He took a deep breath and answered before the phone could ring a third time.

"Jim McGill. Is this Don Ramsey?"

"It is."

Ramsey's voice echoed and McGill knew Don's end of the call was on speaker.

"I'm sorry to bother you so late, Mr. McGill. I wanted to wait until tomorrow morning to call, but neither Sheri nor I could sleep, and she said she didn't think you'd mind … so here I am."

Reading between the lines, McGill knew they didn't have any tragic news for him, and Don was calling to see if he had any for them. Praying he didn't, no doubt. Hoping that there might be some hopeful development he could share.

He gave them what little he could.

"We've discovered that the kidnapper Carrie …" McGill searched for the right word.

Sheri joined the conversation. "The man she killed?"

"Yes, him. We found a photograph of him watching a film shoot in which my daughter, Caitie, was playing a part."

"He was stalking her?" Don asked.

"Yes."

"Why didn't the Secret Service do something about that?" Sheri asked, a note of anger rising in her voice. "This whole thing might not have happened if they did."

Sheri was overlooking an obvious point. McGill, with regret, was about to tell her what it was when Don saved him the trouble. "Honey, I have to think Carrie was right there. If she didn't notice anything amiss, how could anyone else?"

McGill heard a small sob of dismay from the distraught

mother.

In the hope it might be a tiny note of comfort, he said, "I've watched Caitie do film shoots out in California. If they're done in public places, there are always onlookers. The curiosity is normal. People want to see celebrities. They want to watch how the entertainment they consume is made. It would be strange if no one was watching. As long as no one is causing trouble, interrupting the shoot, the security people don't object."

"So how did you get the picture of the kidnapper then?" Don asked.

"A friend of my daughter is a photographer. He was taking shots at random."

"If the kidnapper had a criminal record, wouldn't the police have photographs of him? Wouldn't they know who his associates are?" Don asked.

"The FBI is working on that right now," McGill told them.

Deputy Director DeWitt had shared that information with him. The kidnapper had no criminal record or even a driver's license. The feds were down to looking at horse-drawn carriage drivers now. McGill admired their thoroughness, but wasn't holding out hope that their effort would be successful.

He wasn't about to express that sentiment to the Ramseys and …

He came up with another long-shot idea of his own. He kept that notion to himself. If the combined effort of all the people looking for Carrie Ramsey produced a positive result, he'd be happy to deliver the good news. He wasn't about to raise their hopes on speculation, though.

Which was exactly what Sheri wanted him to do, asking, "Do you think they'll find something helpful?"

"They will, if it's at all possible. They have the best resources available." That was the most he could offer.

Then Don threw him a curveball. "What about the CIA? They have great resources, too, don't they?"

McGill was about to say the CIA worked on foreign threats not domestic ones, but how did they know there was no foreign involvement in the kidnapping? The assumption from the start had been that domestic crazies or criminals had been the perpetrators, but who was to say that was true?

McGill said, "You raise a good point, Don. I'll take that idea to the right people."

"You see why we came to you, Mr. McGill?" Sheri asked. "Who else could do that?"

Nobody that McGill knew. Not even him after Patti left the White House.

There was a sobering thought.

But his future problems would have to wait. There was a young woman's life to save.

Don said, his voice strained, "Please understand that we're grateful for everything you've already done, we just have to … need to have a reason to hold on to hope."

McGill felt at that moment he hadn't done nearly enough.

Didn't deserve to be turning in for the night already.

"Tell him your idea, Don," Sheri said.

There was a moment of hesitation McGill thought, so he filled the void. "What idea?"

Prompted, Don said, "Well, I've been reading up on your daughter. You know, the mentions that have been made of her in the newspapers and magazines. She seems to be quite the remarkable young woman." Don needed a moment to collect himself as he no doubt thought of his daughter the same way. "If you don't mind my saying, Caitie seems to be quite a character. Smart, outspoken and accomplished at a young age."

"She is all that," McGill said, feeling the Ramseys' pain all the more for the mention of his child.

"We've read up on your other children, too," Sheri said. "Such a fine family."

Don said, "Our point is, we don't see anyone who would act against Caitie out of personal enmity."

Just hearing the idea shocked McGill. "No, of course not."

"The obvious target for extortion, if that's even possible, is the President," Don said. "Or maybe such a thing would be done just to horribly wound her."

In a flat tone, McGill said, "That's what we're all thinking."

Sheri said, "But there's someone else to consider. What Don and I thought was: Maybe someone's out to hurt you, Mr. McGill."

CHAPTER 5

Tuesday, March 29, 2016
Number One Observatory Circle — Washington, DC

"Did you know about this?" Frank Morrissey asked.

He and his sister, Jean, the Vice President of the United States, occupied facing armchairs in the first floor sitting room of the VP's official residence. The two of them had just finished breakfast, after the meal was interrupted by a visit from Garner Woodbine, the Vice President's personal attorney.

He'd brought with him a sealed envelope marked URGENT and CONFIDENTIAL. It had been left in his locker at the club where Woodbine played his morning game of squash. The envelope was addressed to Frank Morrissey. Woodbine wasn't Frank's lawyer, but he knew he'd better deliver the mail anyway.

That was, after he'd had the envelope cleared by a private security company to make sure it didn't contain either explosives or toxic biological agents.

Taking the initiative, he informed both the Vice President and Frank that he didn't care to know the contents of the envelope unless it became a legal necessity — for the Vice President. His day had already been thrown off schedule, and now he had to go back to his club and ask for better locker room security without being able to reveal why he was making the request.

Jean had said, "Bill me for your time."

Woodbine simply nodded, but the look in his eyes said there

was never any question about doing that.

Considering that their appetites might be ruined by examining the contents of the envelope, Jean and Frank finished their breakfasts before reading the surreptitiously delivered message. After breakfast, they went into the first-floor sitting room, which was sound-proofed and, as far as they knew, contained no eavesdropping devices.

Jean answered her brother's question. "By reputation, of course, I knew. You know, too. Everyone who didn't just get off a bus from Kansas knows that Galia Mindel runs the biggest spy ring this side of the Kremlin."

"You never spoke about it directly with either the President or Galia?" Frank asked.

"Hell, no. It'd be more polite to ask about their favorite sexual positions."

"Probably more likely to get a straight answer, too," Frank said. "What about your fiancé?"

"Byron? What about him?"

"You never asked him if the FBI knows about Galia?"

"Frank, c'mon. You never accused me of being stupid before. Why start now?"

Frank shrugged. "I still love you as much as I ever have, but I've never seen you so in love this way before. What would I know about how that might affect a straight woman?"

The Vice President sighed. "It affects me a lot, but so far it hasn't destroyed any brain cells."

"Okay, my apology. So here we are. The covertly provided note tells us Thomas Winston Rangel is trying to save the day for the political right wing in this country by exposing Galia Mindel's spy network. He's going to tug on the loose string of how his domestic servant, Elias Roosevelt, whom he accused of grand theft, had the great good luck of having uber-expensive attorney Augustus Wiley spring to his aid."

Jean said, "More accurately, Rangel hopes to have some tabloid TV type do his digging for him."

"Which just between you and me had to come from …"

"Jim McGill. Not that he was the one who broke into Garner Woodbine's locker."

Frank steepled his hands and pressed his fingertips to his chin. "I'd dearly like to know who did that little chore for him."

Jean shook her head. "That's another question you should never ask."

"Probably won't. Anyway, Mr. McGill suggests that the way to undercut Rangel is to get him charged with stealing Edmond Whelan's book manuscript, which, ironically, depending on how highly it's valued, might also be considered grand theft."

Jean smiled. "I like that."

"Mr. McGill also suggests we get Whelan to help us put Rangel in the soup. I think he's right about that, but Whelan will want something in return. Consideration for his own misdeeds."

"So what do we offer him, assuming I become President?" Jean asked. "Sentencing leniency is all I can see. There's no question he's going to prison. The only thing for Mr. Whelan to consider is at which end of the sentencing guidelines he wants to find himself."

"We offer him the minimum?" Frank asked.

"Make it a sliding scale. Just for trying to help us he'll get a little time off. If we can nail Rangel, convict him and put him in a cell, Whelan gets a minimum sentence. Who will you get to talk to Whelan?"

There was no question that Frank would *not* be the one.

He said, "I'll use *my* lawyer. He's just the guy for this sort of thing."

"I won't ask if you'll drop a note in his gym locker," Jean said.

Frank chuckled but didn't respond directly.

He did say, "Maybe we can add some leverage to Mr. McGill's suggestion."

"Like what?"

"Evict T.W. Rangel from his closet, if he tries to fight his grand theft charge too hard."

The Vice President gave her brother a look but didn't say a word.

Even so, he told her, "I hear things. Someone who's lived a lie all his life most likely wants to die that way, too. Make sure people will remember him the way he pretended to be."

"Don't get yourself in trouble," Jean said.

Frank got up and kissed his sister's cheek.

"Of course not," he said. "You'll have a country to govern soon, and you'll need my help."

He gave her a wink and left the room.

Leaving Jean to wonder if Galia Mindel had sold her spy network to Frank or had simply given it to him.

Cheyenne, Wyoming

Dr. Tom Kirby dragged his colleague Dr. Peter Nash out of his house for a run. Nash was a thoracic surgeon, specializing in gunshot wounds. He didn't lack for business. Wyoming led the nation in per capita gun ownership: 195.7 per 1,000 people. They weren't shy about discharging their weapons either. Nash did his best to reconstruct any damage done between the neck and the navel. He made a handsome living doing so.

That morning, shortly after sunrise, the temperature was still two degrees short of freezing. The wind blowing at a steady fifteen miles per hour made it feel even colder. There was no snow falling, but that was all that could be said in favor of a cold, gray day.

Nonetheless, Nash's wife, Pamela, sent her husband outdoors with a merry grin, telling their mutual friend, Kirby, "Run him good and hard now."

Nash replied to his better half, "Did I mention, honey, that I cashed in my life insurance policy? Spent all the money on good liquor and bad women in Vegas."

She laughed. "That's all right. I took out my own policy on you. Ask Tom what he and I have planned after you have your heart attack."

Kirby and Nash had been schoolmates since kindergarten, as had Pamela.

Nash had been the one to get the prettiest girl either of them had ever known.

Now, the chest surgeon gave the ear-nose-and-throat man a suspicious look.

"C'mon, Pete," Kirby said, "all we're going to do is *jog* a little. It'll be good for you."

"Maybe ten years ago," Nash muttered.

Still, he and Kirby set out for what had been described to him as two laps around their mutual housing development, Lab Coat Estates, as it had been dubbed for all the medical practitioners living there.

They moved away from Nash's house at a pace that barely exceeded a brisk walk.

Behind them, Pamela called out, "Faster, boys, faster."

Then she stepped inside and closed the door.

It was too damn cold to watch a couple of middle-aged men trot down the street.

"You ever try anything funny with Pam?" Nash asked.

"No."

"Why not?"

"I love her too much. Wouldn't want her to think less of me."

Nash thought about that for a moment. "In your place, I don't think that would've stopped me."

"Well, you always were the asshole in the group. I only started playing with you as a kid because you lived next door."

"Yeah, same for me." They ran a quarter-block in silence and then Nash asked, "You know why Pam picked me instead of you?"

"I used to think it was myopia. Then I figured out your specialty makes more money than mine."

Nash nodded. "And being a nurse she knew that."

Kirby said, "You're just disappointed the three of us never formed a love triangle, aren't you?"

Nash replied, "More puzzled than disappointed. I mean, you just told me you love my wife but you never made a move on her. That's despite your staying single all these years."

"I'm just being patient. I figure either she'll come to realize her mistake or your bad habits will do you in within a reasonable amount of time."

That was the first time Nash had heard that one.

Sounded plausible when he thought about it.

He gave a dry laugh. "Yeah, that way you could get the missus and my money. Pretty damn sneaky. So how come you dragged me out for a run this morning? You're taking a chance you might extend my longevity."

Kirby shook his head. "Wouldn't dream of it."

"What then?"

"I just wanted to make a point to you at a time and in a place where there are no distractions that might lead to any confusion."

"Ooh, sounds serious," Nash said derisively. "Like I might need a drink and a smoke to face whatever music you intend to put on your phonograph. Now that I think of it, drinking and smoking would make jogging a lot more fun, too."

"Shut up and listen, Pete."

In all the time the two men had known each other, they'd had only one serious, punches-thrown fight. It had started when Kirby had told Nash to shut up. Kirby had suffered two black eyes; Nash had lost a front tooth.

The only reason their friendship had survived was Pam saying she'd be finished with both of them if they didn't shake hands and forgive each other. Now, after decades had passed, that clash echoed in both men's minds.

Nash stopped jogging and asked, "What did you just say?"

Running in place, staying light on his feet, Kirby said, "You heard me."

"You sonofabitch. I never thought I'd hear that from you again."

"I never thought I'd say it. Do I have your attention now?"

"Now, but not for long. This time, you'll be the one to lose your teeth."

Kirby danced backward a step. "That moron you sent to my office, the one who calls himself Lewis Addison Armistead? Do you know what he did?"

Humor pushed anger aside for the moment and Nash flashed a wicked grin.

"I know what he wanted me to do. I told him I don't work below the waist. As a joke, I said he should go see you. Jesus, Tom, I didn't mean to upset you. Hell, there are people who pay good money to look at naked lady parts. You being single, I thought you might be one of them."

Kirby stopped bouncing, just looked at Nash and shook his head.

"You and me, we're done. Tell Pam there's no help for it this time."

He turned and started walking home.

"Are you serious?" Nash called out. "It was just a damn joke, damn it. I wouldn't have done it if ... hell, Tom, I'm sorry, all right?"

Kirby stopped and turned to face Nash.

"Did you see the picture Armistead had?" he asked.

"I didn't have the time. What was so bad about it? Was the woman disfigured or something?"

Kirby shook his head, looking worried. "No, but now you've made me wonder if that's the next thing that's going to happen to her."

"Nothing like that's going to happen. Listen, I —" Nash caught himself, thought twice about offering a further explanation.

He was too late, though, to keep Kirby, his lifelong friend, from intuiting what was about to come next. "So you do know this Armistead asshole."

"Him and his dad, yeah. A few other people, too."

"Pete, what I saw yesterday has me thinking about going to the cops. This loser wanted me to estimate a young woman's age by looking at a poorly shot photo of her genitals. Like a fool, I tried to get rid of him by saying she was in her late teens to mid-twenties. He seemed disappointed that she might be that old. If he's got this poor girl and he's a pedophile, I don't like to think how he might take out his displeasure on her. If he's even worse than a child molester … well, I spent most of last night shuddering at what I'd become a part of because of you. I hoped that maybe you could tell me why I've been wrong to worry. Something more than the fact that you know this cretin. When I get home I *am* going to call the cops."

Nash's emotions made another fast swing. This time fear filled his face.

He held up a hand and said, "Wait, Tom. I'll take care of it. I didn't know it was this bad; I was just playing a joke on you. If there is a young woman in trouble, like you think, I'll make sure it all works out right, okay? But do *not* go to the police. Please."

"Jesus, Pete, what the hell have you gotten yourself into?"

Kirby had heard whispers that Nash occasionally treated people off the books. Not just anybody. Certainly not common criminals. But people whose politics he shared and who found themselves on the wrong end of a heated argument and an exchange of gunfire.

He'd chosen not to believe those rumors.

What kind of fool would Nash have to be to risk his practice and maybe even his marriage to do something that stupid? Thinking how this situation might affect Pam made Kirby sick to his stomach. Should he tell her … what? He had a *suspicion* Pete was about to ruin his life and maybe hers, too. Without any proof, she might slap his face.

Telling her about the photo he'd seen, and Pete's role in it, might produce the same result.

"Just give me one day," Nash said. "One day, Tom, that's all. I'll make it right. I swear to God."

Kirby silently asked himself how you could know a guy your whole life and never see him for who he really was. He turned his back on Nash and started to jog home. After a few strides, he picked up the pace. A heartbeat later, he was sprinting.

Nash couldn't hope to catch him. He had only one alternative.

He turned and ran for his own home, quickly wheezing from the unaccustomed effort.

Rochester, Minnesota

A request from the White House and the fact that Celsus Crogher was a retired, high-ranking federal officer got access for Ken and Caitie McGill and Carolyn Enquist to use the Rochester PD's shooting range. Under Celsus' supervision.

They arrived early when only a few cops and the range manager, Lieutenant William Morgan, were on hand. Morgan shook hands with Celsus and had done him the courtesy of hanging the first target in the range's center lane. Ear protectors and shooting goggles were also provided. Morgan didn't discourage the cops on hand from watching, but he kept them at a respectful distance.

Carolyn told Celsus, "If you don't mind, Mr. Crogher, I'd like to shoot first."

"You go right ahead, ma'am."

Morgan and the other cops were interested in watching Carolyn shoot. So was Celsus. More women were shooting these days than in years gone by. More than a few of them had real proficiency, but this lady, well, she was getting on in years just a bit and looked like she probably drove a Volvo with a "Make Love Not War" bumper sticker on it. A vintage hippie chick.

Nothing wrong with that. You just didn't see many gunslingers who looked like her.

Even so, she had her own Walther CCP 9mm. A compact weapon with an eight-round magazine. Very light recoil. Easy to rack a round into the chamber. A practical, effective gun for a woman who didn't feel she needed to compete with the big boys in either size or firepower.

Carolyn told her children, "When I first learned to shoot, I feared someone might get past all the cops watching out for us and I might be the last person between you and who knew what kind of madmen, I asked Sweetie to teach me to shoot the right way, the way she and your father learned to do it."

Back then, Ken and Caitie hadn't laughed at the dramatic notion of their mother being their last line of defense. Ever since Dad had married Patti and Patti had become the President, they'd had cops and special agents watching over them around the clock. It hadn't taken long at all for the McGill children to understand their world had changed. That perfect strangers might want to do them harm for no good reason.

Good reason, as they came to understand, was an entirely subjective notion.

It might be a political grievance, cultural disharmony, racial or religious animosity or a simple desire for notoriety. You never knew what might fall under the heading of rational thinking for someone. Their father had been shot by a patron of the Chicago Symphony Orchestra because the benefactor of the arts had felt the orchestra's maestro had insulted him and deserved to die. Jim McGill had intervened and took a bullet for his trouble.

So his kids knew from an early age that the world was an uncertain place.

That being the case, none of the McGill children felt anything but happy that their mother was doing all she could to keep them safe. Having reached the years of early adulthood now, and having been taught to be self-sufficient, they chose to put the burden of protecting themselves onto their own shoulders.

Carolyn had been unable to argue with that.

She agreed with Jim that she should go to the shooting range with Ken and Caitie, though not for the same reason. Well, not entirely. She would remind her children about just how awful making the choice to shoot another person might be. Yes, the right to defend yourself was paramount, but carrying the emotional burden of knowing you had injured, maimed or killed another human being would be a heavy and quite possibly lifelong burden to bear.

As Sweetie had told her, "You shoot too soon, you might make an unforgivable mistake. You shoot too late, you might die. So you have to shoot not just straight but also at exactly the right moment. That's part of the moral dilemma of carrying and using a gun."

Carolyn told Ken and Caitie all that and then she added, "We're the guests of the Rochester Police Department and we thank them for their courtesy."

The offspring knew their maternal cues and said thank you to Morgan and nodded to the other cops on hand.

Then Carolyn added, "However, we'll be shooting by the Chicago Police Department's qualifying rules. One hundred rounds at distances of seven, fifteen and twenty-five yards. Seventy lethal hits is the minimum to qualify. Is all that clear?"

Both of her kids nodded.

Carolyn put on her goggles and ear protectors and assumed her firing position; strong side of the body away from the target about 30 degrees, arms thrust forward slightly bent, weapon pointed downrange at a 45-degree angle.

Using a portable microphone, Lieutenant Morgan called out, "Fire when ready."

Carolyn raised her weapon and began shooting immediately, continued at a quick but unforced pace, steady as a metronome. She reloaded without any wasted motion. The targets and distances changed. She kept shooting and reloading in the same methodical fashion. For her, the outside world had ceased to exist … until Morgan ordered, "Cease fire!"

Carolyn lowered her weapon, engaged the safety and let out a deep breath.

Her eyes blinked rapidly as she turned and looked at her children. She handed the weapon to Celsus and embraced each child with one arm. Her voice caught in her throat as she told them, "I, I h—hope and pray that you never have to shoot anything but a paper target."

She kissed each of them and added, "Now, it's your turn."

At Caitie's request, Ken went next. She wanted to see how her older brother handled the exercise. Or so she said. Ken grinned. He wasn't buying that.

He said, "You just want to know what score you'll have to beat."

"That, too, but Mom made it look too easy. I want to see how you handle it."

Ken was smart enough to get coaching. He had Celsus adjust his shooting form and give him pointers. Then he put on his protective gear and took his mother's gun from Celsus. Morgan gave him permission to fire and Ken showed he was a real Mama's boy: smooth, methodical and pinpoint accurate.

His performance earned him a maternal kiss.

He got a pat on a shoulder from Caitie. "Not bad."

Celsus asked her, "You need any tips?"

"I need a holster."

"Why?"

"Well, you don't walk around with a gun in hand most times, do you?"

"Caitie," Carolyn said in a scolding tone.

Celsus held up an interventional hand. "No, she's right. Most people in law enforcement carry their weapons in holsters. You're thinking of your protective detail, aren't you?"

Caitie nodded.

Lieutenant Morgan was watching with interest, too. "Are you thinking a waistband holster or a shoulder holster, Ms. McGill?"

"Waist."

"I think we can help with that, if it's all right with your mother."

Caitie and Morgan looked at Carolyn. She turned to Ken to see if she'd have any support if she said no. He only shrugged. Carolyn sighed and said okay.

Morgan turned to the youngest-looking cop among the onlookers. "A waistband holster for Ms. McGill. The cop returned in less than two minutes with a black leather open-top holster. Caitie slipped her belt through the loop and it rode at her hip with a slight backward tilt.

Celsus handed her Carolyn's Walther. Caitie slipped it into the holster: a perfect fit.

She gave the young cop a wink and said, "Good eye."

He blushed. The other cops laughed. Celsus returned the focus to the business at hand. He explained the technique for drawing the weapon out of the holster: The arm drawing the weapon stayed close to the body and moved backward in a straight line. The weapon was withdrawn only far enough to clear the holster. The weapon was thrust forward to meet the supporting hand. The movement to eye level was a straight line.

Celsus took Caitie through each step twice. She paid close attention and performed as directed. When Celsus wanted to do a third run-through, Caitie said, "I'm good; I've got it."

With a nod from Carolyn, Celsus stepped back.

Morgan gave everyone time to take a breath and then said, "Fire when ready."

Caitie had the gun out, supported, raised and fired in the blink of an eye. Her reloading was unpracticed and slowed her down, but her ability to get the weapon out of its holster and shoot accurately amazed everyone who saw it.

Celsus whispered in Carolyn's ear, "Damn, if she doesn't have your ex's hand-speed."

Carolyn found those words less than comforting.

When the score for all three shooters was tallied, each more than qualified by CPD standards. Carolyn scored 95 hits out of 100 shots, just one short of what was considered great. Ken had 94, one short of Mom. Caitie had a 91, still really good, and with her speed she was sure to register some hits before the other guy even started shooting.

Every cop in the place shook all three shooters' hands.

Morgan slipped his card to Celsus and quietly told him, "If things get scary out there on the farm and you need any reinforcements, just give me a call."

Celsus nodded and said thanks.

Caitie huddled with Ken and the two of them told the lieutenant they'd like to make a donation to the department's favorite charity, whatever that might be. He gave them the name and address and said thank you.

Morgan asked the McGill kids what they thought of their experience.

Ken said, "Mom's right. I hope I never have to shoot anything but a paper target."

Caitie added, "It's not for me either."

Morgan told her, "You took to it really well for a beginner."

"It's not that," she said. "Shooting just seems too … impersonal. I think I'd rather use my hands and feet."

Giving Caitie a curious look, Morgan said, "Well, okay, then."

Everybody shook hands again and the visitors left the range with the better part of the day still ahead of them. Seeing an opportunity, Caitie asked if she might ask another favor.

"What's that?" Carolyn and Celsus asked at the same time.

Caitie told them, "I'd like to see if there's a hair stylist in town who has an opening."

The National Mall — Washington, DC

Dressed in T-shirts, running shorts and shoes, McGill and Sweetie ran along the National Mall, moving at a seven-minute-per-mile pace. Each of them was happy to be able to do that and converse without straining. The years might be passing, but the toll they took was diminished by regular exercise and the lessening appeal of bad habits. Sugar and alcohol moderation had become an easier reach.

Pain-free knees and shoulders were more important than getting a buzz on.

Satisfaction came from family, friends and doing your job well.

Each of their shirts was a gift from their respective spouses. Putnam Shady had given Sweetie a shirt from Cool Blue bearing the new progressive party's logo and its slogan: *Too cool to be fooled.* McGill's T-shirt was a gift from Patti, bestowing on him the unique if unofficial title: PHOTUS. The acronym was explained: *President's Henchman of the United States.*

Deke Ky had been given the option of running ahead of or behind the two old friends. He'd chosen behind, not because he couldn't outrun McGill and Sweetie. It just made more sense to look for a threat ahead of you than to look over your shoulder for bad news sneaking up from behind. Leo, in the Chevy cruising Constitution Avenue, would give Deke a blast of his horn if he saw any bad guys approaching from behind.

While McGill and Sweetie had gone out unarmed for their run, Deke had not. He wore shorts and sneakers, too, but under a nylon windbreaker he carried both his Uzi and his sidearm. On a day with the temperature in the upper 50's, he was comfortable. He ran just far enough behind McGill not to overhear the boss's conversation.

"I tried," Sweetie told McGill, "but I just can't do politics."

McGill said, "After watching Patti up close for seven-plus years, I'm surprised anyone can."

"I can deal with the public," Sweetie said. "I've actually met a lot of interesting people and plenty more who need help. If that was all there was to it, I'd be fine. It's the institutional interests that ruin the whole thing for me. The party's needs come before the people's too often."

"You could be an independent," McGill said.

"I'd still have to work with a party to get things done, and then I'd be serving their interests without even having the benefits of membership."

"Okay, you've convinced me," McGill said. "So what are you going to do? I'd take you back in a heartbeat, if you want, but you were pretty clear you don't want to risk making even the most honest of mistakes anymore."

Sweetie said, "I still feel that way. The idea of being even tangentially responsible for another person's death scares me silly."

"So the solution to your problem is?"

Sweetie caught McGill's eye and they looked at each other for a couple of strides before turning back to watch the path ahead and make sure they neither tripped nor trampled a covey of nuns from Ohio.

"I thought I'd come back to the shop in a new role, one I thought up myself," Sweetie said. "I could be the company's ceo."

McGill shot her a quick look and laughed. "I thought that was my job."

"You're the upper-case CEO."

"And you'd be the fine print version?"

Sweetie smiled. "In a manner of speaking, yes. I'd be the chief *ethics* officer. I'd keep an eye out for the moral principles that should guide the business."

McGill thought about that for a moment and smiled. "That might be a first for this country or anywhere else for that matter. Would part of your job be rapping knuckles with a wooden ruler?"

Sweetie had spent a year in a convent, after all.

"For minor offenses maybe," she said. "To correct more serious misdeeds, a right-cross to the jaw might be required."

"We'd have to stipulate that in all our employment contracts," McGill said.

That earned him a light sock on the shoulder, necessitating a stride correction.

"So what do you think?" Sweetie asked. "Can I come back in that capacity?"

"You can come back and do anything you want except sit in my chair."

"When you're in the office."

"Right," McGill said. "When I'm out, feel free."

"You don't think I'm being foolish?"

"Never."

"But your brow is furrowed," Sweetie said.

"Really? I didn't even know I could do that." McGill sighed. "I think maybe you've come up with exactly the right idea. I've been questioning my own judgment lately."

"Really?"

"Well, in terms of who I've been thinking about hiring anyway. If I open offices far and wide, I'm going to need investigators to do the work. You remember Gene Beck, right?"

"Uh-huh," Sweetie said, keeping her voice even.

McGill heard the note of reservation anyway.

"Well, he served his time out in California."

"Already?"

"Sentencing guidelines out there allow judges to consider individual circumstances. One of Gene's circumstances was that he wouldn't publicly reveal what he did as a government-paid contractor."

"You mean kill people when he wasn't stealing frozen embryos."

"Just between you and me?" McGill said.

"Of course."

"I asked Galia for a favor. I don't know how, and didn't ask, but she got me a look at the names and bios of the people Gene killed. If he'd done the same thing for the military or the CIA, they'd have given him some kind of medal he could never show anyone. But because the government was covering its heinie he did those things as a private citizen."

"He got paid with government money, right?" Sweetie asked.

"With a bit of subterfuge, yes. I didn't tell Patti about my snooping, so don't tell Putnam."

"I won't."

"So how do you parse things ethically on the idea of hiring Gene Beck. He's smart, skilled and didn't do anything the government didn't indirectly ask him to do, and as you said, paid him to do."

"I don't know," Sweetie said. "I'll have to think about it."

McGill might have mentioned that he'd paid Beck to put a note in Garner Woodbine's gym locker, knowing it would spur the Vice President and her brother to take action to discredit Thomas Winston Rangel and undercut his attempt to ruin Galia Mindel and by extension the President.

Also to preserve Jean Morrissey's viability as a presidential candidate.

They'd never covered situations like that in his catechism class back in parochial school. Even so, McGill mentioned it when he'd gone to confession that morning. He figured that was good enough. He didn't need to add to Sweetie's workload as his new chief ethics officer.

Other than to mention: "I was also thinking of hiring Ellie

Booker."

"The TV reporter?"

"Producer and reporter. She's a terrific investigator, but in the course of a recent conversation with her I got the totally unsupported feeling that she might've killed someone."

Sweetie shook her head. "Unh-uh. If you got that feeling, something she said must have supported it."

"Well, yeah, but it wasn't like she said, 'One time I aced this guy.' It was in the context of her life being threatened and if she had to kill somebody in self-defense, she'd do it. Anybody might feel the same, but it was the way she said it that struck me. Like it would be no big deal. As if she knew that from experience."

"She didn't actually come close to saying so, right?" Sweetie asked.

"No, not even close. Maybe I just misread her."

"You do that much, misread people?"

"Not too often."

"Hardly ever that I recall. Did you offer her a job?"

"No."

"Good. Gene Beck is at least a maybe. Ellie Booker, let her stay on TV."

"That was my take, too. Now, let's work on an issue Don and Sheri Ramsey raised with me last night."

"I gave them your private number," Sweetie confessed.

"I figured. Thought you'd do your penance for it."

"I have."

"Okay. Anyway, the Ramseys suggested that maybe the attempt to kidnap Caitie wasn't motivated by politics or a personal enmity against Patti, but —"

"You were the target," Sweetie said.

"Exactly. So you think we can figure out who hates me that much?"

"Tell me how far you've gotten already."

McGill said, "My cop years: twenty in Chicago, five in Winnetka. Thinking in terms of that time period, I can't think of anyone I locked up who a) served his sentence and got out; b) hates me so much he'd come after one of my kids; and c) has the brains and resources to pull off the snatch that took Special Agent Ramsey."

Sweetie had known McGill well for almost all of his time as a sworn officer. Reviewing the worst of the creeps she'd known of from that period she agreed with him, mostly but not quite completely.

"What about Lindell Ricker?" she asked.

Ricker had been the young man who'd been part of the group responsible for killing Andy Grant. His arrest had provided the link to Erna Godfrey. Lindell had plenty of reason to hate McGill, but he had nothing to do with Carrie Ramsey's kidnapping.

"He died in prison," McGill reminded Sweetie.

She winced. "Here we are keeping our bodies fit and it's my mind that's going."

McGill said, "We can start playing chess. If I cheat, as the chief ethics officer, you can scold me."

"I would, but let's get back to who hates you. I can't think of anyone else from your cop years. After that, though, Damon Todd had reason to hate you."

"But we both know he's dead. So is Etienne Burel."

Burel was the hulking French monster better known as the Undertaker. McGill had set him aflame in Paris. He hadn't burned to death, but after he'd plunged into the Seine he'd swallowed enough polluted water to contract and die of a bacterial infection that wouldn't yield to antibiotics.

Sweetie had a suggestion. "Let's think of a bad guy or two who crossed your path and lived to tell about it."

"Gene Beck, as we discussed, but he was semi-bad at worst."

"Okay, but we won't scratch him from the list; we'll just put him at the bottom."

McGill nodded. "Auric Ludwig, the gun lobbyist. He's got to hate me; he's not out of prison as far as I know; he does have the brains and probably enough crazy friends to pull off a broad daylight kidnapping. But why wouldn't he come straight at me?"

"If he's as smart as you say, maybe he'd know that hurting one or more of your kids would be the worst pain he could inflict," Sweetie said.

McGill couldn't argue with that. The only thing as awful would be losing Patti, but she was much better protected than his children. "All right, we'll mark Ludwig down as a real possibility."

"Who else?" he asked.

"How about that militia nut you took down in front of God and the whole wide world?"

"Harlan Fisk. He's in prison and —"

McGill came to an abrupt halt. Thinking he'd either had a seizure or had seen something menacing, Sweetie stopped, too. Deke rushed up in a matter of seconds, Uzi out and looking for any possible point of attack.

Taking note of the fuss he'd caused, McGill said, "Nothing's wrong. Not here anyway. Don't scare the tourists. I just had a thought that brought me up short."

Putting away his Uzi, Deke gave him a look of exasperation.

Sweetie only asked, "Would you care to share?"

"Using the criteria I mentioned," McGill said, starting to count on his fingers, "Although he's in prison, undoubtedly because he's locked up, Harlan Fisk hates me. Chances are he knows enough like-minded crazies on the outside to pull off a brazen crime like a daylight kidnapping. They probably have the resources to take a victim to any number of remote hideouts. But the big thing is, we caused a rift between Fisk and his daughter ... what's her name?"

It took him a moment to think. Neither Sweetie nor Deke interrupted.

"Elvie or something like that, I think," McGill said. "Fisk had abused her trust and we got her to turn on him. Maybe the stupid SOB considers her dead to him or something like that."

"Gave her a new perspective and that ruined her for his cause," Sweetie suggested.

"Yeah, right. But we won't forget about Auric Ludwig —"

"Right. But Harlan Fisk goes to the head of the line, and let's find out what happened to his daughter, too."

The run was over. They all headed to McGill's armored Chevy.

On the ride back to the White House, he called Minnesota, feeling the need to speak with all of his children. He started with Caitie. She told him about her shooting and her new haircut and color. She was no longer a blonde with pink highlights. McGill offered up a silent thank you.

Then he asked Caitie to have her friend Ben send copies of *all* his people photos to Byron DeWitt. Good kid that she was, she said she'd get right on it. Sounded glad she could be of help.

The White House — Washington, DC

When your job was to keep the President of the United States alive, well and safeguarded against everything except the right-wing media, people expected you to be a well-grounded, tightly focused, ready for anything SOB. Pretty much everything Celsus Crogher had been.

Elspeth Kendry was all of those things, but she was also her own woman. She was imaginative in a way her predecessor would never be. She was far more intuitive as well, able to make jumps in logic without having to touch every stepping-stone along the way. One other thing, that she kept to herself, she was a bit of a mystic. Just as the dictionary defined it, Elspeth believed in the spiritual apprehension of truths that were beyond the reach of intellect.

During one of the catnaps she took during her sixteen-hour workday, she'd had a dream. She saw her dear and long-departed friend Nadine Najimy falling past her again, but this time Elspeth caught Nadine's hand and pulled her up into her embrace, immediately making it the best dream she'd ever had.

She'd finally saved her friend, and all would be well. She was sure of that when Nadine kissed her cheek and whispered into her ear, "*Alqiddis. Alqiddis al'amriki.*" The saint. The American saint. Having delivered her message, Nadine slipped from Elspeth's grasp yet again, but instead of falling she slowly rose above Elspeth.

Leaving her with a benediction: *"As-Salaam-Alaikum."* Peace be unto you.

Peace but not a moment to lose. Elspeth's eyes popped open and she knew immediately who the American saint was. She'd met him when she was a little girl. He'd been a friend and a colleague of her father.

Dominic Mancuso had been both a lecturer at the American University and a diplomat at the U.S. embassy in Beirut. Elspeth had made her parents and Mancuso laugh when she'd shared her impression of his appearance.

"He looks like Santa Claus after he went to the beach."

Mancuso had gray hair going white and a matching beard. His Sicilian complexion had absorbed years of the Middle Eastern sun and made his skin tone indistinguishable from many of the local people. Even dressed in Western clothing, he'd often been mistaken for a Lebanese businessman or a visiting Syrian military official traveling in mufti. While his ethnicity might have been mistaken by those who saw him pass by, the fact that he was someone important was lost on no one.

While he smiled at almost everyone he met and spoke fluent and polite Arabic in a soft voice, it was impossible not to think this was a man you would never want to anger. His wrath would make Shaitan —the devil — cower. Unfortunately for Mancuso, his sense of quiet menace was not evident as he and his wife sat among the one hundred and fifty-five other souls attending mass one Sunday in a West Beirut church on the eve of the Lebanese civil war.

Most Christians had fled the area. Those at mass that day might have been thought of as either the stalwart faithful or the suicidally stubborn. In either case, the mob who regarded them as infidels fire-bombed the church and tried their best to kill them all. They missed by one.

Less than one, really, because they cost Dominic Mancuso his left arm below the elbow. He managed to survive, though, and unlike so many of his coreligionists he didn't flee the country. In a move that shocked everyone, he went the other way.

He became a Muslim.

His public explanation was simplicity itself. Would God have allowed a genuine place of worship in his name to be destroyed? Of course not. So Mancuso had better make his change of religious affiliation while he was able. He would also beg for mercy upon the soul of his wife.

Mancuso's transformation met with an even division between wholehearted approval and dark suspicion. Those who regarded him warily were dissuaded from becoming actively hostile when Mancuso resigned from both the university and the embassy and used his "family fortune" to help the poor and the countless others who had suffered the grievous wounds of war as he had. For his kindness and generosity he became known as *"Alqiddis."*

The saint. Some Muslims believed in saints. Others considered the very idea to be idolatry. In the Middle East, nothing was ever simple.

With his linguistic fluency, his native appearance and now also local garb, many people came to forget Mancuso was ever an American. But the ghost of Nadine Najimy hadn't when she appeared in Elspeth's dream. Elspeth called her father.

"Dad, it's me."

"My one and only daughter," he said with a laugh, "whose voice I'd know immediately, even if I was dead and buried."

Her father's joke of after-life awareness sent a chill through Elspeth, coming as it did on the heels of Nadine's appearance in her dream.

Sticking to her reason for calling, though, she asked, "Dad, do you know if Dominic Mancuso is still alive?"

There was a pause long enough to make Elspeth uneasy, before her father finally replied, "What made you think of him?"

She answered truthfully.

"Nadine Najimy?" he asked. "Oh, my. The past never lets us go, does it?"

"Daddy, are you all right?"

"Yes, I'm fine."

"So do you know if Mr. Mancuso is still alive?"

"Let me ask him. He's sitting here in the kitchen with your mother and me."

Booker Productions — Washington, DC

"You're an ambitious broad just like me," Ellie Booker said, "FBI agent or not."

It had taken Ellie only a glance at Abra Benjamin to make that assessment.

"*Special* agent," Abra replied.

The two women were sitting in Ellie's Washington office. She had another in Manhattan. When she wasn't in one of them, she was usually on the Acela going to the other.

Ellie said, "Yeah, I've often wondered about that special part. I've never met or even heard of a regular, ordinary or plain old FBI agent. I think what happened was, one day somebody on the payroll went in to ask for a raise and the boss said, 'Can't spare any money, but how 'bout I make you a *special* agent?' You think that's what happened?"

"You're not funny," Abra said.

"Maybe I'm an acquired taste."

"Or just an asshole."

Ellie sighed. "Are you the best they can do? I wouldn't mind a rookie if, you know, she's 50 percent more human than you."

"You're stuck with me or you can take your own chances."

"Fine. Thanks for stopping by. I'll fly solo."

Byron — Deputy Director DeWitt — had told Abra she'd be a mortal lock to get his job if she found out what happened to Representative Philip Brock on top of bringing in Tyler Busby. It was a testament to Abra's ambition that she couldn't make herself walk out on Ellie Booker.

"See," Ellie said with a grin, "you're hating yourself right now for not telling me to fuck off. Get up and go. I know because there have been times I've felt the same way. You want what you want, and you'll put up with just about anything to get it."

"Maybe *do* anything, too," Abra replied.

Ellie's eyes narrowed as her smile widened. "Oh, I know all about that, too."

Doing her level best to keep her face from showing a trace of emotion, Abra got the uneasy feeling she was dealing with someone who was even more dangerous than she was annoying. It had never occurred to her to think Ellie Booker might have a criminal record, but she decided to check out the possibility as soon as she was out of the woman's presence.

Even if Booker hadn't been caught, she'd all but copped to doing something wrong. Possibly *very* wrong. Maybe Abra could get the lowdown on Phil Brock *and* nail one of the movers and shakers in the modern news biz for unsuspected villainy.

Wouldn't that be a coup? Put her in Byron's seat while it was still warm from his backside. That would be delicious. It might even be the starter's pistol for her run at the director's job.

Ellie Booker saw again that she was right about Abra being an ambitious broad.

She had to admit to herself that Abra could also keep a good poker face when she wanted. Not that a blank expression could keep Ellie from hearing the wheels turn in someone's head. They were always turning in hers. An objective evaluation of the woman sitting across from her noted Abra's good looks as well as her intense drive to succeed. Ellie had no doubt that Abra Benjamin at one time or another had used sex as a tool to achieve professional advantage.

Wouldn't it be fun to expose that on television? *G-Woman Gone Bad.*

Ellie kept herself from laughing at the notion by asking a question. "Since you're going to stay, after all, *Special* Agent, why don't we go talk to this woman Tyler Busby was bunking with? Sometimes people will talk to me when they'd never speak to the likes of you."

The idea of putting Ellie Booker into a cell with Ah-lam had its appeal for Abra.

See if Ellie could best Ah-lam in a fight.

But she decided to go another way.

"You might be right about Mrs. Busby being more willing to talk to you," Abra said. "You must have video facilities here."

Ellie nodded, suspicion now filling her eyes.

"Uh-huh," she said.

"I'll have her brought here. You can see if you're as good as you think you are."

"You're going to have a federal prisoner removed from wherever the hell you're holding her and bring her to a commercial office building for an interview?"

Ellie was more than a little suspicious, and Abra enjoyed putting her off balance.

"Yeah, take it or leave it. Add my protecting you to the package just to make it interesting."

"There'll be lots of your federal colleagues here with her, right?" Ellie asked.

"Platoon strength anyway."

The idea of having so many feds on the premises held zero appeal for Ellie, even though she never brought anything incriminating into the office. But there were *lots* of story ideas on file that her competitors would kill to see. Who knew if the FBI wouldn't pilfer them and leak those gems to the competition just to stick a finger in her eye?

Still, the idea of getting Tyler Busby's honey to break down on camera about how the rich old bastard had plotted to kill the President … hell, she didn't have *any* story idea bigger and better than that. Pretty damn smart of the lady fed to bait her with that deal.

The special agent was good.

Well, so was Ellie Booker.

"Deal," Ellie said.

Cheyenne, Wyoming

After his confrontation with Pete Nash, Tom Kirby stayed home that day, calling his office and pleading a debilitating headache, asking Karen, his office manager, to reschedule his patient load for that day.

"Are you all right, Doctor?" she asked. "I could ask Dr. Kelly to stop by and see you or if you think things are more serious, I could send an ambulance."

"No, no, don't do either of those things. I'll just pop a couple of NSAIDs and get some bed rest. I'll be fine by tomorrow."

"Are you sure?" Karen still sounded uncertain.

"I am, thank you. I'll be fine." He said goodbye and hung up.

Kirby understood his associate's concern. He'd never missed a day of work before. There could be a blizzard, as there often was from early autumn to late spring, and he'd get into his Grand Cherokee and let the four-wheel drive plow through the highest drifts. He was understanding if patients called to cancel appointments in really bad weather, but he held himself to a higher standard.

If somebody needed him, he was damn well going to show up.

He'd felt the same sense of responsibility when he was in school. From kindergarten through med school, he'd never missed a day of class. One of his profs had joked that with his respect for obligation Tom would be first in line on Judgment Day, even if he wasn't going to like the verdict.

That, of course, was an exaggeration, because right now what truly kept him at home was indecision. He couldn't bring himself to do what he knew he ought to do. What he'd said he would do. Call the cops and tell them his old friend, classmate and colleague, Pete Nash, was up to his eyeballs in something criminally wicked.

He wanted to make the call. He was leaning that way almost to the point of falling over. But a lifetime of shared memories, most of them good, pushed back. God have mercy, how could Pete have been so stupid to get involved with whatever was happening to that poor young woman?

There could be no good explanation for it. No way it didn't involve some sort of horrific crime. Pete had hinted at times that he'd gotten involved with characters he'd described as *true patriots*. That term might describe any number of people depending on the speaker's point of view. In Wyoming, though, it was unlikely to be applied to anyone to the left of the local VFW — Veterans of Foreign Wars — post.

Every minute he delayed ate at him. His reluctance might be a contributing cause of that young woman's death. Or to her continuing agony. Right now, she might be —

He could withstand the pressure no longer.

He reached for his phone. It rang just before he picked it up.

Karen calling back? No, the ID screen showed it was Pam.

How the hell could he talk to her? For that matter, what might Pete have told her?

The thought that Pete might well have lied to Pam about what had happened made Tom answer the phone. His voice was hoarse as he said, "Hello."

Pam, by contrast, was borderline panicked. "Tom, what the hell is going on?"

He answered truthfully. "I don't know. I wish to hell I did."

"You don't know? This is crazy."

"What did Pete say?"

Pam didn't answer, the silence lasting long enough for Tom to ask, "You still there, Pam?"

He heard the sounds of sobbing before she came back on, her voice filled with pain. "He didn't say anything to me, but I overheard him talking to someone else. He said he was sorry it had to come to this, but they'd have to get you … *kill* you if it came to that."

"Holy Christ," Tom said.

There was no question now what he had to do. Save himself. Try to get Pam clear of the fallout, too. Go to the … no, not the cops. Whatever was going on had to be bigger than a local matter. Patriot was a word with implications that were national not municipal. He'd have to go to the FBI.

"Tom, are you still there?" Pam asked.

She was trying to choke back her tears, rebalance her emotions if not her world.

"I'm here. How did you know to call me at home?"

"I tried your office. Karen told me you stayed home sick. I knew that wasn't right because you don't go out running first thing when you're sick. I didn't let on, but I had to find you. So I called the only other number I had. Tom, please tell me, why would Pete talk about killing you or anyone else? I feel like I'm cracking up."

Tom told her about Lewis Addison Armistead and the photo he had with him.

"That's disgusting."

"Pete sent the man to me, and when I confronted him about it this morning, he begged me not to go to the police about it."

"Oh, my God. What's he involved in?"

"I don't know. I'm going to talk to the FBI."

"The FBI? You think it's *that* bad?"

"I do … Do you want to come with me?"

"Wait, wait just a minute."

He heard the phone being put down. In that instant, Tom had a sinking feeling in his gut. Was Pam setting him up? Getting him to delay his departure while Pete and his friends came for him?

The moment before he was about to end the call and run Pam came back on the line and said, "I found it, I got it."

"What?"

"That awful picture you told me about. Pete had it in a manila envelope in his home office, where he hides things when he's trying to be sneaky. He doesn't know I know about it."

"Why would he have the photo?" Tom asked. "I gave it back to Armistead."

They both paused to think, and Tom came up with the answer first.

"I was no help to Pete, so he's looking for another medical friend to involve."

Pam moaned. "Oh, my God. What should I do?"

Tom cut to the quick. "Don't let whatever this is taint you."

"I should go to the FBI with you? Turn in my own husband?"

"I'll come right over and pick you up," Tom said.

"I don't know if I can do this."

"Pam, you know something bad is going on now. You either do the right thing or you become a part of it. I'm sorry."

"Me, too. Only a lot more than you."

Ten minutes later they were pulling up at the FBI office on Airport Parkway.

J. Edgar Hoover Building — Washington, DC

Hope my cooperation will let me skate if I get arrested for protesting global warming or something. — Ben Nolan.

Attached to the note was a link to a cloud server where Ben stored his photographic images. Caitie McGill's friend had sent it to the deputy director. A smiley-face emoticon was appended to the desire for relief from future legal jeopardy.

Also noted was the fact that 3,485 distinct head shots were available for the FBI's review.

That and the fact that each picture was copyrighted.

DeWitt grinned. He liked people who had a sense of humor.

He said to himself, "We get any worthwhile return from your pictures, kid, I'll let you pie the faces of the entire on-air roster of Satellite News America and get a walk."

SNAM, with its persistent ultra-conservative bias, had been giving Jean Morrissey a heavier than usual torrent of grief lately. DeWitt had already wondered if he could get away with pie-ing those pinheads himself.

He forwarded Ben's link to the techies who'd run comparisons first against the Bureau's database of criminal mugs and thugs. If no matches could be found there, comparisons to state photo records would be surreptitiously run once more. DeWitt had briefly thought it might be more expedient to feed the link to the omnivorous maw of the NSA and see if they could find any matches, but those people had so much data on everyone and everything that other federal agencies took a perverse pleasure in withholding information from them.

Counterproductive though that might be.

Ah, government. DeWitt couldn't say goodbye fast enough.

Then again, sometimes there were moments that satisfied you right down to your soul. Or the core of your rational mind, if you preferred a humanist take on existence. In either case, the computer search of FBI photo database turned up, in a pleasantly short time, four facial matches out of the 3,485 possibilities available.

That was a .0011% positive return but it was more than enough to give the FBI a running start on finding out who might have kidnapped Special Agent Carrie Ramsey.

The quartet of Turner Bidwell, Kyle Nance, Dolph Finster and Axel Bing, between them, had records for crimes including manslaughter, arson, assault with a deadly weapon and false imprisonment. That last offense was defined as: *restraint of a person in a bounded area without justification or consent.* Making it an element of holding someone who'd been kidnapped. The first offense, manslaughter, meant: *killing a human being without malice aforethought or in a circumstances not amounting to murder.*

Killing a human being was the important part to DeWitt. Whether impulse, reflex or recklessness was the impetus, taking a life had to leave a mark on the perpetrator's psyche. With some people the response could well be: *I'll never let anything like that happen again.* With others the feedback might be: *Now, that wasn't so bad.*

You threw that false imprisonment into the stew of the four felons' crimes, though, and a benign response to taking a life would be unlikely. The arsonist might come in handy for the disposal of the remains. If these four had their hands on Carrie Ramsey, the FBI would have to move fast to make sure her life wasn't the next to be taken — assuming that she wasn't already dead.

Before DeWitt could make his first move, his phone rang.

Jim McGill was calling. "Sorry to intrude, but I've got something for you that needs to go into your thinking about Special Agent Ramsey's kidnapping."

McGill, in DeWitt's experience, hadn't been one to throw around imperatives, husband of the President or not. He was also a pretty smart ex-cop. So the deputy director chose to take the directive as being helpful.

"What's that?" DeWitt asked.

"Looking back at the list of people who wish me ill, two names top the list: Harlan Fisk and Auric Ludwig."

"The militia nut and the gun lobby cynic."

DeWitt had long since made a study of McGill's exploits.

"Right. Both of them have reason to hurt me, but Fisk's estrangement from his daughter makes him my top choice. You remember her?"

"Elvie," DeWitt said. "I remember her well. I questioned her. I handed her the phone to speak to her father. He screwed himself out of any Dad-of-the-Year prize with that call."

McGill asked, "How many guys like that ever take responsibility for anything bad?"

"We're waiting for the first one, as far as I know."

"Do you know where Elvie's being held?"

"I do. You'd like to talk with her?"

"Yes, right away."

"Will do. We've made a bit of other progress as well."

He told McGill about the four IDs culled from Ben Nolan's photos.

"Do you think Caitie might remember seeing them if she gets a look?" DeWitt asked.

"I'll loop her in and we can talk to her when you bring Elvie to town."

"Maybe ..." DeWitt bit his tongue.

"What?" McGill asked.

"Well, do you think it would be helpful if Caitie spoke with

Elvie if Elvie's reluctant to speak to you or me?"

McGill took a beat and then replied, "I'll ask Caitie if she'd like to help with that."

Without saying so, they both knew she would.

The White House — Washington, DC

Despite the Savile Row suit he was wearing, Dominic Mancuso looked more like a prophet to Elspeth Kendry than a poobah from either the State Department or K Street. His hair was a nimbus of white hovering around gleaming brown eyes and a face of burnt umber. He kissed both her cheeks and beamed at her as if he'd just seen the gates of heaven open at his approach.

"Elspeth: so beautiful as a child and now even more so as a woman."

The special agent who'd accompanied Dominic to Elspeth's White House office knew better than to laugh or even grin when he saw the boss blush. He simply slipped away without a sound, closing the door behind him. Not that the good manners required for professional survival would keep him from sharing a laugh with the rest of the troops, Elspeth knew.

She didn't have the time to worry about that. Or for the usual amenities of offering food and drink that a guest from the Middle East might expect before they got down to business. She gestured Dominic to a guest chair and took the seat behind her desk.

She politely expressed her regret about the loss of Aunt Luisa all those years ago. There was no blood relationship between the Kendrys and the Mancusos, but the affection between them was familial in nature.

Dominic placed his remaining hand over his heart, closed his eyes and bowed his head.

As if the name of an angel had just been mentioned.

Both Christians and Muslims believed in angels.

When Dominic opened his eyes, he said, "Your father told me about the dream you had. Seeing your friend, hearing her mention the title that was far too generously bestowed upon me. Did your dream comfort you?"

Elspeth nodded. "It did. Very much."

"I understand completely. Luisa visits my dreams regularly. The first time I saw her that way, I was delighted. I thought she'd come to me because I was going to leave this life and rejoin her. When I woke up I was bitterly disappointed to be alive."

Looking at him across the breadth of her desk, Elspeth realized just how old Dominic was. He had to be well into his nineties. The glow in his eyes didn't come from vitality; it came from serenity. His soul was at peace and his body would soon take its rest.

"What did you do after that, Uncle Dom? After you saw Aunt Luisa."

He smiled with a brilliance that made Elspeth think maybe he had a bit more time after all.

"I made sure to take as many naps as I could," he said with a laugh. "Luisa came back to me. Not every time I closed my eyes or even as often as I wanted. But enough to sustain me. More than enough to assure me that the last time I see her in my sleep she will take the one hand I have left and off we'll go."

He gave Elspeth a wink. "Or, who knows, maybe she'll bring a replacement hand for the one I lost."

Elspeth smiled, her heart warmed by the old man's story and glad none of her people could see her with tears in her eyes.

"But you want to hear about more than that, don't you?" Dom asked.

Elspeth blotted her eyes with a tissue and nodded.

Dominic told her his story, as much as he could without giving away the store.

Even so, her eyes were wide by the time he finished. "You were a *spy?*"

With a small smile of satisfaction, he nodded. "Bureau of Intelligence and Research."

"Okay, that's State Department, but what about your teaching positions?"

"Covers, fairly effective ones at the time."

"And your ... sainthood?"

"The best cover any spy could hope for."

"Your piety and generosity were all an act?" Elspeth asked.

"Only at the start, when hate and the desire for vengeance motivated me. But you play a part long enough, the strangest thing happens. You *become* the person you're pretending to be."

"So are you a Christian or a Muslim?"

"Both. I practice elements of each faith. Both agree there is but one God. Beyond that, what matters? It's just a difference of customs and details. I've talked about it with Luisa. She says I won't have to worry about how things turn out for me. On balance, I won't be found wanting."

"I can't imagine hearing better news than that," Elspeth said.

Dominic chuckled. "Especially at my age. With that in mind, why don't we get to why you're really so glad to see me after all this time?"

Elspeth told him about the kidnapping of Special Agent Ramsey.

"What I need to know is whether the bad guys are foreign or domestic," she said. "If they're jihadis, we won't have to waste time looking at domestic terrorists. If the kidnappers are locals, we don't have to look for foreign sleeper agents."

Dominic understood the logic, but asked, "What if it's a collaboration?"

Elspeth reflexively started to object, but stopped herself. "That seems so unlikely, but I just remembered one time hearing Mr. McGill speculating on that possibility."

Dominic smiled and bobbed his head. "I'd be happy to meet him. I've heard stories. Very interesting fellow. He saw that both foreign and domestic terrorists want the same thing: to bring down the federal government. Once that's achieved, each side can take on the other. Both sides are sure they won't have to put up much of a fight to emerge victorious."

"Both sides are crazy, if that's what they think," Elspeth said.

Then she asked the big question, "Uncle Dom, do you know of any jihadi group aiding and abetting local crazies. People who'd think that kidnapping a teenage girl could advance their cause?"

Dominic Mancuso nodded. "People tend to speak freely in front of a saint, especially when they want their own sense of righteousness validated."

"Can you tell me who they are or do I have to get the President's go ahead?"

"I spoke with the President on the drive over here. She called me. A delightful woman. I hope I have the chance to meet her, too. She told me to feel free to speak with you on this matter. So, here, my dear Elspeth, is everything I have on what you want to know."

Dominic began his recitation. Elspeth made an audio recording and took handwritten notes.

When Dominic finished, she nodded her head and said, "This could help, a lot. But you can't go back to Lebanon now. Somebody will put it together how we got the information."

"Of course they will but I am, as of this minute, officially retired. My time overseas has ended. My time everywhere else isn't far behind."

Elspeth came around her desk and took Dominic's hand in hers.

"Are you going to miss playing the person you became?"

"I think so, but it had to be. I developed a very bad habit for a spy."

"What's that?" Elspeth asked.

The Saint grinned. "According to what I was told, I began to talk in my sleep."

The White House — Washington, DC

McGill thought it would be only fair to speak with Carolyn before he talked to Caitie, and get his ex's take on the situation. He explained how the investigation was making progress and how Caitie might help advance the cause.

"So you want to bring her to Washington?" she asked.

"Yes."

"In a private airplane?"

"Air Force executive aircraft. Military pilots and security personnel aboard."

Carolyn surprised McGill with a chuckle. "Fighter jets escort?"

McGill laughed, too. "I think that might be arranged, if it would make you feel better."

"Are you going to miss all this, Jim?"

"The perks? I have to admit that despite my best efforts I have become a bit spoiled. Nobody in the world has the resources at her fingertips that a President does. I only get the overflow and it's mind-boggling. But the demands that come with the job are more than I could ever bear. I'll be clicking my heels when I see Patti pass the torch on Inauguration Day."

"I'll be happy for the two of you, too. And I appreciate your consideration, speaking to me first about Caitie."

"You're our kids' mom. Nobody is more important to them than you."

"Yeah, sure."

"Don't ever doubt it, Carolyn. How are the offspring doing?"

"Well, the last I saw, Abbie was showing Ken and Caitie the finer points of knife-fighting she learned at Georgetown. Firearms might not be for them, but paring someone into itty-bitty pieces, that'd be cool. I never thought I'd have raised such a bloodthirsty brood."

"You can blame me," McGill said. "I'd like to see them practice. I might learn something new."

"Great. Now, *I'll* be the only one to bring a gun to a knife fight."

"Carolyn, just between you and me —"

"Jim, if you're going to tell me how to use a knife to fight a gunman, let's save that for another time."

He was going to tell her exactly that, and these days maybe Abbie could tell her, too.

Instead, they each said goodbye and McGill waited for Caitie to pick up the phone.

"Hey, Dad, Mom says you want me to come to DC."

A note of excitement rippled through his youngest's voice.

"If you can tear yourself away from your edged-weapon training."

"Yeah, sure. It's fun, but I never would have thought Abbie'd be the one to show me."

"Me either."

"Abbie's good, though. Ken is, too. But the practicing lacks verisimilitude when the knives have rubber blades."

Verisimilitude, McGill thought. There was no getting away from the cinematic vocabulary.

He said, "Yeah, well, there are two reasons for rubber blades: One is so you don't die or dismember yourself or your training partner; the other is so you don't give any concerned adult a fatal heart attack."

"Right. I'll remember that."

While writing her next screenplay, no doubt.

"Getting back on subject," he said, "do you think you'd be helpful speaking to a young woman about your own age? In case she won't talk to any of us old fogies, I mean."

"What do you know about her?" Caitie asked.

"Her father is an incarcerated right-wing paramilitary loon who pimped her out to a child-molesting out-of-work rocket scientist, and then wouldn't come to her aid when it would mean giving himself up to the FBI."

Caitie thought about that for a moment. "Yeah, I think I can help, if you need me."

"Humor me a little here. Why do you think you can help?"

"Because her father sounds like the kind of jerk-parent who's the exact opposite of you and Mom. Patti and Lars, too."

"Tell your mother that. It will make her feel good."

"Okay. What I mean is, knowing you, I have a pretty good idea of what she wishes she had. I'll play to her motivation."

McGill had to smile. "You're going to make a truly fine film director someday, kiddo."

A bright note entered Caitie's voice. "You really think so?"

"Absolutely, unless you sell out and go commercial."

Caitie blew a raspberry McGill's way.

They laughed and made a plan. McGill would send a plane to Rochester as soon as possible. Celsus would take Caitie to the airport and McGill would meet her at Joint Base Andrews in suburban Maryland.

"I'll look just like you remember me," Caitie said. "Only my hair is shorter."

That was when it hit McGill. At some point, if things broke a certain way, his daughter wanted to show Carrie Ramsey's kidnappers that they'd fucked up and grabbed the wrong person. And then what?

She'd cut their hearts out?

Wouldn't that be filmic? To use the lingo of the art form.

Sioux Falls, South Dakota

Special Agent Carrie Ramsey opened her eyes and looked around. She was in a new small blank-walled room. She could tell because this one had a tinge of pink to its gray paint. A soft whoosh of heated air came from a vent in the wall opposite the cot on which she lay. A steel door stood at the far end of that wall, wedged tight into its frame.

Not that she could even get that far because she was chained to the bed.

No, wait a minute.

Turned out she wasn't restrained. Neither her wrists nor her ankles were shackled. That was a heartening first. Suspicious, too. Was somebody testing her, watching to see how she'd react to her increased freedom of movement? Or had they mistakenly assumed she'd abandoned all hope? If so, she had to encourage the idea until it was time to make a move.

She closed her eyes and drifted back into sleep, wondering

why she was so tired all the time. Just as the answer was about to come to her she lost consciousness. But it was right there when she woke up sometime later feeling a bit less sluggish. They were gassing her, that was it. Spiking her air supply with an inhalant that put her under. The situation had been covered in her training. She couldn't remember the countermove, though, if there was one.

She had the feeling that idea — that she was being gassed — had already occurred to her, at least once and maybe more. But who could tell for sure when your mind was muddled?

Her thoughts drifted back to her undergraduate days, studying criminal justice. She recalled reading about an anesthesiology resident in Phoenix who drugged the drinks of young women he met in bars. He'd take them home, bind them, wait for them to wake up and sedate them again with Desflurane and Sevoflurane: anesthesia gasses.

He didn't take sexual advantage of them; that wasn't what he had in mind at all. After he had been caught, he claimed he was simply trying to further his education. That and make sure he'd never lose his medical license nor be driven out of business by astronomical malpractice insurance premiums. To further his goals, he'd subjected the captive women to surgical stimuli: small incisions in inconspicuous places. See if they felt any pain at given levels of anesthesia. Check the efficacy of his work.

He kept meticulous records — a big part of his undoing.

At his trial for kidnapping and capital murder, the defendant admitted he'd subjected his victims to unnecessary surgery — inadvertently causing the deaths of three of them — but only because his professors had instructed him that nobody really knew how anesthesia worked once it reached the brain. How it induced unconsciousness, lack of sensation and the inability to see, hear or feel anything was a mystery. Moreover, knowing just how much anesthesia to provide at any given point in a procedure, he was informed, was as much an art as a science.

"An *art*," the defendant exclaimed incredulously. "Who the hell's going to insure an artist? I had to protect myself. I had to have real-world practice."

It didn't help his case that he'd characterized his victims as people who wouldn't be missed. The jury decided neither would he. The defendant was sentenced to death. Arizona, ironically, administered capital punishment by using a gas chamber. The executioner got his dosing right. Artfully, a wag in the viewing gallery said.

That story passed quickly through Carrie's mind. At least, she thought so. But how could she know really? She doubted that the assholes gassing her had ever gone to medical school. The next time they put her down might be the last time. Hell, the effects could be cumulative. She might live, all right, as a vegetable.

Before any more morbid thoughts could register, the steel door opened and a tall, overweight SOB stepped inside, bringing a steel chair with him. He sat wrong way around with his meaty forearms resting on the back of the chair. The guy's head was shaved and he had scars on both cheeks and through his right eyebrow.

In a deep but mellow voice he told Carrie, "You haven't been eating. You're losing weight, and you didn't have all that much to start."

Mr. Basso Profundo. Was he the boss, Carrie wondered.

She was about to snap out a reply, but she caught herself and wondered …

What would Caitie McGill say to this golem? Something snotty and elitist? Probably.

Carrie said, "Bring in a new chef and we'll see."

Triple XL liked that. The fat on his face rearranged its wrinkles into a grin.

"I heard you were a spitfire."

"You have no idea."

Carrie thought that line worked for both her and Caitie.

"Well, we do have some notion. You took out one of our boys, someone we considered real able-bodied, and you did it with your teeth. We're wondering if he's still alive."

"Alive and talking?"

The big man chuckled, a surprisingly pleasant sound coming from such an ugly mug.

But Carrie saw a new light in his eyes like he'd just scored a point with her. Her head was still fuzzy but she soon realized her question sounded like something a cop might ask. But then Caitie McGill had grown up in a cop's house.

So she went with, "You think my dad's not going to find you? You and all your half-ass friends. He will, and we'll see if you're all fat and happy then."

"Won't do you any good, calling me names. I've heard 'em all. Though I hear you can give 'em to me in French. Well, we're going to see about that. I've got a friend coming in from Quebec. We'll see how much French you know. And don't tell me to go screw myself. I already had that one translated, thank you."

Carrie blinked. Foggy-headed or not, she felt her guts chill. Any French speaker would find her out in a heartbeat. She had only one way to go, make the bastard doubt himself.

She leaned forward, pushing her face at him.

"Wait a minute. Who the hell do you think I am?"

He looked at her closely. "We were aiming for Caitlin McGill, and you sure do look like her, but there's this one little problem?"

"Your arms are too short to reach your dick? Gotta have someone help you pee?"

That one got to him. He started to rise from the chair, quickly and with little effort, surprising Carrie with his agility. But then he settled back onto the chair. Shook a fat finger at her.

"Almost got me there," he said. "Never heard that one before. Maybe you are little Miss Hellraiser."

Carrie smirked as she thought Caitie might.

The big man said, "*Maybe* you are and maybe you're not. See there's this one little problem. We had people watching Abigail McGill out there in Washington, DC, and you know what?"

The chill in Carrie's stomach turned frigid.

She knew what had to be coming but didn't say a word.

Big and ugly leaned forward again.

"Our people out in Washington didn't see just one Abbie McGill, they saw two. How about that? Now, we didn't get that word until we'd already taken possession of you. Ever since, we've had to wonder: Are there two Caitie McGills and did we get the right one?"

The huge man stood, picked up the chair in one hand.

"You need to eat. We won't put anything in your food."

"How about the air? You going to stop poisoning that? My head's starting to hurt."

That brought a look of genuine concern to the big man's face. Whatever his plan for her was, it wouldn't do to lose her too soon. "We'll cut that out, too. You figured that out all by yourself, did you? That's interesting."

Carrie did her best to imitate a teenaged eye-roll.

"What the hell else could it be? I feel like my head's filled with gauze and my throat's dry."

The man offered what appeared to be a genuine smile.

"They said you were smart. So what do you want to eat? I'll have some carryout sent 'round, whatever you want. Nothing in it worse than MSG."

If the guy thought he was going to ingratiate himself ... no, shit, he was just testing her. Seeing if she asked for something Caitie McGill might order. They may have seen the kid eat for all she knew. Well, so had Carrie.

She said, "Shrimp Pad Thai. Stir-fried thin rice noodles with bean sprouts, egg, green onion and crushed peanuts in a sweet and sour tamarind sauce. Iced green tea to drink. You can keep the fortune cookie." The last snotty bit was to stay in character.

Her dinner order might be had in minutes in any big city.

If she was in some Podunk town, though, or maybe even out in the woods, Pad Thai could be an impossible reach. Failure to provide the dinner she'd requested might give her some bearings on her location.

But Basso Profundo just nodded and said, "Sounds good. Think I'll have some, too."

"No MSG," Carrie told him. The fat fucker.

Booker Productions — Washington, DC

Shortly before Ah-lam arrived in handcuffs and leg-irons at Ellie Booker's office to audition for her debut on big-time American TV, Special Agent Abra Benjamin told Ellie the story of her confrontation with the Asian woman in Montevideo.

Ellie listened with rapt attention, not interrupting.

It played better that way; a camera was rolling.

After Abra had finished her story, Ellie said, "Come on, Special Agent Benjamin, you swatted a baby in mid-air so you could head-butt the kid's mom?"

"Exactly. I can't say I consciously knew the infant's father, Tyler Busby, would catch him, but that's what happened. I trusted my instincts, knowing that they often operate efficiently on a level my conscious mind can't discern. Everything worked out for the best: The child was uninjured and two lawbreakers were taken into custody."

Ellie's unspoken takeaway was that Benjamin was both ruthless and lucky, a formidable combination. She'd have to watch herself around this woman. Not that she would ever be hesitant when it came to asking pointed questions.

"Was there ever a time your instincts failed you, Special Agent Benjamin?"

"Not so far." Abra sure as hell wasn't going to get into her relationship with Byron DeWitt. How she'd erroneously thought he'd remain her lover even after she gave up the child they'd conceived. That had been the worst mistake of her life, losing him to Jean Morrissey.

Christ, Byron was anything but a ruthless careerist. His greatest ambition was to catch a perfect wave while emptying his mind of all earthly concerns. Zen surfing. And now the guileless SOB was going to marry the woman who was likely to become the next President.

Where the hell was the fairness in that?

"You think of something to regret after all?" Ellie asked, noticing a shadow of rue in Abra's eyes.

"Only that a woman can't have it all."

"For instance?"

"Well, it's not as easy as it used to be, but some men can still pursue their career goals and count on a woman to maintain a home-life for them. How many women can find a man to play that role for them?"

Domesticity interested Ellie about as much a playing badminton did. She was about to cue her videographer to stop recording when she heard a cluster of outsized men pour into her outer office. She could tell from their tromping footfalls they were many in number and shopped at the big and tall store.

One of them called out, "U.S. marshals with a prisoner for Special Agent Benjamin."

Ellie's receptionist might have provided the same notification with far less theatricality. The showy way was fine with Ellie. Her cameraman had jumped up instinctively and captured the better part of the marshals' entrance with a relatively small Asian woman in an orange prison jumpsuit in their midst doing her best to look tough.

"Right this way, guys," Ellie told the troops.

Abra showed her badge. "I'm Benjamin. Bring her in."

She nodded to an empty chair three feet to her left.

Two marshals deposited the prisoner as directed and stood on either side of her.

Ellie thought that was a shame. Round two of the FBI agent versus the dragon lady from China would have made for riveting television. Still, the two marshals were photogenic and their presence connoted the woman as being a dangerous character.

Adding to that impression, Benjamin told Ah-lam, "You've already been informed of your rights under the Constitution of the United States. Those rights remain in effect. You're here now to see if you would like to waive those rights and tell your story about your relationship with Tyler Busby."

Ah-lam presented a grim face, not to Benjamin but to the video camera, shooting over Ellie's shoulder to give a storyteller's point of view. "I cannot be forced to testify against my husband in this country. He told me that."

"Absolutely true," Benjamin said. "If he really was your husband. We've found the captain of Mr. Busby's yacht, *The Wastrel,* the man who performed your so-called wedding ceremony. He said he was only humoring his boss by reading a script downloaded from the Internet. He said he has neither the religious nor the civil credentials to marry anyone. The Department of Justice will contest the validity of your wedding. If you refuse to cooperate with the FBI, you'll be charged with obstruction of justice as well as assaulting a federal officer: me. You could be looking at 30 years in prison for those charges alone. If you're charged with being an accessory after the fact to Mr. Busby's crimes, you could be looking at life in prison at the least and possibly a sentence of death."

Ah-lam thought the FBI was trying to trick her. The woman she'd fought with in Uruguay talked of imprisoning her for many years. The FBI man who talked with her spoke of the possibility of Ah-lam going free with a large sum of money in her pocket. But he'd wanted her to betray the pinnacle of power in China. That would mean death, not immediately perhaps but inevitably. Ah-lam had said she must consider her choices.

From what she'd learned of life, Ah-lam considered the man to be the woman's superior.

Then again, in this country a woman was the President.

Ellie Booker kept quiet and maintained a poker face, but she thought Abra Benjamin was something else. No raised voice, red face or clenched fists for her. Just a simple recitation of horrifying facts. We can lock you up or even kill you, and we will do one of those things if you don't play it smart and cooperate with us. Ellie had no doubt the special agent could make good on her threats.

Ah-lam, as ever, stubbornly pursued her self-interest.

"What do I get if I help you?" she asked, hoping for a better offer than the last one.

"You'll get the U.S. attorney's statement to the judge that you're a cooperating witness and the recommendation that your prison sentence be far more lenient that it would otherwise be."

"I must have more. I have already been offered freedom and money."

That got Ellie's attention; Abra's, too. The special agent's composure slipped, just a bit and only for the blink of an eye. But the camera never blinked.

Abra said. "I don't believe anyone made you such an offer."

Ah-lam produced an ice-cold smile. "All I had to give up was Jonathan."

Ellie wanted to clarify that for the home-viewing audience. "You were asked to give up your son?"

"I was *told* I would never get him back."

That rang true to Abra, but she knew she had to regain control of the situation quickly.

"If you were given such a generous offer, why are you still in custody?" she asked.

Not wanting to speak the truth in front of a television camera, knowing that to do so would be to sign her own death warrant, Ah-lam responded in Mandarin.

No one present spoke the language, but Ellie would later learn that Ah-lam had told the special agent, "Your mother services the fleet from her knees."

At that moment, she said, "I'm Ellie Booker. Would you mind answering some questions for me?"

"You are FBI, too?"

Ellie shook her head. "I'm a TV producer and a journalist."

Abra held up a hand and looked at Ah-lam.

"Anything you tell Ms. Booker can be used against you in court. If you choose to speak to her, you do so at your own legal risk. Do you understand?"

"Who brought me here, you or her?" Ah-lam asked Abra.

"I did. Ms. Booker thought you might speak to her if you wouldn't speak to me. But what I just said stands: Anything you say to her may be used against you."

After holding Abra's gaze for several seconds, Ah-lam turned to Ellie.

"What do you want to know?"

Ellie got straight to the point. "Was Tyler Busby part of a conspiracy to kill President Patricia Grant — and was Congressman Philip Brock also part of that conspiracy?"

Ah-lam said, "I don't know this Brock person. My husband never spoke of him to me."

Ellie said, "All right, returning to your husband, Tyler Busby: Did he plot to kill the President of the United States?"

Ah-lam felt both fear and anger make her head throb. She might have gone mad. Instead, she felt a sudden stillness: She realized she was already as good as dead. Her brother's unexpected appearance in Uruguay was proof that Chinese agents were watching her. They'd know by now that the Americans had her in their grasp.

The Politburo would assume as a matter of course that she'd already yielded whatever she knew about Donald Yang to serve her own interests. Beijing would never allow *him* to fall into American hands. He knew far more about their plans than she did.

The irony was, she didn't know whether Yang and the Politburo had anything to do with the plot to kill the American President. It might be possible, but she'd never heard of it. All she knew was Yang wanted her husband dead. For what reason, though, she couldn't say.

She told Ellie, "I never heard my husband speak of anyone named Brock." Turning to Abra she added, "We should speak privately."

Ah-lam's tone had lost all its combativeness.

Abra didn't buy the mood change, but she wanted to find out what kind of game Ah-lam was playing now. Might be something that shouldn't be televised. She told the marshals, "Let's get her over to the Hoover Building, guys,"

Stunned, Ellie got to her feet. "What, that's it? This is bullshit."

Abra grinned. "That's showbiz, sweetheart. And remember what you said: You don't want any protection from me."

E Street — Washington, DC

Abra sat in the back seat of the government Chevy Suburban with Ah-lam and a marshal. The vehicle had been stuck in traffic for a couple minutes. There was construction on the street, narrowing the thoroughfare by a lane, and a fire truck had stopped in the intersection a half-block ahead. The gridlock was aggravating for the average motorist. For the marshals transporting a high-value prisoner, it started to fray nerves.

The driver of the SUV holding Ah-lam and Abra radioed to the lead vehicle in the three-car caravan to have a marshal hoof it to the corner and find out what the delay was. "Everybody else," he said, "keep a tight watch on the situation. It's probably nothing, but let's not count on it."

Abra told Ah-lam, "Don't get your hopes up. You're not going anywhere."

Ah-lam laughed.

"You think I'm joking?" Abra asked.

Ah-lam ignored Abra's hostile attitude and said, "I am ready to give you Tyler."

"Why?"

"It is what I already told the blonde man with Mao in his office."

Abra blinked. "The deputy director?"

"Yes."

Abra wondered why the hell Byron hadn't told her that he'd already interviewed the bitch. Jesus. He'd been complaining for some time about burning out. Maybe he really was losing it.

"What else did you say?"

"He wanted to know if China took part in the assassination plan. I said I needed time to think, and then you summoned me."

Abra ground her teeth. Goddamnit, Byron, she thought. Are you trying to cut me out here?

Ah-lam said, "I see now I have only one chance to be free."

"And what's that?"

"To become a target."

"What?"

"I don't know if Donald Yang or China was involved in the assassination plot, but if I walk out of your prison and someone tries to kill me ..."

Abra understood immediately. "It would be because Yang was involved, maybe China, too. They couldn't take any chance that you might know something, even inadvertently."

Ah-lam nodded.

"Why would you do that, risk being killed?" Abra asked.

"Better to die quickly than little by little."

The marshal in the back seat with the two women nodded.

He could empathize with that point of view.

"So if China kills you," Abra said, "that's an implicit admission of their guilt."

"Yes."

The marshal nodded his agreement.

"We'll have to talk to the deputy director about all this," Abra said.

That was when traffic began to move and Abra's phone rang.

Speak of the devil, she thought. Byron was calling.

J. Edgar Hoover Building — Washington, DC

Byron DeWitt thought his fiancée, Vice President Jean Morrissey, was going to be sorely disappointed in him if he died before he could marry her. His state of exhaustion, though, might well be terminal. His demise would become the stuff of legend. Not the heroic kind. The sort where people scratched their heads in wonder and laughed without a trace of humor.

Thinking if not saying, "The putz worked himself to death at his desk. Can you believe it?"

Jean would hardly be able to grasp the turn of events, losing her chance to be elected President, being a single woman, because of his misplaced sense of duty. Hell, if he would forsake his goal of returning to California to teach, surf and play private eye, he could goof off all day at the FBI and Jean would still make him the director. She might even buy him a new Warhol serigraph to put up on his wall next to Chairman Mao.

She'd no doubt feel that'd be a small price to pay for four years in the Oval Office and a place in the history books. He felt sure Jean would become almost as historically significant a figure as Patricia Grant. True, Patti Grant was the first female President of the U.S.A., but he had the feeling Jean would be a real ass-kicking segue. Accomplish a big thing or two for the betterment of the country.

He couldn't think of any examples of what her achievements might be at the moment, but maybe if he could make it over to his office couch, a shameless knockoff of the one James J. McGill had in the White House, he could lapse into a coma for a day or two — maybe a week — and snap out of it to find his sweetheart at his bedside.

They'd call in the hospital chaplain and get married right there.

Lock up the women's vote with a photo of a bedside kiss from the bride.

Then it wouldn't matter if he croaked.

DeWitt's phone rang and he thought maybe it was the emergency room calling to ask if he'd like to skip the nap and head right over. He'd suggest they send an ambulance. He didn't think he should drive at the moment. At his rank, he could have had a driver, but man-of-the-people that he was, he'd turned down that perk.

Dummy.

Turned out he didn't have to worry about going anywhere. It wasn't the hospital calling. Wyoming was. For a moment, DeWitt found it amusing that the Cowboy State had telephones. Ruined his image of the rugged Westerner to think of a tough *hombre* on horseback whipping out his cell-phone instead of a six-shooter.

The mental picture made DeWitt giggle.

"Sir?" a male voice in his ear said.

"Yes, who is this?"

"SAC Caleb Hickok in the Cheyenne, Wyoming office."

"Great name."

"Pardon me."

"Great name for a cowboy, Hickok."

"I'm from Peabody, Massachusetts, sir."

"But you're working in Wyoming?"

"Yes, sir."

"Hold on a minute. I'm going to record this call so I can keep everything straight." DeWitt hoped he pushed the right button on his phone. There were so *many* of them. It almost made him dizzy. "Okay, go ahead."

"Sir, I can't say for sure, but we might have a possible lead on the disappearance of Secret Service Special Agent Ramsey."

A pulse of adrenaline cleared DeWitt's head and made it feel like someone had driven a spike through it, too. He gritted his teeth and pushed the pain as far aside as he could.

"What kind of lead?" he asked.

SAC Hickok told him of a doctor named Kirby and a former nurse named Nash who'd walked into the Cheyenne office with a story. DeWitt did his best to focus on and retain the details of Hickok's narrative. It was hard as hell, though. His head was killing him.

Still, he felt fairly sure he had the gist of it. A man with a photo had approached Dr. Kirby asking him to determine a female's age by the appearance of her genitalia. Mrs. Nash was the wife of another doctor who had directed the information seeker to see Kirby.

Dr. Nash had contacts with right-wing extremist groups.

Hickok said, "Sir, if a group wanting to harm any of the President's step-children had been surveilling them and —"

"They saw one of the children and a decoy," DeWitt said, "they'd want to know for sure who they'd kidnapped."

He was glad he could still draw an inference.

"Yes, sir."

"You're right, Hickok, this could be a break. Keep Dr. Kirby and Mrs. Nash in protective custody. Bring Dr. Nash in for questioning. If he's already on the run, put out an all-points bulletin on him. We want to get our hands on him as soon as possible."

"And if the Secret Service wants to take custody of him, sir?"

"He's ours until we hear otherwise from above, but the Secret Service can participate in any interrogation."

"Should we share any details we learn about Dr. Nash? The Secret Service might use that information to pursue their own search."

"We'll work that out if we get that far."

"Yes, sir."

An unnerving thought occurred to DeWitt. "SAC Hickok, if you're able to arrest Dr. Nash, do you have a secure facility out there that can resist an attack by a hostile force?"

After a momentary pause, Hickok asked with a note of disbelief, "Are you thinking someone might attempt a jailbreak, sir?"

"Can't be too careful," DeWitt said. "You're not in Peabody anymore."

The SAC laughed. "That's for sure. We'll be ready for anything, sir."

DeWitt said goodbye and put his phone down, charged up from the idea that they might be a step closer to finding Caroline Ramsey. God, bringing her home safely would be a great way to leave the job. His head was almost clear now, and if it didn't hurt so much he would have felt two-thirds human again.

The thought occurred that he should get in touch with Abra. Let her carry the load for a while and maybe he could get 24 hours of solid sleep. She was angling for the job anyway. Let her see what she was in for. He picked up his phone and tapped in her number.

No sooner had he done so than something inside Byron DeWitt's head exploded and he felt as if the top of his skull had flown off.

"Mr. Deputy Director? Byron, are you there?"

He wasn't where he had been a moment ago. He'd fallen out of his chair. The phone was no longer in his hand but lay on the floor a foot from his head.

In a thick, clumsy voice, he mumbled, "Abra … I think I'm dying."

Walter Reed National Military Medical Center
Bethesda, Maryland

The gathering in a secure conference room at the hospital complex where the Presidents of the U.S. went for their annual physical examinations — and where Ronald Reagan was rushed after he'd been shot — normally would have taken place in the Situation Room in the basement of the White House.

In the present situation, though, things were different. A senior member of the FBI had suffered a stroke; his fiancée was the Vice President of the United States; she intended to be as close to him as conditions permitted; and the President said, "Okay, we'll take this show on the road."

That was how one of the most important meetings of the Grant administration, and possibly any administration, took place in Bethesda, Maryland.

The topic under discussion was whether the government of China had played a role in the planned assassination attempt on President Patricia Grant. If so, that would amount to nothing less than an act of war. The question then would become how should the United States respond?

The principal figures in the room were the President, the Vice President, Chief of Staff Galia Mindel, Attorney General Michael Jaworsky, Secretary of Defense Martin Dempsey, Secretary of State Helen Hargitay, Director of National Intelligence Gregory Ishida and Chairman of the Joint Chiefs of Staff General Nicholas Mills.

Also present, summoned by the President, was Secretary of the Treasury Cheryl Tyler.

A platoon of the poobahs' respective staffers cooled their heels nearby.

Not present, but in a smaller, no less secure, room down the hall were Jim and Caitie McGill. They had their own fish to fry. Even though it was impossible for them to hear anything beyond the walls of the room in which they sat, neither father nor daughter could keep from, every so often, cocking an ear in the direction of the gathering with global significance.

Addressing her meeting, the President said, "For the sake of discussion, ladies and gentlemen, let's ask ourselves why China might do something so dangerous as trying to kill me. You start with what you learned from the FBI tonight, Jean."

Jean Morrissey looked around the room.

"A Chinese national, a woman named Ah-lam, who claims to be the wife of Tyler Busby, told FBI Special Agent Abra Benjamin that she had no knowledge of whether her former employer Donald Yang or the Chinese Politburo was involved in the planned assassination attempt. Her story changed when she learned …" The Vice President's voice caught in her throat, but she pushed on. "When she learned that Deputy Director DeWitt had been stricken. She thought she had some sort of leniency deal with him, but fearing he would be unable to help her, she said that Donald Yang is an operative of Hu Dai, one of the seven members of the Chinese Politburo's Standing Committee, the center of power in China. She also claimed that Yang told her during pillow talk that he was one of the men who would change the world when they killed the American President."

Everyone thought about that. Pillow talk might be either confessed truth or self-aggrandizing bullshit. In either case, it would have to be investigated. This wasn't a question that could be left unresolved.

Secretary of State Hargitay said, "Hu is the youngest member of the Standing Committee at 52 but he's halfway up the totem pole already as far as his power and influence goes."

General Mills picked up the narrative, "Hu made his bones as a general in the People's Liberation Army, putting down Muslim Uighur uprisings in Xinjiang. He was quick to kill just about any of the locals who stepped out of line, either because they insisted on practicing their religion or they protested the increasing number of Han Chinese displacing them culturally."

DNI Ishida added, "Hu's ruthlessness is in keeping with his given name, Dai. It refers to a martial arts sword technique."

"Off with their heads?" Galia asked.

"Gunfire is more common," Ishida said, "but I wouldn't be surprised if a blade is used on occasion."

Secretary of Defense Dempsey said, "We also think Hu is a moving force behind China's island-building projects as the basis to claim most of the South China Sea as their own territorial waters. At your direction, Madam President, our navy disregards China's claims and continues to cruise in what we and the rest of the world regard as international waters. But Chinese military aircraft continue to harass our vessels with ever closer flybys. It's only a matter of time until something unfortunate happens."

"Or someone blinks," Secretary of State Hargitay said.

"Not us," the Vice President said.

Every eye in the room turned to the President.

She echoed, "Not us. The Chinese have to know that if I died, from any cause, they wouldn't find a soft-touch in Jean. She'd probably bust their chops just for the fun of it."

The Vice President, despite her worry over her fiancé, had to smile and everyone else chuckled.

"Martin," the President asked the Secretary of Defense, "am I correct in thinking both the United States and China have enough nuclear weapons to destroy each other?"

"We have far more than we need, Madam President. They have an adequate amount."

"And there's no chance that either country could ever successfully invade and conquer the other using conventional forces and weapons?" the President inquired.

"None."

The President turned to the Director of National Intelligence. "Do we have any sign, Gregory, that either China's collective leadership or any of its members are feeling suicidal?"

"No, ma'am."

Patricia Grant turned to the Secretary of the Treasury. "Your thoughts, Cheryl? Why would China be lunatic enough to support, in any fashion, an attempt on my life?"

The Secretary said, "In a word, Madam President, face. China's dignity and prestige are on the line, and shame is waiting just around the corner. For years now, we've all been hearing how China will soon surpass the United States as the world's largest economy. Their standard of living has skyrocketed for hundreds of millions of their people in a relatively short time. They managed to combine the gravy train with the bullet train."

"But?" Galia Mindel asked.

"But they've sunk themselves under such massive government debt it makes ours look small and reasonable by comparison. The good times in China are likely to end soon, and when the crash comes it won't be pretty. The ruling class has bought civil harmony among its masses by making them comfortable, affluent or downright rich. When all that buying power goes poof there's going to be hell to pay."

The President turned back to the Director of National Intelligence. "Gregory."

"I agree, but what I'm sure Ms. Tyler knows but hasn't yet said is when China's economy heads south, and its international power and influence do too, much of the world's economy will also go into the dumps."

The Treasury Secretary nodded. "That's right. We'll get hit as well, but our pain will be less than everyone else's and we'll recover first and best."

The President said, "Well, I can see where that wouldn't please the Chinese. It would be taking a cream pie to their precious face. On the other hand, if I had been killed and that caused political turmoil here, maybe that would have put a real crimp in our economy."

"No question about that, Madam President," Secretary Tyler said.

The President said, "Okay then, everybody, let's put on our

thinking caps. See what ideas we can come up with, short of a shooting war, that will put the screws to China economically. Deepen the hole they've already dug for themselves."

Secretary Tyler said, "We can stop letting their billionaires and millionaires buy U.S. real estate. That'd stop distorting the housing market over here and cause big headaches over there. If we can talk the Brits into stopping them from buying up London, too, so much the better."

"There you go," the President said, "I like it. Let's have more."

"Here's one," Jean Morrissey replied, "If the Chinese are buzzing our naval vessels, we should buzz them right back, rattle their teeth good. Give them an idea of what we can do if they really piss us off. Teach them you do *not* fuck with the United States, not ever."

General Nicholas Mills gave that idea a thumbs-up.

"Good," the President said. "As soon as you have a plan, General, let me see it. If I like it, if it's smart, shows a sharp edge and assures a visibly unbeatable military advantage on our side, we'll do it."

"All that and don't spill a drop of blood, correct, Madam President?" Mills asked with a straight face.

"If they haven't spilled American blood first, yes. Feel free, however, to make them wet their pants *en masse.*"

That idea drew laughs from around the table.

Before the discussion could go any further, there was a knock at the door and a military doctor dressed in surgical scrubs speckled with blood stepped into the room. He saluted his superiors: everyone in the room.

"Madam President, Ms. Vice President, I was instructed to let you know. FBI Deputy Director DeWitt is out of surgery."

Walter Reed Waiting Room

Sitting on a sofa, sipping ice green tea, Caitie McGill asked her father, "Do you ever worry about Mom anymore?"

Sitting next to his daughter, McGill looked up from the iPad in his hands. He'd been trying to distract himself by reading the sports section of that day's *Chicago Tribune*. A baseball columnist had written that after a 108-year wait the Chicago Cubs would likely win the World Series. The White Sox, the baseball team in his hometown he'd always rooted for, were predicted to finish at the .500 mark, with a bit of luck.

As his father would often comment about such situations: "What a revolting development *this* is." Borrowing the line from an ancient TV show. That memory had no sooner come to mind than McGill thought how often it might apply to circumstances found at the pinnacle of the federal government. What had happened to Byron DeWitt, though, he saw as a tragic development.

A bright young guy like that in his mid-40s, a stroke was the last thing you'd worry about for someone like him. Jean Morrissey had to be eaten up inside and —

He heard Caitie ask him a question, not getting the details. He'd told her it'd be all right for her to watch the television in the room. It wouldn't bother his reading. She'd just shrugged and shook her head. Put her feet up on a table holding an unruly collection of old magazines. She hadn't brought anything to read from Minnesota. Said she had too much on her mind.

She just sat there quietly next to him thinking her own thoughts.

Maybe writing a screenplay in her head.

Until she asked McGill again, at his request, "Do you ever worry about Mom anymore?"

"Not too often." He knew without asking she'd meant Carolyn not Patti.

"Why not?"

"Well, it's pretty much Lars' job now," McGill said. "That's only right, don't you think?"

Deliberating on the question for five seconds, Caitie said, "Yeah, it is. Back when we all lived together, what did you worry about?"

McGill laughed. "I suppose the first thing I worried about

regarding your mom was whether she'd say yes when I asked her to marry me."

Caitie rolled her eyes. "You didn't have her at hello?"

A movie reference: *Jerry Maguire*. Even McGill knew that one.

"Well, sure, if we'd gotten married in elementary school. As time goes on, as I'm sure you've already seen, things get more complicated. So an element of doubt, albeit a small one, had crept in by the time I asked the question."

"Did you feel the same way about asking Patti to marry you?"

To McGill's surprise, he realized he hadn't. "No. Not to sound cocky, but it never occurred to me she'd say no. I think we both realized if we could have our hearts broken in the same way by the same tragedy we must be pretty compatible. Besides that, as a mature man by that time, I'd come to understand my considerable animal magnetism."

Caitie choked on the iced green tea she'd been sipping. Then she laughed. Which didn't keep her from saying, "That's more than I really wanted to know."

"Be careful what you ask then."

"Did you worry about anything else when you and Mom were married?"

"Of course. Like most people, we worried about paying our bills. We were very careful each time your mother got pregnant. Those were largely unspoken worries: Were we doing everything right to make sure nothing went wrong with either Mom or you guys? Once you were born, there were all the usual worries. Would one of you kids put a loose button in your mouth and choke on it? Would an older kid set a younger one on fire? Would we ever find a trustworthy baby-sitter so we could go on a date once or twice a year?"

Caitie smiled, knowing there were measures of both truth and nonsense in her father's answers. She asked, "Do you worry about Patti?"

McGill nodded. "Not so much about outside threats these days, more about the constant grinding pressure. People can take only so much of that before they're worn down to a fine powder."

"*Illegitimi non carborundum,*" Caitie said.

Don't let the bastards grind you down. The Latin reference made McGill smile. His kid knew more than movie dialogue.

"*Facilius dixit quam fecit,*" he replied. Easier said than done.

It took Caitie three tries but she guessed the translation.

"What about you, Dad?" she asked. "What worries do you have about yourself?"

All signs of humor fled from McGill's face. His eyes were serious in a way his daughter couldn't recall seeing before. The lack of play-fulness almost scared Caitie.

He told her, "I've always had one abiding worry: that a time will come when my help might make the difference between a good outcome and a bad one, and I'll come up short. Like I did with Andy Grant."

Caitie took her father's hand. "Mom told me you did everything you could for Mr. Grant. You know what? Patti told me that, too."

"She did?" McGill had never heard that before.

"Yes. I was talking to her, one day, just the two of us. We were at Camp David for Thanksgiving. All you guys who know how to cook were in the kitchen. Patti and I were taking a walk. I told her how happy I was that she was part of my life, my step-mom."

A smile came back to McGill's eyes.

"You, Abbie and Ken make her very happy. Me, too, some-times."

"Patti's crazy about you, Dad. But we did get to talking, and Mr. Grant came up. Patti blames herself for his death, not you."

"Another thing she and I have in common," McGill said. "Hogging the blame."

"Dad, do you know why I'm asking all this?"

"Because you have something devious in mind, what else?"

"Yeah, of course. But I mean specifically."

"I haven't worked that out yet," McGill said.

"You would, if I didn't tell you, but I'll save you the time."

"Okay."

"Celsus and I think whoever grabbed Special Agent Ramsey is going to attack Lars and Mom's place in Minnesota."

That sat McGill back on the sofa. "You do, do you? You and Celsus?"

"Yeah, we both worked it out individually, but then we talked."

"The two of you are pals now?"

"Sort of. He's really changed for the better, you know?"

McGill said, "I do. It's amazing the effect a good spouse can have."

A sparkle appeared in Caitie's eyes as if she knew just what he meant.

Neither of them got into that at the moment. They had other business to tend to.

McGill asked, "How would the bad guys even know about the Minnesota house?"

Caitie shrugged. "They did their homework."

"Meaning?"

"Well, they were watching me, and presumably Abbie and Ken, right?"

"Yes."

"So who does that leave? Not Patti. She's got too many people protecting her. She's kept too far away from casual looky-loos." California-speak for gawkers and snoopers. "Besides all that, there are easier targets."

"Your mom and Lars," McGill said.

Christ, he should have been thinking more about Carolyn than he had been.

Caitie asked, "Do you know what kind of protection the Evanston PD is giving Mom and Lars these days."

He didn't, not in detail. What with the kids off on their own. "I'll have to ask."

"Ask if they've been taking any pictures of people passing by Mom's house. If so, maybe we could compare them to the photos Ben took of the people watching me."

McGill looked at his youngest in quiet amazement.

He thought if she needed extra spending money when she was off at film school, she could work part-time at his Paris office. He felt sure Yves, Gabbi and Odo would be glad to have her.

Then Caitie took McGill's unspoken admiration a step further.

"Celsus and I asked the Rochester police and the Olmsted County Sheriff's people to take photos of out-of-state travelers who catch their eyes. We can feed all the images into one big database.

"Have I ever mentioned that you amaze me?" McGill asked.

"Pretty much since I learned how to talk, yeah."

"Have you talked about any of this with your mom and Lars, you or Celsus?"

Caitie shook her head. "We don't want them to worry."

McGill laughed. "Good on you."

"There's one more thing, Dad."

There always was. "What's that?"

"I'd like to talk with Special Agent Ramsey's parents, if they'll meet with me."

Suspicion crept into McGill's eyes and Caitie saw it.

"It's not about gathering material for a script. I want to tell them how sorry I am all this happened. It might mean something to them ... what with the two of us looking so much alike."

McGill put an arm around his daughter's shoulders and kissed a cheek.

"I'll ask. If they say yes, I'll take you to them myself."

"Thanks, Dad."

Before they could say anything more, Patti stepped into the room.

She hugged both McGills as they stood to greet her and told them, "Byron DeWitt is out of surgery. The doctors are hopeful he'll make a good recovery. Not perfect, they think, but good. He'll have to do a lot of work and he'll need a lot of help."

"Good for him," McGill said. "How will all this affect Jean?"

"She's going to campaign harder than ever, without leaving this hospital until he does."

J. Edgar Hoover Building — Washington, DC

Special Agent Abra Benjamin had to leave Walter Reed while her former lover, Byron DeWitt, was still on the operating table. Presumably with part of his shaven skull sawed off. If that was how they did brain surgery. Maybe it was, maybe it wasn't. She didn't know, hadn't had the time to Google it.

Perversely, her first thought wasn't how challenging the surgical procedure might be or how long Byron would be under the knife. She thought of how sadly grim he must look right now. He'd always been so handsome with his bright eyes, clean features and that beautiful mop of surfer's hair.

The really great thing was he was never stuck on his own good looks. He took his appearance in the same nonchalant stride with which he glided by everything else. Sure, there were people who mattered to him. Her to some degree, a great measure at one point. But he made his relationships seem like a breeze, too. Coming or going, knowing him was as easy as sipping lemonade on a hot day.

Christ, what was she going to do if Byron died?

Take his job, for one thing. She was already sitting behind his desk. FBI Director Jeremiah Haskins had taken her aside when he first arrived at Walter Reed. Told her, "Step in for the deputy director. Use his office, speak with his authority. You're now an acting deputy director. Don't let anything fall into a crack."

Good soldier and cunning careerist that she was, Abra did as she was told.

Did it despite the biggest promotion of her life leaving nothing but a bitter taste in her mouth. She tried telling herself she'd done everything she could for Byron. Alerted the office staff of a medical emergency involving the deputy director. Made sure both an ambulance and a medevac helicopter were on hand to transport him to any hospital that could best help him.

She'd arrived just in time to board the chopper that took Byron to Walter Reed. Nobody aboard even thought to tell her she couldn't ride with them. Not with her badge, sidearm and a look of grim determination on open display. After Byron had been rushed into the operating room, the flight nurse had the courage and the kindness to put a hand on Abra's shoulder, look her in the eye and tell her, "Time is critical in situations like this. Whatever his outcome, you gave him the best chance he could have."

Abra had been unable to respond verbally. She only nodded her head in thanks.

And now she was sitting in Byron's chair, behind his desk, in his office with Chairman Mao looking serenely down at her. What more could an ambitious woman ask for? Director Haskins would likely leave with the change of Presidential administrations. One more big professional coup and his job would be hers. Just what she'd always wanted.

Better yet, with Senate confirmation, she could serve for ten years.

Wouldn't that be ... something she just didn't give a shit about right then.

The subject that occupied her mind at that moment surprised her. She was thinking about the child, the little boy, she and Byron had conceived and she'd given up for adoption. The adoptive parents were Mayor Ron Ketchum and his wife Keely Powell of Goldstrike, California. They'd named the little boy Matthew. Abra thought he would be starting kindergarten in the fall.

She wondered if he looked like Byron.

She wanted to see if he did.

God help her, she wanted him back. If she lost Byron ... Well, then she'd have lost both of them. Of course, there'd be no way to reclaim the son she'd given up. No court would allow it. You couldn't just say, "Oops, changed my mind." Not five years later. It wouldn't be fair to the little boy.

The irony of her determination to see that Ah-lam never got her son back hit Abra like a kick to the gut. Talk about how what goes around comes around. Too damn bad for both of them.

The stubborn tug of her relentless ambition refused to let Abra sit idly by in a funk of self-commiseration. There was work to be done, and if it was done well she might as well claim credit. If she was going to be a wretch, she might as well be a successful wretch.

She'd be able to buy more flowers for Byron's grave that way.

Have the freedom to schedule visits on days when Jean Morrissey wouldn't be there.

While holding those bitter thoughts in mind, Abra's intercom buzzed. Byron's secretary had gone home long ago, but when Abra arrived at the office a relief staffer was already waiting to help with her needs. The secretary had introduced herself as Nita.

Her manner had been courteous, serious and aware of events.

Now, though, speaking to the new boss, she seemed cheerful, even happy as she said to Abra, "Good news, Ms. Deputy Director."

There should have been an "acting" preceding deputy but Abra didn't object.

"What's that?" Abra asked, trying not to get her hopes up.

"Director Haskins says Deputy Director DeWitt is out of surgery and his outlook is favorable. Lots of hard work ahead, the director says. No certainty as to how complete his recovery will be, but he's going to make it."

Abra said a silent, "Thank you," to the God of the Covenant.

Even if he winds up with Jean Morrissey, she appended.

To Nita, she said, "That is wonderful. Will he be here in the morning then?"

There was a drawn out silence before Nita said, "Are you kidding, ma'am?"

"I am. Sorry for the inappropriate humor. I guess … I guess I'm just so relieved."

"All of us are."

"Is there anything else?" Abra was almost her old self again. Wanting to pad her record of accomplishments. Meaning work her tushie off, but not quite as hard as Byron had.

"Yes, ma'am. A jpg file of pictures of licensed carriage drivers from around the country has just been sent to the deputy director's server. Do you know the password?"

Abra did, but she let Nita tell her anyway.

Not just anyone had to know how closely she and Byron had

worked together.

The idea of crossmatching the photos of carriage drivers from around the country against that of the creep Special Agent Ramsey had chewed out of existence wasn't a thrilling prospect. But it had been Byron's idea. She'd honor it, and the photo recognition software would make the job less onerous. She set about the task immediately.

And soon struck gold.

Sioux Falls, South Dakota

Special Agent Carrie Ramsey woke up feeling … almost normal. Her head was clear. So was her vision as she opened her eyes. She didn't even need to look down to know that neither her wrists nor her ankles were bound. The lack of pressure on and the relief from the constrictions on her limbs was one of the best feelings she'd ever known, even if there was still some lingering soreness.

The chipping paint on the ceiling above her held no fascination so she turned her head to see what else might come into view. Mr. Big and Ugly was back, sitting on his chair again, this time the proper way. His fingers were interwoven on his lap, almost in a slovenly prayerful manner. He looked at her without blinking: *creepy.* Almost like the opening moment of a horror movie. All you'd need to complete the scene would be some scary soundtrack music. Shrieking violins and whatever.

The cinematic characterization reminded Carrie of whom she was supposed to be. Caitie McGill. That little brat, she assumed, would have a more sophisticated set of movie references for the situation … but, hell, the kid wasn't the one who'd given her the assignment that put her in this fix. Caitie hadn't twisted the special agent's arm to make her take the job either.

For a disturbing moment, Carrie wondered if her oversized captor had removed all the hardware so he could get unencumbered access to her body. She ran a quick mental scan of her anatomy and didn't feel as if anyone had laid hands on her in any intimate area. She was relatively certain she remained sexually unmolested.

Better than that, she actually thought she might be able to spring off the cot where she lay and get to her jailer before he could react. He was way too big to grapple with or even to trade blows. But if you put a thumb in someone's eye you'd be pretty much free to attack other vulnerable spots: knees, crotch and throat.

Thinking that way brought its own measure of satisfaction, but even if she left the big bastard bleeding and rolling on the floor that didn't mean she'd be able to get away. There could be five guys with guns waiting on the other side of that door. If they heard their outsized friend moaning in pain, they might shoot her just to get even. With morons you could never expect more than knee-jerk reactions.

Carrie looked at her captor and came up with Plan B. She'd lie on her side. If he came at her, she'd have no choice but to fight. If he just wanted to talk, she'd keep playing her role as Caitie McGill. As feisty and prickly as the kid could be, even that offered some satisfaction.

"Got nothing to say?" the ogre asked in his bottomless bass voice.

"Go fuck yourself. How's that?"

"It's a start. Talk to me some more. You like that Pad Thai I got for you?"

Carrie had enjoyed it. Objectively, it was okay not great. Compared to the crap they had been feeding her, it was manna from heaven. Still, she felt as if the guy was fishing for something more than a compliment for the cuisine or a thank you from her.

By the grace of inspiration and a cooperative digestive system, Carrie came up with exactly the right response. She belched loud and long at the mountainous SOB. To her surprise, he laughed in response.

"You are a pistol, I have to say that," he told her.

"More than you can imagine."

"Now, that's the girl. Let's keep the conversation going."

Carrie immediately clammed up. If he wanted to talk, to hell with him.

The big man leaned forward, planting a broad elbow on a tree-trunk thigh.

"Okay," he said. "You're not going to cooperate, I get that. Problem for me is, I need you talking in your normal voice, not shrieking in pain or blubbering through a river of tears. That won't do me no good. Not yet anyway. You sure you don't want to talk? I'll guarantee your food will be better than it might be otherwise. I'll leave the cuffs and shackles off you, too, so you can at least dream you can get away. How's that for a deal?"

It sounded pretty damn good to Carrie.

The guy really didn't understand how well she could fight. Even if she didn't get away before they killed her, taking out at least one of that giant bastard's eyes would give her some satisfaction. So she said, "What's your name?"

The big man smiled again. "Now, there you go. My name's Dallas Reeves. Was born in Oklahoma not Texas, though."

Carrie thought he'd answered truthfully. As long as she was going to say anything to him, she thought it would help to learn as much as she could. By learning the bastard's real name, he'd also just told her the kidnapper's didn't plan to let her live.

Having seen their faces, at least two of them, and now knowing a specific identity, they'd have to kill her. A chill accompanied that knowledge, but she'd also learned she'd need to take any risk possible to get away, and if she managed to get hold of a weapon she'd have to use it with lethal intent.

At that point, she felt there was little to lose by continuing the conversation.

"Why'd you take me?" she asked.

"Why do you think? Give me a guess, and try to make it a good one."

Carrie remembered she had to answer in character as Caitie McGill. "To hurt Patti and my dad and my mom."

A smile wormed its way across Reeves' fleshy face.

"That's what you call the President of the United States, Patti?"

"Yes, she's my step-mother."

Reeves looked at his prisoner closely. "Yeah, well, I suppose a child can't choose who their blood kin will take up with. Now, your real mama, we didn't give her the same amount of thought."

"And you don't give a shit that you're hurting her anyway."

Reeves shook his massive head. "I'm afraid you got me there."

"So you want to hurt Patti and my dad."

"Mmm-hmm."

"Why?"

"What's your guess this time, Missy?" Reeves asked.

"You came in a distant second to my dad in the most-popular-boy-in-school contest?"

Reeves liked that even less than the crack she'd made about his dick.

He got to his feet.

Carrie swung her legs over the side of the cot, ready to dart out of the way of any charge Reeves made at her, doing whatever she could to hurt him as she zipped past. He saw her readiness and didn't like his chances of catching her. Not without a long, tiring effort.

He backed off to the door, nodding in time to the thoughts running through his head.

"I've heard enough," he said. "You know why I wanted to hear you?"

Carrie was through talking.

Reeves explained himself anyway.

"My French-speaking friend from Quebec? He got himself arrested, the dumbass. But just today some of my other friends and I were listening to a song on the radio. You're probably too young to know it, but it's a good one. Been sung by more than a few folks. Question among the boys was 'Who's that singing it now?' I told them. I got some disagreement but I was proved right by the disc jockey. Everyone agreed I have quite a keen ear on me."

He waited for Carrie to say something but she didn't cooperate.

"Anyway, now I just heard you talk, and I was paying strict attention. We weren't able to get any TV or movie DVDs with Caitie McGill talking on them. Not yet. But we will, and probably before too long. I'll take me a good listen to those videos, and then we'll know who's keeping us company."

Carrie showed no emotion, at least she hoped not.

Even so, Reeves told her, "Know what my bet is? I think we've got ourselves one real fine understudy. That's so, we'll have ourselves a talk, you and me, and find out who you really are."

He opened the door, stepped out, leaving Carrie to consider what she might do now.

CHAPTER 6

Wednesday, March 30, 2016
The Newseum — Washington, DC

The news museum was located on Pennsylvania Avenue between the White House and the U.S. Capitol. For those with the heart and lung capacity and good knees, it was within running distance of the biggest sources of headline news stories in the country. Not that any of the name network correspondents would ever hoof it. They traveled in the back seats of company cars while their drivers fought traffic for them.

Besides that, big time TV reporters weren't known to hang out at a museum.

Even one dedicated to their own trade.

That midweek morning in March was an exception. On the eighth floor, the museum's Knight Conference Center was packed. Two hundred and fifty domestic and foreign newsies were gathered for what was billed as a "head-to-head news conference" between the two leading conservative candidates of the Republican party for the presidency of the United States, Senator Oren Worth and General Warren Altman.

Worth and Altman were expected to give their individual responses to questions from the audience of journalists. Not that every newsy would get to ask his or her own question. The candidates had agreed to answer ten questions. Beyond that point, additional questions would be accepted only by mutual consent.

The over/under on the number of questions that would actually be taken was 12.

A dozen was judged to be both the equivocation limit for the candidates and originality limit for the media pack. Beyond that number, the volume of hot air coming out of the pols might cause one or both of them to collapse a lung, and the mind-numbing repetition of the same questions by the press might make the zombie apocalypse look like a real possibility.

Still, the event was billed as both an exercise in democracy and great fun for the whole family. It would be shown on monitors throughout the museum and on TV stations across the country and around the world. That being the case, the organizers of the news conference were more than a little disappointed — really pissed off as they'd later admit publicly — when Senator Worth's chief of staff had phoned in his regrets earlier that morning.

She'd said the senator was feverish, had a temperature of 102 degrees.

He needed to get well, and not infect anyone else.

The call was taken by an intemperate former newsy who'd caught on at the museum after getting canned by his paper. He said, "Watch out if his temperature gets up to 350 degrees."

"I beg your pardon," the chief of staff said, her voice stiff with indignation.

Unfazed, the newsy told her, "That's the temperature you cook chicken."

He'd later use that tidbit as the headline for a blog post.

General Altman, after he'd been informed that his political opponent wouldn't be attending due to illness, had kept a straight face and said, "Poor guy has a frail constitution, doesn't he?"

His subtext was clear. Oren Worth was a sissy unfit to be President. The general wouldn't have let *anything* keep him from being on hand that day. He would have come to the Newseum if he'd had a full-blown case of Ebola. Especially if he could sneeze on a pack of left-wing media wienies. That would be more fun than he had bombing Iraq in 1991.

One of the things Altman was really looking forward to if he became President was getting the media to behave themselves. They hadn't really been objective for some time now. SNAM, where he'd worked until recently, made no pretense of being anything but a bullhorn for the right. Broadcasting a message of which he approved. You worked hard, you played by the rules, and if your family had been in the country long enough, you got ahead. You made good.

You were new to the U.S. or you had other disadvantages, you had to work even harder and be patient. Maybe this wasn't your generation's turn to get ahead. But if you stuck it out, had kids and grandkids, your family's turn would come. Even if yours, personally, never did.

That's the way Altman sincerely felt things should be. Anybody didn't like it, tough. He wanted to be President and thought he'd be good at the job. But he'd get there his way or not at all. If he didn't make it, so be it. He had his Air Force pension and a lot of the money he'd made being a straight-talking guy on TV the past six years. He'd be comfortable if not altogether content.

Especially if another damn woman wound up in the White House.

Jesus Christ, what would the country come to if that happened? Sooner or later the Russians and the Chinese were going to challenge America. When that day came, a man, preferably one with combat experience and senior officer rank, had better be sitting in the Oval Office.

The general heard his name announced. Show time. He stepped out onto the stage. He didn't smile but he gave the audience a wave that approximated a salute. That was more than most of them deserved but he felt the gesture served him better than —

Mary, Mother of God. That little shit Welborn Yates, washout of a fighter pilot, was sitting in the front row, and the SOB was in full uniform. A colonel now. And next to him was ... holy shit. Altman's step faltered for a moment. He had to force himself toward the podium.

Carina Linberg was sitting next to Yates. This was an ambush.

Altman made a tactical maneuver. He stepped to the microphone before he was even introduced and said, "I'm sure you've all heard by now that Senator Worth won't be joining us this morning."

He'd been hoping for a few boos but all he got was silence. Bastards.

"He isn't feeling well, so let's hope he won't have too long a convalescence."

Altman was reaching for a laugh with that one, hoping to conjure an image of Worth sitting in a rocking chair on a sun porch with a blanket wrapped around him. He didn't even get an audible chuckle. At that moment, he knew the flop sweat of the would-be stand-up comic.

In the best tradition of that craft, he pushed onward.

"Since I'm the only speaker here, I think it's fair that I limit myself to five questions, that being half the number that two of us would have taken."

That idea drew a roomful of *stony* silence and dirty looks.

Altman almost gave in and said, okay, he'd accept ten questions after all.

But that would make *him* look weak. Able to be pushed around by a bunch of liberal arts majors. If he did that, Putin and Xi Jinping would hand him his ass anytime things got tense. Worse, Jean Morrissey would make him out to be a wimp when they debated in the fall.

"Five questions," he reiterated. Fuck 'em if they didn't like it. "Who's got the first?"

Didi DiMarco was seated in the front row next to Carina Linberg.

Carina was whispering into Didi's ear, and then the TV host stood up.

"I won the lottery, General Altman," she said, "I get to go first."

The newsies on hand all participated in the lottery to see who'd get to ask the candidates questions. Numbers 6-10 were especially pissed off that Altman had eliminated their turns in the spotlight. Besides that, there was much *sotto voce* grumbling that the drawing of numbers had been rigged.

Altman recognized the fellow television personality. He didn't like her lefty politics at all, but that concern paled next to the fact that Carina Linberg had just whispered into her ear. There was no way that the message could have been good news for Altman.

He still managed to suck it up and ask, "What would you like to know, Ms. DiMarco?"

"General, if you can remember your final year as Chief of Staff of the Air Force —"

"Of course, I can."

He knew what was coming now, and it was going to be bad, but he couldn't plead a faulty memory. He was in his late 60s. If he said he couldn't recall something important, he'd leave himself wide open to phony accusations of dementia or some such thing.

"I'm happy to hear your faculties are sharp, sir, and I bet your eyesight is still good, too."

"It is," he said in a flat tone. "Do you have a question or is this just a stroll down memory lane?"

Didi smiled. "It's both, actually. The woman in the seat next to mine is Carina Linberg. She was a colonel in the Air Force when you were the chief of staff. You pressed to have Colonel Linberg charged with adultery, a crime as viewed by the Uniform Code of Military Justice at the time."

Altman ground his teeth together. Any more pressure from his jaws and they'd start to crack audibly.

Didi continued, the whole room paying rapt attention by now. "Colonel Linberg was accused of having sex with a married naval officer, the late Captain Dexter Cowan. The charge was dropped when Captain Cowan died in an automobile accident."

"Are you ever going to ask a question, Ms. DiMarco," Altman said. "If not —"

"Here's my question, General. What will you say when Colonel Linberg, seated next to me, publicly admits that she slept with both you and your late wife while you were the Air Force chief of staff?"

Altman's fingers turned white as he squeezed the lectern in front of him.

A sense that the man might go berserk rippled through the room.

That didn't stop Ellie Booker from standing up.

"I have question number two, General. Did you know that the late Captain Cowan sent a letter to his brother, Stephen, shortly before he died, and when Stephen passed away with the envelope unopened it passed into the hands of Captain Cowan's estranged widow, Arlene? She in turn forwarded it unopened to Colonel Welborn Yates who is attached to the Air Force's Office of Investigative Services. He tells me he intends to have the envelope opened today under crime laboratory conditions. Would you care to speculate, sir, what might be in that envelope? Do you think it might have something to do with your activities at the time you were pressing for Colonel Linberg's court martial?"

Altman literally threw the lectern aside, making most of the people in the room jump.

His chances of ever becoming President were tossed aside with it.

He stormed out of the room without having answered even one question.

Metropolitan Detention Center — Washington, DC

When McGill and Caitie got into his armored Chevy, Leo asked Caitie, "Any music in particular you'd care to hear during our drive, Miz McGill?"

"What's Dad usually listen to?" she asked.

"Classic rock, a little alt rock and a bit of country I spoon feed him now and then."

"And what do you listen to when you're in the car alone?"

"Same thing only in reverse order."

"What about you, Deke?" Caitie asked.

Sitting shotgun, McGill's personal special agent said, "Police radio."

McGill told his daughter. "He doesn't mean Sting and his friends."

Caitie laughed, but said, "Deke always makes me feel safe."

The compliment was rewarded with a rare on-the-job smile from its recipient.

"Let's go with your playlist, Leo," Caitie said.

Willie, Waylon and Kris serenaded them on the relatively short drive to Southeast Washington and the detention center. The federal government didn't pipe in any music to either the staff or the inmates in the building. The architecture, lighting, furnishings and even the feel of the air in the structure was oppressive. Nobody serving time was supposed to enjoy even a minute of their time there.

Caitie shook hands with the warden when they were introduced and then surprised McGill when she took his hand as they made their way to the interview room where Elvie Fisk was waiting for them. He recognized his child's nonverbal message from years gone by: *This is scary. Keep me safe.* McGill had seen any number of lock-ups from his days as a cop, but even he had to admit a federal prison rated high on the intimidation scale.

And yet people kept doing things that landed themselves there.

Even little Elvie Fisk. Now twenty years old, she still had over a year and a half to serve on her five-year term. In federal prisons, an inmate could earn only 54 days of Good Time Credit for every year of incarceration. From the Bureau of Prisons report McGill had been given, he saw that Elvie had been a model prisoner, but seemed to be deteriorating both mentally and emotionally.

Initially interested in pursuing educational opportunities, and receiving her high school equivalency certificate, she'd stopped attending classes for college credits. While respectful and obedient in her conduct with prison staff, she'd developed the habit of spending personal time simply staring off into space, not speaking to anyone.

Her incommunicative posture had provoked a beating from an inmate who'd attempted to engage her in conversation. Elvie had declined to offer testimony on her own behalf regarding the incident, saying, "The both of us are still in here. Ain't that enough?" A staff psychologist had diagnosed Elvie as verging on chronic depression and expressed concern her condition might become resistant to treatment.

Caitie had read the report, too, and like her father was determined not to forsake the opportunity to see the young woman. Either she'd talk to them or she wouldn't. They still had to see what they could do.

When they entered the interview room, Elvie had her head on the table to which her hands were shackled and her eyes were closed. Upon hearing the warden speak her name, though, she sat up and looked at him. "Yes, sir?"

"Your visitors are here. See if you can find the strength to talk with them, okay?"

"Yes, sir."

Turning to McGill, he asked, "Would you like a corrections officer in the room with you?"

"No, thank you."

"The officer will wait just outside then."

"That's fine. Thanks for your help."

The warden stepped out and closed the door behind him.

Elvie looked at McGill. It took her a moment but she remembered him. Gave him a nod to let him know she'd made the connection. She turned to look at Caitie. Studied her for a moment and then looked at McGill. She saw the resemblance, understood their relationship.

"You're his," she told Caitie.

"I am. My good luck. May we sit down?"

Elvie produced a feeble laugh.

"Something funny?" Caitie asked.

"Uh-huh. Thinkin' anybody needs my say-so for anything."

"We'd like to sit and we'd like to talk."

"Still don't need to ask me."

Elvie put her head back on the table and closed her eyes.

Caitie looked at her father. He nodded. He was letting her take the lead. They sat and looked at Elvie. She was quiet and her breathing was regular, but neither of the McGills got the idea she was asleep.

They let a moment pass in silence.

Then Caitie asked, "You like movies?"

Elvie opened her left, uppermost, eye. "You bring me one to watch?"

"Tell me what you like. I'll see what I can do."

"Just like that, huh? You must be *special*." Elvie closed her eye.

The McGills looked at each other. Both of them took the sneering tone in Elvie's voice to be a good sign. To give somebody attitude, you had to care at least a little.

Caitie said, "I am special. I always have been."

Not bothering to look up, Elvie said, "Yeah, shit. Throw yourself a party."

"I have people who do those things for me," Caitie said with Hollywood hauteur. "I'm in the movies."

"None I've ever seen. Leave me alone."

Caitie pushed her chair back with a loud squeak. "Come on, Dad. This loser isn't going to be any help."

Elvie gave Caitie the finger.

McGill realized the script was being improvised on the spot.

Only he didn't know what his part required of him.

Caitie gave him his cue, gesturing to him to shove his chair back, too, and get up. He did. They got as far as the door before Elvie said, "I like slasher flicks."

Her head still lay on the table; her eyes were still shut.

"*A Nightmare on Elm Street* and *Friday the 13th,* stuff like that?" Caitie asked.

Elvie opened her eyes and lifted her head, looked at Caitie like she might actually be for real with her movie talk. "Exactly like that."

"*Freddy versus Jason* was the biggest one," Caitie said.

Eyes downcast, Elvie muttered, "Never got to see that one."

Caitie glanced at her father, asking a silent question.

McGill felt he knew what Caitie wanted and gave a nod.

Looking back at Elvie, she said, "You want to see it?"

Daring to hope, Elvie focused on Caitie. "You can really do that?"

"I told you: I'm special. You want popcorn and a Coke while we watch the movie?"

The White House — Washington, DC

The CIA, in the person of counterterrorism officer Deena Wilkes, came to the White House saving Elspeth Kendry from having to truck down to Langley. The two women shook hands politely. Neither of them felt the need to show she worked out harder than the other. They were both tall, fit and self-confident. More than smart enough to know they didn't have to show off.

Elspeth got her guest seated and asked if she'd like a drink.

"Water would be good," Deena said.

Elspeth put in a call and a bottle of San Pellegrino, a glass and a coaster came promptly.

When they were alone again, Deena said, "The good stuff. You do all right over here in the White House."

"Personal stock paid for out of pocket. One of my few indulgences."

"Good one to have. Smart to stay hydrated. What can the agency do for you, SAC Kendry?"

"It might be what we can do for each other. Have you ever heard of Dominic Mancuso?"

Deena hesitated. "I suppose you can pick up the phone and get whatever clearance you need from the Oval Office."

"Would you like to see?" Elspeth reached for her phone.

"Not necessary, unless I get real nervous. Which doesn't happen too often. Yes, I've heard of Mr. Mancuso, aka *Alqiddis al'amriki*. The American saint."

Deena's pronunciation of the Arabic title caught Elspeth's attention.

She asked, *"Hal tatahaddath alerby?"* Do you speak Arabic?

"Nem fielaan." Yes.

Switching back to English, Elspeth asked, "You studied it in school?"

"Refined it in college. Learned it at home. Dad converted to Islam when I was little. Mom kept singing in the band Dad used to front, and he got me as a parting gift."

"Did you convert, too?"

Deena shook her head. "Even back then it was too late for that. When both my folks were on the road, Grandma took care of me. Had me singing in the church choir at three. I lost my heart to Jesus and gospel music. But I respect how my Dad's new faith got him sober and responsible. He's the best man I know."

Elspeth nodded. "You checked me out to know how I learned the language?"

"Yeah. Growing up in Beirut, that must have been an experience."

"It was. Among other things, Dominic Mancuso became an unofficial uncle. He and my parents are old friends. And quite recently Uncle Dom told me something I thought I should pass along to the Agency. That and ask for a bit of help from the Agency."

Deena offered a noncommittal smile. "Anything the boss approves. Mine or yours, I guess."

"I'll make the call now. Won't take long," Elspeth told her.

Within a minute, Deena had been told: "Tell SAC Kendry anything she wants to know."

"Impressive when you can get the President to write you a blank check like that," Deena told Elspeth, after saying, "Yes, ma'am," and thanking the President for her time.

With the obstacle to speaking freely removed, Elspeth said, "Uncle Dom told me there's a new group of jihadis starting to come into their own amidst all the madness going on in Lebanon. They call themselves *Suq Allah.*"

"God's marketplace?"

"Yeah, the top dog is supposed to be a graduate of the London School of Economics." Elspeth gave Deena a name. "The idea is to create a stock exchange of ideas on how to bring down the Great Satan or the good old USA to you and me. They came up with a plan that's a variation on an idea that James J. McGill thought about a few years ago."

"What's that?"

"An unholy alliance between the jihadis and American terrorists, right-wing crazies. Mr. McGill got the part right about the jihadis funding the homegrown assholes. He thought, though, the domestic pricks would do the dirty work and the foreign assholes would claim the credit."

"I can see that," Deena said. "What's the new wrinkle?"

"The overseas shit-heads claim credit only when they're sure the local creeps didn't screw up and look like chumps. If people got the idea the jihadis couldn't outsource their threat effectively, it would make them look bad, too. "

Deena said, "Yeah, that makes sense. But if the mutts they hire get away clean, and the jihadis take credit, that makes them look even scarier. Their global reach extends even to their biggest enemy. And the how-the-hell-did-they-do-that factor really builds fear."

Elspeth nodded. "Uncle Dom said the incentive for the locals not to screw up is they get money for their next attack only if they make no mistakes with their first opportunity. If the locals fail, they own the mess, and the jihadis disavow any participation."

"Damn," Deena said, "what're they teaching in business schools these days?"

"Machiavelli maybe. We probably should look into it. See who's recruiting the best and the brightest besides the investment banks. Anyway, now you and the Agency have some important information you might have had to wait for if it went through channels."

If we ever got it at all, Deena thought.

"And we're grateful," she said. "It's pretty easy to see what favor you'd like in return."

"Right," Elspeth said, "we'd like to know who's on the receiving end of the jihadis' funding here at home. Uncle Dom didn't have that. The sooner we know, the better chance we have of getting Special Agent Ramsey back alive."

"Amen to that," Deena Wilkes agreed.

Then she offered the caveat, "We'll have to liaise with the FBI, though. You know, if by some chance we have the information and they don't. That can happen every once in a while."

Exactly what Elspeth had suspected. "I'll ask the President to smooth that over so there are no delays. We really need to work fast here. No time for bureaucratic delays at all."

"Yeah, well, must be nice when you can pick up a phone and get the Oval Office."

"Does help," Elspeth said. "Let's hope it's enough."

Metropolitan Detention Center — Washington, DC

They had Cokes and a DVD player in the building; they had to send out for the movie and the popcorn. The screening of *Freddy vs. Jason* took place in the warden's conference room. The warden asked McGill if he might stay and watch the movie.

"I'm a fan," he said. "I've been wanting to see this one for a while."

If he could do it while earning his salary, so much the better.

The two McGills were thinking about the advisability of that when Elvie spoke up.

"It's okay," she said. She even pushed a can of Coke the warden's way.

After more than three years of incarceration, she knew it never hurt to have someone look out for you, especially the guy who ran the joint. He could pass the word along to his colleague at FCI Coleman Medium Security, Elvie's full-time lockup. "The kid's all right. Keep an eye out for her."

At least Elvie hoped he might do that.

The critics called the movie, "The same old slice and dice."

Elvie and the warden thought it was top notch.

Both McGills felt a little queasy. The movie made them think of what Carrie Ramsey might be enduring at the hands of her captors. Yet another spur to move quickly.

The warden gave Elvie's spirits an even bigger boost than the movie did.

"Thank you for allowing me to join you, young lady."

Not inmate, young lady. The guy might've been putting on a show for her visitors, who obviously had the kind of pull Elvie couldn't even imagine. Yanking her up to DC from Florida. Getting her permission to watch the movie. The Coke and popcorn, too. She felt almost like a real person again.

It boosted her hope that maybe things would improve for her back at Coleman.

When the warden left her with the McGills, though, she was still savvy enough to ask.

"What do you want from me?"

She directed her question at McGill not Caitie. She'd bet he was the one made the final decisions. Just like her old man always had. And that's when it hit her.

Before McGill could answer her question, she said, "This is about my father, isn't it? He tried you on for size, and you laid him out cold. I know about all that."

She'd heard stories from both the inmates and the correctional officers.

"He never lost consciousness that I know of," McGill said. "He took a run at me; I got out of the way, did some damage as he went past and put him on the ground. And, yes, we'd like to talk with you about him."

Elvie pointed at Caitie. "You brought her along because she's a girl like me. Maybe a little bit younger."

"Yes," McGill said.

"You think I'd tell her something I wouldn't tell you?"

"Would you?" Caitie asked.

A smile formed on Elvie's face. "A girl learns to take care of herself when she gets locked up. Even someone little like me. I've taken some beatings, but I've given some, too. So how about —"

"My dad leaves the room and we see what happens?" Caitie asked. "Listen, these days, *I* could put your father on the ground. You wouldn't last two seconds with me."

His daughter's vehemence surprised McGill. He didn't know whether she was acting or being sincere. It had been months since he'd worked out with her. She may well have been honing her Dark Alley skills. But he didn't think putting Elvie in traction would look good for either of them.

"Easy, Tiger," he told her.

Caitie just shook her head in disgust. "You try to be nice to people ... some jerks just don't get it. Don't know when someone's trying to help them. C'mon, Dad, let's go."

She got to her feet.

Elvie said, "You used that one already, remember?"

This time Caitie gave Elvie the finger. She knocked on the door. A corrections officer let her out.

"You going, too? Thanks for the good time. Stop by anytime."

McGill stayed seated and said to the officer, "You can close the door."

He did. McGill and Elvie stared at each other. She looked away first.

"Who hurt you worse," he asked, "your mom or your dad?"

"What the hell do you know?"

"I know what I've read about you. Your mother let you go with your father when he set off on a fool's errand. Your father used you to seduce a man more than three times your age. Then he sold you down the river when you could have gotten a much lighter sentence. Despite all that, you started out making the most of serving your time. Then you fell off a cliff and got depressed. Something bad happened. What was it?"

"Fuck you," Elvie said.

She didn't look away, though. Kept her head off the table. Gave McGill another run at a staring contest. He had to admire that.

"One of your parents hurt you again," he said quietly. "Which one was it?"

Her mouth twisted as if to spew another expletive, but then the tears came in volume. Her anger could no longer hold back her despair. "Both of them."

Now, she crossed her arms and put her head down, sobbing.

McGill waited without saying a word. He watched the door with the intent of waving off anybody who opened it, be it Caitie or the warden. A look would do with his daughter; he took out his temporary FBI badge to show the warden.

Turned out, he didn't have to use either.

He and Elvie were left to themselves. When she exhausted her grief for the moment, she looked up and seemed surprised to see he was still there. "You don't give up, do you?"

"Hardly ever," McGill said. "Did your father get in trouble inside prison? Was he foolish enough to get in a fight with a guard?"

Elvie said, "What he got was lung disease."

"Cancer?"

"No, that obstructive kind that chokes you out."

"Chronic obstructive pulmonary disease?"

"Yeah, that. They got him on an oxygen tank already and he still can't get enough air. It won't be long is what he wrote me, and that was a month ago. He might be dead already for all I know."

McGill thought about that. A dead man couldn't plot to take vengeance, but if a plan had already been set in motion maybe it would be a comfort in Harlan Fisk's last gasping moments.

"Would you like me to find out for you?" he asked Elvie.

She shrugged. "It don't really matter."

"Because he didn't apologize to you in his last letter?"

She finally looked away. "He *never* apologized. He thinks it's right, the two of us jailing at the same time. What he told me the last time he wrote was, 'Stay true, darlin.'"

"And what did your mother do? If your father never changed from what you knew of him, she must have been the one to put you in your tailspin."

"My what?"

"The one who made you miserable."

Elvie nodded. "She was the one, all right. I was doing pretty good with my schoolwork, better than I ever did *in* school. The job counselor said I had skills that could earn me a paycheck, but it's always easier if you know someone who can recommend you for a job."

"You wrote to your mother," McGill said.

"I did. Told her what good grades I was getting, and asked maybe could she help me. She wrote back. Said no. I made my choice going off with my dad. So don't come 'round. She has a new husband and new kids. Doesn't want me *stressing* her marriage or being a bad influence on her children. So when I get out, I got nobody. Makes me wonder what the point is."

McGill said, "Go back to your studies. Keep getting good grades and I'll give you a job. That or pay for your college. Your choice."

She looked at him with more intensity than she'd shown so far.

"Yeah, good grades and telling you something you want to know about my dad."

"No, the grades are enough, but here's the situation. Someone is trying to hurt me by hurting my children. Do you think your father would like to hurt me before he dies?"

"Damn right. Knowing him, he'd go to hell smiling if he could do that."

"Okay, the other thing is some people grabbed a young woman they think is one of my daughters. Kidnapped her. Maybe they've killed her already. If they haven't, I'd like to get her back. If they have, I want to see them put in prison."

"Not killed?"

McGill asked, "What's worse, dying quickly or living inside for a long, long time?"

"Living inside. The longer you've got to go, the worse it is."

"My feeling, too."

"Why'd they kidnap the wrong person?"

"She looks pretty much like the right person. The one you met today. That's all I can tell you. Except that she deserves being confined even less than you do."

Elvie thought about that. McGill could tell she wanted to hear his promise to help her again, but she went with taking him at his word. "How can I help you find this girl?"

"A lot of the men who came to the National Mall with your father were let go. Do you know anyone among them who might do something as bad as a kidnapping?"

Elvie searched her memory.

Then she started giving McGill names.

Sioux Falls, South Dakota

The door to Carrie's captivity room opened and the guy in the Smokey hat was back. Now that she thought about it, his whole outfit, including the little kit bag he carried, reminded her of something. Took a moment because his get-up didn't have any of the usual patches or insignias, but what he looked like was a Boy Scout leader. A den father? No, that was Cub Scouts. She couldn't think of the proper title, but that was what he resembled.

She asked, "Where's Dallas? Doing something important and he sent the B-team?"

Smokey didn't like that. They hadn't parted on the best of terms last time, and old Dallas had promised Smokey he'd get to have his fun with the female prisoner by and by. Had that time come?

If so, Carrie had been left unshackled last night. She didn't know if that had been intentional to see what she might try to do or if it was just negligence. But if keeping her alive was no longer a part of the bad guys' plan, she was surely going to take as many of them with her as possible, and bless their pointy little heads, they'd made it easier. Smokey would go for sure.

Since she already had him irritated, she pressed harder.

"Maybe you just came to dump the slop bucket. Haven't pooped recently but there is some fresh pee in there. Maybe you can sniff it, imagine where it came from and get a thrill."

Smokey ground his teeth, making his jaw muscles bulge.

They looked pretty strong, too. Wouldn't do to underestimate him. Take him out fast, she thought, and then maybe abuse the remains to get the others angry and off balance. That might be a way to go.

But Smokey found some unsuspected self-restraint.

"We're moving before long. Time to get you back in chains." That was when he couldn't stop himself from going too far. He reached into his bag for the shackles, grinned and said, "Think we'll leave 'em on when the two of us have our little ron-day-voo. That's coming up soon, too."

Carrie had come to the decision, even before Smokey had entered the room, that she wasn't going to let her limbs be bound again. These SOBs meant to kill her. Maybe use her for some vile purpose and then kill her. Even if she never got a chance to escape, she'd be able to put up a much better fight with her hands and feet free. If she was going to die anyway, better to do it fighting.

She told Smokey, "You come near me with those things, I'll strangle you with them."

The bastard only smiled at her, like he had a trump card to play.

He was *really* going to enjoy putting her in her place.

He dropped the manacles and leg irons and reached into his bag, lowering his eyes to make sure he grabbed the right thing. He looked up as he pulled out a Beretta 92 FS, the standard sidearm of the U.S. Army and many domestic police forces.

It was also the weapon Special Agent Carrie Ramsey used.

Smokey gasped when he saw that Carrie wasn't cowering in a corner. She was right there, so close he could feel her breath on his face. Her left hand closed around his right wrist like a steel clamp. Her right hand wrapped itself around the barrel of the gun from above. Before he could even chamber a round, she snapped the barrel downward.

The trigger-guard fractured Smokey's index finger, the bone breaking audibly.

It was a classic gun disarm. With the weapon in Carrie's hands now, the follow-up move could range from letting the would-be assailant run away to putting a round between his eyes. Carrie chose to shoot Smokey in his right foot. He howled loudly enough to wake the comatose.

Whoever else was in the building, and it sounded like at least four or five of them, came at a run, some shouting questions, others trying to think of orders to give. Then the foghorn bass voice of Dallas Reeves bowled hubbub aside. "Stop, damnit, just stop."

Before anyone dared to take a look through the open doorway, Reeves called out, "How you doin' in there, Lem?"

Lem? Perfect name for a goober, Carrie thought. He was now lying on the floor moaning, his leg bent, knee pulled up to his chest, so he could hold his bleeding foot in his hands. That process was made more difficult by his broken finger. He was about to respond to Reeves when Carrie pointed the gun at him and shook her head.

"Lem's having a bad day," Carrie yelled. "He's going to need some quiet time."

"You got his gun, sweetheart?"

"Poke your fat head through the door. See for yourself."

"I'll take that as a yes."

Carrie said, "If you don't have the balls, pick a sacrificial lamb. I promise not to shoot more than once, likely to his head."

"You're sounding less 'n' less like a teenage girl, honey," Reeves said.

Carrie thought *oops,* but she said, "You have no idea how tough McGills are."

"Still have my doubts, darling."

"I've got none about you. You're a tub of chickenshit. Probably not looking like a profile in courage to whatever nitwits you talked into following you."

Carrie hoped the insult would change the subject.

It did, but not helpfully.

"You know, we don't hear from Lem, maybe he's dead already."

The implication was clear. If they didn't have to worry about harming one of their own, they could charge her in numbers. She'd get a few of them, but they'd get her, too.

So Carrie kicked Lem's bleeding foot.

His howl left no doubt as to its authenticity.

It was also loud enough and long enough to use as cover for the other creeps to rush her, but they didn't stick so much as a nose into view. The first wave assaulting Omaha Beach, they were not. A small favor, but good to know. These guys were going to look for a way to get her back — or kill her — without risking their own skins.

If they could help it.

If time or some other constraint didn't make them desperate.

Maybe even if old Dallas didn't make them doubt their masculinity.

Without ever calling his own into question.

"So we got ourselves a standoff here," Reeves said.

"Or you could all give up and go home. Try to tell yourselves you're not pathetic losers."

"Whoever you are, girlie, you got one nasty mouth on you."

"Yeah? You get kidnapped by a bunch of assholes, see how your manners hold up."

Reeves had no reply for that. So Carrie filled the opening.

"Hey, you other dickweeds out there, think about this. If you come charging in here, old Lem gets it right in the head. And if fat boy is willing to sacrifice him, he'll do the same thing with you. So if he comes up with any risky plan, tell him to lead the way."

The ploy was an obvious attempt to sow dissent in the ranks, but that was okay. Carrie didn't think subtlety was the way to go with this motley crew. And they had no direct rebuttal.

Reeves obviously didn't want to continue a battle of wits. But he was muttering something to his followers. Carrie crouched behind Lem, with no objections from him once she pressed the Beretta against the back of his skull. She'd never so much as fired a weapon in the direction of another person before shooting Lem, but she had no doubt she could dispatch him and then shoot anyone else who came into view.

It was amazing the changes circumstance could force upon a person.

If she somehow got out of this damn situation alive, she was pretty sure she wouldn't be able to go back to her job. The idea of self-sacrifice, taking a bullet for someone else, now seemed foolish beyond belief. What she deeply wished at the moment was that she could plug Lem, run out of the room and kill anyone who got in her way.

The world would be a better place if she could manage to do that.

Didn't look like a new day was about to dawn, though. Reeves was doing his best to thwart her getaway without exposing any more of his people to a direct line of fire. Somebody had tied a loop into what looked like an electrical cord and managed to throw it over the room's doorknob. With a tug, an unseen hand pulled the door shut.

Carrie thought of shooting through the door in the hope of hitting someone.

She chose not to, not wanting to inspire a return fusillade.

Of course, if Dallas' men shot randomly through the door or wall, they might hit old Lem.

Then, again, maybe Lem was expendable. If not immediately, soon enough.

Shit, she knew she could hold out for a while, but there was no way to make it all the way to a happy ending unless she got some help. The assholes wouldn't even have to burn the place down around her. Just wait for fatigue or dehydration to make her pass out. If she felt things were heading that way, she'd make an assault of her own.

Take Lem out first and do her level best to get fat Dallas Reeves, too.

The idea of going out in a blaze of glory only distracted her for a moment.

Then she obsessed on the one thought she'd sworn to herself

she would avoid: That someone was going to ride to the rescue in the fucking nick of time. Like that ever happened.

The Ramsey Apartment, Washington, DC

McGill thought it was a good thing Caitie had her hair cut before he introduced her to Sheri and Don Ramsey. The difference in appearance was small but just enough. They saw Caitie standing in the doorway to their temporary residence and they both experienced a moment of elation. Their eyes went wide with delight, smiles gleamed and arms rose to embrace … someone who *wasn't* the child they'd thought they lost. They'd been fooled but only momentarily. Then they realized the miracle they'd been praying for had yet to be realized.

It was exactly what McGill had feared.

He tried not to let disappointment linger.

"Sheri and Don Ramsey, this is my daughter, Caitlin."

Caitie took it from there. She stepped forward and embraced Sheri. With feeling and physicality. She kissed Sheri's cheek. Then she greeted Don the same way.

"She's always been bashful," McGill told them.

Don smiled. "Just like our girl."

"So much like Carrie," Sheri said, reaching out for another hug.

Caitie accommodated her immediately.

Then she told the Ramseys, "Thank you for seeing my dad and me. I wanted to tell you how much I think of all the Secret Service people who look out for me. They're family as far as I'm concerned."

Don ushered them into the living room. Sheri brought soft drinks. Caitie sat between the Ramseys on a sofa. They both seemed pleased to have her there. McGill looked on from an easy chair.

Caitie picked up her earlier thread with characteristic bluntness.

"When I said the Secret Service and I are like family, I mean that in more than one way. You can ask my sister Abbie and my brother Ken, I can be a pain in the butt."

McGill nodded.

Caitie saw him and added, "My mom and step-parents would also agree. It's unanimous. I can be a handful … and I make things harder for the people who keep me safe than I should. I feel terrible about what happened to Special Agent Ramsey."

McGill saw tears form in Caitie's eyes, but she didn't yield to them.

She cleared her throat so she might continue, but Don intervened.

"You don't think you had anything to do with it, do you?"

"Maybe I did," Caitie said.

She told the Ramseys about changing her appearance so she could stand out again.

"It was a stupid thing to do, feeding my ego, nothing more. If I hadn't done that, Carrie wouldn't have needed to take the time off to get her appearance redone."

Sheri took Caitie's hand. "If you hadn't done that, the two of you would have looked so much alike that Carrie might have been mistakenly taken anyway."

McGill had the same thought, but he knew sometimes wisdom is best received from a source other than Mom and Dad.

Don had another idea to offer. "It's possible if the two of you were spotted together without any other special agents nearby you *both* might have been grabbed."

That suggestion made Caitie blink twice. Then she laughed so hard that she shook.

McGill kept a straight face but he was sure what was coming next.

Caitie said, "Carrie and me both being taken at the same time? The Mongol Horde wouldn't have a chance."

The Ramseys looked to McGill for his opinion.

"Maybe if Genghis Khan was having an off day," he said.

Sheri asked, "So you're a tough young lady?"

"Yes, ma'am."

Hearing that, the Ramseys told their guests about all the times Carrie had stood up for classmates and younger children in schoolyard situations. Caitie's eyes gleamed and she laughed in all the right places. Watching her with the Ramseys, McGill felt a chill. He was getting a better idea than ever how much losing Carrie would hurt the Ramseys.

When the exchange of family lore wound down, he said they should be going.

The Ramseys stood to see them off. Everyone shook hands and exchanged more hugs.

Don asked, "Are you getting anywhere?"

"Yes, thanks to you."

He nodded to Caitie and she told the Ramseys about talking with Elvie Fisk and the names she'd given McGill.

"I think you were right about someone wanting to hurt me," he told the Ramseys. "A man named Harlan Fisk has it in for me. He's dying, just barely hanging on, I was told on the way over here. I think he put this whole plot in motion and is just hoping he can last until he hears it has succeeded. I emailed the names I was given to the FBI. They should be looking for these men right now."

"That's wonderful," Sheri said.

Don was quiet.

"Mr. Ramsey?" Caitie said.

He looked at her and then at McGill. "You know what worries me most? Not that Carrie will break down under whatever her circumstances are. I fear that she's going to decide she's had enough and force the issue. Either try to make an escape or say 'To hell with this.' And try to take down as many of the bastards as she can. Force them to kill her before she kills them."

The expression on Sheri's face made it painfully clear that Don hadn't shared that particular horrifying idea with her, and now it took hold of her, too.

McGill looked at Caitie and saw her nod, perhaps without even being aware of what she was doing. She agreed with Don's surmise. Could see herself also doing exactly what he had described.

McGill felt more pressure than ever to bring things to a quick conclusion.

The least awful one he could.

Florida Avenue — Washington, DC

Sweetie and Putnam sat in the facing living room chairs they used whenever having a serious discussion. Their daughter Maxi was at school so they could speak freely without scaring the wits out of a child who'd yet to learn all the awful things adults could do to each other. A situation like the abduction of Special Agent Ramsey was hard enough for people who'd logged more than a few decades of life to handle.

"You were really able to access Eugene Beck's prison record?" Sweetie asked her husband.

"You know I know people," he said. "I don't have to hack anyone's computer. I pick up a phone and make a call. Someone answers and we talk. Voilà, and you don't have to know how to write a line of code."

"Doesn't hurt that you're Darren Drucker's fair-haired boy, I bet."

"Actually, people keep pestering me for stock tips."

Drucker was the best stock-picker who ever lived. He stacked up billions faster than he could give them away, and he worked hard at his philanthropy.

"He give you any recommendations?" Sweetie asked.

"Buy low, sell high."

"Let me write that down," Sweetie said.

Not that she bothered. Sweetie didn't care about money. She'd once taken a vow of poverty and had allowed herself to backslide only to the point of frugality. Having a roof overhead, adequate food and a few changes of clothing were all she asked of the material world.

"Back to Eugene," she said.

"Model prisoner. Obeyed all the rules. Even volunteered to teach interested inmates how to speak Russian."

"How'd that go over?"

"Class was filled to its limit. Most students didn't get much beyond learning the Cyrillic alphabet, but some useful stock phrases were memorized: 'I'm innocent. I'm an American. I have rights. I want to go home.' Like that."

"Useful, if you decide to go to Russia at all. Jim told me Eugene has killed people."

"He told me the same thing." Anticipating Sweetie's next question, Putnam said, "Yeah, I called him. He said the only people he killed were all targeted by the government."

"How can we know that?"

"I wondered the same thing. So I called the President and asked her."

"What?"

"Patti and I get along famously. She said she'd look into it and get back to me. She was interested to hear her husband is bringing the guy into his growing empire."

"How'd you know that?"

"I talk to people and you talk in your sleep."

"I do not."

Putnam said, "I have recordings."

Sweetie bought it, just for a second. "Good thing for you I don't believe in cursing."

"Just kidding about the recordings, but not about the talking. Well, it's not so much talking as praying. You *pray* in your sleep, for Maxi and me mostly. So I never interrupt."

Sweetie could believe that. "Thank you for the courtesy."

"Right. So the President got back to me and without going into detail said I could trust Gene Beck, as far as she could determine. You want me to see if the gun lobby's former top dog has a hit out on James J. McGill — with Gene Beck along to watch my back."

"You think you'll need him?" Sweetie asked.

"I'd feel better having a guy like that nearby."

Sweetie sighed. "And I'd feel better if you check out Auric Ludwig. Jim said he thought it was possible that Ludwig might come after him. But he's understandably hung up on the threat to his kids, and he likes Harlan Fisk for that."

Putnam said, "You and I would be more concerned about a threat to Maxi than one to our own sweet selves."

"Yes, we would. That's why I'm asking you to do this."

"And I'm happy to do it. But you know what lurks just below the surface here, right?"

"What? You think I'm itching to go back and do my own investigations?"

"Let's just say you haven't laid that demon to rest, and I don't have the free time to be your steady proxy."

"I know. I'll work it out."

The doorbell rang. Putnam said, "That's Gene. Want me to introduce you?"

"You've met the guy?"

"Yeah, kind of like him, too. He whistles a merry tune."

"Maybe another time," Sweetie said.

They got up and she gave him a kiss. "Be careful."

"Always."

The White House — Washington, DC

Caitie McGill, over the years, had seen a good many rooms in the Executive Mansion. She knew the place far more intimately than the tourists who took the guided public excursions. She hadn't seen either the John F. Kennedy Conference Room, better known as the Situation Room, or her father and step-mother's bedroom. Some places were simply off limits.

She had been allowed into the Oval Office a number of time. This time she was there with her dad. Patti was on her way and would join them shortly. McGill saw Caitie examining her surroundings with a more critical eye than she'd previously employed. She was taking in details. The placement of the furniture, the window treatments, the rug with the Presidential seal. And probably the fact that there wasn't a speck of dust anywhere in the room.

"Figuring out the lighting and the camera placement?" McGill asked.

Caitie snapped out of her reverie. "What?"

"You were thinking about how to shoot a scene in here, weren't you?"

She bobbed her head. "Pretty obvious, wasn't I?"

"Uh-huh. You get carried away by these cinematic moments often?"

"Only when I'm in a safe place or I have someone trustworthy with me."

"So you won't wander into traffic," McGill said.

Caitie rolled her eyes. "Dad, you've taught all of us to be alert when we're out in public. I've taken that to heart. Besides, when you're watchful you see more *interesting* things, too. Not just potential threats."

"Good." McGill looked as if he might say something but held his tongue.

Caitie saw the hesitation with no trouble. "What? What were you going to say?"

"Well, since you asked. I got the feeling you were doing more than just lifting the Ramseys' spirits when you told them you and Carrie could have beaten the snot out of the Mongols."

"What more was I doing?" Caitie asked.

"You were thinking how well you might have done if you'd been in Carrie's place."

Caitie fixed her eyes on McGill's. "You're scary sometimes, Dad, you know."

"Why? Because I know you think in many of the same ways I do?"

"Is that what you were thinking, too?" Caitie asked.

"Yeah. I think I could have gotten two of the bad guys before they got me," McGill said. "Three when I was younger. The last guy might even have taken off."

"I think I could've gotten two, too. Three when I reach my physical prime."

"You're that good?"

"I've been practicing with a stunt guy I know. He teaches Jeet-Kune-Do in his spare time. That's the martial art Bruce Lee devised."

McGill grinned, and wondered why he hadn't heard about that from the Secret Service. Maybe because he hadn't asked. He knew enough to respect reasonable boundaries of privacy with his off-spring.

"Maybe you can show me a few new tricks sometime," he said.

"What new tricks might those be?" Patti asked, walking in unannounced.

Being President, she could do that.

Galia was with the boss and closed the door behind them.

"Patti," Caitie said with a smile, rushing to hug her step-mother.

She did the same with just a bit less enthusiasm to Galia.

"*Ça va?*" Patti asked. How goes it?

"*Ça va,*" Caitie said. It goes.

McGill knew the multi-purpose French colloquialism, but once his wife and his child got going in their common foreign language he was lost. It was a situation he intended to remedy after he and Patti left the White House. He'd study French privately, and keep his new fluency secret for a year or two. See what he might overhear.

Patti took the seat behind her desk. The McGills and Galia sat in guest chairs.

Caitie understood the significance. "We're talking official business here?"

"In a minute. What are these new tricks you mentioned, Jim?"

McGill inclined his head toward Caitie. "The kid is studying a new martial art."

"Jeet Kune Do," Caitie said. "The way of the intercepting fist."

"Bruce Lee's brainchild," McGill said.

"No kidding?" Patti said. "Well, he was pretty fierce, though he left us far too soon."

"Do you wear protective gear?" Galia, the only Jewish mother in the room, asked.

Caitie nodded and then hedged, "Sometimes. When we spar. If it's just learning forms and movements, we wear street clothes. What's great about it is you're free to improvise if a new technique pops into your head. It's like jazz that way."

"Like springing off a bent knee and head-butting someone?" Patti asked.

Caitie winced. She knew her step-mother wasn't just making a wild guess.

McGill could only say, "What?"

Caitie glanced at her father and decided she'd rather face the President of the United States.

"You've heard from the Secret Service?" she asked Patti.

The President nodded. "Only very recently."

"What's going on here?" McGill asked, hoping to hear from one of his two family members, and not in French.

Caitie sucked it up and told McGill of her attack on Special Agent Godwin.

McGill brought a hand to his forehead as if experiencing a migraine. "Do you know you might have killed the man?"

In a small voice, she answered, "I didn't at the time. My new sparring partner told me about what might've happened. I felt sick. I won't do it again …"

McGill heard the abridgment. He looked at his daughter and asked the relevant question, "Unless?"

"I have to."

Galia said, "Maybe I should step out."

Both McGill and Patti shook their heads.

Uncharacteristically chastened, Caitie asked, "You want *me* to go?"

"I want you to study ballroom dancing and flower arrangement," McGill said.

"It's a little late for that, Dad."

"That's what I was afraid of. Okay, that's your secret; here's mine. The President, her chief of staff and I spoke with former SAC Crogher last night. He told me of the idea you and he shared that the kidnapping of Special Agent Ramsey — the bad guys mistakenly thinking they'd grabbed you — was the opening move to get all the McGill kids to take shelter at the Enquist home in Minnesota. I had some doubts about that at first, but after talking to Elvie Fisk, I buy it."

Patti picked up the thread. "So I said, 'Let's move everyone to Camp David. Carolyn and Lars included. They'll all be safe there.'"

McGill added, "Meanwhile, Abbie and Ken's stand-ins can take their places in Minnesota."

Caitie saw the script unfold in her mind. "You want the creeps to attack a strong target, not a weak one. Very Sun Tzu."

McGill said, "We want them to give up when the trap springs and they see how overmatched they are. And I take it you learned about Sun Tzu from Mr. Jeet Kune Do."

"Yes."

"How many boyfriends do you have?" McGill asked.

"Just one, maybe. Ben. Charles looks middle-aged but he's older than Mr. Miyagi. He's a friend and a mentor but that's all."

"Glad to hear it," McGill said. "A maybe boyfriend is better than two of them."

"Dad?"

"Yes?"

"I'm here right now because you can't use *my* stand-in in Minnesota, right? You want to tell me I have to go to Camp David, too."

"Uh-huh."

"And you've got reinforcements." Meaning Patti and Galia.

"I do."

"I'm surprised you didn't bring Sweetie."

"She wasn't available."

"But there's a catch, isn't there?" Caitie said. "Or you would have just packed me off with Abbie and Ken."

Patti said, "What's the problem, do you think?"

Caitie took the time to look at the situation from several angles. Ignoring the three old folks looking at her.

She concluded, "Uncertainty is the problem. How do you keep the ruse going? The bad guys can't possibly be dumb enough to just attack Mom and Lars' house without at least one of them taking a good long look at it first. See what the conditions are.

"If they see Abbie and Ken," Caitie said using air-quotes for each of her siblings' names, "the stand-ins might fool them. But if they don't see me or someone who looks like me, that might be a giveaway. If I'm not there, they might think it's because they already have the real me.

"Or if they have someone who has a few brain cells to rub to-gether, they might think: You know what? Those bastards aren't going to take a chance exposing the real Caitie McGill. Those other two McGill kids are phonies, and so is the one we kid-napped. We should probably get rid of her right now because those SOBs probably have us figured out.

"On the other hand," Caitie said, "if I'm there, the ambiguity remains in place and Carrie Ramsey has a better chance of staying alive."

Patti and Galia nodded. McGill hated the choice he faced: risk his child's safety or possibly increase the danger to the Ramseys' daughter.

Caitie saw his pain and took his hand in hers. "I can do it, Dad. I won't screw up."

McGill was less than convinced, but he said, "Don't tell your other mother."

Caitie nodded. "Of course not. But she shoots better than I do."

When Caitie left the Oval Office, McGill walked her out and gave her two choices of places to go: the Residence or the White House kitchen. Knowing she'd better play along or her chance to play a starring role in Minnesota might go poof, she said, "I'll go to the Residence and get some room service."

She made her choice in front of the President's secretary, Edwina Byington. A look from McGill was all Edwina needed.

She'd see to it that the Secret Service made sure there were no detours either within the building or to the outside world.

Parental solidarity.

With Caitie's well-being secured for the moment, McGill assumed the responsibility for ushering in the next guest waiting to enter the Oval Office: FBI Acting Deputy Director Abra Benjamin. She was observant and intuitive enough to have read the subtext of the scene between McGill and his daughter: Kids, even ones on the verge of adulthood, could be problems. You had to lay down the rules.

It made her feel a little bit better about not being a hands-on mom.

Who had the time for that stuff?

"After you," McGill told her. He closed the door behind them.

Once they were seated and Abra had been greeted, the President asked her, "You have news, Ms. Deputy Director?"

"Yes, ma'am. Positive on two fronts. We've identified the kidnapper who died when Special Agent Ramsey was taken."

"That's good. Have you shared that with the Secret Service yet?"

"Not yet, ma'am. My thought was to come directly to you."

"Thank you, but we'll hold things up for just a moment." The President buzzed Edwina and asked to have SAC Kendry come to the Oval Office directly. Then she turned back to Abra. "While we're waiting, what can you tell us about Deputy Director DeWitt?"

Abra did her best to maintain a professional demeanor, but she fooled no one in the room. They all saw she had personal feelings here. But no one said a word about that.

"I called Walter Reed to see if there was anything new while I was on my way to the White House. A doctor at Reed told me, in layman's terms, that the brevity of the time between the incident and the initiation of treatment with medication and surgery made things a lot better than they'd have been otherwise."

Abra had to clear her throat and rein in her emotions. "The doctor said even a marginal delay in getting the deputy director to the hospital might have been fatal. He also said that Byron's—"

She caught herself a beat too late on that, speaking with a personal familiarity. "He said that the deputy director's otherwise robust health should help with his recovery. He spoke in terms of functional independence measures and the activities of daily living. In that context, there are progress markers to watch for at three months, twelve months and two years. It's going to be hard, but I … we all have confidence the deputy director will make a substantial and likely complete recovery."

Galia reached out and gave Abra's hand a brief squeeze. "I've had friends who've suffered the same type of misfortune. What I was told, and what I've seen, is the prognosis is far better for patients who have the company of a caring companion."

Abra blinked and said, "He didn't tell me that."

"He might've thought you'd know," McGill said. "I can't imagine anyone who's laid up not doing better with someone to care for him or her on hand."

Before that idea could be discussed, Edwina buzzed to say SAC Kendry had arrived.

Elspeth walked in and at the President's bidding took a seat.

The President told Abra, "We'll talk about Byron again soon, just you and me."

"Yes, ma'am." Abra felt grateful for the President's use of her former lover's first name. It took a bit of the burden off her doing the same thing.

The President told Elspeth, "The FBI has identified the man who died in the kidnapping of Special Agent Ramsey." She nodded to Abra to continue.

"His name is William Anderson. He owned a horse-drawn carriage business in Virginia; still took the reins himself on certain occasions, usually big-money weddings. Normal rates were $500 for two hours or 50 miles. I mention the money because this man was neither poor nor ignorant.

"He went in front of a judge two times, once in criminal court, once in civil court. The criminal offense was simple battery, a bar fight. The other guy started it and threw a first punch that broke

Anderson's nose. From that point, though, it was all Anderson. He would have gone uncharged with a self-defense justification except he kept hitting the other guy even when he was helpless. The police report said witnesses told the cops that Anderson was holding the guy up and hitting him even after he was unconscious. Three of Anderson's friends finally pulled him off or he might have killed the man.

"In court, his lawyer pleaded diminished capacity, claimed his client lost all sense of control after he'd been struck first and didn't even realize how badly he was hurting his attacker. The judge said that didn't absolve Anderson but it was a mitigating circumstance. He didn't impose jail time but he did fine Anderson $10,000 and ordered him to pay whatever medical expenses were not covered by the other guy's insurance company. And since that company wasn't going to pay for a fight started by their own insured, Anderson wound up paying the whole tab, just north of $200,000.

"He was said to be highly irate about that. Blamed all levels of government for being stupid and corrupt. It's rumored that he got more money in donations from like-minded … well, citizens, to be polite about it than he put out."

McGill said, "If that's the case, he not only got more than even with the guy who hit him, he made money in the bargain."

Galia saw another angle. "He also probably felt the intoxication of becoming a leader of sorts." She turned to the President. "No offense, ma'am."

With a straight face, the President said, "None taken. I've enrolled in a twelve-step program. Please continue, Deputy Director. Why was Anderson in civil court?"

"William Anderson was not this man's birth name. That was Roderick Faircloth."

McGill smiled. "Hardly the name for a guy who's a brawler at heart, but then neither is William Anderson, unless it refers to a specific individual."

Abra nodded, silently impressed by McGill's intuition. "It does, we think. The most likely William Anderson we came up with, given our man's brutality in the bar fight and his participation in a kidnapping, was Captain William Anderson, a Confederate guerrilla. He first served with Quantrill's Raiders in Kansas and Missouri.

"Anderson later split with Quantrill and set up his own guerrilla group, one of whom was Jesse James. By today's standards, Anderson and his men would be considered war criminals. Anderson was nicknamed Bloody Bill. He attacked 22 unarmed Union soldiers who were on furlough, going home to their families. He massacred them and mutilated their bodies. On another occasion, he and his men ambushed 150 Union soldiers and slaughtered them, too. He was known to scalp his victims and decorate his horse with those scalps.

"We feel the namesake of that historic monster was the man Special Agent Ramsey took down in Los Angeles," Abra said.

Elspeth Kendry gave a nod of approval.

McGill knew Elspeth would have liked to do as much to the man.

"Anderson might have been the one designated to be Carrie Ramsey's personal jailer," he said. "She might have spared herself a lot of grief, getting rid of that guy."

"Assuming the others weren't his kindred malign spirits," Galia said.

"In a way we hope they are, ma'am," Abra replied to the chief of staff.

"How's that?" the President asked.

"Both the historical record and the FBI regards the Civil War as an armed rebellion against the United States. William Anderson, the original one, certainly qualified as a rebel. We feel the man who assumed his name was emulating him. With that in mind, we're now conducting a search of criminal records in which the offenders' given or assumed names match those of prominent figures in the Confederacy."

"Do you think that's likely?" Galia asked.

McGill nodded. "I bet it is."

"We've already come up with one instance," Abra said.

She told them about the man who visited Dr. Thomas Kirby in Cheyenne, Wyoming with a gynecological photo. "He called himself Lewis Addison Armistead."

The President said, "I think I remember that name from college. He was a Confederate general, wasn't he? Died in battle?"

Abra nodded, "Yes, ma'am. He was the officer who led the deepest advance in Pickett's Charge at Cemetery Ridge in Gettysburg. Armistead's effort was seen as the military high-water mark of the Confederacy."

At that point, McGill asked Abra, "May I have your cell phone number, Deputy Director?"

She didn't ask why, not aloud, but McGill saw the question in her eyes.

He told everyone about the names Elvie Fisk had given him that morning.

McGill said, "I remember Robert E. Lee and Stonewall Jackson's names from high school history, but I didn't know about Bloody Bill or Lewis Armistead. Maybe some of the names Elvie gave me will help expedite the FBI's search. I'll text them to you right now, Deputy Director."

As McGill was doing so, Elspeth Kendry spoke up. "I have a list of names, too, from Dominic Mancuso. Middle Eastern immigrants who have become Canadian citizens and are known to make regular visits to the United States. Mr. Mancuso says they're to be watched closely. Perhaps in case they visit with people here who are nostalgic for the Confederacy."

Abra looked at Elspeth. "Does the FBI know about this?"

"You do now," Elspeth said. "I'll send you the list of names and bios I have."

"And the CIA knows of this, too?" the President asked.

"With apologies to the FBI, ma'am, I told the CIA first. I was about to call the Bureau when I was summoned here."

"Damn," Galia said, "terrorists using the cover of Canadian citizenship."

McGill expanded on that thought, *"Terrorists with no known connections to the bad guys* coming in from Canada. That is scary."

"A nightmare for another day," the President said. "Is there anything more the FBI has learned from Dr. Kirby?"

Abra said, "Yes, ma'am. Armistead was sent to Dr. Kirby by a friend, Dr. Peter Nash. Nash has friends among the right-wing extremist groups in the Mountain West. Dr. Nash has been taken into custody for questioning. He's refusing to talk, but his wife, Pamela, and Dr. Kirby came into our Cheyenne office voluntarily to tell us everything they know. Mrs. Nash has provided us with several names, but she admits it's possible her husband has other acquaintances he's never mentioned to her."

"Have you shared those names with the Secret Service and the CIA?" the President asked.

"Not yet, ma'am."

"Do so before you leave this office, and copy me, too. I'll forward it to the director of national intelligence." The President took a deep breath. "We're all one team here. Our only goal is to protect our country."

"And get Carrie Ramsey back," McGill added.

The President nodded. "Yes, of course. That, too."

K Street — Washington, DC

Putnam thought having Gene Beck as a traveling companion was like having a Pandora channel dedicated to whistling. There was a a lot of country, a fair amount of pop, a little bit of rock and even show tunes and just a touch of jazz.

Putnam mentioned his musical analysis as they set out on their errand. He was driving. Gene was keeping an eye out to see if anyone was taking a particular interest in them. They were headed to Lobbyist Gulch, otherwise known as K Street. Putnam had once plied his trade there, before meeting Sweetie and leaving the dark side. His departure hadn't left a gap. The population of lobbyists in town continued to grow like springtime weeds.

Even so, there were lawyers with other specialties in the gulch.

Criminal defense was prominent among them. Putnam had made an appointment with one of them.

Satisfied for the moment that there were no immediate threats to their welfare, Gene asked Putnam, "You ever whistle?"

"When I was young and my manners were juvenile, I used to whistle at girls."

Gene grinned. "I think we all did that. What I mean is did you ever whistle songs, you know?"

Putnam shook his head. "Not that I can remember. I only sing in the shower, if no one else is home. As bad as my singing is, my whistling is worse."

"Let's hear it."

Putnam shot him a glance. "I don't think I can. My lips are usually too dry."

"Come on. 'Mary Had a Little Lamb.' Everybody knows that one. Just lick your lips and give it a try."

"I don't know," Putnam said.

"Tell you what. Just give it one try and I'll teach you how to do a truly great wolf whistle. You can impress your wife at just the right moment."

Now, that idea appealed to Putnam. He couldn't wait to see how Margaret might react. He licked his lips and gave "Mary" a try. To his surprise, he managed to do a passable job. He stopped for a red light and looked at Gene.

"Not bad for a beginner. You want to learn the wolf whistle now?"

"No, let's wait a bit on that one. I want to think of the right moment to use it first. Have that for inspiration."

"Fair enough. Tell me again about this lawyer we're going to see."

Putnam said, "His name is Nicholas Kingsbury."

"That's a pretty la-di-da name."

"Well, he added the s-b-u-r-y. He was Nicky King when I knew him in college."

"Law school?"

"Undergraduate. I went to Georgetown Law; Nicky went somewhere in Arizona, I think."

"But you kept in touch?"

"Not especially. But you hear about people through undergrad news sites, what so-and-so is doing these days. And once I started working with Darren Drucker, people came out of the woodwork. Just about everyone I'd ever met. Even girls who turned me down for dates. Nicky told me he'd gone into criminal defense, specializing in white-collar defendants. Like he thought I had to be dipping into Darren's till."

"Any reason he should think that?" Gene asked.

Putnam laughed. "Not with Darren, and not since I met Margaret. Not since I've had the FBI looking over my shoulder since I was a teenager. But that's another story."

"But you never told Nicky about all that?"

"No. If people want to misjudge you, sometimes that can come in handy."

Gene said, "I know all about that. It was how I made my living for a while. That's another story, too. So is there anything I should know about this meeting?"

"Nicky is the third lawyer to represent Auric Ludwig. You know who he is, right?"

Gene nodded.

"Ludwig was charged with and convicted of obstruction of justice. His first lawyer was Ellis Travers. He tried to get Ludwig to give up some bent cops in exchange for leniency. When Ludwig wouldn't play ball, Travers resigned. Ludwig's second lawyer was Spencer Dryden."

"Now, him I know," Gene said. "The cowboy lawyer."

"Right. He got a million dollars for getting the best sentence anyone could hope for. Ludwig got a 20-year stretch instead of the 30-year maximum. There were plenty of rich, grieving parents wanting to see Ludwig do the whole ride. The only reason they didn't raise holy hell was with Ludwig's hypertension he's unlikely to make it through ten years of incarceration, much less do his full sentence."

"So Nicky King is doing what," Gene asked, "trying for an appeal?"

"Yeah."

"Nicky have any chance of winning for Ludwig?"

"I've checked Nicky's record," Putnam said. "It's a lot better than I would have suspected, but I don't see a chance in hell of Ludwig getting off with time served. The sentence might be shaved down to 15 years, maybe even ten. But that's the best I see him getting. There's going to be a lot of push back from those rich parents whose kids got gunned down on a football field."

Gene was quiet. Putnam caught a glimpse of his eyes in the rear-view mirror.

Got the feeling, up close and personal, this was a man who could indeed kill.

If he'd lost a child on that field, Ludwig likely wouldn't have made it to prison.

Whatever his feelings, Gene asked, "How's a jailbird paying for a private lawyer?"

"I asked Nicky. He said donations from supporters. The way I see things, Ludwig knows even if he gets a substantial cut in his sentence, he's still going to die in prison. So what's he got to lose by trying to have Jim McGill killed?"

"I'd ask how he'd pay for a killer but he could probably pass the hat for that, too."

"Probably could."

"You don't really think Nicky's going to tell you he even knows about any such thing?"

Putnam said, "He'd certainly never admit it, especially if he's in on it. You know, placing the help-wanted ad or whatever. But in our college years I played poker many a night with Nicky. The only times he won were when I wanted to encourage him. I know his tells, bluffs and how to make him fold."

Gene smiled and started whistling a happy tune.

"What's that one?" Putnam asked.

"Don't know," Gene said, "I'm writing it right now."

The Oval Office — Washington, DC

After McGill and Abra Benjamin had left the President's inner sanctum, the discussion between Patricia Grant and Galia Mindel turned to politics.

"Do you think Warren Altman is done, out of the race?" the President asked.

Galia said, "We'll know soon enough, ma'am. I'm not usually one to see a supernatural hand interfering in the affairs of us mortals. This time might be different. If Captain Dexter Cowan sent a letter to his brother, Stephen, who didn't open it and that letter was passed on to the former Arlene Cowan, who also didn't take a peek but passed it on to Colonel Yates, well, I begin to wonder. Maybe the murdered Mrs. Altman cut a deal with a higher power to have the letter come to light at exactly the wrong time for her husband. Just as he's reaching for the biggest prize he could ever imagine."

"Becoming commander in chief," the President said.

Her chief of staff nodded. "Up until now, Mrs. Altman's murderer has never been determined much less found."

Patricia Grant thought back to the early days of her presidency. It seemed like a lifetime ago. "Jim had suspicions that Captain Cowan had killed Mrs. Altman at General Altman's direction. There was no proof of that, though."

"Captain Cowan's finale on the Beltway — trying to ram his car at high speed into the one with Colonel Yates and Leo Levy inside — was the last act of a desperate man," Galia said.

"Or someone who'd lost his mind," the President replied. "But even if Captain Cowan did write to his brother that he'd killed Mrs. Altman at the general's bidding, would that hold up in court? Could he be convicted on the testimony of a man he'd never be able to confront?"

Galia shrugged. "That's a question for a lawyer to answer.

Maybe several lawyers and ultimately who knows how many judges. What matters more is how it would play in the court of public opinion. And we both know what that verdict would be."

"Guilty," the President said. "Warren Altman would become a pariah and would never be elected President."

"Even if there's no direct admission of murder by Captain Cowan, there could still be a confession of some lesser but still career-ending crime. In that case, Altman's goose is still cooked," Galia said. "Just by publicly walking away from Ellie Booker's question he implicated himself in some misdeed he doesn't want to talk about."

"All right," the President said, "we'll agree Warren Altman is finished politically. What about Senator Oren Worth? What are his chances of succeeding me?"

Glee entered Galia's voice. "Absolutely none if you resign and Jean Morrissey is sworn in, as Didi DiMarco suggested you might do."

"And failing that?"

"Well, Senator Worth's whining that you'd be playing unfair to give your Vice President a leg up on winning the job undercut his image as a tough, smart, rich guy. If he'd kept his wits about him, he would have laughed and told Didi, 'Let Jean Morrissey have it that way for a few months, if that's what she wants. I'm going to *win* two full terms.' That would have made him look confident. His partisans would be cheering. His poll numbers would have skyrocketed."

Patricia Grant's laugh was mirthless. "I'm glad you work for me, Galia. You'd probably have anticipated that question and prepped Worth on how to respond."

Galia lowered her voice. "Madam President, just between the two of us, I *gave* that question to Didi DiMarco."

The President said, "I should have known." Then she asked, "How hard will it be for Jean to win the Presidency if she remains at Byron DeWitt's bedside instead of going out to campaign and debate?"

"The Vice President would get a great deal of admiration and sympathy from the public, and she'd also lose to Worth, even if he did look like a wimp. But he won't. He'll rehabilitate himself. Jean won't be able to phone in her campaign. Elections in this country don't work that way."

"How much of an edge would it give Jean if I did resign?"

Galia peered at the President to see if she was serious.

She saw no sign of jest.

So she said, "The advantage would be considerable because the duties and obligations of this office would leave the new President no choice but to leave her fiancé's recuperation to others. She'd either be here working on the business of the nation or—"

"She'd be out telling the public why they should elect her for a term of her own," the President said.

Galia offered a note of caution. "If you made the offer, Jean might tell you, 'Thanks but no thanks.' You have to consider that possibility."

"She might do that."

Galia had to know: "How seriously are you about considering this idea, Madam President?"

"I'm not sure. I'll have to discuss it with Jim."

Kingsbury & Knolls — Washington, DC

Putnam's old college pal, Nicholas Kingsbury, didn't keep him waiting five seconds after his secretary announced them on her intercom. "Mr. Shady and a friend are here to see you, sir."

Kingsbury embraced Putnam with apparent sincerity and then stood back at arm's length to take a good look at him. "You look great, Putnam. Better than that photo of you on the bar association website."

"Did you check me out?" Putnam asked.

Putnam had called an hour earlier to see if Kingsbury had time to see him.

"Yes. Wanted to make sure I'd recognize you, but I barely do.

You've lost weight. Hell, you look fit. Happy, even. What's your secret?"

"Marry the right woman."

"*You* are married?"

"I know. Surprised me for the longest time, too. I put an ad up for a basement apartment to rent in my townhouse and the woman of my dreams answered it."

"You always were a lucky SOB." Kingsbury stepped back and extended a hand to Gene. "Nick Kingsbury."

Gene shook hands. "Gene Beck."

Kingsbury turned back to Putnam and asked, "You checked *me* out?"

"Yeah. You going to invite us in, offer us a couple of seats?"

Kingsbury responded indirectly. "I read you're working with Darren Drucker. Is that right?"

"Yes."

"And you haven't taken on a special assignment with the Department of Justice or anything like that?"

Putnam shook his head. Said, "No," too, in case his old pal had a recorder going.

"Should we cut this reunion short, if you're not happy to see me?" Putnam asked.

"Are you in trouble? Do you need a lawyer? Is your friend a lawyer, too?"

"No to all three questions."

Kingsbury looked at Gene, and asked, "You know who Auric Ludwig is?"

"Used to be a gun guy. Now, he's an inmate."

"What do you think of him?"

Gene looked at Putnam, who nodded.

"He's a dick."

Kingsbury gave that a moment's consideration. "Yeah, he is. Come on in."

He pointed to two guest chairs, leaned back and told his secretary, "No calls, please, Judy."

He closed the door and took the black leather throne behind his glass-top desk.

Kingsbury was still focused on Gene. "If you're not a lawyer, may I ask what you do?"

Gene glanced at Putnam again. Got another nod.

"I used to be a contract assassin for the government. Then I was an inmate. Now, I'm trying to see if maybe I can divide my time between becoming a private investigator and writing songs."

Kingsbury had heard everything Gene said, made mental notes of it all, but he fixated on the first line of Gene's résumé. "You *killed* people?"

"Only bad ones. Guys stamped 'Null and Void' by the government."

"*Our* government, the federal government?"

"That's the one. Of course, sometimes I just BS folks for the fun of it. You decide."

While Kingsbury was working on that, Putnam redirected the conversation.

"You did an in-depth search on me, didn't you, Nicky?"

Turning his gaze away from Gene, Kingsbury said, "Sure, it's only natural to see how old friends turned out."

"So you already knew I'm married and who my wife is."

"Margaret Sweeney and, yeah, I know she's a longtime friend of James J. McGill."

"She's like a sister to him. One time she even took a bullet for him. If somebody like, say, Auric Ludwig were to try to involve you in a plan to do violence against Mr. McGill, it would be an awful mistake on your part. You don't have to worry about dealing with Gene but as for Margaret, I can't make any promises."

Kingsbury stared at Putnam, trying to see if he was blowing smoke.

Before he could decide, Gene said, "Hey, he might worry about me, too."

"See, Nicky, your troubles are multiplying already," Putnam said.

"Hey, wait a minute. Who said I'm —"

"Scheming with Auric Ludwig?" Putnam asked. "Violating professional ethics and maybe conspiracy laws? Not me. But you know how it is in our profession. You do your due diligence or you fold your tent, right? The sad truth, I found out, is somebody ratted out Ludwig's scheme. Told me you're his lawyer, too."

Kingsbury immediately wanted to know who the informer was.

And just as quickly he knew that Putnam would never tell him.

"I did not, I do not violate any laws," Kingsbury said. "You're the guy traveling with a possible hitman in tow."

Without asking Putnam's permission, Gene said, "That *was* true, what I said. But I'm retired from that line of work, just to be clear."

Kingsbury couldn't let it go at taking Gene's word. Lawyers lived to argue.

"Retired at a relatively young age. Probably keeping your skills sharp all the same."

Gene shrugged. "Have to admit you're right about that. It's a dangerous world out there."

"Jim McGill got into a tussle with Gene once," Putnam told Kingsbury.

His eyes brightened with interest. "Yeah?"

Gene answered, "He planted me. Never saw it coming, what he did."

"What'd he do?" Kingsbury asked.

"Out-whistled me."

That baffled the lawyer.

Putnam said, "You don't need to know the details, Nicky, only that it's true. If you further an illegal act on behalf of Ludwig, you'll have Mr. McGill to deal with, along with everyone else. It won't work out well for you."

Kingsbury sat mute behind his desk compressing his lips until they almost disappeared. He became the picture of a poker player holding a bad hand. Showing everyone at the table his tell, too. As if experiencing an epiphany, Kingsbury suddenly understood what he was doing. Figuratively showing his cards. Maybe even a guilty conscience.

Both Putnam and Gene saw it as clear as day.

"Oh, Christ," he said.

"How bad is it, Nicky?" Putnam asked.

His voice small, he said, "Not so bad, yet."

"Tell me."

"That would be unethical."

"Make it hypothetical," Putnam said.

Kingsbury thought about that and nodded.

"Say a lawyer is given a sealed envelope by a client."

"A client who's incarcerated."

Kingsbury said, "Can't say," while nodding ever so slightly.

"Continuing hypothetically," Putnam said, "we both know inmates can speak privately on the phone to their lawyers, but there are long lines to use the phones and who the hell knows if someone isn't actually listening in? Inmates can send private postal mail to their lawyers, but who knows how long it will take to be delivered, and maybe that's being snooped, too. E-mail is out because some prosecutors have used incriminating e-mails in court, and judges have allowed it."

"The bastards," Kingsbury said. "That has to be unconstitutional."

"Possibly someday, but not right now," Putnam said. "Back to the hypothetical. The stationery available to jailbirds, to write home to mom or to some lonely woman who's not choosy about her pen-pals, that stuff is really cheap. You hold it up to a bright light, you can read right through the envelope."

Kingsbury knew where Putnam was going and squirmed in his seat.

Another tell, Putnam saw. He was getting to the man.

"So," Putnam said, "if our hypothetical lawyer received a fancy parchment envelope with a privacy lining from the inmate, guess what? The inmate didn't get it legitimately. He conspired with a prison staffer, the two of them committing a small crime. Unless the inmate is contracting with someone on the outside to commit a murder. Then it's a great big crime. For everyone involved."

Kingsbury's nervous energy departed. He sank into his plush seat and muttered, "Jesus."

Gene nodded. "Probably even a lawyer could be in a real bad spot, huh?"

"It's no place I'd want to be," Putnam said, "especially if I'd been paid a big fee."

Kingsbury whined, "The money I was paid was for Mr. Ludwig's appeal of his conviction."

"Of course," Putnam said, "but the prosecutor will show the jury statistics on how often such appeals succeed. Not very is the answer. Next, he'll bring up the fact that a murder or at least the plan for a murder ensued from the lawyer's actions and he'll ask the jury to decide if that was all a big coincidence. But, hey, this is all hypothetical, right? And maybe Ludwig does just want to send an Easter card to his mother. No, wait. I checked. She's dead."

Putnam stood and said, "Come on, Gene, let's go. We've taken up enough of my old friend's valuable time. Good to see you again, Nicky."

They made it to the door before Kingsbury called out, "Wait, what should I do?"

Putnam said, "Get yourself a good lawyer. Someone honest and careful."

Putnam and Gene got into an empty elevator, and Gene asked, "There are lawyers like that? Good and honest."

"Sure, at least half of us, I'd say. Me only since meeting Margaret."

"So what do you think he's going to do?"

"Assuming he hasn't delivered the message yet, he's going to pay cash for a box of envelopes that matches the one Ludwig gave him. He'll open Ludwig's envelope to make sure what's inside isn't really something innocuous. And then —"

"Wait," Gene said, "do *you* know what's in the envelope?"

Putnam shrugged. "No. I only know what Margaret told me

— that she thinks Ludwig could be going after Jim McGill. I found out Nicky is Ludwig's lawyer and things played out from there. You might have noticed back there who the better poker player is."

"Yeah, that was obvious. But we did all this because your wife had a hunch?"

"When you get to know Margaret better you'll come to appreciate her intuition."

"Okay, but if it is just a greeting card in the envelope, Nicky puts it back into another envelope and passes it along. If it is a solicitation to kill somebody, he puts it back into a new envelope and takes it to another lawyer, one representing him?"

"Yeah," Putnam said.

"Well, what if Ludwig has contacted somebody on the outside about this deal, maybe even hinted how to pick up a payment, and that guy doesn't get the envelope? Nicky might get a visit from somebody who'll give him a real bad time."

They left the building and got into Putnam's car. "You know, Gene, I should have thought of that. I'm glad you did."

"You going to call him?"

"Yeah," Putnam said, "but I'll let him sweat a little first. Remind me in half-an-hour, okay? In case it slips my mind."

"What if Nicky has delivered the envelope already and some guy with a gun has started making plans?"

"Then the lawyer Nicky consults will tell him to get in touch with me to give Mr. McGill a heads-up. But I'm not going to wait for that. I'll tell Margaret about our visit with my former school-mate, and she'll tell her old friend to go on high alert."

"There's one more thing," Gene said.

"What?"

"You considered there might be some risk in all this for you, too, right?"

"Yes."

"So you brought a self-admitted killer along with you. That would make most people think twice about trying to mess with you."

Putnam saw an opening in traffic and pulled onto the street.

He glanced at Gene. "Margaret has brought me a long way down the path of righteousness, but I'm not sure I'll ever cross the finish line."

Gene laughed. He could relate to that.

Then he went back to whistling the new song in his head.

The White House — Washington, DC

McGill was on the phone in his Hideaway. "Caitie ratted me out."

"She didn't," Abbie, his elder daughter, said.

"Not at all," Ken added.

Two-thirds of McGill's offspring were on a conference call with him.

The one-third he'd just accused of treachery was flying back to Minnesota.

Before McGill could explain his position, Abbie continued, "Caitie didn't call us; we called her."

Ken said, "We wanted to know if she was able to help you. Move things along. Get us all back to normal. We miss our regular lives."

"Caitie said maybe she helped a little, suggesting a movie to watch to that girl you talked to, but you did the heavy lifting, Dad," Abbie said.

"The movie was awful but it was important," McGill told his children, "and Caitie knew instinctively to play the bad cop, leaving me to be the good cop."

"Wish we could have seen that," Ken said.

"I'll provide all the details once you get to Camp David."

There was a drawn out silence that McGill didn't like at all.

"What?" he asked. "What are the two of you thinking?"

Abbie said, "It's gone past the thinking stage."

Ken added, "Once Caitie told us she's going to stay here in Minnesota, in case there is a confrontation here …"

Abbie said, "Ken and I have decided we're staying, too."

McGill felt a steel band tighten around his head. He knew better than to issue a paternal edict. That stuff wouldn't work anymore. His children were nominal adults now. They might politely decline any direct order or just tell him to buzz off, depending on their mood.

But he could ask, "Why?"

"It's what families do," Abbie told him. "Stick together."

Ken offered another reason. "If Mom and Lars don't know what might be coming, we have to watch out for them."

"That's right," Abbie said. "You asked Caitie not to tell Mom and she didn't. She only told us. Mom and Lars will be caught by surprise if some bad guys try anything stupid. We have to be there for them. See they don't get hurt."

Ken continued the onslaught. "You really should tell Mom and Lars, Dad. They should have time to prepare. Make their own choices. They might want to go to Camp David."

"Without you? Without their three children?" McGill asked, incredulous.

"It's a possibility," Ken said.

Abbie added, "We are all adults, Dad. Even Caitie, the youngest one of us. Who you already gave permission to be here."

Now, McGill understood, at least a little.

The senior offspring had their noses out of joint about the junior member receiving privileged status. Truth was, though he would never say so aloud, of the three of them, he thought Caitie had the most instinctive street savvy. And now Jeet Kune Do training, too. On top of her Dark Alley training. More of his own personal ruthlessness, too.

Put all of his kids in a bad situation, he'd bet money Caitie would come through it in the best shape. McGill did the only thing he could in a no-win situation.

He said, "Let me talk to your mother."

Carolyn came on the phone, quickly enough that McGill knew Abbie and Ken hadn't pled their case to her first. She said, "Tell me there's some good news, Jim."

McGill repressed a groan and gave her the only news he had.

Carolyn took it well, in that she didn't scream or rage. On the other hand, she went all cool and determined, telling him, "We're not budging, any of us. Somebody comes looking for trouble, between the Secret Service and us, they'll get it."

Sweet Mother of God, McGill thought. Was there something in the water up in Minnesota?

"Carolyn, I know you've toughened up over the years. Caitie tells me you're a respectable shot with your handgun."

"I'm better than respectable; I'm really good."

"Okay, I understated it. Sweetie has told me you're very skilled." McGill could almost feel his ex-wife's glow. "But as far as I know you've never shot at another person, especially one who's shooting at you."

If not deafening, the silence from his ex was palpable.

McGill made a diplomatic concession. "I imagine that to save the kids, Lars or yourself, you could do whatever is necessary."

"Even for you, Jim. You're on my list, too."

McGill knew she was sincere and that touched him. "Thank you."

"I know you'd do the same for me."

"I would, but wouldn't you prefer to avoid that necessity?"

"Of course, but if you'll remember we went through this drill once before, not long after Patti was first elected. Well, in all the years since then, we've all changed. And what if we were to face a situation like this *after* Patti leaves the White House? We won't be able to scurry off to Camp David then."

McGill thought they could *build* their own sanctuary but he kept that to himself.

He only said, "I pray fervently that things will calm down for all of us with a change of administrations, but I see your point."

After a beat, Carolyn said, "So I expect you'll be joining us soon."

Not having a real choice, McGill said, "Yeah, even if I have to parachute in."

McGill was still stewing when Patti entered the Hideaway with two bottles of beer in hand, Beck's Sapphire, his new favorite. She hadn't brought any glasses, just the beer. Handed him one and sat close beside him.

They clinked bottles in a wordless toast and drank.

McGill said, "This is just what I needed. How'd you know?"

"I didn't. I asked Blessing what he thought you might like."

The White House head butler was good at anticipating needs.

"Let's take him with us when we go," McGill said.

"That's one of the things I want to talk to you about, what comes next and when. But tell me what's bothering you first."

McGill told her about the anticipated confrontation in Minnesota and how his offspring and former missus intended to man the ramparts, even if three out of the four were women.

"The only thing I can think to do in the face of such reckless courage is ask you to call out the National Guard to back up the kids and Carolyn," McGill said. "Even if it puts Secret Service noses out of joint."

Patti took another swig of beer and said, "I think special forces would be a better fit than weekend warriors."

"SEALs?" McGill asked, nodding his approval.

"Them or Delta Force or Rangers, whoever's handy. I'll call the Secretary of Defense in just a minute. This does sound serious."

McGill kissed his wife. "I'm going to need another plane, too. So I can get to Minnesota fast."

"You gave the plane you already had to Caitie?"

He nodded.

"Maybe you can fly with the special forces guys."

"I'm okay with that."

Then Patti told McGill the idea of resignation was growing on her.

36,000 Feet Above Michigan

Caitie McGill knew she was being spoiled. It was impossible to think anything else. Her father, through the good offices of her step-mother, had provided her with a private jet and an Air Force crew, including a steward to serve food and drinks, to take her as the only passenger from DC to Rochester, Minnesota.

Abbie and Ken had promised to meet her at the airport. That was a normal family-type thing to do. But at the moment she felt more like a studio head than a soon-to-be film student. She thought she'd better watch out. If she got accustomed to the luxe life it might mess with her artistic values and sense of esthetics. She'd be blinded by glitter and wouldn't be able to see the beauty in ordinary life any more.

If she let that happen, forget about movies, she'd be directing television spots for De Beers diamonds, airing on AWE, formerly Wealth TV. Yeesh.

Fortunately for her, she'd had a great idea in applied cinema to take her mind off any professional pitfalls. She needed to get Ben to Minnesota to make it work, though. She rang for the steward.

"How may I help you, Ms. McGill?" he asked.

The guy was *cute,* Too old for her but not for Abbie. Looked great in his uniform.

Before she got too carried away, she asked, "Is it all right if I make a phone call?"

"Of course. One phone isn't going to interfere with our navigation or communications systems. On commercial flights, if you had hundreds of people using their phones at the same time, that would be a concern. Plus the babble would be maddening."

Caitie laughed. "Yeah, I can see that. It'd be like getting stuck in a giant phone booth."

"Exactly. Would you like something to eat or drink?"

"I'd love a ginger ale, thanks."

"Coming right up."

The steward brought her drink with a straw.

"I'm sorry," he said. "I forgot to ask if you'd like a cherry with your ginger ale."

Caitie smiled and said what she had was just fine.

But she'd like to get a picture of herself with the crew after they landed.

Ask Abbie what she thought of the handsome steward.

She called Ben and asked, "How'd you like to get on a plane right away and make a movie with me in Minnesota?"

He said, "Who wouldn't, but who's paying?"

"I am." Caitie always stashed at least half the pay of every acting job she did, a savings plan made possible by parental subsidies. "Get the first flight you can to Rochester, Minnesota. Fly business class and bring every camera you own, motion and still."

"Sounds exciting already," Ben said.

Then Caitie told him what she had in mind and he said, "Holy shit, that'll be great."

"You're not scared?"

Ben took a moment to think. "Yeah, a little. How about you?"

"I told my dad I wasn't … but, yeah, I'm kind of scared, too."

Walter Reed National Military Medical Center
Bethesda, Maryland

FBI Acting Deputy Director Abra Benjamin got bumped out of Byron DeWitt's hospital room by Vice President Jean Morrissey. Rank had its privileges and all that. Abra was polite, correct and said, "You're welcome" to the Vice President when Jean Morrissey thanked her for sitting with Byron. She referred to him that way, by his first name. Bitch.

She left the room telling herself that being booted out was for the best. She had a massive amount of work to do. Supervising scores of agents running down the known associates of the late Bloody Bill Anderson and the list of cretins that Elvie Fisk had given to James J. McGill now belonged to her. It was a time-devouring job when Special Agent Carrie Ramsey might not have … well, who knew if the clock on her hadn't run out already?

That was where Abra's focus should have been all along.

If Ramsey was still alive, she couldn't have much time left.

To hell with Abra's own screwed up personal life.

She had just about crossed the building's lobby when a woman stepped in front of her, bringing Abra up short. The woman was well dressed, short and slight. She looked Arabic. All of that was incidental. Abra was just about to sidestep her when she spoke in a gentle voice.

"Forgive me, please, for intruding, but are you Deputy Director Benjamin? The Vice President described you to me, if I understood her correctly."

That raised an obvious question for Abra.

"You spoke to the Vice President?"

"Yes, I'm sorry but I had to be terribly forward with her. I am Dr. Hasna Kalil, the new personal physician to his excellency Karim Kamal, the Hashemite Kingdom of Jordan's ambassador to the United States."

For the moment, that didn't mean anything to Abra.

"Is Ambassador Kamal ill? Is he in the hospital here?"

"No, no, Deputy Director. Thankfully, he is in good health. His excellency simply wishes me to deliver a thank you note, and now his best wishes for a speedy and complete recovery to Byron DeWitt. I was told that I am not allowed to see him, but I can give the card to one of the people who have that honor. The Vice President gave me your name."

She reached into her handbag and extended an envelope to Abra.

"If I may impose on you, ma'am, the ambassador would be most grateful."

Abra accepted the envelope but was more than a little curious.

"Dr. Kalil, I'm an investigator, so I have to wonder what the reason is for Ambassador Kamal's gratitude."

The doctor spread her hands in a gesture of helplessness.

"I would be happy to tell you, if only I knew."

"I also wonder why the ambassador would use you as his courier."

Dr. Kalil smiled. "That I can tell you. I was speaking with the ambassador in his office, telling him how pleased I was to be posted to America. I said I would like to learn my way around Washington as soon as I can. He said I could start with a trip here."

Plausible but Abra didn't buy it for a minute.

Not that she had the time to solve a new mystery.

She simply said, "Thank you, Doctor, and please tell the ambassador I'll see that Deputy Director DeWitt gets this card."

"May I walk out with you? My car is just outside also, if that is your vehicle at the curb."

"It is. How did you know Deputy Director DeWitt was in this hospital?"

"The embassy called his office. This is what we were told."

The Bureau traced every call that came into the Hoover Building, so identifying a call to Byron that originated at the Jordanian embassy would back up the doctor's story.

She wondered how the doctor's ride was allowed to park in a tow-away zone. Then she saw. Dr. Kalil had arrived in an embassy car with diplomatic plates, and there was no need at the moment for the medical center security to cause a fuss. So the woman was gaining a bit of credibility.

Abra said goodbye and got into the back seat of her car. The driver knew where to go, back to the office. She fingered the envelope addressed to Byron. She worked it over several times. Feeling for wires and possible explosive material. She felt nothing but paper and card stock.

The driver had his eyes on the road and didn't know what had transpired in the hospital lobby anyway. So Abra took a risk and opened her former lover's mail. Rationalizing that it might be important for her to know what the Jordanians were up to.

They stymied her, though. Whatever the message was, it wasn't written in English. Or even Arabic. What she saw was a block of ideograms. Kanji. Might have been Japanese.

Knowing Byron, though, it was probably Chinese. That would make it hanzi.

Sioux Falls, South Dakota

Dallas Reeves gathered his people. The baker's dozen of them clustered together in the living room of the house on the edge of town. Interstate 90 was just a stone's throw away, and from there it was a straight shot east to Rochester, Minnesota. Two hundred and thirty-six miles, three hours and thirty-seven minutes doing the legal speed limit.

The room's curtains were drawn, but that was just being extra careful. The house was at the dead end of a quiet block and the neighbors were the early-to-bed variety. They certainly wouldn't be partying as midnight on a work night approached. It was possible somebody might be taking the pooch out for a late whizz, but that would be no big deal.

All that guy would see was a couple of friendly looking vans rolling quietly past. If the dog-walker waved to them, the drivers would wave back. Smile, too. Leave the onlooker with a nice, warm feeling. Never giving him any reason to think he'd seen an armed-to-the-teeth troop convoy pass by.

Not that their weapons would be on display. Most of them were hidden in the floors and wall panels of the vans. The drivers were under strict orders to obey all traffic laws. No speeding, but no dawdling too far under the limit either. If, for some reason, one van got stopped, the other would continue to the next highway exit and loop back on the other side of the road.

If the cops had everyone out of the stopped van and it looked like the van was about to be searched, troops from the second van would take out their weapons and eliminate the cops. Each vehicle would then race off on its planned escape route. The mission would be scrubbed.

That would be a bitter disappointment. One everybody would work hard to avoid.

Reeves took them all through the plan once more.

Then he asked, "Any questions?"

A hand went up. The youngest member of the group, a kid named Cole, asked, "Are you sure you want us to kill that Lars Enquist guy? I know it's to let everyone see we're serious, but couldn't we just maim him some and prove our intentions that way? We kill him, it's going to boil their blood. Make it more likely they'll think we'll kill the others even if they give us what we want. For sure, make them shoot to kill us rather than take any of us prisoner."

Doubts as to the wisdom of the plan weren't supposed to crop up at this late hour, but Reeves didn't lash out. The points raised were good ones and Cole was the smartest of the ones who were going to do the actual fighting.

"Well, Cole, it's like this," Reeves said. "We have to go with the psychology that works best. You hurt someone but don't kill him, you give the other side the idea you don't have the stomach to take a life. That could lead them to think all they have to do is come at you hard and you'll cut and run. Then they can pick you off or lock you up at their leisure.

"You can also pretty much take it for certain that they will shoot to kill once we show up carrying our weapons. For them, the simple appearance of armed men will be a capital offense, and really that's as it should be. We're in a war here. We either rally the American people to our side or die trying.

"To me, in the end, a quick death is what I'd prefer to being put in a cage for God knows how many years. Hell, they might even put us on display like we were zoo animals or something. Have kids throw peanuts at us."

That drew laughter, but its tone was nervous.

Reeves had conjured the image of a life none of them would want to endure.

Cole's hand went up again. "After we kill Lars, if they still need convincing, the mother is next?"

Reeves nodded. "Miz Carolyn Enquist, yes."

"And that youngest girl, she has to go too because she's seen you and Lem."

Reeves said, "That was always the plan, to kill one of the McGill children. That way they'll know we're serious when we say that if they come for us after we exchange the other two for the people we want freed, we'll come back and kill them, too. We got that girl first so she was the one we chose. So it didn't matter if she saw us or not."

"That's a lot of killing," Cole said.

"You were told what was going to happen."

"Yeah. Hearing it's one thing, doing it's another."

"You're not up to it, Cole?"

"I'm up to it. What scares me is if I start, I might not know when to stop."

Reeves said, "I'll tell you when."

The big man went over the few remaining details. They'd drive to Rochester and then cruise past Carolyn and Lars Enquist's house out in the country at first light. Go to the Minnesota safe house, eat and sleep. Go back to the Enquist house at sunset, take the Secret Service by surprise, kill them and Lars, and grab all the people Jim McGill loves most in the world.

McGill was the sonofabitch they wanted to feel the most pain.

The only change in the plan was Reeves had Cole stay with him, instead of one of the others. Cole said he could kill? He was going to get the chance to prove it. With Caitie McGill or whoever the hell she was.

Carrie Ramsey had been raised as a Methodist. Mom and Dad didn't go to church every Sunday, but they went more often than not. They contributed a fair chunk of money every year to keep their church and the larger Methodist community going. Dad had traveled to Central America four times with mission groups to provide free medical care to the local people.

If anyone deserved to go to heaven, she thought, Mom and

Dad did.

As for her, she wasn't at all certain heaven existed. She didn't see death as the final curtain, simply lights out and nothing more. Self-awareness probably shifted, she thought. It might not be as discrete as living within an individual body in a particular place. Awareness might become a Zen flow of sensation, energy racing all over creation. The sum of all knowledge might be a certainty that you were rushing ever closer to the source of ... everything.

And once you were there?

Who knew? Maybe you got to ride the roller coaster again.

Carrie's contemplation was interrupted when she saw Lem trying to crawl away. She'd allowed him to take off his shoes and use both of his socks to bind the entry and exit wounds in his right foot. The wounds hadn't seemed to bleed all that much, but then it wasn't *her* blood.

Perspective mattered.

She'd probably closed her eyes while thinking about what happened next if she didn't get out of this damn room alive. It said something that her prisoner was now trying to escape rather than take his gun back and shoot her. Said he knew he was over-matched.

She cleared her throat and when he looked back with fear in his eyes she crooked a finger at him like he was a little kid trying to escape Mom's notice. Get back here, Junior. He hesitated. The doorway was still a good fifteen feet away and he'd have to open the door, too. He didn't have a hope in hell of getting away, but he wanted to be free so bad.

Welcome to the club, asshole, Carrie thought.

She raised the Beretta to make the choice easier for him.

A guy who'd been shot once already, he didn't want to get plugged again.

Especially not pointlessly.

Lem turned himself around, crawled back toward Carrie. She watched his eyes until he lowered his head and looked at the floor. Then she waited for him to gather his muscles in preparation to spring at her, try to get the gun back after all. But he didn't. He stopped ten feet or so short of her, the spot where she'd positioned him earlier.

It would have been okay with her if he'd curled up on the floor like a cat, but he pushed his torso upright with his back against the wall and his legs extended. He looked at his wounded foot and winced. The thing still throbbed with pain. On top of his legitimate discomfort, Lem added a layer of self-pity.

Still, he knew better than to look to Carrie for commiseration.

Having said he was going to rape her, he was lucky she hadn't shot him in the balls.

Carrie was seated with her legs drawn up to her chest and her back against the wall facing the door to the room, a distance of a bit more than twenty-five feet between the two points. If the door was thrown open and someone — please let it be Reeves — charged in, she'd shoot him first, get Lem second and then target anyone else who was foolish enough to try to gain entry.

What she worried about, and tried to push from her thoughts, in case there was any mind-reader nearby, was someone being smart enough to open the door a crack, toss in a firebomb and let both her and Lem get charbroiled. That idea was enough to inspire a personalized prayer: *Please, God, anything but that.*

Just as Carrie swept that horror from her consciousness once again, the door did open a crack, and Fat Dallas Reeves spoke. "Everybody doing okay?"

Carrie didn't say a word. She only pointed the Beretta toward the door.

Lem looked at Carrie, silently asking if he could speak.

She nodded.

"I'm hurt awful bad, Dallas," he said, doing his best to sound piteous.

"She just shot you the once, right?"

A look of indignation hardened Lem's face.

He shared it with Carrie: *Do you believe this asshole?*

Receiving no sympathy, he looked back at the door.

"Yeah, she shot me just once," he said, amping up the volume. "How the hell many times you been shot?"

"The same number I let anyone grab my gun from me."

"You fat bastard."

"Mind your manners, Lem. I'm tryin' to get you out of there. She's still alive, isn't she?"

He looked at Carrie and got another nod.

"Yeah, she's alive."

Carrie heard Reeves and someone with a higher voice whispering.

Then Reeves said, "She doesn't want us getting a fix on where she is unless we give her a shot at us, huh?"

Lem said angrily, "Can't blame her for that, can you?"

"You gettin' sweet on her, Lem? Can't think she's much taken with you, puttin' a bullet in you."

His tone changed to sulking, Lem said, "I don't blame her for that either. Maybe gettin' shot is what it took me to learn a man shouldn't think about doin' wrong to a woman."

"Ain't that sweet?" Reeves asked with a rumbling laugh.

While Reeves was enjoying his wit, Carrie made a series of gestures to Lem. He could leave if Reeves took his place as her hostage. Lem smiled at that notion.

"Hey, Dallas."

"What?"

"She says she'll swap me for you."

Carrie and Lem heard the two voices converse again.

Softly, so the two men — or the man and a boy — outside wouldn't get a fix on her position, Carrie said, "*Bawk, bawk, bawk.*"

That made Lem laugh. "Hey, Dallas, she just called you a chicken."

Carrie held her arms out to her sides.

Lem said, "A big, *fat-assed* chicken."

"Shut the fuck up, Lem," Reeves bellowed. "I'm sending someone in with his hands up. He's just a kid. You kill him, honey, you got that on your conscience. If you got one."

Before Carrie could respond the door swung open. She almost shot in anticipation of someone entering. But she held off. A moment later a kid stepped in with his hands in the air. Carrie focused on a point between him and the doorway. She might have to shoot both the kid and Reeves in the next moment. While not forgetting about Lem either.

The kid figured out what she was thinking with no problem.

He told Carrie, "You don't have to worry about Dallas or Lem. Dallas is good at giving orders but not much else that I've seen. Lem isn't good for much at all."

Lem hadn't moved a muscle since the door opened.

"So which one of us do you want?" the kid asked. "My name's Cole, by the way. In case you want to know who you might shoot next."

Lem looked at Carrie, hoping for mercy.

Keeping her eyes on the kid and the door, Carrie told Lem, "Go ahead, go. Just remember Dallas wouldn't risk himself for you. He doesn't give a shit about you. He's just playing a game here."

"Now, now, young lady," Reeves called out. "Lem knows I love him."

"Yeah, sure. Just remember, Lem: Don't drop your drawers and bend over while Fat Boy's in the room."

Cole grinned.

But Reeves' voice rumbled like thunder. "You got one foul mouth on you, you little bitch."

"Come in and do something about it."

Cole looked in Reeves' direction. Then he turned to Carrie.

"He ain't comin'. Lem, you better get out before he lets her keep both of us."

Lem crawled out as fast as he could. Cole saw a gesture from outside the room. Carrie's Beretta tracked him in case he tried to run. But he only kicked the door shut.

Carrie told Cole, "I don't care if you are a kid, I'll shoot you if I have to. Put your back against the wall. Put your hands on your head and slide down the wall until you're seated with your legs straight out in front of you."

Cole did as he was told.

"You have a gun on you?"

Cole nodded.

"Take it out with a thumb and finger."

"It's in my pants, in back, under my shirt. If I put my hand back there —"

"I'll shoot you. Lie on your stomach with your hands stretched out above your head."

He followed Carrie's instructions. She took the gun away from him and quickly patted him down. He didn't have any other weapons on him. She stepped back and let him sit up with his legs stretched out again.

He looked up at her and said, "You're not eighteen. You're older and you're some kind of cop."

Simple as that, Carrie thought.

You didn't need anything fancy to tell her from Caitie McGill.

Just bring in a teenaged boy.

CHAPTER 7

Thursday, March 31, 2016
J. Edgar Hoover Building — Washington, DC

Deputy Director Abra Benjamin, acting with Director Jeremiah Haskins' approval, had been up all night, directing teams of FBI agents to raid forty-nine American homes in fourteen states. To help in her efforts, she'd consumed caffeine every way but intravenously. She was wide awake, mentally exhausted, highly pissed off and scared silly she might have ended her career within the space of eight hours.

She'd ordered each team from regional offices to make exigent entrances — break down the doors — of all the known militia affiliated associates of Roderick Faircloth, a/k/a William Anderson, a/k/a Bloody Bill Anderson, the man Special Agent Carrie Ramsey had chewed to death in Los Angeles.

Being both thorough and meticulous, Abra had extended the raids to the thirteen named persons on the list James J. McGill had given her, the associates of imprisoned militia leader Harlan Fisk, as provided by his also incarcerated daughter Elvie.

What had Abra gained from her efforts and those of all the men and women she'd mobilized on such short notice? Nothing whatsoever. She'd gone 0-46, with three houses found to be empty. So she'd likely compiled what would undoubtedly be the single largest onslaught of lawsuits brought against the FBI in its history. The offenses ranging from false arrests to property damage to disturbing the peace.

Given sufficiently outraged judges and juries, the damages awarded to the plaintiffs might exceed the Bureau's annual budget.

The monetary awards, though, would be small change compared to the public loss of faith in federal law enforcement. The national ire wouldn't be limited to just the FBI. Everyone from postal inspectors to park rangers would be tarred by the same brush.

If Abra hadn't been so dehydrated, along with all her other personal deficits, she might have cried. Unable to find that avenue of emotional release, she cast about in her mind looking for someone to help her. The first name to occur to her was still under heavy sedation: Byron.

What would he advise her to do in this hellish situation?

Read "The Art of War?" See what old Sun Tzu had to say.

If she'd had the time, maybe she would have done just that. But she had little if any time at all. She couldn't keep scores of people in custody without finding sustainable charges. The longer she held on to them the worse off she'd be.

Forget about law enforcement; the whole of the federal government would suffer.

Good God, she was doing the extremists' work for them.

She had to find someone to help her before her head exploded and she wound up in a hospital bed next to Byron. Then again, maybe that wouldn't be such a bad thing. Become incapacitated and unresponsive while she still had health coverage.

She might actually have tipped into irrationality if she didn't have Special Agent Ramsey's file on her desk. She flipped open the cover and saw Carrie Ramsey's personnel photo. She really did look like Caitie McGill. Abra had never met the President's stepdaughter in person but ...

Damn, if that wasn't the answer right there. Not to the whole problem, but who she could ask for help in Byron's absence: the newly appointed presidential consultant to the Department of Justice, James J. McGill. She'd heard he was even carrying an FBI badge these days.

Close enough to a colleague in calamitous times.

Abra didn't have McGill's personal number so she called the White House public number and pled her case to a switchboard operator. Once the woman verified that she was calling from an executive office in the Hoover Building, she put Abra through, bless her.

Her luck held when McGill answered, but there was a buzzing, rushing noise in the background. "Jim McGill. Is this Deputy Director Benjamin?"

"Yes, sir. We seem to have a bad connection. Should I call back?"

"The connection won't get any better. I'm in flight."

Abra's heart sank. She'd hoped to see McGill in person.

He said, "Something I can do for you, Deputy Director?"

"If you have a few minutes, I could use some advice. I have a bad situation here."

"Whatever I can do," McGill said. "What's the problem?"

She told him what she'd done and the disastrous results.

McGill listened closely and when she finished he asked, "You found absolutely nothing incriminating in any of the 49 homes your people raided. Nothing pertaining to the matter we're both focused on at the moment or anything else?"

McGill was intentionally vague because he didn't know if it was possible to tap into someone speaking from an airplane. He felt it likely was. Wouldn't do to make a bad situation worse.

"No, sir," Abra said. "At the risk of sounding paranoid, it was like they were expecting us and made sure they were ready. Hell, it was like they were expecting a rich aunt to come for a visit. Everything was cleaned and polished. Every last place, that's what I was told."

McGill wanted to reconfirm. "Both the list relevant to the West Coast and the one I gave you?"

Joseph Flynn

"Yes, sir. Both lists."

McGill thought for a moment. "We have a saying in Chicago, one that applies to a lot of places, 'The fix was in.'"

"I agree, but the people we thought might be suspects were right where innocent people should be, at home in bed. Not hatching midnight plots. I have the feeling that as we check further we'll find they were following their usual routines for quite some time."

McGill said, "If the reports from your people are accurate, that would fit."

"I trust my people, sir."

"I do, too. I was just thinking aloud. What about guns?"

"What about them?" Abra asked.

"The people on the list I got from our young friend were members of the armed group that came to Washington. Part of the deal for their release was they had to leave their weapons behind. But that was years ago now. They aren't the kind of people to live in houses without guns. Some of them, I'd think, would even do illegal modifications."

Abra knew McGill meant: convert a semi-auto rifle to fully automatic.

No great feat for a skilled gunsmith.

Abra was quiet long enough for McGill to ask, "Still with me, Deputy Director?"

"Yes, sir. I was just scrolling through some of the reports from the incursion teams. No weapons were fired. I don't even see the mention of any weapons being found on any of the premises."

"None at all?" McGill asked. "Not in *any* of the houses? Not even from the list my young friend provided? That seems impossible, unless —"

"Unless they knew we'd be coming to see them," Abra said.

"Yes," McGill said. But he was thinking of something else.

He was thinking how Elvie had been used and then abandoned by her father, Harlan Fisk. Who was to say others like Fisk wouldn't also use their children to serve their own ends?

"Deputy Director," McGill said. "did your agents report seeing any teenaged children or even young adult children in the homes they raided? If not, check the public records and see if there should have been people in that age range in those homes. If the records say yes, ask Mom and Pop where their kids are? Don't let the any of the adults go before you confirm their children's whereabouts."

Abra understood what McGill was suggesting, but she wanted to be sure.

"You think they're using their kids?" she asked.

"Let's find out," McGill said.

He gave Abra a number where she could reach him directly.

McGill's notion gave Abra a small hope to which she might cling. People abusing their children was one of the gut-roiling things cops at every level of government saw all too often. Simple beatings were only the beginning of the long list of horrors. Gang-bangers using little ones as lookouts for open-air drug markets was common. Pimps luring young girls into prostitution when Mom was busy with her own problems and Dad was a complete unknown.

From what Abra had read in Elvie Fisk's file, she'd been the victim of a variation of sexual exploitation. So, really, it wasn't hard to think that adults might send their kids out to commit a terrorist act or two. Just look overseas. You had child soldiers in Africa and jihadis around the world had started using little kids as suicide bombers.

It was enough to make a normal person gag and then think…

Could happen here.

Abra sent out an email blast to all the offices that had conducted raids. Find out where the children of the people they'd arrested had gone. Off to war maybe? With all the guns that should have been found in their homes? Report back with any information. Let the parents know they'd be charged as accomplices for any illegal acts committed by their children.

That might get their attention, Abra thought.

She'd no sooner sent her email than she received one.

It came from Santa Barbara, California and the desk of Professor

Emeritus Hiram Chen, Byron's mentor and cultural father figure for all things Chinese. Byron had told her how the professor had meant more to him than anyone outside his family when he was growing up. Professor Chen was the only one Abra had thought she could trust to do the translation of the hanzi on the card that Dr. Hasna Kalil had given her.

The FBI did have agents other than Byron DeWitt who were both fluent and literate in Mandarin, but Abra had no idea whether the message from Dr. Kalil was flattering or critical of Byron. She wasn't going to take the woman's word that the message was a combination thank you and get well card. That kind of message could have been penned in plain English.

The idea that a native Arabic speaker would write a message in Chinese to a highly placed FBI official told Abra she should handle things with care. Even to the point of safeguarding Byron from office politics. Professor Chen was the only one she knew who could be relied upon to both do the translation and keep Byron's best interests at heart.

His message to Abra was concise: "Byron has told me, in the past, I may trust you. So I shall. The message you sent to me reads in colloquial translation: 'I owed you one. Here's payment in full.'"

Abra felt a chill reading that. Had Byron done something illegal? For money? She couldn't believe that. For a great piece of modern art? No, not even for that. Professor Chen said there were two URL links in the message and he provided them.

"I have not visited these sites, and I would be wary of using them, if I were you. Also, this hanzi was done by an artful hand. Someone educated and powerful. Make of that what you will.

"I assume you've communicated with me because Byron is unable to do so. I would be most interested to learn what has happened to him, if that is permissible." He signed his name and then added his own message in hanzi characters.

Abra decided to leave the professor's private note untranslated. Byron could read it when he was able.

She only replied to the professor that his message had been

received and she was grateful. Then she took out her personal MacBook Pro and booted it up. She connected to a Wi-Fi network the Bureau reserved for using potentially dangerous hyperlinks. It was discrete from all other systems and any Trojan Horse malware would reap only a mountain of nonsense data. An attacker would be gumming up his own works beyond repair.

The first URL apparently involved no malware, but it almost made Abra vomit nonetheless. Fugitive, former U.S. Representative Philip Brock's head rested on a silver platter between two similarly situated pig heads. A scrawl of Arabic hovered above the three heads.

Fighting back the bile in her throat, Abra wondered how the hell that could be any kind of repayment. With more than a little hesitation, she went to the site at the other URL.

This time she found ten driver's licenses with photos, names and addresses. Four belonged to U.S. residents; four more in Canada; two in Mexico. A thrill ran through Abra. She recognized three of the men immediately. They were wanted terrorists. Big names, the guys she knew.

Abra immediately made screen captures of all ten in case, as she suspected, the site would soon be taken down. She printed out the images, too, in case her laptop somehow became disabled. With more than a little reluctance she returned to the other site and printed out Philip Brock's farewell photo.

The question now was what she should do with all her newly found information.

She did what was expected of any responsible executive. She took things up the chain-of-command and called Director Jeremiah Haskins' office and told his secretary she needed to see him right away. But she did that only after she made copies of everything and sent them to Galia Mindel at the White House.

En Route to Olmsted County, MN

Until the terrorist attacks of September 11, 2001, the use of American military forces within the United States was forbidden by the Posse Comitatus Act of 1878. The act stated that federal troops may not be used to enforce domestic policies. Originally applicable only to the Army, the act's reach was extended in 1956 to the Air Force and by implication, if not specificity, to the Navy and the Marines.

The implicit rationale behind the act was that the nation's armed forces should not become the instruments of a chief executive intent on imposing his notions on the American people.

The act did not apply to the National Guard acting within its own state's boundaries at the direction of state authorities. So McGill's impulse to think of the National Guard first was on the money.

Post 9/11, however, a Department of Justice memorandum reinterpreted the constraints of the Posse Comitatus Act. The memo said the President had the authority to deploy troops to deter terrorist threats within the country. So while having the military act as a domestic law enforcement agency was still out, using it to perform military functions within the country, e.g. foiling terrorist attacks, was in. *Affirmed* in the wording of the memo.

That meant President Patricia Grant had operated within the bounds of her authority when she put twenty Delta Force special operators on a military cargo plane to Minnesota with McGill and SAC Elspeth Kendry. Elspeth's job was to coordinate with Colonel Arlen Gregory, the Delta Force's commanding officer. Their mutual goal was to make sure the McGills and the Enquists came through any hostilities alive and well.

McGill sat quietly to one side as SAC Kendry and Colonel Gregory laid out their plans. They were aided by bird's-eye photographs of the Enquist property and the surrounding roads and farms. The "birds" in this case were spy satellites operated by the NGA, the National Geospatial-Intelligence Agency. Among other things, the NGA functioned as a combat support agency by providing imagery of conflict environments.

The standing joke was that the only thing the NGA couldn't

see was what was in the hearts and minds of the enemy — but they could tell that, too, by how the opposing forces were arrayed.

The way Elspeth and the colonel worked things out, the Delta Force special operators would form the outer ring around the Enquist property. The Secret Service special agents would form the inner ring around the house. They'd sync their communication channels with each other, and summon the county sheriff's deputies to arrive after any belligerents had been captured. The cops would hold the prisoners until U.S. marshals arrived to take them into federal custody.

SAC Kendry and Colonel Gregory shook hands on their plan. Then they both looked at McGill.

Elspeth told him, "You'll be your family's last line of defense, sir."

"Fine by me," McGill said, "but there are a few more things to consider."

"Sir?" the colonel asked.

"That phone call I took a few minutes ago. It was from FBI Deputy Director Benjamin."

McGill told Elspeth and the colonel that all but three of their primary suspects had been found peacefully occupying their own homes.

Colonel Gregory asked, "All this is a false alarm?"

"I doubt it," McGill said. "The three people the FBI couldn't find? My thinking is they were the other members of the team that kidnapped Special Agent Ramsey. Those three are taking no chances. They're hiding somewhere, possibly abroad. The rest, I think they're just playing coy."

The colonel remained focused on what interested him most. "Where's the danger here? What's the threat?"

McGill briefly explained how Harlan Fisk had used his teenage daughter.

"What I think is happening here," McGill said, "is the enemy will be a bunch of kids."

Both SAC Kendry and Colonel Gregory had seen such things.

"Well, shit," the colonel said. "I hate the idea of killing kids."

"Me, too," McGill said. "There's one more thing."

"What?" both Elspeth and Gregory asked.

"We need to give the local police notice of what might happen. If by some small chance one or two of the attackers sees their situation is hopeless and decides to make a run for it, and they still have, say, assault rifles, they might shoot a motorist to steal his car or break into someone's home and take hostages."

The look in Gregory's eyes told McGill he was thinking he might need to kill some kids.

If any of them tried to run off carrying weapons.

"Something to think about," McGill said. "I can call the cops, if you want."

The White House — Washington, DC

The President sat on a sofa in the Oval Office with Jean Morrissey sitting to her right and Galia Mindel sitting to her left. Patricia Grant held the print-out of the image of Representative Philip Brock's grisly death. None of the three most powerful women in the country flinched upon looking at the picture. They were inured to such things. Barbarities happened across the world every day. With increasing frequency, they were photographed and distributed on social media.

The opportunities to be appalled by inhuman acts were available to anyone.

In terms of volume, though, nobody had as many chances as the President of the United States to see in detail the depths of immorality to which people might sink. The government spent billions each year collecting information from around the world. Much of it was both graphic and gruesome.

Much of it was also necessary viewing for the President to determine the right response.

"Are you sure you want this job, Jean?" the President asked.

She shrugged. "Someone has to do it. Someone who can handle it."

Galia nodded at what she thought was the right response.

The chief of staff said, "I had the Arabic script on the photo translated. It comes out roughly as 'two pigs and one swine.'"

The President said, "My guess is Dr. Kalil isn't really Ambassador Kamal's private physician."

Galia said, "No, ma'am, I verified that, but the ambassador knows of her. Says she's done great work with Doctors Without Borders. The CIA says she might also apply her surgical skills for various Middle Eastern terrorist cells. Might even have decapitated the congressman herself. Right now, no one knows where she is."

"Why would she kill Brock?" Jean asked.

"Her twin brother was murdered," Galia said. "Could be possible Philip Brock had something to do with that."

The President said, "You saw this woman, Jean. What was your impression?"

"Small, polite and determined. She wanted to get in to see Byron, but she knew better than to raise a fuss. So she's also smart. I sicced her on Abra Benjamin. I'm not supposed to know how close she and Byron once were, but I do. Frank told me."

Galia said nothing, but she approved of Frank Morrissey vetting his sister's lover.

Washington was that kind of town.

He'd make a good chief of staff.

"Did Frank ever mention Dr. Kalil and a connection between her and Byron?" the President asked.

Jean Morrissey shook her head and sighed. "I'll have to ask."

Galia moved the discussion along. "One thing's for certain; we'll never be able to get Phil Brock to testify against Tyler Busby about Busby's part in the assassination plot against you, Madam President."

All three of them knew the flip side of that coin. Jean and Galia deferred to the President.

"Yes," she said, "but we could show Busby this picture of his co-conspirator. Ask him if pleading guilty might not be the lesser of two evils."

As they considered the possibility of using that strategy, the intercom buzzed.

Edwina Byington said, "Sorry to disturb you, Madam President, but Mrs. Bettina Hurlbert is calling. She seems to be on the verge of hysteria. She's begging for a moment of your time. How would you like me to reply?"

Bettina was the widow of the late Senator Howard Hurlbert, who'd been murdered in his Virginia home. More than a few conspiracy theorists among the opposition thought the President had had him killed. Patricia Grant picked up the phone and put it on speaker.

"How may I help you, Bettina?" she said in a compassionate voice.

"Patricia, I just received the most awful ..." She stopped to sob and then catch her breath. "It's horrifying, really. A picture, a photograph of Philip Brock."

"Oh, my God," the President said.

"You *know* what it is?"

"I just saw a photo sent to me by the FBI."

"Philip's head between two pigs?" Bettina asked.

"Yes. Was there an inscription on yours?"

"There was. It says, 'You, too, are avenged.' I ... I always thought you were in on it, Patricia. Howard's death, I mean. But this is too cruel even for politics."

"It is, Bettina. Please turn the photo face down. I'll have FBI agents at your house in minutes."

Olmsted County, Minnesota

The average age of an infantryman who fought in World War II was 26. In Vietnam it was 22. The eldest of the "soldiers" gathered in the farmhouse eight miles up the road from the Enquist place was nineteen-year-old Darin "Daring Mac" MacTeague. He stood 6'2" and weighed 195 pounds. He was an All-State (2nd team) defensive end on his high school football team. He liked thrash metal bands, had a job application in at Winn-Dixie and had put $253 aside from previous summer jobs for an engagement ring he'd wow Dana Mercer with when he got home.

He was already signed up for classes next fall at the junior college. His plan was to work, study and land a good job in retail management someday. Have a wife, kids, and his own home. Be somebody substantial in his community.

At the moment, though, he was a captain in the FreeMan Militia, a multi-state group of armed patriots that intended to make a real difference in the direction of the country. Not that they thought they could take over the whole United States. That kind of thinking was for fools. What they could do, what they would do, was commit *influential* acts. Things that would shift the political thinking of everyday Americans.

Make them realize they had power, too. It wouldn't be just a bunch of conniving crooks with billions of dollars who got to call the shots in Washington anymore. People who took real shots — gunfire — would have to be taken into account as well. You crossed real patriots, they'd show you all kinds of hell could break loose.

Not that they'd try direct confrontation like massing troops on the National Mall anymore. That had led to prison sentences for militia leadership and humiliation for everyone else. Getting their guns taken away from them still stung to this very day. Darin's dad, Huey, had been one of them.

He'd worked two shifts for years to replace all the guns he could.

Including the Bushmaster XM-15 he'd given Darin for his 18th birthday.

All of the troops in the farmhouse had one model or another of the same assault rifle.

Even Eddie Pike who just turned sixteen.

As senior officer, Darin called all his men together in a prayer circle. They asked for divine guidance and protection. That and victory, of course. They'd have to take care of — kill — whoever it was protecting those McGill kids. What they'd been told was, it'd likely be Secret Service agents they'd be going up against, and those fuckers carried Uzis. Well, all of the weapons Darin and the boys carried had been modified. They could rock 'n' roll, too.

After the communal moment of divine supplication, they all reviewed the video they shot with their cell phones as their vans had rolled past the Enquist property. Darin laid out his plan of attack, but asked for suggestions how his thinking might be improved. He got a couple of good ideas, too.

Everybody felt they had a real good chance of pulling this thing off.

They took out the sandwiches, chips, cookies and soft drinks they'd bought back in South Dakota and stretched out on the farmhouse's beds, furniture and floors to get some rest before they headed out that night. Darin told his boys to sleep tight and wake up ready to kick some ass.

The guys roared as fiercely as they knew how in response.

When Darin plopped down on the big bed in the upstairs room, his mind whirled. They'd done okay so far. The sympathetic farmer who was letting them use his place had left the key right where he said he would. He'd bugged out himself the day before. Darin would make it look like they broken into the home before they left for their raid. If the cops braced the farmer, he could claim it wasn't his fault.

The farmer was the least of Darin's worries. What preoccupied him was the thought of killing Lars Enquist. He felt he had no choice but to take that job on himself. He didn't worry about shooting Secret Service agents or them shooting him. He felt sure he was bigger, stronger and faster than anybody on the other side.

Hell, he'd had 35 quarterback sacks in a twelve-game season. One more and he felt sure he'd have been *first team* all-state. Gotten some scholarship offers. Even so, he was positive he could raise holy hell charging the enemy line firing an automatic weapon. He just didn't see *anybody* standing up to him.

He could even accept that by pure bad luck some dumbass on the other side might shoot him.

What he had real trouble with was the idea of killing somebody who'd probably be unarmed and wetting his britches in terror. A guy named Lars? He'd probably be crying and begging for mercy, too. It was going to be damn hard to pull the trigger on someone like that.

But he'd said he could do the job.

As Darin drifted off to sleep, he wanted a real grown-up to talk to.

He wished the problem was something he could discuss with his mom.

The Enquist Property — Olmsted County, Minnesota

As McGill arrived at the driveway of his ex-wife's homestead in the company of a woman who carried an Uzi to work and one of the deadliest men in the world, he saw his youngest child and a male who looked no older, despite his wispy beard, having a grand argument with Celsus Crogher, McGill's own former nemesis. Both Elspeth and Colonel Gregory began to exit the armored government Chevy Suburban that had transported the three of them from the Rochester airport.

McGill held up an interdictory hand.

"I've got this," he said.

Technically, he had no authority over either the Secret Service or the military.

Practically, such fine distinctions didn't matter when you were married to the President.

McGill exited the vehicle while everybody else stayed put. The kid with the beard saw his approach first and gave Caitie a nudge. She looked and saw her father. Celsus turned and saw him, too. The look on his face said he couldn't determine if an ally or an enemy was approaching.

"Having a difference of opinion here, are we?" McGill asked.

The young man, who had a sizable trunk sitting next to him, extended a hand to McGill and said, "Ben Nolan. I'm the innocent bystander in this scene."

McGill shook his hand. "Jim McGill."

"My dad," Caitie added.

"Saw the resemblance," Ben said.

The kid looked like he was having a fine time; Celsus less so.

McGill focused on the aggrieved party. "There's a problem?"

"He shouldn't be here." Celsus darted a look at Ben. "No civilians should be here. Only armed professionals."

"My sentiments exactly," McGill said.

Celsus was pleasantly surprised to hear that. The look on his face said, "So?"

McGill told him, "I lost the battle. Couldn't even get my ex-wife to leave. Or her husband, and I think he's one of the voters for the Nobel Peace Prize."

He was trying to lighten the moment. The young people liked the joke; Celsus didn't.

McGill headed him off at the pass with the ultimate argument ender. "Even the President couldn't get them to change their minds." Then McGill threw Celsus a bone. "I understand if you want to pack it in, and I won't hold it against you, but I think we'd all be safer with you around."

Looking slightly mollified, Celsus asked, "Holly G. couldn't bring the hammer down?"

McGill confided, "The way we worked things out, the kids became community property." He nodded at Caitie. "She's the President's child, too, and you know how kids get over on their parents."

Caitie had the smarts not to gloat. Ben kept a straight face as well.

McGill advised Celsus, "You might not think so now, but if you and Merilee have a child or two you'll come to understand."

That idea reached Celsus. Wanting to maintain a measure of honest indignation, though, he asked, "Do you know what these two want to do?"

McGill sighed. "I'm sure I'll find out." Before Caitie could launch into her explanation, he added, "Wait. We'll get everyone together, and then you can make your pitch."

"Okay," she said.

"Fair enough," Ben seconded.

McGill gestured to Elspeth, Gregory and the special forces guys blocking the road to move onto the Enquist domain.

Irrepressible as ever, Caitie just had to get in one question: "Dad, have you ever seen the movie *Witness?*"

Sioux Falls, South Dakota

"You missed my iPad," Cole said. "It's one of those little ones."

He was still sitting on the floor, back against the wall, legs straight out.

"What?" Carrie asked.

She sat tailor-fashion against the opposite wall, facing the kid and the door to the room. She had the gun she'd taken from Lem in her hand with the safety off. The Beretta she'd taken from the kid lay on the floor next to her right hip. She was sure she could hit the kid or anyone who came in through the doorway with no trouble.

Unless she fell asleep. Then she might be in trouble.

She didn't feel drowsy now, but who was to say she could stay awake longer than the kid? Or someone outside the room who might be taking a nap right now and waiting for an opportune moment to bust in. All she could do in either case was hope they made enough noise to wake her.

Gave her at least a second to locate her target and fire.

Cole said, "Got it against my stomach under my belt and shirt. You felt me up about everywhere else, but not there."

Carrie didn't want to get her hopes up, but she had to ask. "Does it have Wi-Fi?"

If it did, she could make a FaceTime connection and summon help.

But Cole shook his head. "No data-pack. That's why they let me keep it. I use it to play games and read."

Disappointed though she was, Carrie asked, "Read?"

Cole grinned. "Yeah, more than just comic books, too. My mom teaches high school math. Encourages me to stay mentally active. Got a couple interesting TED Talks on it, if you want to watch."

Carrie pointed the Beretta at Cole and said, "Show me the iPad."

She didn't bother to tell him to move slowly. If the kid was smart enough to watch TED Talks, he'd know he better be careful. Carrie knew he was also evaluating her. Seeing if she was smart enough to make an obvious mental leap about modern communications.

Cole raised his shirt, exposing the top half of the tablet computer.

He drew it out of his waistband, not reaching for any other hidden object.

"Why did you bring that in here?" Carrie asked.

The boy shrugged. "I figured if you didn't shoot me right off I might get bored just hanging around waiting."

"Waiting for what?"

Cole smiled again. "Well, that's the interesting part. Seeing what happens next."

"Slide the iPad over to me. Give it a nice hard shove so I don't have to walk far."

The boy put his back and shoulder into it. Got the iPad within Carrie's reach. Cole was stronger than he looked. Carrie brought up the home page with all the icons for the resident apps. FaceTime was there. So were the TED videos, games and books. She scanned the titles of several novels. The kid liked Kurt Vonnegut and Joseph Heller.

"You want to distract yourself a while," Cole said, "I'll sit tight. You have to be bored stiff, as long as you've been cooped up."

That simple statement brought Carrie up short. She asked, "How long have I been held? What day is it? What time is it?"

"Time and date are on the homepage there. You were grabbed last Saturday. Didn't hear the exact time."

Carrie saw it was Thursday, March 31st, midmorning. So she'd been held prisoner a little over five days. That was all? It seemed like an eternity. Good God, how did some people manage to survive years of captivity? She knew she'd never make it that long. Hell, she wouldn't last another few days.

With that in mind, the question arose: Would Cole be a help in making an escape or was someone using him to con her? Fool her into trusting him and then lead her into a trap. Break her spirit. Maybe even make her think that death wouldn't be such a bad outcome.

"What are you doing here, Cole?" she asked.

"You mean in this room or with the rest of the guys?"

"Both."

"I'm in the room because I said I could kill somebody and the boss wants to see if that's true."

"You came in here to kill me?"

"*Well* ... I wasn't really sure myself. I'm fairly smart but not entirely right in the head or so I've been told. Honestly, it was an open question until I stepped into this room."

"And now?" Carrie asked.

"I like the way you handled Bad Fat."

"Reeves? You call him that?"

"Not to his face. Not yet. But you know, nutritionally, there's good fat and bad fat, right?"

"Yes. And he's bad fat?"

"That's more imaginative than just calling him a dick."

Carrie smiled.

"There you go," Cole said. "You smile, you look closer to the age you're pretending to be."

"I'll keep that in mind. So what are you doing with the rest of these creeps?"

"My dad's in the army. Career guy. Mom and I made about eight different moves with him, all the hell over the world. Then we had enough. Mom got a divorce and I went with her. Last thing Dad said to me was to sign up as soon as I could. Go infantry. Get combat pay. Pretty strange coming from a quartermaster guy. But wouldn't you know it, the first school where I knew I could stay a few years, I met these guys whose dads were in the FreeMan Militia. I thought, hell, maybe it was fate and I should give this bearing arms thing a try. You know, before I saw whether I should do it for real."

"And?" Carrie said.

"And I sure as shit hope our real army's better than these guys or we're all in trouble." He laughed but only briefly; then his face took on a reflective expression. "I also keep getting this feeling in my stomach like I ate spoiled meat or something. Makes me think of the old people I've heard talking about something they'd really like to do over. I thought I was *way* too young for that shit."

Carrie tried to evaluate Cole's sincerity. If he was bullshitting her, he had a gift. Of course, some people who had that gift did it because it was so much fun for them. Made them feel superior.

"I didn't know it'd work out like this," Cole said, "but we've got close to a fair fight here. What with most of the other boys gone. Except Bad Fat does have at least one automatic weapon."

"They've gone somewhere, the ones who grabbed me? Where did they go?"

"Most of them went … well, the plan is they're going to grab your …" He made air quotes. "Brother and sister."

"You're kidding."

"Nope. That's the plan. They get snatched. You get it in the head."

"Why kill me?" Carrie asked.

"To show what badasses they are. They want to swap your sibs for some guys the feds have locked up. They shoot you to show what'll happen to what's their names — Abbie and Kenny? — if the FBI or someone else comes after them."

"What the hell are these guys smoking? They'll be hunted down no matter what. No matter how long it takes."

"Yeah, well, airtight logic isn't their strong suit."

Carrie said, "But you understood what your gut was telling you, didn't you? You manipulated Reeves. You got him to put you in here with me. You're hoping to help me and cop a plea."

Cole only shrugged and grinned.

Then Carrie made the leap the boy had wondered about earlier.

"You know there's somebody nearby with a cell phone," Carrie said. "We can use that to make a call. Better yet, we can use it to make a Wi-Fi hotspot and I can do FaceTime with my people."

"You mean the McGills?"

"Them, too." Carrie got to her feet. She said, "Who stayed behind and who went on the suicide mission?"

Cole stood up, too. "Everybody was supposed to leave for one place or another. Except you, of course. The great minds figured you'd be discovered later. But with you and me still alive, I'd say Bad Fat and Lem are still on the premises. If BF has half-a-brain, and I think he just might, he kept one of the other guys with him. Maybe even two. But I don't see Lem being any use at all. So that means the odds are three-to-two at worst, and maybe even-steven. Of course, those AR-15s on full auto put a lot of lead in the air. It's hellacious."

Carrie started to think about that. How best to overcome fire-power with brainpower. The fact that her gears were turning was obvious to Cole.

He interrupted Carrie's scheming. "So you going to trust me with whatever you're cooking up? You sure I don't have something sneaky up my sleeve?"

The kid was toying with her. Maybe something was wrong with his head.

"You ever want to see your mother again?" Carrie asked.

"Uh-huh. Wouldn't mind that."

"Good. Don't forget it. You try any sneaky shit with me, I'll rip your arm right out of your sleeve and beat you to death with it."

Cole blinked and then laughed. "Now, that's what I call leader-ship. So what's the *real* Caitie McGill like?"

The question hit Carrie's pause button for a second. Then she found the right answer.

"Damn near as tough as me."

Florida Avenue — Washington, DC

Putnam met Sweetie at the front door of their townhouse with drinks in hand. He kissed his wife, gave her a glass, ushered her inside and closed the door. He said, "We have lemonade to sip. One of the glasses has a finger of vodka, too, but I forget which one."

Sweetie got the feeling Putnam wasn't just fooling around. She didn't often get that vibe. Much to her consternation, she thought she still had good cop instincts. When she wasn't pushing ideas that wound up getting someone killed, that was. But now wasn't the time to think about that.

She and Putnam sat in their serious discussion chairs.

"I think I have the vodka," Putnam said.

"It's *really* that serious?"

He nodded. "But first things first. You dropped Maxi at school? She's blazing new trails in scholarship?"

Sweetie said, "All's well with you, me and ours. So tell me what's going on."

"Well, unfortunately, you were right about Auric Ludwig. He not only wants Jim McGill dead but is actively working to further that aim."

Sweetie squeezed her eyes shut for a moment. Another bit of cop intuition validated. Well, if she saved Jim's life maybe that would mitigate some of the guilt she felt for causing Erna Godfrey's death.

"What did you find out?" she asked.

Putnam told her of his visit with Gene Beck to the law offices of Nicholas Kingsbury.

"Nicky called me back not five minutes ago," he said.

"That was fast," Sweetie said. "I know you wouldn't point a gun at the guy. How about Gene?"

"As an aside, my dear, I would in fact both point and fire a gun to guarantee your or Maxi's well-being. In this case, however, neither Gene nor I flashed any firepower. But Gene did mention to Nicky that he was an assassin."

"Oh, boy."

Putnam shook his head. "There was no legal exposure in doing that. Anyone trying to verify Gene's admission would run smack into the Great Wall of National Security. But Gene did put Nicky on edge a bit."

Sweetie said, "I bet. You planned that, of course. 'Look at the friends I've got. Don't ever think of messing with me.'"

"Great minds," Putnam said, "think alike and all that. In the way of direct motivation, though, I pointed out to Nicky he'd legally be considered part of a murder conspiracy if he acted as a conduit between Auric Ludwig and a hitman. I recommended he seek the advice of wise legal counsel to extricate himself from his dilemma."

"He couldn't rely on you, of course, because you want to keep your distance," Sweetie said.

"Just so. He turned to the venerable Murray MacMurray, Esquire."

"Who?"

"Exactly. Murray keeps a very low profile. I thought he'd died years ago. He might be Washington's original fixer and courtroom wheeler-dealer. I think he had a law office in DC before Pierre Charles L'Enfant laid out his designs for the city."

"Yeah?" Sweetie asked. "So this guy still wears a tri-corner hat?"

"The last time I saw Murray he was wearing a Borsalino Panama. He looked like a gangster who just flew in from Havana. You know, pre-Castro. Anyway, Murray came over to Nicky's office, accepted the offer of a glass of water, and being a few centuries old he happened to spill the water on the envelope Auric Ludwig had given to Nicky. Which just happened to be lying on Nicky's desk."

Sweetie saw where this was going. "MacMurray said they had to open the envelope to make sure the contents weren't damaged. If they had been, what, made illegible, Nicky would have to go back to his client, report the regrettable accident and ask Auric Ludwig if he'd care to reconstruct his message."

Putnam gave Sweetie a wink. "Beautiful and smart."

"Only the message was still easily read," she said, "and it

concerned killing Jim. And as an officer of the court, Nicky —"

Putnam held up a hand. "Don't get ahead of yourself here, Margaret. The applicable disciplinary rule says a lawyer *may* reveal the intention of a client to commit a crime and the information necessary to prevent the crime. It doesn't impose the obligation to do so."

"What?" Sweetie asked in disbelief.

That wasn't how she remembered things from her days as a cop.

Putnam said, "Lawyers being lawyers, though, there's a foot-note to the rule to consider. If the facts in the attorney's possession indicate beyond reasonable doubt that a crime will be committed, the attorney has a duty of disclosure."

"That's better," Sweetie said.

"Yes, well, 'beyond reasonable doubt' is a standard subject to vigorous debate. But with the intended victim of this crime being the President's husband, my guess is most lawyers would choose to be pro-actively cautious. Unless, of course, they were die-hard political opponents of the President."

"Or felt a *personal* dislike for Jim," Sweetie said.

"That, too. Anyway, Nicky wanted no part of being involved in any attempt on Jim McGill's life. He asked Murray for a moment of privacy so he could call me and say thanks. By now, he and Murray should be explaining the mishap with the water and what they saw to the cops."

"What details about the plot, if any, did Nicky give you?" Sweetie asked.

"Only that the killer-to-be is someone called Corona Moe and the job is supposed to be completed before Inauguration Day next January."

Sweetie said, "Auric Ludwig didn't find this guy online." She thought about that for a moment. "He doesn't have Internet access, does he? I've heard you *can* find killers on the Dark Net."

"The cops will look into that," Putnam said, "but I'm sure you know what's more likely."

"Yeah, some jailbird Auric Ludwig met in prison gave him a name."

"What's even more likely than that? Aubrey Gadsden, the criminal defense lawyer to whom Nicky was supposed to give the message, knows this Corona Moe guy. Either Moe is one of his clients or one of his clients knows Moe. You see the problem with that?"

Sweetie did. "Gadsden won't be liberal in his interpretation of 'beyond reasonable doubt.' He'll fight any attempt to name the hitman."

"Yes, and he might have the American Bar Association supporting him."

Sweetie got up and kissed her husband. "I've got to call Jim."

"You do that," Putnam said, "and I'll call the President."

Olmsted County, Minnesota

The McGill clan, the Enquists, mister and missus, Ben Nolan and more than a score of the nation's most highly trained and effective Secret Service special agents and Delta Force special operators had gathered in the Enquists' living room to listen to Caitie McGill make her pitch.

Caitie had lost her fear of public speaking long ago, but this did look, in more ways than one, like a tough crowd. Without having heard a word, Celsus Crogher already appeared skeptical. Ever the trouper, though, Caitie hewed to the credo of her chosen profession: The show must go on. And it did.

She started by making direct eye contact with Mom and Dad.

"Do you remember that great scene near the end of *Witness?*"

McGill and Carolyn had seen the movie, but were unsure of the particular scene their offspring meant.

Ken jumped in with a possibility. "The one where Danny Glover gets buried in the corn silo?"

That sparked memories in several members of the audience and heads nodded.

But Caitie shook hers. "That's not the one I meant."

Abbie said, "I know which one you mean. The scene where the old man starts ringing the bell."

Caitie beamed and nodded. "Eli Lapp as played by Jan Rubes."

McGill's memory clicked and he recalled the scene. "Yeah, Eli rings and rings the bell. It's the Amish version of calling 9-1-1. All the neighbors drop whatever they're doing and come on the run."

"Right," Carolyn said. She and Jim had seen the movie on a date before they were even married. "All the neighbors surrounded the corrupt cop while he had the drop on Harrison Ford."

"Chief Paul Schaeffer," Caitie said, She looked for the actor's name but it didn't come to mind.

"Josef Sommer," Ben supplied.

Caitie smiled at him with a warmth both of her parents noticed.

"Right," she said. "So Chief Schaeffer had every intention of killing John Book, but now there are all these people, these witnesses, watching. Is he going to commit murder with all of them looking on? Will he kill all of them, too? He doesn't have enough ammunition for one thing, but more than that he doesn't have it in him to become a mass-murderer."

"So what do you want us to do," Celsus asked, "round up a bunch of Amish and have them waiting in the wings?"

Caitie stepped over to Celsus and completely disarmed him by giving him a kiss on the cheek.

McGill had to repress a laugh. Not everyone was that successful.

"That's exactly what I want to do," Caitie said, "only we won't need actual Amish." She looked at the Secret Service people and the Delta Force guys. "What we will need is some costuming. Jeans and flannel shirts. Redwing boots and Carhartt coats. Things to make all you hard guys look like Minnesota natives."

Colonel Gregory laughed. "I *am* a Minnesotan. I know just what you mean."

Caitie smiled at him, gave a thumbs-up, hoping she'd found an ally.

She turned to her father. "Dad, you essentially faced down a whole army on the Mall. Took care of one guy and that was that."

McGill corrected the record. "There were military snipers behind me, making sure nobody pointed a rifle my way."

Caitie blinked. She hadn't heard that before. Neither had his other children or his ex-wife.

He continued, "And after I put Harlan Fisk on the ground, the President of the United States was the one who delivered the ultimatum to the militia guys. They took *her* word as gospel."

Caitie said, "You're right. I should've remembered Patti's role, but we're not going to be dealing with that many armed men, are we?"

McGill shared a questioning glance with both Celsus and Colonel Gregory.

They both shook their heads.

McGill said, "The considered opinion is no, we won't." He sighed. "In fact, I think we'll be looking at a relative handful of teenagers, the children of some of the men who were in Washington."

That surprised Abbie and Ken, Carolyn and Lars.

It seemed to delight Caitie. "That's perfect."

"In what way?" McGill asked.

Caitie laughed. "At the risk of hyping my own generation, Dad, we're not dumb. We know who has the upper hand, the money and the power. We might resent that at times, but we usually don't forget it. There are even times you still scare us. Some grown-ups might think they have nothing to lose and put up a fight. But teenagers, I don't think so."

Colonel Gregory cleared his throat. Everyone looked his way.

"Ms. McGill, I enlisted in the Army at 17. I was *eager* to get into a fight, *any* fight. Any of you gentleman have similar feelings?" the colonel asked his men.

They all raised their hands.

In a less certain voice, Caitie said to the colonel, "Okay, I stand corrected. But being in special forces, how many of you think you really are special?"

All the hands went up again. Even the colonel's.

"And how many of you think kids in an untrained civilian militia are anywhere near as special?"

None of the men raised a hand.

The colonel hedged his bet. "There might be one."

Caitie looked at McGill. "One last question, Dad?"

"Go ahead," McGill said.

"This is for both the Secret Service and Delta Force," Caitie said. "In your expert opinions, would teenagers with guns and a grudge against the government be more likely to open fire on people in uniform or people dressed more like them? Or the way they usually dress."

McGill thought she had a real point there.

So did Colonel Gregory by the look on his face.

Even Celsus seemed to think she had things right.

"What I'd like to see, what Ben and I would like to film, is a situation where *nobody* gets shot."

Carolyn blew her baby girl a kiss as tears of pride formed in her eyes.

"I'm going to need approval for anything outside of our normal parameters," Colonel Gregory told McGill.

He nodded and said, "I'll get the commander-in-chief on the line for you."

The colonel said, "I thought you might say that. I'll still need the freedom to tweak any plan we lay out here. I can't trust my people or yours to someone who's … less than special."

McGill nodded. Caitie shook the colonel's hand.

Once the colonel took McGill's phone and was speaking to his ultimate superior, McGill put an arm around his youngest's shoulders and took her off into a corner. "I am so proud of you. You amaze me no end."

In a quiet voice, Caitie confessed, "I have an ulterior motive, Dad."

A surprised McGill said, "What?"

"The possibility that the other side might be sending their kids couldn't be better."

"Because they'll be easier to intimidate, quicker to surrender."

"That, too. But what I'm thinking? The bad guys have Don and Sheri Ramsey's child? We'll have even more of theirs. What better chance can we have of getting Special Agent Ramsey back safely?"

Well, he had just said she amazed him.

Still, he had to play the devil's advocate.

"What if the bad guys say they'll kill Special Agent Ramsey if we don't let their kids go?"

"We'll tell them they'd be making their children accomplices to the murder of a federal agent. That's a death penalty crime. They'd be killing their own kids."

That made McGill think of a Bible story.

God telling Abraham to sacrifice Isaac.

There were some people who *would* do the unthinkable.

The Oval Office — Washington, DC

Shortly after having Galia dispatch the FBI to Virginia to interview Bettina Hurlbert and take possession of the card she'd received saying that she'd been avenged, Edwina announced another call for the President.

"Mr. McGill, Ma'am. He says he has a Colonel Arlen Gregory with him and the colonel needs a word with you."

"Very well, Edwina. Put him through."

"Madam President?"

"Speaking."

Colonel Gregory introduced himself by name, rank, unit and current mission. Then he explained Caitie McGill's idea and how he wasn't about to undertake it without clearance from her or at least a general officer.

"How would you like to handle this situation, ma'am?" Gregory asked.

"I'll take responsibility, Colonel. Wouldn't do to waste time here."

"No, ma'am."

"What do you think of Ms. McGill's idea, Colonel?"

After a moment of silence, he said, "I'm conflicted, ma'am. I think the young lady's likely right that whoever we might face will be less hostile to men dressed in civilian clothing than men in uniform. But I know for a fact things in real life don't work out like things in the movies. At least most of the time. There's also a bit of ego and stubbornness on my part. I take pride in my uniform. My men and I have earned the right to wear it when most don't. Taking it off would go against our grain."

The President considered that a legitimate concern.

She came up with an idea. "Do you think a draft would work, Colonel?"

"Beg pardon, ma'am."

"Well, I'm no military tactician, but what if we conscripted, say, several local, county or even state police officers, women included, and asked them to play the roles originally conceived of for your men? Police officers are known to work in plain clothes. Then you and your men, in uniform, could take up concealed positions to provide cover fire for the others if necessary. Would something like that work?"

Gregory was quiet again and then he began to chuckle. "Ma'am, it is an honor and a privilege serving under you. Just talking to you is something I won't ever forget."

"So you like my idea?"

"Very much, ma'am, if you can get the police to accommodate us."

"I'll make a call to the governor. May I have your personal phone number, please?"

Gregory gave it to her.

"You should be receiving a call soon," the President said.

The President asked Vice President Jean Morrissey to go to her White House office, call her successor as the chief executive of the state of Minnesota and ask for his help. Jean knew the man and

Patricia Grant figured he'd rather talk to a prospective President than a departing one.

That task had no sooner been deferred than Edwina buzzed the Oval Office again.

"Attorney General Jaworsky and Colonel Welborn Yates, ma'am."

"Together or queued up, Edwina?"

"Together, ma'am, on speaker at the AG's office."

"Very well. Put them through." Once the connection was made, the President asked the Attorney General, "Bad news, Michael?"

"That's often the specialty of this office, Madam President, and this time definitely."

"Tell me."

"If you don't mind, ma'am, I'll have Colonel Yates give you the details."

"Go ahead, Colonel."

"Yes, ma'am. Laboratory analysis shows that the envelope the late Captain Dexter Cowan mailed to his late brother, Jeffrey, was not opened before the lab techs unsealed it. The same applies to the envelope the attorney for Jeffrey Cowan's estate posted to Arlene Cowan, the captain's ex-wife. The same applies to the envelope the former Mrs. Cowan sent to me. All the canceled stamps are contemporaneous with the accompanying postmarks."

"So nobody fiddled with the mail," the President said. "And the contents reveal?"

Welborn Yates said, "Captain Cowan wrote that he killed General Warren Altman's wife in return for General Altman's sponsorship for lucrative private sector employment for Captain Cowan after he left the Navy."

"God help us," the President said quietly. "Michael, where does this leave us in terms of a possible prosecution of General Altman?"

The Attorney General said, "It leaves us with a heck of a mess. Captain Cowan's written confession is not really a dying declaration. He didn't expire immediately after authoring it. No one witnessed him writing his statement. On the other hand, handwriting analysis confirms he wrote the note, and the last act of Captain Cowan's life was his attempt to take the lives of Colonel Yates and Leo Levy by ramming their car with his at a high speed on the Washington Beltway. That clearly shows the man was capable of using deadly force."

The President said, "So the evidence, while not conclusive, is too compelling to ignore."

"Exactly," the AG said. "At this point, I'm reluctant to ask for an indictment, but there's no way we can or should avoid opening an investigation."

"A homicide investigation of a Presidential candidate by the administration of an opposing party," the President said.

She felt her face grow hot.

Galia, sitting across the President's desk from her, gave her a look of concern.

One that was personal, not political, in nature.

The President's face was getting red. The chief of staff walked over to a drink cart and poured a glass of water. She placed it within the President's reach.

"It's your call, Madam President," the attorney general said, "but I strongly suggest we open an investigation — even though its conclusion will almost certainly be reached by the next administration."

"Yes, there's that, too. Very well, Michael, go ahead. We'll do what we must."

"A final question, ma'am. Do we go about our business strictly in-house?"

The President heard Colonel Yates speak softly in the background.

She said, "Tell me what's on your mind, Colonel."

"Yes, ma'am. The fact that Dexter Cowan sent a letter to his brother and its eventual arrival on my desk is already public knowledge. I'm sure both Ellie Booker and Didi DiMarco are waiting eagerly for the other shoe to drop. If the Department of Justice doesn't acknowledge publicly that it's conducting an investigation, we'd be asking every reporter in Washington to dig for the story.

When it leaks, it won't look good."

"No, it wouldn't. I don't think we can leave that can of worms for Jean to deal with."

"There's another benefit," the AG said. "If, say, Oren Worth were to win, he'd have a harder time killing a publicly known investigation than one that was kept in the shadows."

"Small cheer, but thank you for trying, Michael. Very well gentlemen: start the investigation and announce it publicly. I'll take the heat for what little time is left to me in this job."

The President ended the call, and Galia immediately said, "Drink some water."

The President thought she'd never had a more refreshing glass of water. It was so cool and pleasing she actually seemed to feel her body temperature go down to a more comfortable level. She didn't think she'd been experiencing the onset of a fever. She didn't feel weak or have any aches in her head or joints. It was more like someone had lit a fire within her. Not the kind associated with amorous pleasure.

"May I have a bit more water, Galia?"

"Of course, Madam President." The chief of staff refilled the glass.

Before Patricia Grant could take a sip, though, Edwina buzzed yet again.

"I'm sorry to disturb you once more, Madam President, but Mr. Putnam Shady is on the line. He says the matter is urgent and it involves Mr. McGill."

Magic words, the President thought: urgent and McGill.

"Put him through, Edwina." Covering the mouthpiece of her phone, the President added to Galia, "Let's hope the next call isn't news of a declaration of war against us."

The chief of staff forced a smile, but she was worrying once more.

The President's face was growing red again.

"Mr. Shady," Patricia Grant said, "you have some important

news?"

"Very important, ma'am, and equally unpleasant."

The seriousness of his tone of voice was unmissable.

"Someone's been hurt? Margaret or Maxine?"

"No, ma'am. They're both fine. This development concerns your husband."

Jim? But he was in Minnesota. How would Putnam even know where he was much less —

"Madam President, Margaret told me that when she and Mr. McGill were thinking about which of his past ... adversaries —"

"You were about to say enemies, weren't you, Mr. Shady?"

"Yes, ma'am. Which of his enemies might try to hurt him by abducting his children. They came up with two names that stood above the others: Harlan Fisk and Auric Ludwig. I'm sorry to say both of them, individually, have plots in motion. Fisk went after the McGill children; Ludwig plans to retaliate against Mr. McGill himself."

He told her about the letter from Auric Ludwig to criminal defense attorney Aubrey Gadsden, via Nicholas Kingsbury, soliciting the services of a man referred to as Corona Moe to kill James J. McGill before Inauguration Day 2017.

"I have reason to believe Nicholas Kingsbury, the lawyer who'd been hired to handle Auric Ludwig's appeal of his obstruction of justice conviction, and Mr. Kingsbury's new lawyer, Murray MacMurray, have gone to the Metro Police Department with their information. For the preservation of a possible defendant's life, I think Auric Ludwig should be moved into an isolation cell. I'm sorry to have to be the bearer of such unhappy news, Madam President. Margaret is relaying this development to Mr. McGill directly as we speak."

The President felt as if a volcano was about to erupt inside her.

The heat was awful and she began to feel unsteady.

"Thank you for calling, Putnam. You and Margaret are such good friends."

She put the phone down and Galia was there with the water

glass in hand.

"Drink," she said.

The President consumed all the water in one go.

Then she said, "Galia, please call Dr. Nicolaides."

Artemis Nicolaides was the White House physician.

Sioux City, South Dakota

"Do you think you can take him, Buddy?" Dallas Reeves asked.

Buddy Legrand smirked. "Little Cole? I could take him, his mama and daddy and six of their closest kin." Buddy was six feet tall and went two hundred and twenty pounds.

The two of them looked across the width of the basement from the stairs leading up to the first floor of the house where Carrie Ramsey was being held captive. Buddy was seated; Reeves stood two steps below him and kept his eyes pointed at the room where Cole had been expected to execute the prisoner, but as of yet had failed to do so.

"There's the woman in there to think of, too," Reeves told Buddy.

"That little gal? She'll be *no* problem. Only she is pretty cute. Seems a waste to kill her."

Reeves gave him a critical look, but Buddy's notion of reprimand started at a smack to the face.

So Buddy continued, "One of the boys told me she's even been in the movies. You know, guys like me can only *dream* of bedding a movie star. Having one nearby, almost close enough to touch, I tell you, that's tempting. I wonder how I might shoot holes in Cole but not hit her. That could be tricky, but if I apply myself, I bet I can find a way."

Reeves laid his hands on Buddy's shoulders, pulled him to his feet. He had six inches and a hundred pounds on the younger man. His intellect dwarfed Buddy's by an even larger ratio. For sheer recklessness and bravado, though, Buddy was in a league of his own. You had to tolerate those qualities when you were trying to develop a killer.

"Listen, Buddy, what I want you to do is wait four hours minimum, six if your patience can possibly last that long, and then shoot right through the wall of that room over there where we've got Cole and her. It's only drywall. Your rounds will go right through it like it's Kleenex. You understand?"

"Blow my nose too hard at it, the snot'll make a hole," Buddy said.

"Right. You start shooting right to left about the height of your own belly and then come back the other way about knee high. You're bound to get them both. If you only wound them on the first try, that's all right. You put a new clip in your weapon, go in and finish them off. You got all that?"

"Got it. But why do I have to shoot Cole? Never liked him much, but he's on our side ain't he?"

"I thought so," Reeves said, "but I sent him in there to kill … whoever that woman is and he hasn't."

"What? I thought you told all us she's that Caitie McGill girl."

"Maybe but maybe not."

"Then who?"

"A Secret Service agent," Reeves said.

"They got government women who look like that? Damn, that's almost enough to make me think those people are doing something right."

Reeves squeezed the young man's shoulders hard enough to tighten his focus.

"I gave you a thousand dollar bonus, right?"

Buddy was smart enough to say nothing more than, "Yes, sir."

"Tell you what. You take care of things the way I told you, I'll take you down to this place I know in the Caribbean. Little French island. They got gals like you've never seen. Doing things you've never even heard of. You can have a week with however many of them you can handle. How's that sound?"

Buddy grinned. "You got me excited already."

Reeves didn't want the young fool over-primed.

"Remember, you give me and Lem the time we need to get down the road first. We gotta catch up with the others over there in Minnesota, and I gotta find a doctor for Lem on the way. I want four hours minimum. That's why I gave you that watch."

The thing on his wrist was cheap with a plastic band, but it had digital numerals, not minute and hour hands that might confuse the semi-literate.

"I got just one more question," Buddy said.

"What?" Reeves asked, his impatience seeping through.

"Well, I don't care a bit about Cole dyin', but what if some of the other boys do? What do we tell them? What if they get mad at me?"

Reeves said, "Don't worry. Nobody likes Cole. He's a smart-ass. What you can't forget, Buddy?"

"What?"

"That woman in there, she's got Lem's gun for sure and most likely Cole's, too."

He handed Buddy a Bushmaster assault rifle with a 40-round magazine. As a precautionary measure, Reeves equipped his protégé with a second magazine. Even an idiot, he figured, should be able to kill two people with 80 rounds.

"They ain't got nothing like this," Buddy said, smiling at the weapon in his hands.

Olmsted County, Minnesota

Carolyn Enquist heard the phone ring in the kitchen of her new home. A land line. Old fashioned as could be, but she and Lars liked it. They felt low-tech was homey. She went to answer it.

Her ex-husband, Jim McGill, was in the family room working out strategy or tactics or whatever they called it to defend their children and her home. Lars was with them to represent the Enquists' interests and to report to her at timely intervals just what the heck was going on.

The very idea that a group of armed men — well, boys, really, but still — might soon attack the place where she lived should have scared her silly. Would have done just that not so long ago. Now, she mostly felt sad and determined as hell to protect what was hers.

Of course, having the Secret Service, U.S. Army commandos or whatever they were and Jim on hand helped her to stay unflustered if not exactly calm. Lars had told her how the plans to defend the house were shaping up. The army guys were going to form an outer ring of defense, the Secret Service would be the inner ring and Celsus Crogher and Jim would be the last line of defense between any bad guys and their own sweet children.

Lars, bless him, had told her, "Carolyn, we should be right there with Jim and Mr. Crogher."

Unlike her, Lars had taken up marksmanship only as a shared spousal activity. He was a fair shot, true, but Carolyn was sure Lars never imagined being in a gun fight. He had a shotgun somewhere in the house, but it was more a symbol of cultural solidarity than anything else. Everybody in rural America had a shotgun in their house, so he did, too. But the thing was never loaded. She wasn't sure there were even any shells on the premises. You'd have to club somebody with the weapon for it to be dangerous.

Then, again, there *was* a weapon under their roof — other than her handgun — that could do real damage. On a vacation trip to Norway, Lars saying he wanted to explore his ethnic roots after watching the *Vikings* TV series on the History Channel, they found a shop in Oslo that sold what was billed as traditional weaponry. Lars had been almost giddy when they went inside.

Carolyn had played the role of the sensible mother: One toy, no more.

The item Lars had bought, though, was no plaything. He purchased a double bit ax with a four-foot long haft. The two blade heads were so sharp they would have made a real Norseman swoon. The forty-eight inch sure-grip pebbled oak handle made for a huge killing radius.

As the weapon was being packed for international shipment, Carolyn had joked, "I hope you're not going to reach for that thing anytime we have an argument."

Lars had laughed, kissed her and said, "It falls into the same category as one of those really expensive guitars some old guys buy even though they know they'll never learn to play it."

"But they can still fantasize they're rock 'n' roll stars getting all the cute groupies?"

"Exactly. A love-life placebo. Probably as effective as Viagra."

Well, as a pharmacist, he should know, Carolyn thought. As long as he didn't plan to make her Anne Boleyn, she was okay with the ax. And once Lars hung it over the fireplace in their bedroom, Carolyn had to admit things got more vigorous and interesting between them.

"Mrs. Enquist, are you there?"

Talk about being lost in reverie. She'd picked up the phone without even saying hello.

"Yes."

"This is Lieutenant William Morgan of the Rochester Police Department. The firing range manager. We met the other day when you and your children came in to shoot."

"Oh, yes, Lieutenant. How are you?"

"I'm fine ma'am. The chief of our department got a call from the governor asking for volunteers to help with a situation you may be facing out at your place. The chief passed the request on to me as I've already met you, and I did offer my services when we met at the range."

"Yes, you did. That was very kind of you."

"Thank you, ma'am. Anyway, I've talked to a number of officers in our department, and I've been in contact with colleagues from the Olmsted County Sheriff's Department and the state police. I've rounded up 60 volunteers so far. Twenty from each law enforcement agency. Do you think that would be enough or should I scout up some more?"

"I think that would be enough," Carolyn said, "but I'll get Mr. McGill for you. He knows more about this kind of thing than I do. But tell me, Lieutenant, some of your volunteers are women, aren't they?"

"Yes, ma'am. The governor heard about all this from Vice President Morrissey. They both think gender equity is important. So does my wife. We've got 24 women among our volunteers."

Acting on a spur-of-the-moment impulse, Carolyn said, "I'd like to be part of your group, too."

There was a lull before Morgan asked, "Do you have any police experience, ma'am?"

"I was a cop's wife for fifteen years."

Another silence ensued.

Carolyn filled it. "I assume you and the other officers will be inconspicuously armed."

"Yes, ma'am. Sidearms concealed by clothing."

"And you'll all wear armored vests, of course."

"Yes, ma'am."

"And you'll all have communications gear."

"Yes, ma'am."

"But you won't be marching in parade formation like it was a holiday."

"No, ma'am. We were told we should arrive like a gaggle of neighbors coming on the run to help friends in need. We'll be staggered and a bit spread out. "

"I could be at the back of the crowd," Carolyn suggested. "Lars and me, that is."

"I think we'll need to get permission from ... someone."

"No, I don't think you will. This property belongs to my husband and me. We're the ones giving permission for everybody else to enter our land."

Carolyn could almost hear Lieutenant Morgan think. Trying to detect a flaw in her reasoning. Finding none, he said, "I guess I should ask what size vests you and Mr. Enquist need."

That was more like it, Carolyn thought. She gave him their sizes and said she'd have Jim call him to see what he might have to add.

A moment later Lars entered the kitchen and Carolyn told him about the call from the police and what she'd done.

He thought about it for a minute before asking, "Can I bring my ax?"

Sioux City, South Dakota

Turned out Cole had three TED Talks on his iPad. Two of the speakers were male, one was female. Carrie Ramsey and Cole had worked out a plan on how to use the videos an hour after Dallas Reeves had left the building, putting his trust in Buddy Legrand to become a multiple murderer. Given the history of young psychos in America armed with weapons of war, Reeves had felt the chances were good Buddy *wanted* to shoot somebody. Hell, why else would a kid join a backwoods militia?

Throw in the false promise of tropical island hookers being made available to service the boy's every wish and Reeves had been fairly sure his young gunman would shoot the girl, too, without any particular regret.

Inside the makeshift cell, Carrie was anything but certain who her opposition was now.

She and Cole sat side by side on the floor, backs agains the wall, knees drawn up, in the corner of the room diagonally opposite the door. Ten minutes earlier, they'd each used the waste bucket. They were lucky neither of them needed to do more than pee. Cole had to endure the indignity of having Carrie watch him urinate, if only from behind. He had to go to the far end of the room and turn his back while she peed.

Modesty had been a minor consideration for Carrie. Shooting straight while squatting and making water had been the major one — in case Cole thought it would be a funny time to try to get the upper hand. When she was finished she had Cole move the bucket, about half full now, to a point just short of the door. If someone entered and wasn't paying close attention, he might put a foot into the bucket, getting both distracted and disgusted.

Also probably getting shot for looking the wrong way.

Carrie didn't need to hold a gun on Cole. She'd told him once more she'd break some part of him if he tried to do something stupid. His neck at the worst. His nose at the least.

He gave her the peace sign, which actually made her smile.

Speaking quietly, Carrie said, "How'd the militia creeps know the McGill kids, their mom and step-father went to Minnesota?"

"Bad Fat said they'd checked into the parents, learned about them buying the house there, public records and all that. They've got a sympathizer in the area was what he said."

"Well, what if they'd gone someplace safe, like Camp David?"

Cole shrugged. "Back to the drawing board?"

"I know you told me already, but give it to me again, what the big plan is."

"Kill you, first off," Cole said.

"They'd do that even if they knew I wasn't Caitie McGill?"

"Yeah, well, I'm the only one who's seen that for sure. Bad Fat has his suspicions. The others don't have a clue. Getting past all that, BF told me the plan was to kill one of the McGill kids regardless, and since they caught you first, you were elected."

Carrie frowned.

Cole explained again the idea of using two of the McGill kids as ransom for adult militia leaders who'd been locked up. Executing one of the McGills would show what could happen next if any other militia people were arrested.

Carrie was incredulous. "They really think the government will be too *scared* to go after them?"

Cole shrugged. "Bullies bully until someone kicks ass."

The kid had a point. Sounded like he knew from personal experience, too.

"Did your father hit you before you and your mother split?"

The boy looked away but answered. "Some. Not too bad."

"Your relationship with your father have anything to do with your being here now?"

Cole looked back at Carrie and nodded. "I've thought about killing him for a long time now. So the opportunity to get some training and take possession of a weapon seemed to fit with my plans."

"You were going to track him down?"

The boy smiled and shook his head. "Wouldn't have to bother. He wrote me. He's coming back to the U.S. soon. Finally getting out of the service. Said he wants to see me."

"Welcome home, Dad. *Kapow?*"

Cole laughed. "That's funny. I was thinking I might be just a bit sneakier."

"Sure, you don't want to get caught."

"Like I am now. Truth is, I came in here actually thinking I could shoot you." He shook his head. "One look and I knew I couldn't. Him I could kill; you, no."

"Would you be disappointed if you found you couldn't kill your father either?"

"Yeah, very. Especially if he ever raises a hand to my mother again."

"Her, too?"

He nodded.

Carrie sighed. "Let's get back to our present situation. You said there were thirteen young guys who came out here with Bad Fat and Lem as adult supervision. You really think either of those two assholes will stick around for a pitched battle?"

"No."

"And the other young guys' parents: What was their thinking, if any?"

"They already tried their hand in Washington. Got caught. Some went to jail. Maybe they think their kids will do better. Run faster to get away if nothing else."

"Were you really thinking of going through with it, fighting the Secret Service?"

Cole shook his head. "I saw this movie about the Civil War. Those fools used to march right at the other side's riflemen, even the other army's cannons, too. Got their shit scattered something awful and the ones still on their feet just kept marching. That's what I got to feel like I was doing, and I had no way to get out."

"Why'd Bad Fat choose you to come in here?" Carrie said.

"I asked too many questions. I was starting to make him nervous. Maybe creating doubts for the one or two other guys who were paying attention. That and I told him I could kill you."

Carrie said, "Yeah, that must've been an important detail. In general, though, how were you regarded for your military skills compared to the other guys?"

Cole laughed again. "Top of the class in smarts, bottom in warrior skills."

"Okay, let's assume Reeves doesn't want to be on the premises when a multiple homicide goes down."

"You 'n' me?"

"In Reeves' dreams, yeah. Who would he leave behind to try to kill us, assuming he didn't want to lose anyone with skills that were needed for the attack on Fort Enquist?"

"That's easy, Buddy Legrand."

"What's his problem?"

"Ate a lotta lead paint, I think."

Carrie grinned "If we didn't have to shoot our way out of here, I wouldn't think that was funny. I take your point to mean Buddy's not too smart."

"No smarts at all. Lots of strange ideas, though. Thinks he's got a lot more going on than he does. You going to let me help you shoot our way out of here?"

"That was a figure of speech. What I can't understand is how these kids think they're going to get past the Secret Service agents guarding the Enquist house."

"Didn't I mention that?" Cole asked.

"Mention what?"

"They're all gonna be dressed up as Boy Scouts. Uniforms top to bottom. You notice my haircut?"

"Yeah, it's neat and short."

"Just like all the other boys. We all brush our teeth every day, too. We're All-American. Even our vans, they say Boy Scouts of

America. Got the right emblems and all that on them. Who's gonna shoot a Boy Scout troop in this country?"

Carrie smiled ruefully and shook her head.

Something like that wouldn't fool the Secret Service for more than…

A few seconds might be all they'd need.

That many shooters with the automatic weapons they had.

God, even if they didn't succeed the carnage would be awful.

For the first time since she'd been grabbed in L.A., Carrie had a reason beyond her own survival to break free.

"You know what the only smart thing about this whole mess is?" Cole asked.

"What?"

"Somebody found some old bumper stickers that had never been used and put them on the front and back of each van. They say: *Patti Grant for President.* How's that for a good joke?"

Carrie didn't like it at all.

That might actually be a smart ploy.

Buy the shooters a few extra seconds to open fire.

Olmsted County, Minnesota

Carolyn and Lars asked McGill if he could spare a moment to talk with them. He excused himself from the meeting with Celsus Crogher and Colonel Gregory and accompanied the Enquists to their kitchen. Carolyn had a cup of coffee and a cinnamon roll waiting for him. McGill knew a set-up when he saw one.

He'd been expecting some kind of special pleading from Abbie and Ken after Caitie had stolen the show so far, but he hadn't anticipated that his ex and her husband might have some possibly loopy idea in mind. He took a sip of coffee and a bite of the roll anyway.

Might as well get something out of this little confab.

"What's on your minds, Carolyn, you and Lars?"

Having grown much more forceful in the past several years, she came right out with it.

"When the local police appear to play the roles of our helpful neighbors, Lars and I are going to be out there with them."

McGill was sure Carolyn had a reply ready for any criticism he might offer.

So he only said, "Because?"

Carolyn took a moment to think. She hadn't been ready for so basic a response.

"Well, because Abbie, Ken and Caitie are our children, too." She took Lars' hand to indicate his paternal role.

McGill said, "Agreed."

His concise manner only made Carolyn suspicious.

"You aren't going to object?" she asked.

"Do you have any other reasons?" McGill asked.

"Well, we're all at risk here," she said.

McGill kept any hint of fault-finding off his face.

That didn't stop Carolyn from saying, "Yes, I know we all could be safe at Camp David now, even if we won't have that option much longer. But this is our life and we have to deal with it, confront it, if it comes to that."

"You're absolutely right," McGill said.

Carolyn stared at the man she'd once married and suspicion seamlessly melted into sadness.

"Don't you care any more, Jim? It doesn't matter to you what might happen to me?"

McGill looked at Lars. "With your permission?"

Lars didn't know what was being asked of him, but he nodded.

McGill took Carolyn's shoulders in his hands and kissed her cheek.

He told her, "Things aren't what they once were between us, but you will always matter to me. And right now? This is the first time I have even a hint of how scared you used to be when I was a cop in Chicago. But I respect your right, and Lars' right, to make your own decisions."

Not asking her current husband's approval, Carolyn hugged her former spouse.

When she stepped back, McGill asked, "You'll be wearing body armor?"

Carolyn nodded. "Courtesy of the Rochester PD."

"Try to position yourself in the middle of the pack," McGill advised, "next to some cops who look alert and dependable."

"We will," Carolyn said.

Assuming a hang-dog expression, Lars said, "Carolyn won't let me bring my Viking ax."

Caitie had texted a photo of the weapon to McGill some time ago, so he knew what Lars was talking about.

"Probably wouldn't be a good idea to wear a horned helmet either," he said.

Carolyn gave McGill a peck on the cheek, and Lars shook his hand.

Never one to be wasteful, McGill sat down to finish the coffee and roll.

That was when he got the phone call from Sweetie.

Sweetie, another stout soul, got straight to the point: "Auric Ludwig tried to put out a hit on you."

"Tried to or has put?" McGill asked.

"Good question. Here's the deal. Ludwig tried to get the lawyer he's using on his appeal of the obstruction of justice charge to convey a letter confirming the job — killing you — but Putnam intervened. What the letter says is the hitman will be receiving his payment in full soon."

McGill was curious. "How much is the fee?"

"Five hundred thousand."

"I'd probably have been worth more earlier in Patti's presidency," McGill said.

"You really think ego is your first worry here?"

"I'd be happy to go beat the mean out of Auric Ludwig, and a full confession, too, only someone might think that was a crime."

"Jim, let's get real."

"Okay, do we have any idea who the hitman is?"

"We have what has to be a moniker: Corona Moe."

Corona? A thin brew in McGill's view. Who'd be scared by someone using that name? Now, if the killer was named Snake Venom, after Scotland's 135-proof beer, there might be something to worry about. Thinking Sweetie might not approve of that sentiment, though, he kept it to himself.

Sweetie misinterpreted his silence. "You're starting to take this seriously?"

Attempting to find patience with a world that was trying him sorely, McGill said, "Margaret, I'm dealing with a threat against my children's health and welfare at the moment. If someone comes after me while I'm busy with that, the phrase *short work* will apply. As in that's what I'll make of the jerk. With no regrets about whatever the outcome is."

"You won't mind if I look into this then?" Sweetie asked.

"You're ready to get back in the game?"

"I'll start by helping the people I love most. See how that goes."

"Thank you, Margaret. I'd do the same for you."

"I know."

"Did you call Patti before you called me?"

"Putnam called her. I called you first."

"Maybe *you* should beat the truth out of Auric Ludwig. I'll go your bail."

"I think I'll work the investigation my way. Maybe get Putnam to help."

"As you wish, Margaret."

"The President is seeing Dr. Nicolaides," Edwina Byington told McGill when he called the White House.

His heart began to race. "What's the problem?"

None of the doctors who'd examined his wife three years ago had ever determined the reason she almost died under anesthesia while donating the bone marrow that had saved Ken's life. The cause of the event was left as being idiopathic. Medical jargon for we don't have a clue.

Patti had been examined weekly, monthly and then semi-annually to guard against a recurrence of the mystery condition. But as time passed with the President demonstrating outward good health that was confirmed by lab and imaging tests the medical regimen was relaxed to a President's annual physical exam with a report to the nation that all was well.

So what the hell was happening now, McGill wondered.

"Is she being taken to the hospital?" he asked.

Edwina told him, "No, sir, both Dr. Nicolaides and the President told me that won't be necessary. They asked me to share that with you in the event that you called. The doctor also said the President would be unavailable to speak to you for an hour or two while he runs some routine tests."

To McGill's ear, Edwina sounded calm. Even so, he asked, "You wouldn't try to keep anything from me, would you, Edwina?"

"Never, sir. You're the only drinking buddy I have around here."

McGill laughed. He had, in fact, taken Edwina out for a drink on a handful of occasions.

He said. "Please ask the President to call me whenever she can."

"Of course, sir."

McGill said good-bye with the words "routine tests" still echoing in his ears.

In his mind, it was always preferable not to need any medical tests, routine or otherwise.

Still alone and seated at Carolyn's kitchen table, McGill spent a moment in silent prayer, "My children, my wife and myself, are all in jeopardy of one sort or another: Was it something I said or did, Lord? I could use a little guidance here. Give me a hint. I'm a reasonable guy. I'll work with you."

Almost as if he'd gotten a direct response, McGill experienced a small epiphany.

If Carolyn and Lars could go out to confront the enemy, he should do the same.

McGill gathered his children, with Ben Nolan tagging along, and brought all four of them back to Lars' den where Celsus and the Colonel had just finished working out the details of how to shoot the would-be kidnappers, if necessary, without mistakenly hitting each other's people. They halted their discussion as McGill and the young people appeared.

"Okay, Dad," Caitie said, "we're all here. So what's up?"

McGill held up a hand, calling for a moment's patience.

He asked Celsus, "The local cops will have their representatives here soon?"

"Yes, a captain from the Rochester PD, another captain from the Olmsted County Sheriff's Office and a major from the Minnesota State Patrol. They should all be here in the next fifteen minutes or so. The colonel and I will go over things as we see them and ask for their input."

Celsus had become far more amenable to taking suggestions since leaving the White House.

"You good with that, Colonel?" McGill asked.

"Yes, sir."

McGill looked at Caitie. "You and Ben have positioned all your outdoor cameras?"

Caitie gave Ben a nod. He said, "We've got 360° coverage of the approaches to the house and one wide-angle lens pointed straight up from the roof in case anyone sky-dives in."

Elaborating, Caitie said, "We have Bluetooth feeds to both my MacBook Pro and Celsus' laptop. Both computer displays will feature a grid of the camera shots. If either Celsus or I want to watch the feed from a single camera, we can do so independently, even if we choose different shots. All the video that's shot will be stored in real time on a secure server."

McGill looked at the two young filmmakers and the two guys

in charge of the people with the guns.

"Were there any disagreements on how to proceed with creating a visual record of what happens here?" he asked.

"Only one," Colonel Gregory said, "and we got that worked out."

Celsus explained, "There was a question of who, if anyone, should have the final say about releasing any of the video to the public. We arrived at a mutually agreeable choice of an arbiter."

McGill knew the answer to that one. "The President."

All four of the parties directly involved nodded.

McGill kept his concerns about Patti's health to himself.

He did tell his children that their mother and other father would be out among the plainclothes cops during this little drama.

Abbie's response was, "What about Ken and me? We're adults, too."

McGill turned to his son. "How do you feel?"

Ken said, "I've almost died young already. I'll take a pass this time. I can help Caitie and Ben do their thing."

"Abbie," McGill asked, "are you sure?"

Firming her jaw, she said, "I want to be with Mom and Lars."

Both Celsus and Colonel Gregory looked on with interest.

McGill said, "It's okay with me if it's okay with your mother."

"Which one?" Abbie asked.

"Both, but wait for me to set up a call to the one in the White House. I have to go out for a while."

All of his children, Celsus and the colonel asked McGill in near simultaneity, "Where?"

He crossed to the doorway of the room before turning to answer. "We've heard from the local, county and state police agencies that they're already looking for the bad guys, hoping to stop them before they get this far."

"Stop them without starting a firefight at the mall," Celsus added.

"Yeah, that, too," McGill acknowledged. "Well, since everyone else around here wants to pitch in, I thought I'd do the same. Go out and see if I can spot the bad guys. Talk sweet reason to them."

Celsus put a hand on the side of his head to listen to a message coming in on his earbud.

He responded and then said to McGill, "Perfect timing. Special Agent Ky and Leo Levy just arrived from Washington. Your Chevy is at the front door."

"You goin' out?" Knox Williamson asked, entering the bedroom Darin MacTeague was using.

Darin looked up from the shoelaces he was tying.

"Yeah. I want to do some last minute scouting. Make sure those government people at the Enquist house haven't brought in an army tank or something."

Knox's jaw dropped at the idea.

"Hey," Darin said with a grin, "I was just kidding."

Knox forced a laugh, sounding louder than he'd intended in the otherwise quiet house. He was the militia unit's second in command. He had a question in mind, the kind anybody would hate to ask, but ask it he did, "Darin, I was thinking, what should I do if, you know, you get killed?"

Darin didn't much like *hearing* the question, but he kept his voice as calm as he could.

"Take over is what you should do. If it looks like we have a chance, bust into the house and grab those McGill kids. Then get back to where everyone can jump into that semi-truck Dallas'll have waiting for us."

"You think Dallas will really be there, the way we planned it?"

The doubt in Knox's voice chilled Darin.

"What, you don't think he will?"

"I'm probably just worrying too much."

Knox had been the quarterback and the captain of their football team. He *had* a scholarship offer to play big-college football. On top of his athletic skills, he got great grades, too.

"I've never known you to worry," Darin said. "You think. Think rings around most of us. So what are you thinking now?"

Knox sat on the bed next to his teammate. "It's crazy, maybe, but what if we don't have a chance? What if we were sent out here to get killed?"

"What?" Darin's voice came out louder and shrill.

They heard stirrings from the rest of the house.

Darin got up and closed the door to the bedroom. He looked back at his friend.

"You think our mothers and fathers would do something crazy like that?"

"Not your mother or mine. Or any of the other moms, I guess. But my dad and yours? You put the two of them together, they own more guns than Canada. Most of the rest, the fathers I mean, are pretty much the same. They feel shamed by what happened to them up in Washington. They want to get even."

"And sacrificing us will do it?" Darin asked.

"Martyrs to the cause, if a bunch of kids get killed by the federal government. Money and recruits would pour in. Nobody dies in vain anymore if you call them martyrs and make them heroes."

Darin sat back down on the bed.

"My dad loves me," he said.

"Yeah, so does mine. As long as I do what I'm told. All the hell I want to do is play college football. I know I'm not tall enough to ever go pro, but I could do just fine in college. Meet some nice girls, make contacts to get a good job. Have a real life. Can't do any of that if I die tonight."

Darin nodded. "I was thinking about my future, too."

He took out his wallet and looked at a picture of Dana.

"You've already got your girl," Knox said.

Then he shook his head, looking sadder than anyone ever should at eighteen.

"What?" Darin asked.

"You know, it's too late for us. We're already fucked."

"What do you mean? We haven't done anything yet."

Knox laughed. "No? We've been holding a kidnapped girl whose daddy is married to the President of the United States. How do you think that's going to work out for us? Shit, we'd be better off shooting ourselves."

Darin couldn't help himself; he had to laugh.

"So that's your answer, suicide? Maybe we should take the time to write a sad poem first."

That made Knox laugh. "If you don't think we should kill ourselves, maybe we could go on a bank-robbing spree, get the cops chasing us at a hundred miles per hour and … shit, we'll figure the rest out later. Or we could just take one of the vans and make a run for the border."

"Mexico?" Darin asked.

Knox said, "You speak Spanish?"

"No."

"Neither do I, and Canada's a hell of a lot closer."

"What'll we do for money?"

Knox said, "How about we sell as many fully automatic assault rifles we can. No questions asked. We could make some good money doing that."

"What about the other guys?" Darin asked.

"You like any of them?

"Not especially. Only met them a week ago. You're the only one I know."

"Then let's just leave them here. Maybe some of them will come to their senses, too."

Darin said, "And if they don't?"

"Well, let's hope they won't be blowing any college scholarships."

As Darin and Knox made their getaway, taking with them all but three of the assault rifles, the other recruits of the FreeMan Militia did what teenagers everywhere were wont to do: sleep until someone yanked them into consciousness. Even when the engine of the van started, none of the sleepers awoke.

Darin told Knox, who'd be driving the first leg of the journey north, to wait just a minute.

He used his knife to puncture all four tires on the other van.

They'd left three rifles and ten magazines of ammo behind in case the boys needed to defend themselves. That was only fair. But if there were some hard-core assholes who wanted to carry on with the original plan, well, they'd just have to hoof it eight miles down the road. Even dressed as Boy Scouts in rural Minnesota, Darin and Knox didn't like their chances to make it to the target.

That was the best they could do.

Until Knox had another idea.

The White House — Washington, DC

Stepping into the Oval Office, the President told her chief of staff, who was waiting there, "I'll never be the same but I'm all right." Galia embraced her and said, "Thank God. No President should ever die in office, especially you."

The President took her seat behind her desk and Galia closed the door to the office. "So tell me, please, what did Dr. Nicolaides say? Unless you'd rather not tell me, of course. I'll understand."

Galia's words proclaimed one sentiment; her face expressed another.

'Fess up, sister.

"I'd rather not," the President said, "but I need your help, so I will."

When Galia heard the diagnosis, she couldn't help but laugh.

The President let the merriment go on for several seconds before asking, "Do you think we should alert the news media?"

Galia laughed even harder at that but shook her head. "No, no, we might set our cause back years."

The President had to smile. "It does sound funny now. In the moment, it was anything but."

"Half of humanity sympathizes with you. At least those of a certain age."

"Sympathy doesn't do me a bit of good," the President said. "I'll never run for office again. But …"

Galia stopped laughing and started paying attention. The President had found a political angle to play here? The chief of staff wanted to know what it was. Right away.

"Without knowing what you know now, Galia, how would you describe the events of the past hour-and-a-half in this building, as others might have seen them?"

Galia took a minute to formulate her description. "The President was working in the Oval Office when the White House physician was summoned to attend to her. Dr. Artemis Nicolaides then rushed the President to his suite in the building. Several medical tests were administered there ... I assume."

The President nodded.

Galia continued. "The tests were administered and initial results allowed the President to return to work. Definitive results are still pending. Unless the tests indicate the President is unable to perform her full range of duties, specific results will not be made public."

The chief of staff reached her hand across the President's desk and Patricia Grant took it.

"You're not anticipating any bad news are you?" Galia asked.

The President shook her head. "Except for that one thing, Nick says I'm in the clear."

Sighing, Galia took a seat. "So, tell me, Madam President, how can we make all this work to our advantage?"

"First, we wait for the leak about what happened here today to hit the news."

There was no question that it would, and soon. Thousands of people worked in the White House: over 3,000 full-time employees and a near equal number of part-timers and volunteers. How many took notice of the President being rushed to the White House physician's medical suite was anybody's guess. The number had to be measured in three digits and possibly four. More than a handful would speak directly to members of the media. Others would spread the word on social media.

"Then once the leak becomes news," Galia said, "we use an approximation of the wording I just came up with as a press release."

"Yes, and the payoff is?" the President asked.

Galia needed only a heartbeat to come up with the answer. "The President has come down with a mystery condition. Nothing serious enough to invoke the 25th Amendment and put Vice President Morrissey in charge full time, but Jean will have select opportunities not only to *act* Presidential but also to perform Presidential duties. That's …"

Galia was going to say brilliant, but she stopped to look for pitfalls.

"What could anyone do to us?" the President said.

"Legally, nothing. Politically, argue against a woman ever becoming President again."

The President gave a mirthless laugh. "Good luck with that."

Galia had to agree. "Personally, though, you can expect mud to be flung at you."

"A small price to pay if we can get Jean elected. I'll have to clear this with her, of course. But I'm going to do everything I can to see that neither General Altman nor Senator Worth ever sits in this office."

Galia said, "We both know there's no worry about General Altman."

"What, just because he initiated a murder for hire and the victim was his wife?" the President asked in mock seriousness. "That and sleep with a subordinate officer he later tried to drum out of the service."

"I know political parties like to protect their own," Galia said, "but these misdeeds strain even those limits, don't you think?"

"Possibly. No, probably, but only because Carina Linberg has become a best-selling author and a celebrity under her pen-name. When she starts talking about the general, he'll be sunk."

"So that leaves Senator Oren Worth," Galia said. "I don't think he's going to like your pre-positioning Jean for the job. He'll think it's *unfair, wah-wah-wah.*"

Both women laughed.

"You know who that leaves to attend to?" the President asked.

The choices were many but the chief of staff intuited whom the President meant. "Tyler Busby. We can't leave his mess around for anyone else to clean up."

"No, we can't. The time has come to deliver a copy of the farewell photo of the late Representative Philip Brock to Mr. Busby's lawyer. See what kind of reaction we get."

Galia had only been waiting to get the go-ahead on that move.

The photo in question was already in an addressed and sealed envelope.

It would be delivered by courier within the hour.

"Is there anything else, Madam President?"

"Not for you at the moment. I have to return Jim's call."

Edwina had slipped her the phone message on the way into the Oval Office.

Olmsted County, Minnesota

For the first time that he could remember, McGill was at the wheel of his official U.S. Government Chevy. He was impressed how a light touch on the accelerator sent the car roaring up the road. It took a moment to get in tune with the car and stay anywhere near the speed limit. Deke was sitting shotgun. Leo was stretched out across the back seat snoring lightly.

He'd made the drive out from DC nonstop, Deke said.

McGill shook his head. "You had to stop for gas. A beast like this has to get awful mileage, between the monster engine and the weight of armor all the way around."

Deke said, "Nah, Leo just called in a KC-135 and we refueled on the fly."

The KC-135 was also known as the Stratotanker, McGill knew. It was the aircraft that refueled U.S. fighter jets in mid-air. It could do the same thing for Air Force One should the need arise. But it wasn't an option on anybody's Chevy.

"Yeah, right," he told Deke.

"Okay, I pumped some gas, but Leo only let me pee every

other stop. Not that that took very long. I'd close my eyes for what seemed like a few minutes and when I opened them again we'd be in another state. The only thing that was different from Star Trek's going into warp drive was the special effects weren't quite the same. Pretty close, though."

"I take it then, you're a bit wired," McGill said.

"A little," Deke admitted, "but fully functional if we catch up with those bastards who took my sister-in-arms." Meaning Carrie Ramsey.

McGill told him of all the forces arrayed at the Enquist spread.

"I like it," Deke said. "Shouldn't we get back there? Wouldn't want to miss the fun."

"The considered opinions of all the great minds, including mine, is that when the bad guys come it'll be dark outside or close to it."

"When's sunset around here?" Deke asked.

"A little after 7:30 p.m." McGill had checked.

"Sunrise?"

"A little before 7:00 a.m."

Deke peered through the windshield at the sky. "Heavy clouds. Filtering out a lot of light already. If the assholes are waiting 'til dark, they could make their move earlier than what the clock says."

"Yeah," McGill said.

"What do you think these fools look like?"

"Kids." He explained the reasoning.

"That sucks, but okay, kids. Still, they won't be dressed like the military. Not unless they're truly stupid. They'll have some kind of disguise."

The great minds, McGill realized, hadn't gotten around to that possibility.

But both he and Deke were busy watching oncoming traffic. A lot of it was pickup trucks, SUVs and minivans. Blue collar tradesmen making their workday rounds, city workers with homes out in the boonies and moms running the myriad errands family life demanded of them.

Neither man saw any vehicle that struck him as suspicious.

"It's too early in the year to pick crops up here," Deke said, "or I might suspect these guys could have the smarts to pass themselves off as migrant workers riding in the beds of pickup trucks."

McGill looked at him. "Really? Even if it was harvest season, I don't see this particular group trying to pass as people of color."

Deke, whose primary ethnicities were Asian and African-American, deferred to McGill. "You probably know more about rednecks than I do. Of course, all they'd really need is a box truck. You could pack whatever kind of dipshits you want in one of those and nobody would know."

McGill wasn't about to let the crack about rednecks slide, but he had to slow to allow a passenger van to pull out of a driveway ahead on the right. Both he and Deke had the visual acuity to recognize the emblem on the driver's door and read the lettering that encircled it.

"Boy Scouts of America," Deke said. "You think these mooks could be devious enough to use the Scouts as a cover?"

McGill didn't. Not until he saw the bumper sticker on the back of the van.

Patti Grant for President.

"Jesus," Deke said, spotting it, too.

McGill remembered that he'd asked for guidance from above.

"Does that bumper sticker look like it's been out in the weather for over seven years?" he asked.

"No way," Deke said. "It's a lot fresher than the rest of that damn van. Somebody thinks he's really funny."

As they passed, Deke got the house number of the place from which the van had departed.

Another van was parked there. Its tires looked flat. More Boy Scouts.

McGill said, "The dumb ones just have to give themselves away."

"I'm going to get a UAV in the air."

"A drone?" McGill asked. "What, with Hellfire missiles?"

"Yeah, if they have one like that available. What I'm thinking, though, is we want to see where that vehicle is going, and we don't want to lose it if we run out of gas before they do."

"Good point," McGill said. "We need to call in the location of that house back there, too."

At that moment, a phone call reached the Chevy. The console display said POTUS. President of the United States. Not that McGill had ever needed it before but the Chevy had hands-free calling.

He tapped the button and said, "Madam President, we may be on to something here."

Great Falls, Virginia

Senator Oren Worth traveled to Thomas Winston Rangel's house in his classic 1961 British Racing Green Jaguar XKE. He had the top down and wore a snap-brim hat and aviator sunglasses. That was his idea of blending in with the environment. He felt sure not one person in a thousand would recognize him.

He kept both the hat and the glasses on after Rangel admitted him to his home.

"No need for cloak and dagger here, Oren," Rangel said. "I have the curtains drawn."

The old man's words were only mildly biting, but his expression told Worth he was a putz. Embarrassed him into removing the glasses if not the hat. Rangel led the Senate majority leader to his study and indicated a loveseat where he might sit. He would have been pleased if Worth had ignored his direction and took the armchair that was clearly the seat of power in the room, but the senator sat where he'd been pointed.

"Would you care for sparkling water," Rangel asked, "or something stronger?"

"San Pellegrino, if you have it."

Being a good host, Rangel obliged his guest, while personally opting for two fingers of Pappy Van Winkle. He took the chair

Worth should have grabbed for himself. He silently admitted that the senator didn't look half-bad in the hat. It was the glasses that were the over-the-top element.

Worth took a sip of his Italian sparkling water. "You said you have something important to tell me, Thomas."

"A few things, actually. Let's start with Warren Altman. He's withdrawing from the race. You should have the conservative vote for President all to yourself."

The senator smiled, briefly. Then he picked up on the potentially bad news.

"Altman actually did it? He had that Navy man kill his wife?"

"So the note from the late Captain Dexter Cowan claims, my spies tell me. By itself it's not likely to be enough to cook Altman's goose before a judge. In the public's credulous mind, though, he's done. He'll never hold *any* elective office. No private employer of any significance will ever hire him. If a future, hostile administration decides to yank his military pension, he might wind up on the street, literally."

A small chill ran through Worth as he thought the mighty could indeed fall.

He fought off any sense of personal peril by reminding himself he had *billions* to his name.

Politically, though, his risk was rising fast.

Rangel was glad to see that Worth understood the implications. "What would we do, Oren, if some liberal candidate for the presidency found himself in General Altman's position?"

"We'd crucify him and spread political guilt by association as far as we could. But…"

Rangel wanted the senator to finish the thought for himself, but when he let it dangle, the old man stepped in. "The Democrats and Cool Blue aren't as tough, mean and nasty as we are? That was true once, but no longer. Do you think there's *anything* Galia Mindel and Patricia Grant won't do to get Jean Morrissey elected?"

Senator Worth shook his head. "They'll do whatever it takes."

"Exactly. They won't accuse you of murder, of course. They

will put a photo of you next to one of Warren Altman and outline one-by-one all the policy positions the two of you hold in common. Maybe finish the comparisons with an ellipsis … inviting the voting public to say, yeah, Worth probably had someone killed, too."

Spots of red appeared on the senator's cheeks.

"They couldn't do that."

The words were no sooner out of his mouth than he knew of course they could. They would. There was no stopping the people who made the ads and the voters who saw them from doing and responding in whatever fashion they wanted. Welcome to politics in the U.S.A.

"What should I do?" Worth asked.

"I was thinking I should tell you to grow a pair, but that wouldn't be quite apt. I know you didn't make your fortune in the mining business without having both brains and balls. So what you need to do is find them and to paraphrase an old ad campaign, 'Don't leave home without them.' Be tough but never threatening. And never, without exception, complain that anything is unfair. I don't care if Patricia Grant does resign and make Jean Morrissey President. Draw on all the resources you possess to laugh off any challenge and overcome it. Remember who you were *before* you came to Washington."

Worth sat up straighter and his jaw muscles firmed.

He was looking in Rangel's direction but seeing the man he himself used to be.

He liked what he saw and told the old man, "I want you with me every step of the way."

Rangel laughed softly. "There's your first challenge. I won't outlive this day."

"What? How can you know that?"

"Because I'm going to put a bullet in my brain an hour or so after you leave. Long enough, at any rate, so there won't be any connection to you."

Worth was genuinely shocked. "Why would you kill yourself?"

"Because I've heard my erstwhile protégé Edmond Whelan is going to testify that I paid a thief to steal an embarrassing document from him."

"Did you?"

"Yes."

"Why?"

The old man only laughed and Worth got the message.

"Because you didn't want to be embarrassed. You want people to think of you as better than that. But what will they think after you commit suicide? Oh. Yes, by then you won't be capable of caring."

"Now, you're starting to think like your old self," Rangel said. "I don't want to spend my last days in court, much less in prison. So I'm going to depart in the manner I choose, at the time and place I prefer."

Worth wanted to know more. "You must have had inside sources to learn about both Whelan and Altman. Did you simply pay these people or did you have other leverage?"

"A little of both," Rangel said. "There must have been times when you could look at someone across the negotiating table from you and see what their personal defects were and how to make use of them."

"Yes, there were times like that." Worth began to remember just how powerful he was. All the petty courtesies of the Senate were just play-acting. Manners to be observed but not values to be internalized. God, he felt wonderful, as if he was being reborn.

Rangel saw that renewal and offered a note of caution.

"Shortly after I die, my lawyer will release many years worth of my files to various media outlets. Every piece of dirt I have on liberal members of Congress, their donors in the private sector, their pet journalists, their tame intellectuals and other hangers-on will be released. Crimes and sins of every stripe will be exposed. The other side will call it a gigantic smear and they'll be exactly right."

"Sounds like heaven to me," Worth said, "only …"

Rangel smiled. The man's mind was actually working the way it should.

"Galia Mindel will do the same thing to our side," Worth said. "Mutually assured destruction."

Rangel nodded and laughed. "Who knows, Cool Blue, as the newest political party with the least time to corrupt itself, might be the only one left standing."

"Well, shit," Majority Leader Worth said, "we can't have that."

He got up and put his sunglasses on. Time to go. There was work to do.

"Thank you, Thomas," he told Rangel. "A parting word?"

"What's that?"

"When you put the gun to your head? Make sure you get the job done."

Interstate 90, Westbound

"I don't know about this," Darin MacTeague said for maybe the 45th time.

Knox Williamson sighed. He'd already asked who the quarterback in the van was. Darin had parried by asking who the ranking officer was. Knox had pointed out that nobody outside of a group of yahoos recognized any legal standing for that militia. At least his credential had the recognition of their state high school athletic association.

A grim ten-minute silence had followed that point of the discussion.

They hadn't gone 20 miles down the highway and already the bonds of amity were fraying.

Knox broke the silence, proposing a compromise. "Look, if we can find a driver at the next truck stop who has an NRA sticker on his rig, we'll sell him two fully automatic assault rifles for $500. I'll use the money to pay somebody for a quick ride to Sioux City."

"You really think you can pull this off? *Rescuing* Caitie McGill?" Darin asked.

That had been Knox's big idea, why they weren't already headed for Canada.

Knox said, "Dallas told us he left Buddy and Cole to watch her."

"To *kill* her."

"Yeah, well, if she's dead already or I get there even a minute too late, then we're fucked. We go to Canada and try living anywhere but in the woods, they're going to find us."

"Canada's got a *lot* of woods, I hear."

They looked at each other and laughed, friends again. For the moment anyway.

"Even more ice and snow," Knox said. "Spending a winter outdoors up there with only you for company isn't my idea of a good time."

Darin said, "I think we're only going to get sent to prison sooner if we go to Sioux City."

"Okay, so we sell a couple of rifles and go our own ways then."

"You wouldn't even have to sell two. Barter just one to a driver for an express run to Sioux City. Keep the other rifle for yourself, in case you need it."

Knox liked that idea. "You're not too dumb for a defensive lineman."

Darin snorted. "Speaking of stupid, you think those two guys up there in Sioux City are fools enough to kill a young girl?"

"Not Cole. My guess is he has about a step-and-a-half on me in the classroom. Buddy? He'd do it. I only pray to Jesus he hasn't already."

Darin sat in silence for a minute. "I'll go with you to Sioux City."

Knox glanced at him. "How come?"

"You might need help."

"Thanks."

"And you've got about a step-and-a-half on me in the smarts department."

Knox put his eyes back on the road. "I didn't want to come right out and say so."

"That's smart, too. You really think they'll cut us some slack on our jail time if we bring Caitie McGill back to ... where? The cops?"

"Yeah, the Sioux City police. Let them call the FBI or whoever. Will we catch a break? Well, we say we fell under the bad influence of a bunch of grownups and when we realized how wrong we were to get involved, hell, we set the girl free. Got her home in one piece. Whatever they do to us, it won't be as bad as what'd happen if we try to run and hide out."

"You know what else I thought, Knox?"

"What?"

"If it was my Dana somebody grabbed, I'd be praying someone would do what we're gonna do."

"*Try* to do. I think we're good for five miles per hour above the limit without the cops giving us any grief about speeding. Let's hope that gets us there fast enough."

"Amen," Darin said, already praying for success.

Following a half-mile behind the two repentant kidnappers, keeping them in sight, McGill maintained a steady interval. He glanced at the gas tank. It was down to half full. Deke was listening to someone on his earbud. Leo was awake by now, looking uneasy that someone else was at the wheel of the car he considered to be his.

Not that he'd say so. His mama didn't raise no fools.

Deke said, "We've got a bird taking off from Ellsworth AFB near Rapid City."

McGill asked, "Is it armed?"

"Not armed but fast. Has to cross South Dakota and part of Minnesota to take up station."

"Fast and sharp-eyed will do," McGill said. "The President wants to keep the body-count to a minimum. So do I."

During her call to the McGill-mobile, Patti had also told him that she'd had a minor health issue that was quickly resolved. When she heard where her husband was and that Deke and Leo were in the car, she wasn't about to go into details. McGill shared her sense of discretion. Sticking to business, he told her he'd yet to notify the troops at the Enquists' home about the second van parked outside the farmhouse down the road. Patti said she'd take care of that.

Nothing like hearing directly from the commander-in-chief to make military personnel perk up. Before ending the call, Patti said, "Stay safe, Jim."

She hadn't cared who heard that.

After saying goodbye to Patti, McGill called Eugene Beck.

"How's it goin', boss?"

McGill said, "Keeping busy, Gene. There's something I'd like you to do."

"Let me guess. See if I can put my hands on Corona Moe."

"See if you can find him," McGill said. "Hand him off to the Secret Service, if you do."

"Roger that." Being ex-USAF, Gene got to say that.

"Just curious, Gene. What kind of beer do you like?"

"Cold."

"Not particular, huh?" McGill asked.

"No, sir. Not in that way. Are you thinking Corona refers to beer?"

"Don't you?"

"Could be Corona cigars or the aura around the sun. I wrote a song about that last one once."

McGill didn't smoke and hadn't thought about the sun.

"Okay, Gene, whatever works. Keep in touch."

"Roger that."

Leo said, "You've got an old boy who writes songs working for you now, boss?"

"Yes."

Deke said, "You're not going to put him in my office, are you?"

Meaning DC, after the two of them moved to the private sector.

McGill replied, "What, you don't like music?" Before Deke felt he had to respond, McGill added, "I was thinking L.A. Gene would probably be a better fit out there."

Deke kept his sigh of relief as quiet as he could.

The Enquist House — Olmsted County, Minnesota

"Mr. McGill's gone where, ma'am?" Celsus Crogher asked the President.

She'd called his cell phone and he put it on speaker at her request so Colonel Gregory could share in the conversation. The two men were still in Lars' den. He was completely hospitable about the security people and the military taking over his space.

Celsus wondered why more people couldn't be like that.

"Jim's headed west on Interstate 90, following a large white Chevrolet passenger van, approximately ten years old. The van has Boy Scouts of America markings on it. Based on what Jim could see at a glance, a young man was driving with another young man in the passenger seat beside him."

"And the reason Mr. McGill decided to follow these guys, ma'am?"

"Jim saw a 'Patti Grant for President' bumper sticker on the van. One that hadn't been exposed to the weather for years and looked freshly applied. Jim thinks it's an inside joke played at my expense."

Colonel Gregory nodded. He liked the hunch McGill was playing.

Tactics and strategy were all fine, but special forces guys knew there were times you had to go with your gut.

Celsus, though, still had his doubts. "So you're saying, ma'am, we should not count on Mr. McGill taking part in any action that might occur at the Enquist property?"

"I don't think he'll be back anytime soon, Celsus, so yes, don't count on him until you hear otherwise."

Colonel Gregory asked, "Madam President, is it your feeling Mr. McGill hopes he's being led to wherever Special Agent Ramsey might be held? If so, how might you want my men and me to redeploy?"

"Jim didn't come out and say so, Colonel, but my guess is, yes, he thinks he might find the special agent. That or be led to the people behind her kidnapping. Would you like me to have the Minnesota National Guard lend you and your men a helicopter? In case you need to move elsewhere quickly."

"That'd be just the ticket, ma'am, thank you."

"Wouldn't do to station it on the Enquist property where prying eyes might see it."

"No, ma'am."

"I'll ask Carolyn Enquist if she has a neighbor, say, a mile or so away with enough land to tuck a helicopter away inconspicuously."

"That'd be first class, ma'am."

Celsus said, "Just to be clear, Madam President, the special forces people might move out but the Secret Service will remain in place until advised otherwise."

"Yes, Celsus. But Colonel Gregory, I'd like you to send some of your men to a house down the road." She gave him the address and the satellite coordinates she'd obtained. "Jim spotted a second van there. I'd like to know if anybody's at home."

"Absolutely, ma'am, and the rules of engagement are?"

"Watch, listen and don't let anyone leave without talking to me first."

"Should I notify local law enforcement or will you, ma'am?"

"When I call the governor about the helicopter, I'll have him pass this word along." The President was quiet for a moment. "I'll call the county sheriff, too, to make sure there's no confusion."

"Thank you, ma'am. That's reassuring."

"Celsus, you have enough people in case the special forces troops leave?"

"We'll be fine, Madam President."

"Good. Well then, I have other calls to make."

The next call the President made was to Carolyn Enquist on her personal cell phone.

"Carolyn, it's me, Patti."

The first Mrs. McGill always blinked when her successor

called. It had happened before, maybe two or three times a year. But having the President call on a first-name basis always made her heart flutter. She'd never dreamt such a thing could happen … and then there was the fear the President might be calling with tragic news: somebody's death. Jim was always the first person who came to mind.

But Carolyn heard neither anxiety nor sorrow in Patti's voice.

So she said, "Hello, how are you, Patti?"

"I'm well, thank you. And you and Lars?"

"We're good, thanks. To what do I owe the honor?"

"You've heard our suspicion that the people who might attack your home could well be quite young."

"Yes."

"I was wondering what your feelings as a mother are," Patti said.

"I'm horrified. I think of the news stories I've read about adults using children as soldiers in other countries, and I think that can't be happening here. We can't let it happen here."

"I think the same thing, and I see a lot more awful stories than just about anyone."

Shaking her head, Carolyn said, "I could never do your job. You must have to be *so* strong."

"It isn't easy. I'll be ready to pass the torch when the time comes." Turning to another subject, she said, "Jim told me a long time ago to think of his children as my children, too. But I've never spoken to you about that."

Carolyn chuckled. "Don't worry. I've told Lars the same thing. He's come to accept it. I hope you have, too."

Clearing a throat suddenly filled with emotion, Patti said, "Thank you. That means more to me than I can tell you. So, as two mothers, what do you think we should do if we catch up with the young men involved in this awful situation?"

Patti explained how Jim had seen a house down the road from Carolyn where the amateur militia might be getting ready to launch their attack.

"If Jim's right about that," Patti said, "how do you think we might avoid bloodshed?"

Carolyn's initial reaction was to think: *You're asking me? How the hell would I know? I'm not exactly a —*

But acting on a pure gut reaction what she said was, "You know what I'd do, as a mother? If I could find those boys' mothers, I'd call them. Have them tell their kids to put down any damn guns they might have and come out with their hands on their heads and do whatever the hell they were told."

Carolyn's voice filled with emotion. "I'd also tell them I was sorry I hadn't done better for them. I'd do my best to make it up to them. I'd say I loved them, and please don't do anything that will get yourself killed."

After a moment of silence, Carolyn asked, "You think that'd do any good?"

Patti was gone; the President was the one who replied in a decisive tone.

"We're going to give it a try, Carolyn. Thank you."

Sioux City, South Dakota

Buddy Legrand wasn't real good at waiting. Passing time idly, waiting for something exciting, made him itchy. From his flaky scalp to his ingrown toenails he'd feel like he had a monster case of prickly heat. He couldn't endure that shit for more than a minute or two. And Dallas wanted him to wait four, maybe six, hours? His head would explode.

On the other hand, he was real good at snoozing. He could cat-nap like he was the damn king of the jungle. Do it anytime he pleased and often when he didn't. Sure as hell, he could fall asleep anytime nobody was looking his way. He'd done so through eight years of school. It got to the point where teachers would put him at the back of the class because he slept peacefully and didn't disturb anyone.

If he was awake, he'd be itching and scratching like he was

about to spread some horrible disease throughout the classroom and maybe the whole school. The faculty and the administration took the easy way out. They let him sleep and gave him his elementary school diploma honorarily. Nobody ever suggested he should go to high school.

When he turned 17, his dad told him he should join the military and he gave it a try.

Only the Army was far less tolerant of sleeping on the job. They even told him there were times when sleeping on duty could get you shot. What kind of shit was that? By mutual consent, Buddy was given an administrative discharge for poor duty performance. But not until he'd gotten halfway through basic training and had proved that, while conscious, he was more than a fair marksman.

His shooting was what got him into the FreeMan Militia. They provided him with a small salary and three square meals a day. The private sector military was also far more understanding about the need for nap-time. Dallas Reeves hadn't caught on to Buddy's peculiarities because he wasn't a commander from Buddy's home state. Dallas was just a guy who'd been brought in to hold on to that little McGill gal.

So as soon as Dallas had bugged out Buddy decided the only way to obey his orders was to catch a few Zs. He leaned his assault rifle against the wall to his right, maybe five feet from where he sat, his back against the same wall, his legs splayed out in front of him. Not the best position in which to drowse but he'd nodded off in stranger places.

Buddy had once fallen asleep on the back seat of a motorcycle while Uncle Gaston was giving him a ride. Buddy came flying off when the bike hit a bump in the road. Woke up only when he hit the asphalt and started tumbling. Only reason he didn't break apart in million pieces was he'd been so relaxed.

Nobody had ever diagnosed Buddy with either narcolepsy or psoriasis, but other than his induction physical in the Army, through which he ironically stayed awake and obeyed the physician who told him, "Stop that," when he had started to scratch, he'd never seen a doctor. Medical care hadn't fit in with his family's budget, and his father thought Medicaid was for communists.

When Buddy woke up in the Sioux City house he was momentarily refreshed. He leaned right and took hold of his assault rifle. He sniffed the barrel. Detected no odor that any rounds had been fired. He was pleased about that. He'd heard that people did all sorts of crazy things in their sleep: walk, talk, even eat. So why not shoot, too? He was glad he hadn't done anything foolish. He knew that most people already thought he was a retard.

If he started firing an automatic weapon with his eyes closed that might be cause for another discharge, and if the militia turned him out he wouldn't have anywhere to go.

Daddy had said, "Come home a hero or don't come at all."

Remembering the duty Dallas had assigned him, Buddy stood up and called out, "Cole, you still in there with that girl? You better come out quick. I gotta shoot her. Dallas told me so."

After a moment, he heard Cole reply, "Hey, man, give me a little time, will you? I think she's just about ready to come across. You wouldn't stop a friend from getting some, would you?"

Buddy had never thought of Cole as his friend. As far as he could remember, he'd never had one. Well, maybe his uncle. Gaston had even taken Buddy to a *putain* once back home in Louisiana. The woman had a really hard old face but her body still looked ripe as a peach. Hot enough to get him excited just staring at her. Then he woke up in a smelly old bed lying naked beside her.

"How'd I do?" he asked.

She patted his cheek and lit a cigarette. "Honey, you gotta wake up to get it up."

The woman said she'd tried to rouse him in all sorts of ways, but now their hour was over.

When his uncle asked if he'd had a good time, Buddy had only smiled and winked.

Buddy told Cole, "I'll give you as much time as you need, if you tell me all about it."

At that moment, Buddy just wanted to know what he'd missed. Cole yelled, "You bet."

The look in Carrie's eyes was as merciless as the two Berettas she pointed at Cole.

"You might 'get some' and you're going to tell Numbnuts out there all about it?" she asked in a flat quiet voice.

Cole kept his voice down, too, but he didn't look scared.

"He was going to start shooting, if I didn't come out soon. You know that, right?"

"I was thinking about shooting first."

"Where?" Cole asked.

"Pillar to post."

Cole had never heard that expression before but he drew the proper inference. Wall to wall. Probably real fast, too.

"Okay," he said still whispering, "that might've worked. But maybe it wouldn't. You shoot at Buddy and miss, he's going to open up on us. We'd have to be out-the-wazoo lucky not to get hit."

Carrie couldn't argue with that.

Still, she didn't like the idea that she was dealing with another wiseass kid.

Cole took no notice of her displeasure. He said, "If we can get Buddy thinking we're having sex in here, what's he going to do? One of two things. Open the door to see if he can get in on the action or stay out there and jack off. He sticks his head in here, you pop him. He jacks off, he'll probably make more noise than we do. Give you a chance to catch him with his pants down. Pop him or just wound him while he's dropping his cock and reaching for his rifle."

"What about Reeves?" Carrie asked. "Him or someone else?"

"The boys are off playing army; that's the plan. Bad Fat? You take away that Darth Vader voice, he's just the biggest tub of chick-enshit you ever saw. My money says he's split."

Carrie gritted her teeth. The kid made sense. He'd come up with a better plan, off the top of his head, than she had. If they both got out of this, she'd have to introduce him to the real Caitie McGill. The two of them would deserve each other.

Then without giving the matter conscious thought Carrie produced a loud, rapturous moan.

Wouldn't make the grade in a *bad* porn flick, she felt sure.

But Cole beamed and with equal measures of volume and ham got into his part.

"You like that, huh, baby?"

Federal Detention Center — Washington, DC

The story about Wilbur Teasdale, criminal defense attorney to the pinnacle of the high and mighty, was that he didn't charge by the hour, he got either first place in your will or your first born. Whichever had the greater market value. Actually, he took his portion of a client's net worth up front. Only when the check with the long string of zeros and commas cleared did he go to work.

Tyler Busby had secreted enough of his billions overseas in countries that would not budge on inquiries by the IRS, the FBI or any other federal agency to pay Teasdale a truly staggering fee. On his own initiative, Busby had doubled the lawyer's original asking price. It had comforted him to pay what he felt was truly a king's ransom to the man he expected to secure his freedom.

Despite the severity of Busby's crime, conspiring to kill the President of the United States, he was still unable to imagine himself being made to pay for it. Not in the long term anyway. He was too wealthy and too influential to face actual punishment. Hell, the reason he'd tried to have Patti Grant killed in the first place was she was laboring so hard to displace the primacy of the ultra-wealthy in American society. The plutocrats had worked too long to co-opt an entire political party, to lobby endlessly for their tax breaks and to actually write their own laws to allow that meddling woman to succeed.

Busby has simply been the one among the elite with the balls to say that Patti Grant must be stopped. What better way to achieve that goal than to kill her? That would not only take care of the immediate problem, it would send an unmistakable message to future presidents.

They were but water-carriers for their betters.

The shills in Congress were even less, lickspittles.

Tyler Busby was certain his fellow titans would soon rally to his cause. He would be released from incarceration and he would never suffer such an indignity again. The only thing he truly worried about was the possibility of James J. McGill coming after him, killing him even.

The man was a true wild card, unquestionably dangerous.

Well, Busby would make sure he had more than adequate security. Then one day in the future, when all his present concerns were far behind him, he'd have McGill put down. Like the mad dog he was.

Tyler Busby's view of the world and his preeminent place in it changed when Wilbur Teasdale entered the interview room, sat down at the table opposite him, opened his briefcase and slapped a check on the table. Busby looked at it and blinked. The amount equaled half of what he'd paid his lawyer.

The bonus that was supposed to motivate Teasdale to go above and beyond.

Do any damn thing necessary to free Busby and right smartly.

"What's that?" Busby ask, nudging the check back Teasdale's way.

The lawyer said, "It's something I've never given anyone before, a rebate."

Busby sat back, trying to distance himself from what had to be an unwelcome development.

"I don't want it," he said.

Teasdale shrugged. "Perhaps the correctional officers here can use it to fund their softball team."

"That's not funny, damnit!" Beads of sweat emerged on Busby's forehead.

"Then you really won't like this." Teasdale took a manila envelope out of his briefcase and put it on the table. "Open it."

Busby shook his head. Teasdale didn't bother arguing. He opened the envelope, took out a glossy 8x10 photo and put it where Busby couldn't miss seeing it.

Philip Brock's head placed between those of two pigs.

Busby took one look, gagged and swept the photo and the check off the table.

Unimpressed, Teasdale told Busby, "A copy of that photo was sent to the FBI. Another copy was sent to the widow of the late Senator Howard Hurlbert. Hers bore the inscription, 'You, too, are avenged.'"

"Howard Hurlbert, the True South founder? I never had anything to do with him."

"The late Congressman Philip Brock did, and Brock was also a well known companion of yours. Do you see your peril here, Mr. Busby?"

"This is madness."

"It's more than a little strange, I'll grant you, and it only gets more so."

The lawyer took a sheet of paper out of his case and slid it over to Busby.

"My petition for a bail hearing for you. The government is not opposing the request."

"They're not?" Busby was incredulous.

Teasdale stood, picked up the photo and slammed it down on the table.

"No, they're not and this is why. My advice to you is not to bail yourself out. I think you'll be signing your own death warrant if you do. I called Attorney General Jaworsky. He's still amenable to making your time in prison somewhat less awful than it might otherwise be."

"He said I'd die in prison," Busby said.

"But probably not as badly as Congressman Brock did."

Looking for a way to escape both grim fates, Busby said, "I'll be safe if I can get to China."

Teasdale sighed, showing only the slightest hint of pity for Busby.

"The FBI told me your wife, Ah-lam, gave up Donald Yang's connection to Beijing."

Busby appeared to shrivel.

"Also the geopolitical situation between the U.S. and China is looking bad. Mr. Busby, my best professional advice is to take whatever deal I can negotiate for you with the government."

Busby's eyes glazed. His mouth fell open. His world turned into ashes.

Still, he managed to nod.

Interstate 90 Westbound

McGill had stopped for gas and Leo was back in the driver's seat. McGill rode shotgun, and Deke, to his smoldering displeasure, had been relegated to the back seat. Leo was quickly making up the time and distance lost to the necessity to refuel. Better still, the drone sent from Ellsworth Air Force Base had locked on to the faux Boy Scout van, and watching from an altitude of 5,000 feet, was invisible against an overcast gray sky.

Inaudible, too, even if the young fools in the van weren't listening to music.

Besides the video of the vehicle they were chasing streaming on the Chevy's dash monitor, the drone provided a digital road map indicating each vehicle's location, the distance between them and the speed Leo would need to hit to catch the van within a given length of time. The former NASCAR driver was in his element.

He'd told McGill moments ago, "Haven't had any sport like this for quite a spell."

Now, Leo was humming "Maybellene" by Chuck Berry.

If he wanted to, he could catch the van like it was "sittin' still," but that wasn't the plan.

In fact, both the Minnesota and South Dakota state cops had been advised to let the van pass even if it was doing 110 like the

Cadillac in Chuck's song. A traffic stop wasn't going to get Special Agent Ramsey home. So far, though, the read-out from the drone said the van was doing only a steady five miles per hour over the limit and sticking to the right-hand lane.

That told McGill the van's driver was smart enough not to call undue attention to himself.

When Leo closed to within a half-mile of the van he'd ease off the gas and match the van's speed.

They'd be ready to catch it within a matter of seconds if the driver tried to run and hide.

A call coming in on McGill's phone diverted his attention from the road ahead. Patti was calling. He said, "You have good news, I hope."

"I'm happy to say I do. Three of Colonel Gregory's men, moving with great stealth, spotted what they describe as nine young men of parental consent recruit age: 17 to you and me. They're wearing Boy Scout uniforms."

McGill said. "So we've got it right about our guys being kids doing their elders' dirty work. That and we're not dealing with pros here."

"Well, three of them were carrying assault rifles. We wouldn't want to take that too lightly."

"Never," McGill agreed. "Did the special ops guys offer any opinion on the chance the kids might do the sensible thing and surrender before there's any bloodshed."

"They didn't say, but Carolyn and I had an idea about that."

McGill did his best to maintain a neutral tone. "You and Carolyn?"

Mustn't have offended because Patti told him the plan and he liked it.

Moms pleading for reason from their offspring. Might work.

McGill had a suggestion to offer, though.

"How about adding just a bit of a 'dad' element?" he asked.

He told Patti what he had in mind.

She said, "I'll run that by Colonel Gregory."

"Bet he'll like it."

"Probably. Where are you and the guys right now?"

McGill saw a highway sign. "Coming right up on Sioux City, South Dakota."

The Oval Office — Washington, DC

The President asked her second in command, "Any news on Byron?"

Patricia Grant and Jean Morrissey were alone in the Oval Office.

"The doctors say his underlying health must be remarkable because he's bouncing back at a phenomenal rate. Not that doing his recovery therapies won't be Herculean labors, they said."

The President smiled. "Doctors using a classical reference?"

"I think they did that for me, knowing my background as a jock. I asked them if they could rewire Byron's brain to prefer ice hockey to surfing. They said maybe that was asking a bit too much. I guess I'll just have to accept him however he turns out."

The President smiled. "A wise course more often than not."

"How are you, Madam President?" Jean asked. "Word reached me that you saw the White House physician."

"That's the reason I asked you to stop in, Jean. Here's what happened."

She told the story with a straight face.

Jean Morrissey both winced and laughed. "My sympathy. You'd think we could have been designed better."

The President said, "Dr. Nicolaides tells me things should get better eventually, and gave me the name of a specialist to see, but for the short term at least I'll just have to tough it out."

"Did you tell Mr. McGill?"

"I haven't been able to catch him when we could speak freely. But now that you know, I think there will be times in my remaining months in office that I might genuinely need you to step in for me. I feel optimistic it won't rise to the point of invoking the 25th amendment, but you will likely be asked to perform some of my duties, possibly even make a big decision or two. What with helping Byron and campaigning, do you think you'll be able to handle that additional burden?"

The Vice President shrugged. "Isn't that what women do? Take on more responsibilities than a sane person would ever attempt. If I don't get much sleep for the next ten months, or the four years after that if I'm elected President, so be it. Maybe the time will come when I'm ready to lie on a beach and watch Byron ride the waves. But thank you for asking."

"I'm not trying to change any of your plans, Jean, but I certainly wouldn't blame you if you decided your personal life came before doing this job. You already have an idea of how draining it can be."

The Vice President said, "I did think about chucking it all. Just heading off to Santa Barbara with Byron. Helping him get well and then enjoying our time together. But the truth is I don't see anyone, anywhere I think could do the job as well as me."

Patricia Grant smiled. "That's the first prerequisite for getting to this office."

The two of them talked about how best to work things out.

For each other and future presidents.

Sioux City, South Dakota

Special Agent Carrie Ramsey climaxed, dramatically speaking.

Her acting chops had been improving by the minute. She'd honestly thought the first moan of faux passion she'd delivered was hokey beyond belief. She might've fooled a complete moron once or twice with a rendition like that, but anybody with two brain cells to rub together would catch on quickly that he was being conned.

Ironically, that little imp Caitie McGill came to the rescue.

On numerous occasions, Carrie had overheard the kid talking about Lee Strasberg's method acting system. How an actor had to tap into her own experiences to produce the emotions the script demanded. That made sense to Carrie. She could do that.

What she had to get past, though, were her inhibitions.

She could easily remember her better sexual experiences: the sights, scents and sounds. The tactile sensations, too, of course. But they wouldn't come into play here. Credible vocalizations were what she needed to voice.

Except by doing so she'd be giving Cole a peek into her real life.

Who she truly was at her most private of moments.

The little bastard was smart enough to know she wouldn't just be faking it.

The practical side of Carrie's nature booted her past that impediment. Embarrassment was preferable to death. So get going, and be damn quick about it. Carrie quickly selected her three most favorite amorous encounters and created a greatest hits compilation: moans, gasps and whimpers that she recalled with stunning clarity.

Cole took immediate notice of not only of the newly dense and varied erotic tone but also the sudden electrical charge in the air. "Oh, Jesus," he said, his own acting performance veering strongly to realism. "Jesus!"

Carrie tucked one of her two Berettas into the waistband of her jeans at the small of her back. She held the other in her right hand. With her now free left hand she moved Cole backward. He covered her hand with both of his, pressing it to his chest.

Her initial impulse was to pull free, but she realized the physical contact only heightened the memories she'd been drawing on and made her performance even more authentic. It had the same effect on Cole. The two of them would have aced any audition in Hollywood.

She pressed Cole up against the wall that would be behind the door to the room when it opened. She withdrew her hand and stepped back, clear of the door's arc should it swing open. Then Carrie gave it her vocal all, revealing her primal self and ...

The door popped open and there was Buddy.

So moved by Carrie's performance he'd forgotten to bring his assault rifle.

She touched her Beretta to his nose and said, "Hold your applause."

Olmsted County, Minnesota

"No," Carolyn Enquist said.

Lars in his other father role seconded his wife's decision, even at the risk of alienating his step-daughter.

"I'm eighteen," Caitie McGill countered. "I'm legally entitled to make my own choices."

"Not in this case," Celsus Crogher said, holding his right hand up to forestall any further discussion of teenage legal emancipation. "You have no right to accompany a military unit heading into what might become a combat operation."

"What about reporters who are embedded with combat troops around the world? There's a long history of —"

Celsus shook his head. "Are you a journalist? No. Even if you were, reporters are allowed to accompany combat troops only at the discretion of the commanding officer. In this case, that would be the commander-in-chief. What do you think she'd have to say about your request, Ms. McGill?"

Caitie knew exactly what her other mother would say: *No way, kiddo.*

She'd accepted with good grace that changing circumstances wouldn't allow her and Ben to film their twist on the Amish rescue scene from *Witness*. Things like that happened in the movie business. Financing fell through; the script got a last-minute rewrite. *C'est la vie.*

But there was no reason why she and Ben shouldn't be allowed to film the denouement at the farmhouse up the road. That situation might produce its own dramatic moments. *Cinema vérité* at its most exciting and possibly poignant.

Just the thing to take with her to film school in Paris.

Show the profs there what she could do.

That thought had no sooner entered her mind than Caitie realized maybe she was being just a bit self-centered. Feeling stymied but not defeated, she asked, "What about Ben?"

"What about him?" Celsus replied.

Caitie looked at her friend and he gave her a small nod.

Turning back to Celsus, Caitie asked, "Can he go and film what happens?"

Celsus closed his eyes as if trying to hide from a headache.

When he rejoined the others in the room, he looked first at Carolyn and Lars.

She shrugged; he nodded.

Celsus looked at Ben. "How old are you?"

"Twenty-two, sir."

"Are you an only child?"

He shook his head. "Two brothers, one older, one younger."

"Have you ever been exposed to hostile gunfire?"

"No, sir."

"Ever been in *any* life-threatening situation?"

"I saved a little kid who got caught in a rip-current and was drowning. That was kind of hairy. I was fourteen at the time."

That made an impression on Celsus. Risking your life to save another. Self-sacrifice was what the Secret Service was all about.

He said, "I'll ask Colonel Gregory. That's all I can do."

Sioux City, South Dakota

"Hold what?" Buddy Legrand asked.

"Put your hands on top of your head," Carrie told him.

"Is that how you start things out?" he asked, doing what he was told.

"What?"

"You know, like what you did with Cole."

Cole said, "We were faking it."

Buddy looked at each of them, his expression of betrayal almost heartbreaking.

"Well, shit."

With that, Buddy promptly blacked out and collapsed.

Carrie stepped back but kept her gun on Buddy. "What's wrong with him?"

She could tell already the boy wasn't feigning unconsciousness. His muscle tone was too slack. Drool slid from a corner of his mouth. Just to be sure, though, she stepped on one of his ankles with a bit of weight.

He groaned and then began to snore when she eased off.

Cole told her. "He does that sometimes from what I've seen. One minute he's here, the next he isn't. There's a word for that, I think."

"And I bet you know what it is."

Cole grinned. "Narcolepsy. Buddy's got some real problems."

Carrie had Cole tug his unconscious comrade further into the room.

"Sonofabitch is heavy," he complained.

Carrie ignored the gripe and asked Cole if he knew of any particular danger that might be awaiting her elsewhere on the premises. He shrugged and shook his head. "It's just an old house that hasn't been kept up real well."

Carrie told Cole she'd be back for him and Buddy, assuming nothing bad happened to her.

"You gonna bring ice cream?" Cole asked.

The kid was something else, Carrie thought. "Sure, what do you like?"

He told her and ordered for Buddy, too.

Carrie locked the two boys in the room where she'd been held. She saw the adjoining space was an unfinished basement. It held no laundry appliances, but there was a tiny water closet. Bastards could have let her use that. The narrow windows on either end of the room were covered with aluminum foil. To her left was a stairway leading up to a door on the first floor.

At the foot the stairway leaning against the railing was an AR-15 type rifle.

Carrie stashed the second Beretta in her waistband with the first. The combined weight and bulk of the two handguns was uncomfortable as hell. But if you were going to fire an assault rifle accurately you needed two hands. She checked the weapon and was pleased to see the safety was on and the magazine was full.

She pulled the charging handle to chamber a round and took the safety off. Before setting foot on the first step, she looked up the stairway, listened and sniffed. All of her senses failed to report the nearby presence of another human or other animate being. Even so, Carrie found it hard to believe there were no adult bad guys on hand.

The four creeps who'd grabbed her — what seemed like a million years ago now — hadn't been clumsy, inept kids. None of them had fallen asleep on the job. None of them was a fat slob with an operatic voice. So where the hell was the disconnect?

Why use competent SOBs to do the kidnapping and then turn things over to clowns and newbies still wet behind the ears? The only answer that came to mind was that the malignant minds behind the whole set-up not only wanted her to die, they wanted their own guys — hell, their children — to be slaughtered, too, when the grown-ups working for the federal government caught up with them.

That would create their own band of martyrs to inspire a wider movement and boost the fundraising and recruiting efforts. Maybe they hoped to build monuments to Cole, Buddy and the other boys someday in a glorious future. That thought alone was enough to make her gag.

Even so, there was a practical aspect to that line of conjecture. If she was right, the house might be booby-trapped to keep Cole and Buddy from getting out alive. Otherwise, what were the two boys expected to do? Hitch a ride home? Wait for a helicopter to pick them up?

Damn, that last thought was scary.

Militant lunatics with their own air transport.

Carrie pushed that notion aside. But the idea that the kids

might be sacrificed for the cause grew in her mind. Before mounting the staircase, she took a peek at the underside to see if an explosive device had been set to go off when someone's weight pressed down on a step.

No, there was nothing like that she could see.

Still, she did her best not to make a sound as she crept up the stairs. Her silence allowed her to hear the rumble of an out-of-tune engine drawing near. Brakes squealed as a vehicle came to a halt. She couldn't help but think, "Please let it be the cops."

If they'd somehow found her and …

Christ, what if the front door to the house had been booby-trapped?

She couldn't let a police officer be killed. Carrie heard an approaching male voice call out, "I'll be right back." She threw open the door at the top of the stairs and yelled, "Wait, don't —"

The bomb blast's pressure wave threw Carrie down the stairs, back into the basement.

She lost consciousness before she came to rest flat on her back.

The irony being the thunderclap of the detonation woke Buddy.

He and Cole began to hammer on the door to their cell.

When it wouldn't yield, they began to kick the drywall.

McGill, watching the video feed from the drone on his Chevy's dashboard monitor, saw the Boy Scout van pull up into the driveway of a house at the apex of a cul-de-sac. The driver jumped out, leaving the engine running, and called out to someone who was still in the van. Then with an athletic stride, the kid ran to the house, leaped up four steps to the front porch and pulled open a storm door.

He took the doorknob to the entry door in hand, a bomb went off and he was gone. Atomized. All McGill saw was an expanding cloud of red. Had to be blood, he realized. The video feed had no sound component, but everyone in the Chevy heard the explosion directly from the source. Everyone in the neighborhood must have heard the bang.

It had the jarring quality of thunder directly overhead.

"Go," McGill yelled at Leo, "Floor it."

The Chevy accelerated like it was rocket-powered. Leo steered around a bend in the road with no perceptible loss of speed. McGill's heartbeat was still climbing when Leo brought the car to a smooth stop blocking the entrance to the driveway. The fake Boy Scout van wasn't going anywhere.

McGill told Leo, "Get some cops, bomb disposal people and firefighters here right away. Let them know who I am, and be sure to tell them I'm with the FBI at the moment."

"Right, Boss." Leo got busy making calls.

McGill got out of the car and saw Deke was already yanking a big kid out of the van's passenger seat with one hand and holding his Uzi on him with the other. The kid was prone on the dormant grass of the front lawn when McGill arrived. Deke put his cuffs on the kid and rolled him over.

McGill looked at the house, saw flames just starting to crackle in the gaping hole where the front entrance used to be and asked the kid, "What's your name?"

"Darin MacTeague."

"Who was that at the door when the bomb went off?"

The kid's eyes flooded with tears, he said, "My friend, Knox. Knox Williamson."

"Who's in the house?" McGill asked.

"Cole, Buddy and that girl."

Deke kicked the kid on his thigh. Hard.

McGill didn't intervene.

"What girl?" Deke shouted.

"Caitie McGill."

Carrie Ramsey, the two men knew.

"Is she still alive?"

No kick this time. Deke had his Uzi pointed at the kid's head.

McGill leaned in close, ready to push the muzzle aside if the kid came up with the wrong answer and Deke lost control.

"She was the last time I was here. Knox and I came back to set her loose, honest to God. We'd had enough. Knox even thought we might have been set up to fail, but … we never expected this."

The kid started to sob and looked as if he might welcome being shot.

McGill caught Deke's attention and shook his head.

They weren't going to start killing teenagers.

McGill beckoned Leo.

"Don't let this kid go anywhere," he said.

Leo took a telescoping metal baton out of a pocket and flicked it open.

"I'll give him a rap on his knees if he tries to run."

McGill lowered himself, looked at the kid and chose to lie.

He hoped that would be more productive than telling the truth.

"If you really returned to right a wrong, you'll cooperate with me. My name's James J. McGill. That's my daughter down there. So, tell me, do Cole and Buddy have weapons?"

The boy nodded. "Handguns and probably at least one assault rifle. There are more weapons in the van. We took all but three rifles from that farmhouse back in Minnesota."

"Why leave any?" McGill asked.

"People have to be able to defend themselves."

McGill wasn't about to have that discussion now.

"What about Cole and Buddy? Are they shooters?"

The kid collected himself enough to think about that. "Cole, probably not. Buddy, probably. If he doesn't fall asleep."

"Fall asleep?"

"He does that a lot."

"What other places can you see being booby-trapped?" McGill asked. "Think about whoever must have set them and how he does things."

The kid was clearly picturing someone. "Back door. Windows on the porches front and back."

"Upstairs windows?" McGill asked.

"No, the guy doesn't work that hard."

McGill turned to Leo. "Call Celsus Crogher. Have him get on to the special forces people. Let them know they're facing a group with three assault rifles." McGill looked back at the kid on the ground. "How many people are in that house in Minnesota?"

"Nine, unless some of them have run off."

"Tell Celsus nine kids with three weapons."

Leo hit a speed dial number on his phone.

The kid on the ground asked McGill, "You got *special forces* working with you?"

McGill felt like kicking the young fool himself, but he held off.

Instead he asked, "Who would you want to use if your child was taken?"

In a quiet voice, the boy replied, "Anyone I could."

"Right."

In the distance, McGill heard a wail of sirens.

He and Deke circled around to the back of the house. They found a solid old downspout leading to the back porch roof. Climbing it was easy. From the porch roof, it was just a few steps to a bedroom window. They checked for wiring that might lead to a bomb. Finding none, they broke the glass out and climbed inside.

Heat and the sound of fire consuming wood and other fuel greeted them. McGill grabbed two pillows off the bed in the room and pulled the cases off them. He tossed one to Deke and tore the other into a strip large enough to cover his nose and mouth. Deke did the same. They both tucked the remnants into their belts and left the room.

The stairway leading downstairs branched at a landing halfway down. One set of stairs went to the front of the house, the other to the back. The fire was at the front of the house, for now, but the whole place would go up soon if the fire department didn't make a quick appearance.

McGill and Deke ran down the back stairs and had the good luck to find a stairway leading down to the basement just off the kitchen. Deke, being younger and quicker than McGill, had the lead and poked his head into the doorway.

"Damn, we found her," he said. Then he charged down the stairs, yelling, "Get the fuck away from her or I'll kill you."

That was more than enough for McGill. He ran down the stairs. He edged past Deke and saw Carrie Ramsey, his breath catching in his throat, the resemblance to Caitie was that close. He saw a short, slight kid with brown hair, his hands raised and backing away on his knees.

The kid looked away from Deke and his Uzi to McGill. "I can't leave 'em, but I can't carry 'em either. How about giving me a hand?"

McGill saw a jagged hole in a dry wall panel across the basement.

Just about the size of a considerably bigger kid lying on the floor.

He turned and asked the smaller kid.

"They're still alive?" McGill asked.

"Yeah, but I don't think any of us have long if we stay here," the kid said.

McGill told Deke. "Take the special agent. We've got to get back to the second floor. The kitchen door might be booby-trapped."

Deke nodded. He slung his Uzi to one side and put Carrie Ramsey in a fireman's hold with her head on the other side. He turned and climbed the stairs moving as fast as he could without risking a fall.

McGill took the unconscious kid under his arms and told the smaller kid, "Take his legs and let's get moving."

As he backed up out of the basement, McGill could feel his body getting hot. Reaching the kitchen, he saw flames racing through a hallway toward the back of the house like it was hungry and they were dinner.

"Let's step it up, kid," he yelled to his young helper.

They reached the stairs leading to the second floor. Step by step, McGill felt sure they were racing other flames coming up the stairs from the living room. When they got to the landing, he saw they had a one-stair advantage. Now, the smaller kid was the one to urge speed.

"Faster, faster, I'm about to catch fire!"

They made it to the upstairs bedroom. It offered no shelter, but Deke was climbing through the window back into the room. McGill yelled, "Where's the special agent?"

"Dropped her down to some cops."

Deke took over for Cole, displacing him.

"Out on the porch roof and jump, kid."

Cole didn't need to be told twice. He hopped through the window frame and was out of sight in a flash, yelling, "Hey, here I come! Somebody catch me!"

McGill and Deke lugged Buddy out on the porch roof. McGill felt as if his feet were about to ignite. The fire had to be burning in the kitchen directly below them by now. They lowered Buddy, each of them holding one arm and lowering him to the two cops below who had to be feeling a lot of heat themselves.

The cops receiving the unconscious kid scuttled away with him as fast as they could, just before a jet of flame shot out of the back of the house. McGill and Deke spared a nanosecond to look at each other and jumped off the porch roof trying to get as far out into the backyard as they possibly could.

They were still in the air when the house started to collapse.

Olmsted County, Minnesota

"Got a nice little hill right behind the farmhouse," Lieutenant Welk told Colonel Gregory.

"Not too little, I hope," the colonel replied.

"No, sir. Big enough that even Ma couldn't chew through it."

"Good. We don't want to wipe out some small town over in Wisconsin."

The colonel was joking, but not by much.

"McKinney and Goldberg are in position in case anybody tries to run out the back door."

"Good."

The two men sat in a Humvee borrowed from the Minnesota National Guard, a mile up the road from their target. The road had been blocked off by the State Patrol for two miles in either direction. All the neighboring houses within a mile radius had been evacuated.

Using "terrorists" as an explanation had won immediate and unanimous cooperation.

"We're sure the targets are still on site?" the colonel asked.

"Thermal imaging says yes."

"Medical assistance is ready?"

"Air and land transport, yes, sir. Medical facilities in Rochester have been alerted to receive several possible casualties."

"Let's hope we can say false alarm on that one," the colonel said. "We don't want any of our people to get so much as nicked. That would be no end of embarrassing going up against untrained amateurs."

The lieutenant smiled. "We'd never hear the end of it from the SEALs, sir."

"No, we wouldn't." The colonel looked at his watch. "Okay, it's time. Let's go."

Welk relayed the order. Under a gray sky and fading late afternoon light, a UH-60 Black Hawk helicopter with National Guard pilots and crew aboard took up its position 50 feet above the target farmhouse. The sound of its rotors let everyone in the house know the jig was up. If they'd come to make war, well, the war had just come to them.

Not that the kids in the house could fire at the helicopter without either going outside to get an angle on it — thus exposing themselves to who knew what kind of forces — or shooting straight up through the roof of the house, hoping to get lucky. Colonel Gregory had evaluated both of these possibilities as unlikely, but you never knew.

If any armed personnel ran out of the house, his men had been ordered to respond by firing short of their targets, intending to make them either drop their weapons and surrender or return to the shelter of the farmhouse. Should they fire through the roof of the house at the helicopter, the gloves would come off. The member of the Delta team aboard the helicopter, acting as the door-gunner, was authorized to use the aircraft's M134 Minigun to respond. With a firing rate of 2,000 to 6,000 rounds per minute, the weapon would reduce the house to matchsticks in the blink of an eye.

For those first few moments, though, the arrival of the Black Hawk was enough to give the kids inside the house pause. Perhaps it alone might have been enough to make them reconsider the idea of taking hostile action. When surrender didn't prove immediate, however, the psychological phase of the plan began.

A plaintive, terrified woman's voice boomed from a speaker in the helicopter doorway: "Gerald, Gerald Haney, this is Mama. You stop whatever damn fool thing you're doing this minute. Your father told me you went hunting over in Arkansas with your Uncle Bill. Now, the government people tell me they're gonna kill you dead if you fire one shot at any of them. Stop it, Gerald. Stop it right now. Please, Jesus, just stop it. Do whatever they tell you, please."

The woman broke down, sobbing.

Her distress went on for several seconds.

Then the next mother's voice took up a similar plea in an equal measure of distress, pleading to her son. The audio procession of distraught women beseeching their offspring not to get themselves killed for stupid reasons lasted less than ten minutes, but the barrage of heartache made it seem much longer.

Then that part of the show was over and the helicopter flew off.

After a moment of calculated silence, Colonel Gregory's voice sounded through a loudspeaker. "Now is the time to come out, boys. Walk out the front door with your hands on top of your heads. Walk down the driveway to the road and turn left. You'll be taken into custody and all of your legal rights will be accorded to you. The best thing, though, is you'll get to live to see tomorrow. Exit unarmed and in a single file. Leave five paces between each of you. You have ten seconds."

The sound of a clock ticking replaced Gregory's voice.

Boy number one stepped through the front door by the count of three. He had his hands on his head. His eyes darted right and left as if he expected to be shot any second. The next boy followed moments later, doing his best to maintain the specified interval. All told, four of the teenagers in the house chose to surrender.

That left five to go. The mommy ploy had been a start. Now, it was time to demonstrate McGill's idea of a daddy tack. Show them your power without applying it directly.

Colonel Gregory got back on his loudspeaker. "I'm truly sorry the rest of you didn't have the good sense your friends showed us. I'm afraid we're going to have to cut down that big tree at the side of the house. It's a shame, really, to lose a nice tree like that. Be even worse if it should fall on the house and crush one or more of you. If any of you have changed your minds, you have ten seconds to start coming out."

Nobody did.

The colonel gave the order. "Show them what Ma can do."

From a camouflaged position in the field across the road, a two-man Delta crew opened up with an M2A1 .50 caliber heavy machine gun. "Ma Deuce," as Army men called it. Fired from a tripod, it shot 450-600 rounds per minute. Its specified targets were infantry, lightly armored vehicles and boats, light fortifications and even low-flying aircraft.

The roaring way it cut through the eighteen-inch diameter trunk of the maple tree adjacent to the farmhouse would have done a buzz saw proud. Turned out the tree didn't fall on the house, but it did crush the two-car garage just behind the house.

That was good enough to bring an additional two boys out the front door with their hands on their heads. That left three more behind, and they still had their AR-15s. Colonel Gregory sighed. There were always some hard cases. He worked with them every day. Hell, he was one of them.

If those young guys still holding out had their heads screwed on right, he would have admired them. But they didn't and it was his job to see they got brought in. Upright or zipped up in body bags.

"Okay," he said through the loudspeaker. "We'll have to think of something special for the rest of you. It'll be night soon. So remember this, we can see in the dark but you can't."

To emphasize his point, he had the electricity to the house shut off.

From the shelter of the fixed, concealed spot he'd been assigned, using the one camera he'd been allowed to bring, Ben Nolan thought: *Wow, I wonder if there's such a thing as a special forces cinematographer.*

Sioux City, South Dakota

All the injured, including McGill, were taken to Saint Luke's Hospital. Special Agent Carrie Ramsey showed no signs of either shrapnel or blast overpressure injuries. The fact that she hadn't stepped clear of the vestibule to the basement stairs had saved her a lot of damage and probably her life.

Her heart rate was within the normal range. There was no rupture of the tympanic membrane, but when Carrie regained consciousness she complained of a ringing in her ears that made hearing difficult but not impossible.

She had a headache from what was pegged a Grade 2 concussion as the result of her head making impact with the cement floor of the basement. She also fractured the ulna in her left arm as a result of the fall. But she had regained consciousness within three hours of the explosion, and when McGill was permitted to enter the recovery room she recognized him even though they'd never met.

Her first rasping words to him were, "Is Caitie safe?"

She endeared herself to McGill for a lifetime with that.

He smiled and said, "Alive, well and leaving a wide wake, as usual."

McGill got the impression she understood him as much by lip reading as hearing his voice. He gave her right hand a gentle squeeze with his left. She spotted the cast on his right hand, covering his middle, ring and little fingers.

"What happened to you?" she asked.

"I jumped off a roof and tried to break my fall with just one hand." He held up his injured paw and shrugged. "Could've been a lot worse, I was told."

"I don't remember much," she told him.

McGill said, "Special Agent Donald 'Deke' Ky carried you out of a burning building."

That touched a chord of memory.

"A bomb? … I think I remember that."

"That's what touched off the fire. After Deke took you out of the basement, a kid named Cole and I lugged out another kid named Buddy."

"Cole helped me. Wouldn't have made it without him."

Well, good for him, McGill thought. That will help his case. He'd testify for the kid if the memory slipped away from Carrie.

He told her, "I called your mother and father to let them know we got you back."

She smiled and started to cry. "They hate my job."

McGill didn't say so, but he'd have felt the same way.

"They were trying to find seats on a commercial flight out this way, but the President thought she could do better for them. They should be here in about an hour."

Carrie showed him there was nothing wrong with her tear ducts. McGill dabbed her cheeks with a tissue.

"Don't tell anybody I cried," she instructed him.

"Wouldn't dream of it."

"So everybody made it? Everyone's okay?"

"Almost," McGill said.

McGill sat in a waiting room hoping to hear something more

definitive about Deke soon. The initial word was he'd contused his coccyx in a landing even more unfortunate than McGill's own. The treatment for that, McGill had been told, involved icing your tailbone every 20 minutes you were awake for the first 48 hours and sitting on a cushioned donut the rest of the time.

So you not only got a frostbitten heinie you also became the butt of jokes.

What wasn't funny at all, Deke's lumbar spine might have been damaged. The consequence of that were things he didn't want to think about just then. Leo, sitting across from McGill, had said, "I'll keep watch for you, Boss. Deke 'n' I'll pick you up in Minnesota on the way back to DC, if you want. We'll all see the country a bit, at real high speed."

He was joking about speeding, probably.

Then again, maybe he'd have the Air Force refuel the Chevy on the fly.

McGill thanked Leo for the offer but said they'd wait it out together.

While they were doing so, McGill got a phone call.

"This is Colonel Gregory, sir." The Delta Force officer gave McGill a summary of what had happened at the farmhouse. "I don't think these last three kids are going to go easy. My gut tells me they're in there trying to work each other up to make some kind of move. It's dark here now. I told them we can see in the dark, but I think they might come out shooting in the hope that maybe they can get a few of us and at least one of them will get away."

McGill said, "You could be right, Colonel."

"I hope I'm not but I called because you seem to be a bit of an original thinker, sir. I heard from SAC Crogher you did pretty well over there in South Dakota. I'd love to buy you a beer and hear about it sometime, but right now I'm hoping maybe you might have a way to reach foolhardy kids that I haven't thought of yet."

The colonel's hopefulness sparked an idea in McGill. It grew out of what he'd said to Carrie Ramsey about almost everyone making it. He hadn't been thinking of Deke at that moment; he'd had Knox Williamson in mind.

The poor kid had died so fast he never knew his life was over.

The tragic image of his demise, however, had been caught on digital video.

Throw in some testimony from Cole and Darin MacTeague and you might have something.

"I think maybe I can help, Colonel. You'll need to get an iPad to those kids."

Olmsted County, Minnesota

The Olmsted County Sheriff's Department had a robot they lent to Colonel Gregory.

The special forces officer announced to the holdouts in the house, "I'm sending a robot to deliver an iPad to you. There's a video on it. All you have to do is touch the play icon. You'll see your fellow militiamen Darin MacTeague and Cole Tierney on it. They'll tell you what happened at the house where you stayed in Sioux City.

"You'll also see what happened to Knox Williamson. I have to warn you: That wasn't pretty. But it is something for you to consider because we can do the same thing to you. And we just might have to if you don't surrender peacefully. Come out of the house single file with your hands on your heads.

"You'll have three minutes to watch the video and five minutes after that to make up your minds. If you don't come out, we'll come in, and our firepower will kill you within a matter of seconds. Here comes the robot."

The robot rolled forward on twin treads. Above its ambulatory base rose a cylindrical torso containing its central processing unit and communications electronics. Two headlights and a camera lens composed its ocular array. Four miniature microphones provided its "ears." Each of the machine's two "arms" had four "fingers." It held the iPad without difficulty.

And placed it gently within an inch of the front door.

The sheriff had said he hoped Delta Force wouldn't let the kids damage his robot.

Colonel Gregory said the army would buy him a new one, if it came to that.

The machine rolled backward off the house's front porch, executed a 180° turn and headed home, mission accomplished. Once it was ten feet into its return journey, the front door opened a crack. A hand reached out, grabbed the iPad and the door slammed shut.

Colonel Gregory tapped his heart with a hand and whispered, "Give 'em more brains than balls, please, Lord."

He'd seen the video McGill had sent. Two kids, one big, one small, both young. Each had his own approach to reaching the holdouts. Some people might have wanted to edit the second kid out of the video. Gregory let him stay.

Darin MacTeague, in close-up, looked at the camera and said, "Knox and I ran out on you. You already know that by now. You probably hate us for that, and in your place I wouldn't blame you. Knox and I were trying to save our own asses, but what we wanted to do, and what got done anyway, is our prisoner got saved. She's free now. Here's how screwed up we had things: She wasn't even Caitie McGill. She was a Secret Service agent. We never even got the person we went after.

"Even so, Knox and I thought if we brought that girl back, the law would have gone easier on us. They'd have gone easier on you, too. While we were driving back to Sioux City, Knox came up with the idea that maybe all of us were meant to get caught and killed. That way our dying would raise money and sympathy for the militia. Get a lot of new recruits. A lot more guys than the ones they just lost.

"I don't know about you guys, but my dad would've been proud of me dying for the cause. Even so, I still had a hard time believing we'd all get betrayed by our militia commanders, but wait until you see what happened to Knox. It ain't nothing they faked. I was there. I saw it in person, and I'll never get it out of my mind.

Don't be stupid. Don't let your death be as awful and as good for nothing as Knox's was."

The second kid, Cole Tierney, was terse and even taunting.

"I was there, too, when Knox died. Lucky me, I didn't have to see it. But I sure heard the explosion. Sounded like the end of the damn world, and for Knox it was. Listen, if you have an ounce of brains in your head, you'll give up. You don't give up, you're already an evolutionary dead end. If you'd like to kick my ass for ragging on you, just remember: You'll have be alive to do it."

Then the video showed Knox jump out of the van and speak his last words, the ones he'd never made good on: "I'll be right back."

He went to the door a strong young man and left as a red cloud.

The dispersion of which had been programmed to slow down and last several seconds.

A message was superimposed on the expanding cloud: You have five minutes.

That was four minutes longer than necessary — for two of the hold-outs.

One last kid just wouldn't give in.

When the new prisoners were brought to Colonel Gregory, he asked them, "Who's that left in there?"

"Lawton Stringer," one kid said.

The other added, "He said his daddy told him, 'Don't bring disgrace into my house.'"

"Well, shit," the colonel responded.

Despite his threat to attack the house, the colonel began to wrack his brain: How could he get that last kid out alive?

A burst of automatic fire inside the house eliminated the problem. None of his men reported any shots being directed at them, and none of them had discharged their weapons. The two kids who'd surrendered had tears in their eyes.

The special forces operatives didn't enter the house until dawn. They met no resistance. Lawton Stringer had taken his own life. Whether it was any better than Knox Williamson's death was strictly a matter of opinion.

St. Luke's Hospital — Sioux City, South Dakota

McGill sat in the waiting room with his eyes closed, not sleeping, just thinking his own thoughts, few of them cheerful. Leo, sitting next to him, accepting that with Deke out of the picture he was McGill's last line of defense, gave him a nudge and said, "Boss."

McGill opened his eyes and finally had a reason to smile. "Sweetheart."

He got to his feet and gave his youngest child a hug.

"Dad." Abandoning any pretense of teenage cool or the need to separate from the old folks, Caitie McGill hugged her father with an intensity unlike anything since she'd had a spate of nightmares during her elementary school days.

For a moment, McGill thought she'd come to see him, and he felt there was some truth in that. But he knew there was an even more compelling reason for her to make the trip from Minnesota. Alone? Unh-uh. The picture began to assemble itself in McGill's mind.

Before he and Caitie could talk, though, Leo said, "I'll just step around the corner. Head off any desperadoes at the pass."

Caitie, in her high emotional state, let go of her father, embraced Leo and kissed his cheek.

"My, oh my," he said. "I feel like I should write a country song. Only wish I knew how."

"Check with Gene Beck," McGill said. "Maybe he'll collaborate."

Leo stepped out of sight and the McGills sat side by side.

"What happened and how bad is it?" McGill asked.

He'd barely met Ben Nolan, but he hoped misfortune hadn't hit his daughter's friend.

It hadn't but when Caitie told him the story of Lawton Stringer and the assumed reason he'd committed suicide, it made his heart sink nonetheless.

"How could someone do that to his own child?" Caitie asked.

"Probably learned it from his own father," McGill said. "If not, somebody else filled his head with toxic sludge that he couldn't reason away."

"I am *so* lucky to have you and mom, Patti and Lars."

"The feeling's mutual, kiddo, for all of us."

She told McGill what Colonel Gregory had learned from the boys he and his men had captured: that Special Agent Ramsey was to be killed, not returned after the release of several militiamen from prison. That was to be an example of what could happen to Abbie and Ken if the government tried to pursue them. And Lars and maybe Mom were to be killed to show that threat was serious. If that plan didn't work, well then the boys that had been sent out to do the fighting would likely get killed and become martyrs. So that would be a win for the militia's cause, too.

"What kind of people think like that, Dad?"

"The kind who worry about their kids disgracing them." McGill changed the subject, saying, "You came here with the Ramseys, didn't you? I mean, you didn't just jump in a cab and put the ride on your credit card."

Caitie's eyes went blank and McGill said, "What?"

She held up a hand, thought for a moment and nodded to herself.

"You just gave me an idea for a movie, Dad. A young woman gets in a New York City taxi following a guy. She thinks she'll catch him right away, but she winds up following him all the way across the country, maxing out all her credit cards as she goes. The cabbie's more than just a driver, of course. He's a … grad student. I don't know his area of study yet."

"Traffic engineering?" McGill suggested.

He was glad his kiddo had a muse to distract her from life's far too often grim realities.

Maybe movies were the mind's way of imagining a sweeter life. Some movies, anyway.

"That's cool, Dad. I like that. Who knows from traffic engineering? It's fresh."

"Why is the young woman chasing the guy?" McGill asked.

"I don't know. Maybe it's a romantic comedy, maybe it's a thriller. Maybe both."

Before the creative conference could go any farther, Don Ramsey appeared.

He beckoned the McGills. "Carrie would like to see both of you."

He embraced McGill and whispered, "Thank you. I've put out the word to every heart doctor in the country. You ever need help, the tab's on me."

McGill stepped back and laughed.

"I'm in pretty good shape, but in my line of work, who knows?"

CHAPTER 8

Friday, April 1, 2016
McGill Investigations, Inc. — Georgetown

M cGill made a short stop in Minnesota to drop off Caitie and make sure Carolyn and Lars were starting to reconcile themselves to the fact that people with guns had had it in mind to kill them. Both Carolyn and Lars had experienced the jitters when they'd first heard of the militia plan to do them in, but by the time McGill had gotten to them they'd already arranged with Celsus Crogher to have his executive protection company provide security for the near future.

"He's giving us an exceptionally good rate," Carolyn said.

"That Celsus, he's all heart." Words McGill had never thought he'd say.

Caitie had to deal with the idea of her friend Ben wanting to become a special forces cinematographer. Abbie and Ken would be returning to their respective schools tomorrow.

McGill was thinking about Carrie Ramsey's request: Might she go to work for him, should she decide not to continue with the Secret Service, a move her parents fervently backed. McGill had no doubt she'd be a fine employee, but having someone who looked so much like his daughter with the firm ... well, he could put her in an office on the other side of the country.

He'd thought of going straight to the White House from Joint Base Andrews when his plane landed, but Patti had called and told him she was right in the middle of something big, so he decided to go to his office. Dikki Missirian, his landlord, greeted McGill warmly as always, but that left him with mixed feelings.

He and Patti had yet to decide where they were going to live after they exited government housing, and would McGill be able to run an international chain of private investigations offices from a two-room suite in Georgetown? He had doubts about that.

For the moment, though, those familiar surroundings were a comfort. He pulled up the online edition of the *Chicago Tribune* and clicked over to the sports section. With a sigh he realized he just couldn't get enthused about hometown sports at the moment.

Well, baseball anyway.

Before he could turn to football and basketball news, his phone rang.

A high-pitched female voice told him, "I've lost my henchman, mister. Can you find him for me?"

McGill laughed and said, "I didn't know you did a Betty Boop impression, Madam President. Is it safe to come home yet?"

Patti said, "You know I do things for you that I do for nobody else, and you might as well wait a while. I won't be free for a few more hours, but then I'm all yours."

"I'll hold you to that."

"Hold me any way you want. I thought I'd take a few minutes now to bring you up to speed on what's going on around here, but first tell me how Special Agent Ky is doing."

"No spinal damage fortunately, but he's going to have a pain in the butt for some time. He refuses, wisely, to take any opioid pain meds, but he has agreed to pop some extra strength ibuprofen every few hours."

"And your precious hand?"

McGill said, "I'll never play the violin again, but I can still stick my index finger in a bad guy's eye. Club the mutt with my cast, too."

"Fine, then, practical matters can continue unabated."

"And what's occupying your time, sweetie-pie?"

"The gang of thieves in the House and Senate, the looters of the defense budget, have decided to take a plea bargain, every last one of them."

McGill said, "Nothing too lenient, I hope."

"Twenty years."

McGill whistled. "What made them go for that?"

"Two things. Somehow they managed to see the photograph of their late colleague Philip Brock. Well, his head between those of two porcine friends. There's no hint that the thieves were in on the assassination plan, but the idea that someone of their ilk could suffer such a fate proved persuasive. Better to be relatively safe behind bars than take any chance of losing their heads on the outside."

"What's the other reason they took the deal?" McGill asked.

"Come on, Jim, you've been in this town long enough to know."

Giving it just a moment's thought, McGill realized he did. "They think a new President, one from their party, will pardon them. Way before they get close to serving twenty years."

Patti said, "President George H.W. Bush pardoned Defense Secretary Caspar Weinberger and five other officials for their roles in the Iran-Contra coverup. His rationale was 'it was time for the country to move on.'"

"A perennial favorite," McGill said, "and yet another reason to have Jean Morrissey succeed you in office."

"Yes, well, on that point, I'll mention that our old friend Thomas Winston Rangel committed suicide yesterday rather than face his own legal jeopardy."

"And he'll be missed?" McGill asked.

"That I can't say, but Galia expects a gusher of long-held, politically damning secrets to be released any minute now. Things that will hurt our side of the aisle."

This time, McGill made an immediate leap. "Only Galia's threatening to open her own megaton can of worms, right?"

"Let's just say this Presidential election will either be unusually civil or ugly beyond precedent. And I'm not betting on civil."

"How's Tyler Busby doing?" McGill asked. "He should be scared, too."

"His lawyer says he'll cooperate, but he hasn't so far."

"Once a prick, always a prick," McGill said. "Anything new with Byron DeWitt?"

"He's not verbal yet, but he recognized Jean and remembers how to respond to a kiss."

"Good news at last. Thank you for telling me that," McGill said. "Now, as long we're talking about medical conditions, please tell me about your own."

Patti sighed. "I thought you might have forgotten."

"About your well-being? Never."

"Very well. For a moment, I thought I might be having a heart seizure."

McGill wondered if he could use his credit with Don Ramsey for Patti.

Then she said, "But that wasn't it."

He told his wife, "The suspense is killing me."

"Very well. It was an episode of *fervens fulguris*."

Repressing a laugh, McGill said, "You forget you're dealing with a Latin scholar."

"I didn't forget. It just sounds better that way."

"You had a hot flash. Is that so hard to say?"

"It was volcanic, and think about it. If I let this be known, can you imagine how Oren Worth might use it against Jean?" She pitched her voice impressively close to Worth's tenor. "'How can you trust a woman in the Oval Office when she might be suffering who knows what kind of hormonal imbalance? She might start a nuclear war or surrender the country to Liechtenstein.'"

"You think?" McGill asked. "Because he'd lose 90% of the women's vote if he did. I don't think you can win a national election if you do that."

After a pause, she said, "You're probably right, but it would still sting."

"I defer to an expert."

"You won't think I'm less of a woman?"

"Ask me that when you're within reach."

Patti laughed. "I have to get back to work — and it's going to be hard with all kinds of dirty thoughts running through my mind."

She made a smooching sound and said goodbye.

McGill's mood brightened. He thought he'd go to the White House anyway, enjoy a long hot bath, sip a glass of Italian brandy and make ready for whatever marital adventure might await him.

He didn't get the chance.

Sweetie and Gene Beck stepped into his office.

Neither looked filled with good cheer.

"What now?" McGill asked.

"Tell him," Sweetie said to Gene.

"Corona Moe has decided he's not up to doing you in. Too tough a job in his opinion."

McGill wasn't fooled. "That's the good news. What's the bad?"

"He's subcontracting the job," Gene said. "It's going to be a team effort."

ABOUT THE AUTHOR

Joseph Flynn has been published both traditionally — Signet Books, Bantam Books and Variance Publishing — and through his own imprint, Stray Dog Press, Inc. Both major media reviews and reader reviews have praised his work. Booklist said, "Flynn is an excellent storyteller." The *Chicago Tribune* said, "Flynn [is] a master of high-octane plotting." The most repeated reader comment is: Write faster, we want more.

Contact Joe at Hey Joe on his website: *www.josephflynn.com*

All of Joe's books are available for the Kindle or free Kindle app through *www.amazon.com*.

The Jim McGill Series
The President's Henchman, A Jim McGill Novel [#1]
The Hangman's Companion, A Jim McGill Novel [#2]
The K Street Killer, A Jim McGill Novel [#3]
Part 1: The Last Ballot Cast, A Jim McGill Novel [#4]
Part 2: The Last Ballot Cast, A Jim McGill Novel [#5]
The Devil on the Doorstep, A Jim McGill Novel [#6]
The Good Guy with a Gun, A Jim McGill Novel [#7]
The Echo of the Whip, A Jim McGill Novel [#8]
The Daddy's Girl Decoy, A Jim McGill Novel [#9]

McGill's Short Cases 1-3

The Ron Ketchum Mystery Series
Nailed, A Ron Ketchum Mystery [#1]
Defiled, A Ron Ketchum Mystery [#2]Featuring John Tall Wolf
Impaled, A Ron Ketchum Mystery [#3]

The John Tall Wolf Series
Tall Man in Ray-Bans, A John Tall Wolf Novel [#1]
War Party, A John Tall Wolf Novel [#2]
Super Chief, A John Tall Wolf Novel [#3]
Smoke Signals, A John Tall Wolf Novel [#4]

The Zeke Edison Series
Kill Me Twice [#1]

Stand Alone Titles
The Concrete Inquisition
Digger
The Next President
Hot Type
Farewell Performance
Gasoline, Texas
Round Robin, A Love Story of Epic Proportions
One False Step
Blood Street Punx
Still Coming
Still Coming Expanded Edition
Hangman — A Western Novella
Pointy Teeth: Twelve Bite-Sized Stories

You may read free excerpts of Joe's books by visiting his website at: www.josephflynn.com.

Author's note: In return for a generous contribution to the Prairie Art Alliance [now the Springfield Art Association Collective], the author named two of the characters in this book after Don and Sheri Ramsey.